THE CAMELLIA RESISTANCE

by

A. R. Williams

ISBN 978-0-9912610-0-0

For the Contrarian

TABLE OF CONTENTS

2044

Willow rolled into the warm dent Ven left in the mattress as he slipped out of bed. She watched the muscles in his back flex and contract as he stretched. The man was beautiful. His torso was a perfect isosceles triangle wedged into a pair of long legs with muscular thighs and an ass that fit into her hands perfectly. Had he been in the wild, he would have held court over a pride of satisfied lionesses. In the captivity of a hotel room, there was only one satisfied female, but Willow was sufficiently sated that it seemed there was more than enough to go around. She watched him greedily, as if her starved eyes could make up for years of deprivation.

He stopped halfway to the bathroom and turned a lopsided grin towards her like he was as surprised as she was to be naked in a room with a near-stranger. She returned his half-smile with a coy one of her own as he closed the bathroom door behind him.

With no one left to observe her, Willow allowed herself an unfettered grin of satisfaction over the events of the previous night. Somewhere between the second and third round of lovemaking, he'd leaned against her and she'd run her hand over the plane of his stomach, reveling in the texture differential. Where she was smooth and polished, his stomach was rough with black hair. If she'd thought about it in theory, all that hair would have been a turn off, but in the flesh it was sexy as hell.

That lazy intimacy had evolved like a tango transition until she was lying on top of him, her breasts pressed into his back. She'd kissed the hollow of his spine, tongued the vertebra at the base of his neck, and laughed as he turned under her so he could watch her face. They had turned again, this time so he could pin her body to the mattress.

Their laughter dissolved as the streetlight cast shadows across their features. The openness she'd seen in his eyes changed with a blink. What remained was feral and hungry. Willow shivered under the animal scrutiny clutching at the breath that caught in her throat. Ven leaned over her and nipped at her neck. Willow's pulse stuttered, slowed like a roller-coaster cresting an incline, and gathered speed as it dove off the precipice. By the time Ven breached her for the fourth time, she wasn't certain her heart could keep up. It was then that she left unladylike crescents on his hips, digging her fingers into his flesh and holding on.

She wiggled between the sheets, snuggling deeper into his leftover body heat like a cat burrowing into sunlight. Willow turned onto her stomach, felt the cotton sheets against her beard-chafed thighs, and closed her eyes.

Had it been yesterday? No, more than that. The conference started on Monday, she'd met Ven on Tuesday and now it was Friday morning. In three days, she'd gone from Willow Jane Carlyle, keeper of rules, writer of policy and regulation to this wanton, wild-haired thing she barely recognized. She hadn't even bothered with the blow dryer or straightener for the past two days. She flexed her muscles and stretched. The bruise on her hip ached, but even that held a certain sweetness. A clumsy misstep over some wires, vertigo, the sharp edge of the vendor's table, and Ven's un-gloved hand at her bare elbow. That's all it took.

It was clear she needed the steadying once she looked up into his eyes, as if the shock of his skin on hers wasn't sufficient to knock the wind out of her. Her mouth had opened and closed, like a fish in an aquarium, but no words came out.

"Well, hello." He spoke like he'd been waiting to meet her. Like they were long-lost childhood sweethearts, meeting again for the first time in years.

"Um," she'd said in return, blushing.

"Are you okay?" She'd watched his mouth make the words, she'd heard his voice as he said them, but he hadn't let go of her elbow and that was all she could absorb. She looked down at the edges of his nails, cut close, clean and naked, the pads of his fingers still pressed against her skin.

"Oh, sorry." He dropped her elbow abruptly, apologetic at the social gaffe, but not before she'd caught a glimpse of the bare skin at the base of his thumb. A clean slate.

When she looked up again, he was looking right at her. At her. Not her hand, not her swaddled curves, but at her. It was brand new. She wasn't the kind of woman men approached. It was a self-reinforcing fact. She didn't smile at strangers and only looked people in the eye when she had to. She wasn't ugly, but she didn't have "it," whatever the "it" was: that thing that hooked a man from across the room and reeled him in. Reserve she had in spades. Analysis, observation, method. But the flirtation gene that had served her mother so well had skipped her generation. All she could do was stand there and stare.

"Let's get out of here." He leaned over, a truant conspirator, and extended a hand. Without even thinking, she reached down, pulled off her glove, and wiped the powder and sweat on to her pants. Causal as a six-year-old, she placed her palm in his hand.

He'd steered her through the trade show. They maneuvered past vendors displaying the newest in latex glove technology, body-condom manufacturers highlighting the latest in ionic anti-viral coatings, and signs announcing SaniCheck's sponsorship of the whole affair. She didn't even speak to the staffers at the Ministry's public health education booth as Ven led her out the double doors and into a crowd of protesters.

He'd stared at what appeared to be the leader, a vacant-eyed Asian girl with hair like an inky dynamite blast and an incongruent flower tucked behind her ear like a crumpled tissue, as if daring her to challenge him. The girl had met his eyes coolly, then waved her hand, unblinking. The crowd parted silently, and they passed through the center of the tangle of placards and slogans unmolested. Willow had turned back to look at the backs of the protesters. "There's no vaccination for the IdeaVirus," one sign announced as it bobbed over a hooded head.

What had the weather been? Willow couldn't remember. All of her attention had been focused on the pleasure emanating from the nerves in her palm.

Willow was touching another human being, skin to skin.

Of course, there had been more of that since. Much more. Mouths and hands and eyes and ears. A shower for two, muscles strained to exhaustion then used again. A true mating, a contract coupling, bodily fluids, skin and all.

The first knock sounded like Ven dropped something in the bathroom. The second knock was more clearly a fist. Willow looked at the bathroom door. It showed no signs of opening. So she stood up and scrambled for the hotel robe as the third round of knocking began; now more like a battering ram than a human hand.

She slid the chain from its track. The door flew open, smacking against the thin wall with the sound of drywall crumbling. A uniformed Ministry officer stood in the threshold poised for a fight.

As a Ministry girl, she knew the routine. Don't protest, don't get in the way, and by all means, don't resist. The Ministry got answers first and apologized later, if at all. So Willow watched the officer search the small room, clearly not finding what he was looking for. Finally, he turned to Willow, his two "assistants" blocking the only exit.

"Where is he?" The Officer's voice was calm, almost polite.

The Ministry stayed out of contract relationships, assuming that if you were willing to enter into a contract with someone, you knew what you were doing. She and Ven hadn't put ink to paper yet, but the contract was inevitable. With all the incurables easily identified by tattoo... well, Willow was fairly certain that whatever they were after, they had gotten the wrong room. So Willow looked back at him with calm submissiveness. As a means for disarming the more authoritarian aspects of the New Republic, it was the best she had.

"Who are you looking for?" she asked in her most reasonable, compliant Ministry tones. She leaned against the flimsy hotel desk, crossing her arms across her chest in her best impression of Nate, her boss.

"You know who we're after. There's no point in playing dumb." The Officer glared at Willow as if he could wipe the bland smile off her face by will alone.

"I'm not hiding anything," she replied, still perfectly reasonable. "Look around. There is nothing here of interest to you."

"I think I will," the Officer retorted, and turned straight towards the bathroom.

Willow pulled her weight from the desk for a moment, then thought better of it. If the Officer found Ven naked and shaving, it wasn't going to be her fault. The Officer turned the handle, opened the door, and revealed an empty room. Willow did stand at that, but shock made her legs weak and she sank back to the desk. The Officer pulled back the shower curtain and checked each of the four walls for a window. Once he was satisfied that there was no one in the hotel room but the wild-haired woman in her bathrobe, he returned to Willow.

"Sorry for the intrusion, ma'am. Bad intel, I guess." The Officer at least had the decency to look sheepish, but the apology was lost on Willow. She was too busy staring at the bathroom door, the same door she'd watched Ven walk through not two minutes earlier. The Officer snapped his fingers and the two minions turned to leave the room. The Officer followed. "Be well," he said as he pulled the door closed behind him.

Willow waited for a moment, then forced herself to her feet. Dread shook her hand as she reached for the door knob. She pushed the door open, Ven's name a whisper on her lips, but the room inside revealed the same empty volume to her that it had shown to the Ministry officer.

Nothing.

Nothing more than a toilet, sink, shower, and SaniCheck dispenser. As if her eyes were to blame for Ven's disappearance, Willow touched each of the four walls. There was nothing mysterious or permeable about the cool tile. She sank to the floor, pulled her knees to her chest, and held herself close.

ONE

Doctor Webber leaned back in his chair, a seemingly casual rearrangement of limbs, and studied the slouched woman in front of him. She had dark hair and dark clothing. Standard professional issue. Her latex gloves were not the fashionable sort with painted nails or patterns dyed in. They weren't even fake-tanned, just old-fashioned, plain latex. The back of her hands shone under the fluorescent lights.

It was a shame, really. She was a pretty girl, not in the nearly alien way of the young girls his son brought home, but with an old-fashioned asymmetry. One eyebrow quirked a little. One tooth wasn't exactly aligned with the rest. One breast was probably slightly larger than the other. Doctor Webber removed her clothes mentally one by one. Scientifically, of course. Lovely shoulders, dark nipples, and a thin line of hair connecting her belly to her pubis. As a younger man...

But that was not the business at hand, and what he was about to do would render this woman, one Willow Jane Carlyle, untouchable. As he leaned back and stroked his chin in a practiced gesture, his foot stretched to the button on the floor that locked down his section of the clinic.

In his line of work, cocktail parties were an opportunity to trade horror stories of patients gone crazy with the diagnosis. Everyone knew of at least one case where things had gone badly. Most of the infected wanted to go home and think it over before the tattooing, but that wasn't protocol. His practice had been lucky so far, but then Dr. Webber ran a well-regulated operation. If nothing else, Dr. Webber always did things by the book.

With the button under his foot pressed, the clinic doors all locked and iron caging slid silently into place between the walls. His nursing staff went on high alert, watching his door carefully with the sedatives at the ready, just in case this slender woman burst through it, hysterical. And why shouldn't she be hysterical? Her entire life as an upstanding citizen was over.

He turned his attention back to Ms. Carlyle.

It was a shame, really. She was the kind of woman he would have chosen twenty years ago. Well, he would have chosen her had she not been stupid, a whore, or both. He took a deep breath and shook off the unbidden thought that his job was making him old before his time. Then he spoke.

"Ms. Carlyle, I'm sorry, but I have some bad news. Your tests came back positive. You have Herpes."

Her body stiffened as if struck. Her hands clenched and her nails dug into the latex gloves hard enough to draw blood. But she did not cry. She did not speak or scream or react beyond the initial flinch. This, Dr. Webber was not prepared for. They cried, they cursed, they yelled, they explained how the test must be wrong. He cleared his throat.

"As hard as it is to believe, there are still a handful of people who don't know they've got it. It's possible that your partner didn't know." And then a sentence escaped his mouth that surprised him far more than it surprised her: "This doesn't make you a bad person. It doesn't have to be the end of the world."

He was lying, of course. It did make her a bad person. It was the end of her world.

"I understand," she said softly. "I understand."

And she did. Far more than he realized. She already knew what his casual lean meant. She knew that there were retractable iron bars behind the drywall, that the nurses outside were ready for a crazed outburst from the patient within. She'd written the protocol after a rash of clinic shootings eight years ago. It was at the beginning of her career and it all seemed reasonable at the time. People were spreading the virus. Whether they were malicious, uniformed, or terrified didn't matter. What mattered was stopping the virus' spread.

Working with Legal, the staff deaths had been classified as Herpes-related and therefore under the jurisdiction of the Ministry. So what if it had been decades since anyone had died of the virus itself? The clinic slayings had been added to those numbers. And people had died of the virus. Willow had read the textbook accounts of patients suffering agonizing deaths as the virus attacked internal organs. Health care workers needed to be protected. So did the public. People had the right to know up front, before even an introduction was made.

It wasn't just that you couldn't trust your partner in a casual encounter. There were cases where the infected entered into contractual relationships without first telling their intended. Love and fear were both irrelevant to the question at hand. There were no excuses, not in this. If people wouldn't own up to their status, then the identification scheme was the only way. Willow knew the necessity of the protocols. She'd spent her adulthood tracking the spread of sexually transmitted viruses and their impact on the population.

Therefore, she also knew that this was exactly what she deserved.

It didn't matter that she was the perfect poster child for the Ministry. She'd never had unprotected sex, never showered without SaniCheck, and never allowed shoes on her pristine white carpets. But all it took was once.

And now she was here, her arm unfurling as if compelled, exposing the tender skin on her left wrist.

Willow kept a bitter laugh to herself. Were she running a spot-check of this clinic, she'd have to give them a near-perfect review for their adherence to regulation. It was all happening exactly as prescribed.

Only the tattoo was left. She could see the blister-packs of ink, each one with a registered number and a unique magnetic signature to identify her. Once the tattoo was administered, her name would be entered in the registry, her movements tracked and documented for study by the team she herself led—the youngest cultural epidemiology research director in the history of the Ministry.

Doctor Webber leaned forward, reassuring. He repeated himself: "It doesn't have to be the end of the world." But they both knew he was lying.

"They've chosen this clinic for the updated protocol. The latest technology." He reached into a drawer and extracted a device that looked like the barcode scanners from Willow's youth. "I'm going to need your left hand."

Willow extended her arm over the desk. The Doctor's latex glove caught the small hairs on the back of her arm as he pushed up her sleeve. She winced, but did not jerk her hand away.

She watched his rubber finger stroking the flesh at the base of her palm and found herself in the middle of a memory so visceral she almost doubled over it. Ven's hands had a rough edge to them. Hands that were used, not coddled behind a protective layer. Hands that made things, that touched the world, that interacted with time and material.

Her stomach lurched.

The Doctor pressed a button on the tattooing device and it whined to life, buzzing and pulsing like a pissed-off wasp. When its hum filled the room with a steady undercurrent of panic, he pressed it to her skin. All of the needles shot out at the same time, their tips fed by a single blister-pack of magnetic ink, stamping an X with dots in each of the corners into her skin.

She gasped and bit back the pain. The sting of the tattoo had been a theoretical notion when writing the protocol. People got tattoos all the time in the old era, so it couldn't be that bad. They'd done the allergy testing. It was safe. Certainly safer than unprotected sex. In any case, the gains in prevention and tracking were worth the discomfort.

It had been easy to be cavalier about it from the cool remove of her desk and the meetings with like-minded colleagues. Now, with her hand on fire and her fingers being crushed by the Doctor's surprisingly firm grip, Willow Jane Carlyle thought better of the whole protocol. *Better late than never*, she thought ruefully, then burst into tears.

Doctor Webber was back on solid ground with her tears. This he knew: a patient showing appropriate remorse for straying from regulation. Something beyond the stoic resignation she'd shown before. Cold even, as if she didn't know what she'd done. It had unnerved him; he'd lost his footing. He'd started talking when he meant to keep silent.

Willow's latex gloves did little to cover up the throbbing tattoo. The skin on the surface was oozing up plasma and blood, and she struggled to keep herself from cradling her left hand with her right. The doctor leaned back in his chair, satisfied with his role in the affair: he had punished the morally and hygienically reprehensible behavior. He reminded himself that he wasn't just the keeper of the Republic's health: he was an enforcer of public morality.

He tapped the switch again with his casually-extended foot. *The bars behind the drywall must be new,* Willow thought through her tears. They didn't make a sound as they retracted. The lock on the door didn't click either, but just as certainly as she'd been trapped before, she was equally free to go now.

The Doctor tried to think of something appropriate to say, and came up blank. He fell back on old habit: he rummaged through his desk for prescription samples.

"Here," he said. "Take these. Two a day. They should lessen the outbreaks." He pushed a bottle across his desk and Willow picked it up, looked at it without really seeing it, and put it into her pocket. Dr. Webber extended his hand to shake, as if they had come to some sort of agreement of mutual benefit. They hadn't, of course. Willow was an animal now, to be tracked and managed. She shook his hand anyway, the sing-song voice of Mrs. Carlyle loud in her ears: *be polite to the good doctor, Willow. It isn't his fault you failed.*

Willow paused before she left the clinic. She pulled her coat around her, cinching the belt around her waist painfully tight. Her right hand cradled the bottle of pills as she lowered her sunglasses and pushed the door open with her shoulder. The tattoo tingled, a new sensation layered on top of the pulsing, complaining flesh at the base of her thumb.

So this is what it feels like, she thought clinically as the sensors in the outside door logged her exit. In another twenty-four hours the database would update and every registered building in the Republic would record her coming and going. Willow took a shallow breath and quickened her pace.

No one on the street looked at her any differently; she was just another professional woman of indiscriminate age bundled against the cold. Her interchangeability was intentional. Her heels were high enough to be professional, not high enough to attract attention. Her clothing kept to a limited palette of dark navy, gray and black. Her coat was cleanly cut, no shiny buttons, no unusual details. Even her gloves were boring—the one accessory that a woman could acceptably decorate in whatever outlandish fashion she desired—but Willow kept it simple. Unnoticeable. Untouchable. Unapproachable.

Still, she felt every dismissive gaze like a razor on her back. *No one knows, at least not yet,* she told herself. *They can't tell just by looking at me.* But her face felt hot, and she could feel her pulse throbbing behind her knees. *I just need time to think. It's going to be fine. It has to be fine.*

She repeated the words to herself over and over again, a new word for every step. But it wasn't going to be fine and she knew it. Twenty-four hours until every database in the Republic had her name on it. Forty-eight until her entire world knew what she had done. Herpes didn't happen to people like Willow, but the throbbing in her hand gave lie. She was the same as she had been two months ago, but everything was different now. Now she was one of *them.*

She stepped up her pace even further, not quite breaking into a run back to her office, but close.

The Ministry building stood taller than its neighbors, a black monolith with reflective glass displaying the graying October sky back at itself. It dominated the neighborhood. As long as the Ministry stood, so did order, society, the rule of law, and the public health.

Disinfecting tents covered the doors. *Perfect,* Willow thought. *Everyone will be distracted.*

This latest protocol hadn't been her idea, but she'd sat on the panel that approved the pilot program. Sensors in the toilets performed on-the-spot urine tests. If someone had a bacterial infection, the sensors would lock the bathrooms down until the health inspectors cleared the building. That would only happen after the infected person was found and treated.

At the approval hearing, the genius behind the protocol proclaimed that, with sufficient vigilance, both syphilis and gonorrhea would die out within five years.

For the first time, she felt a small pang of sympathy for the poor schmuck caught in the Ministry's obsession with social hygiene.

Willow pushed through the door with her shoulder, burying her hands deeper inside her pockets. She badged through security without bothering to take off her sunglasses. The tall security guard nodded at her, silently acknowledging her right to pass.

She punched the elevator button impatiently with her right hand. The left stayed in her pocket, wounded. The doors closed around her; the red light on the elevator camera blinked on. She marked it but didn't react as she watched the numerical lights move floor by floor.

The doors opened, hazmat suits nearly blocking her exit. They had some poor fool pinned to the mobile disinfecting unit, his bare ass dancing in the air as the team tried to get a clear target for the pneumatic syringe and the antibiotics. This, like everything else, turned her thoughts back to Ven.

But thinking about Ven pushed her over the edge. Her stomach roiling, she turned back to the ladies' room. She didn't bother to lock the stall; she just collapsed, retching into the toilet. When there was nothing left to heave, she stood up, pulled her gloves off and rinsed her hands, then her face, and finally her mouth. Plasma had coagulated around her tattoo. She soaped her hands again and began scraping the ooze off the black mark. The scraping hurt. Badly. But she didn't stop until it had all washed down the drain.

Willow used the back door to enter the suite that contained her modest office and the cubes of the social scientists that worked under her direction. As soon as the door closed behind her, several inquisitive heads popped up from the cube farm. One of those heads belonged to Devan, her self-appointed right-hand girl.

"Everything okay, Ms. Carlyle?"

Willow removed her sunglasses and tried to remember what muscles she used on a normal day. Certainly not the ones that were currently struggling to hold back her tears. She made a face—a neutral one, she hoped—and responded.

"Everything is fine Devan. Could you have Nyah clear my schedule please? Something has come up that needs my attention."

"Of course, Ms. Carlyle." Devan was glowing with the importance of a message. For a half-second, Willow wondered what would happen if Devan got anywhere near a person of real importance, but she closed the door on that thought as she opened her office. Devan was not the name that concerned her at that moment. She wanted into the infected database and she wanted one name only: Zacharias Vendelin. Ven of the rough, unmarked hands.

She locked the door behind her, unbelted her coat and hung it neatly. Years of discipline didn't vanish just because one's life had condensed to the four square inches of space that comprised one's personal parts. With the coat in place, she took the seat behind her desk. It all seemed so normal: her tidy working space, straightening the pencils and pens, adjusting her gloves.

But the normality didn't wash the taste of vomit out of her mouth. It didn't ease the sensation she was watching herself from the corner of the room. Every gesture, every act seemed to require concentrated thought.

Her hand still throbbed, a sensation that seemed to connect directly to the bump on her labia that had sent her to the clinic in the first place.

Willow typed her password into the system and waited for access. The cursor blinked at her, indifferent. After a long pause, her e-mail program woke up and proceeded to alert her to the meetings that she was scheduled to attend that afternoon. She dismissed them all, diving into the database instead. She typed the name into the computer. The software stuttered, then threw up a dossier.

Name: Zacharias Vendelin

DOB: 29 August 2013

Occupation: Counterintelligence Officer, Defense Ministry

Status: HSV+

Diagnosed: 2038

Marked: Yes

Current Status: Classified

Two

There wasn't much more than that, but Willow couldn't read past the face. His eyes looked directly into the camera: fearless, golden, knowing. She could feel the skin on her elbow glow where he had first touched flesh as he steadied her. A protective, manly gesture. His touch was the first direct human heat on her skin since her mother. He could have thrown her up against a wall and taken her there and then. Willow dropped her head into her hands.

Counterintelligence Officer. A professional. She checked his stats again and paused on the 'yes.' There had been no tattoo. Of course she'd looked. He was beautiful, but habits don't die just because the sight of a man makes your knees weak. There wasn't even a need to be surreptitious about it. He wore no gloves. His shirtsleeves were always rolled up, revealing muscular, tanned forearms that had made her mouth dry and her thighs damp. There had been no tattoo. He had stared into her eyes, never once looking at her hand, never once trying to classify her into clean or unclean.

It had looked like absolute trust. It had looked like the beginnings of being seen as a woman, not her status, not her occupation, not her address or the quality of her cashmere coat.

Willow forced herself to take a deep breath.

He could afford to be indifferent. Who cared what she had, if he was already infected? She might still have taken him as a lover had he been marked, but not the way they did it, skin to skin and mouth to mouth. Fucking was one thing, but you didn't just kiss anyone. And you certainly didn't make love without full body protection. It was tantamount to getting married on the spot. At least that's how it was for normal people. Normal people took nakedness seriously.

Willow hated the irony: the lead sociologist studying the way sexually transmitted viruses aligned themselves with social networks, the woman who designed the protocol for ensuring no one could possibly claim ignorance of the status of their sexual partner, diseased. A failure and failed as well. She looked into the computer, looked directly into Ven's eyes, and for the first time since she sat down on the floor of the hotel's bathroom, she felt something other than an astonished grief: rage.

Then the computer blinked off. He was looking back at her, calm and indifferent, and then he was gone. Disappeared for the second time.

Willow bent to check the computer. It was still on. She stood to see if anyone else was having trouble but before she could free herself of the desk, someone was rapping on her door. Her stomach dropped into her kneecaps and the room began to spin. She sat quickly, afraid her legs would give way. The door opened.

"Willow." It was her boss.

"Nate." She hoped her voice didn't tremble as much in his ears as it did in her mouth. "Come in."

He entered hesitantly and closed the door behind him before taking the seat in front of her desk. "Willow, I just got a phone call." Willow raised an eyebrow and tried a nonchalant response. "Is there something I can help you with?"

"No. Actually, it has come to the attention of the Ministry that you are no longer capable of serving in the best interest of the Republic."

"What do you mean?" she asked, but she knew the answer.

"Willow, you have shown a terrible lack of judgment, the kind of failure in judgment that calls into question your fitness for a position of responsibility."

"But I didn't," she protested.

"I'm the one who insisted on sending you to Atlanta. They wanted to send someone else. I went to bat for you because I was concerned about the hours you were putting in and the toll it was taking on your health. When I told you to go live a little I didn't mean to go whore it up with a marked man." Nate's voice veered between offended and condemning, like a parent who has been hurt by a child's disobedience.

"I hate to be so harsh, but there is no other light to put this in. You let me down."

"He wasn't marked." For the second time that day, a tear slipped from under Willow's eyelashes. "He wasn't marked," she whispered.

"You know as well as I do, that is impossible. You were checking his dossier when your access was cut. He was marked 5 years ago. You saw it with your own eyes. I'm going to have to ask you to clear out your personal effects."

He looked around the bare room. There were no photographs, no mementos, only several special act awards and a plaque recognizing her work in the marking campaign.

Willow stared at Nate, immobile.

"Please Will, make this easy on both of us," he finally whispered. Usually Nate enjoyed exerting his power, but he hadn't come to work prepared for this.

"Grab your purse. I'll walk you out."

She wasn't moving, but the set of her shoulders wasn't defiant.

"Don't make me call security. I don't want to do that to you." He looked down at her with his charming smile, the one that he used when he wanted something that wasn't going to go well for the person on the receiving end.

Willow blinked slowly, then shook her head. She opened the drawer that held her purse and noted the stack of disks beside her black bag. On impulse, she pushed the first three CDs on top of the pile into the open mouth of her purse. She stood slowly. Nate stood too.

"I'm sorry to have to do this, Will. I had big plans for your career." Willow turned a weak smile in his direction and pulled her coat from the hanger behind the door. "I understand," she said.

Nate took her arm in a gesture that might have been friendly under any other circumstance, and pointed her towards the door. They left the same way Willow had come in, Nate's hand insistent on Willow's elbow.

It was a long ride down the elevator. Neither spoke. Willow didn't trust her voice and Nate stared at the elevator doors. When the door opened, he propelled Willow into the lobby, only letting go of her for long enough for her to swipe her badge. The gate swung open.

Outside of the security perimeter, he put out a hand for Willow's badge. She handed it to him without meeting his eyes and turned on her heel to walk away.

"Willow," he said her name in a tone intended just for her. She stopped and waited, but didn't turn back to face him. "If you were going to throw yourself away, you could have at least fucked me. For the love of penicillin, I would have taken care of you." She started walking again, the fear of breaking down in public propelling her forward. The last thing she heard was Nate's mumbled "Be well."

The ink in her tattoo buzzed uncomfortably as she passed through the Ministry's front doors. She hadn't considered what it would feel like to have all those particles under your skin straining towards the magnetic readers. It felt like standing on a foot that's gone to sleep. The further she walked from the door, the duller the sensation became.

Her heels tapped out the same staccato rhythm against the concrete that they always did. She watched the crowd around her through the protective shield of her sunglasses. No one looked at her. They didn't look at anyone else either, but generalized indifference was better than the lukewarm concern that would no doubt disappear if the story were told.

What words would she use to describe this thing that had looked like love? The nights she'd spent watching the minutes shuffle after each other on the alarm clock trying desperately not to miss the heat of his breath against her neck. The dull wakefulness, laying there painfully aware of every inch of skin that touched her sheets.

Ah, but then the twinge, like an unkind pinch. That's where the sympathy was sure to dry right up.

When it happened, she noted the unfamiliar sensation briefly and went back to ironing her shirt. When she woke at three with the empty darkness pressing on her chest, the aching in her heart was joined by an ache between her legs. Walking to the building elevator on her way to work, the ache turned into a scratching feeling that stuck.

By the time she got home that night and armed herself with a flashlight and a mirror, there was a red bump on her labia, no bigger than the head of a pin. She prodded at it, wincing, to see if it ran under the skin like a clogged pore. It didn't. When she swabbed disinfectant onto the little crater, it stung with a pain that rendered her heartbreak irrelevant the way that breaking a toe cures a headache.

SaniCheck, guaranteed to kill all viruses and bacteria upon contact. Like every other child of the Ministry, Willow could sing the jingle on demand. She used it full strength. Not recommended, but neither was fucking a stranger.

The bump was still there the next morning. Willow didn't need an aging doctor to tell her that nothing was going to be the same. She thought back to stumbling into Ven in the exhibition hall at the conference, his bare hand on her elbow to steady her as she lost her footing. Her whole life had been altered by some improperly taped wiring. Had she not tripped, there would have been no Ven, no conspiratorial truancy from the conference, no hidden café for long conversations about nothing and everything…

She walked with her eyes on the ground, her left hand tugging towards every building she passed. Only the ache in her labia and the tingling throb in her palm were real. Those two facts were far more than she was prepared to face. Nothing else existed. Certainly not the practiced jostling of the woman several paces behind her, following in strict adherence to the path

Willow wove through the lunch crowd spilling onto the sidewalk.

Reaching her apartment building, she braced herself for the sensation of the tattoo registering with her building. She felt the pull on her hand again like a tug of nausea at her stomach and shook it off as the door ejected her into her lobby. Behind her, the girl placed her hand on the doorframe before she too spilled into the lobby. The elevator door opened and Willow stepped inside, not once noticing the blond staring directly at her.

THREE

"Tell me about your mom," Ven asked.

Willow picked up the wine glass in front of her and took a deep swallow. "Which one?"

"Do you remember your biological mother?" There was no patronizing condescension in his voice, just a burnished edge of kindness. His eyes were open and curious, like he was asking because he wanted to know her better, not relish in the prurient minutiae of old gossip.

Willow closed her eyes and saw India, her riotous curls barely contained by a handkerchief. Her mother was cleaning the old-fashioned way, with a rag dipped in vinegar and hot water. Her hands were bare and she was smiling. "I remember her," Willow answered, her voice now shy and young.

"What was she like?" Ven watched Willow's hands fidget with the napkin, watched her eyelashes press against her cheek as she remembered.

"She was fearless." Willow laughed uncomfortably. "That gene skipped a generation."

"And your adopted mother?" Dinner was long gone and they were the only people left in the restaurant. Ven had positioned them carefully, selecting a table that was protected on three sides by thick walls. There was no need for anyone but him to hear the answers Willow gave.

"What do you think?" Willow rolled her eyes.

"Damn near perfect and therefore damn near impossible to live with." He gave half-a-laugh, sympathetically bitter. "Nothing like my mother." His tone said his mother possessed the same insufferable perfection. Willow smiled.

"I had her book of etiquette memorized by the time I was twelve. It was required reading, like the Brethren make their kids recite the Bible before bed. That was me. Thou shalt not enter the house without washing your hands immediately upon locking the door behind you. Thou shalt not purchase carpet. Thou shalt not offend anyone, unless they are dirty. Thou shalt not impede the Ministry or the Minister in any way. Thou shalt always offer the polite response." Willow shrugged a little, as if dismissing the differences between her mothers. "Thou shalt not touch. Anything."

Ven reached across the table and caressed Willow's hand. "How did you end up there?"

"I don't know," Willow said. "I really don't. I guess Mrs. Carlyle was looking to put her theories to the test. They didn't have any children of their own. She needed a real kid for the experiment."

Willow thought for a minute.

"That sounds ungrateful. I don't know where I would have landed if they hadn't picked me up from the holding barracks."

"What was the Minister like?"

Willow had an unguarded smile for Mr. Carlyle's memory. "He was kinder than you'd expect. He really wanted to help. He would have died a general practitioner in some Brethren community if it weren't for Mrs. Carlyle. She was the ambition in the family. He was the Minister, the most powerful man in the Republic, and she treated him like a wayward child. When she wasn't watching, he read me kids' books from his childhood. But when she was around, it was all etiquette, all the time."

"No wonder you know which fork to use." Ven gestured at the cutlery scattered askew around his plate.

"Of course. A Minister's daughter can't embarrass herself at the dinner table." Willow laughed. "If there'd been a way to major in cutlery, I'd have been valedictorian."

Ven snickered. "I'm sure that would have come in handy."

Willow put on a serious face. "Of course, young man. I would have been Chief Protocol Officer for the Ministry. For a girl, that's like being the Minister." She picked up her water glass again. "Mr. Carlyle was worth knowing. He's the reason I joined the Ministry. I wanted to help." She took another sip. "Mrs. Carlyle is the reason I've gotten so far. I guess some of her ambition sank in."

She looked up and into Ven's eyes.

"There's nothing wrong with ambition," he replied, and lowered his mouth to kiss the palm of her hand.

She was prettier than he'd first thought. The low light in the restaurant softened her. No longer the angular, brittle creature he'd caught in the cavernous conference center, she was turning into a woman. A woman hungrier than most for the kind of attention Ven could offer. For a fraction of a second, he wished she would put up more of a fight, but the thought didn't last. There would be other compensations.

"Deirdre!" The Minister of Health's voice reached through the intercom, startling his secretary.

She pushed the required button and responded. "Yes, Sir?"

"I want Miles. Now." He dropped the line as suddenly as he'd picked it up. Deirdre smoothed her hair, the only gesture that betrayed her fractured composure. She dialed Miles, pushing numbers that had worn away completely on the keypad.

"Did he say what it is about?" Miles asked without expectation.

"Of course not." Deirdre responded, her tone sarcastic but her words in perfect order.

"I'll be right up."

As good as his word, Miles opened the door to the Minister's antechamber moments later. Deirdre nodded in the general direction of the Minister's door. Miles nodded back, completing their unspoken ritual of exasperated camaraderie.

The Minister didn't wait for Miles to close the door. "What's this about the Brethren refusing the updated vaccines?" Warren looked at Miles as if the Brethren's reticence could be blamed on his Chief of Staff.

"Sir, they are traditionally skeptical about vaccines, preferring 'godly' remedies such as can be found in nature." Miles formed quotes around the word "godly" with his fingers.

"What will it take to get these fucking superstitious idiots into regulation?"

"Well Sir, historically, they have questioned establishment modalities. Even in the old era, there were factions that mistrusted vaccinations. We're working against almost a century of indoctrination." Miles' voice was perpetually reasonable, as if talking to a temper-tantrum prone two-year-old. Warren recognized the tone for what it was and resented it.

"Un-indoctrinate them." Warren pounded his desk with a balled-up fist. "We'd have the flu eliminated if they weren't providing a safe haven for the virus." The Minister glared at Miles, waiting for the protestation that would surely follow. This wasn't the first such exchange on the subject of the Brethren.

"I'm sorry, Sir, but the awareness campaigns have not taken hold like they have with the rest of the population." Miles shrugged, thinking back to intelligence reports with bolded words like "refused," "vehement protests," and "Biblical influence."

"Awareness. It's just a bunch of words. They need evidence! We need to give them proof that clinging to the old mythology won't save them." The Minister drummed his fingers lightly on his mahogany desk. The habit set Miles' spine on edge, which was why Warren did it. It was payback for Miles' earlier tone. "What do we have in the archives?" Warren asked thoughtfully.

"Excuse me Sir?" This was a new twist in an old conversation, and Miles wasn't sure the Minister meant what Miles thought he meant.

"You heard me. What infectious agents do we have in the archives?" The Minister's tone dared Miles to protest.

Miles raised his eyebrows but answered anyway. "Sir, we have everything from the Spanish Flu to the early strains of HIV."

"HIV would be hard to explain. They're all about saving themselves. About the only thing they get right," he muttered grudgingly. The Minister paused, flipping through his mental cache of nasty viral infections. "Find the old H1N1 and get it into the HVAC system of one of the Brethren's meeting houses."

"Sir, H1N1 has the potential to cause fatalities." Miles didn't often protest, but he was very aware of the unpredictable consequences of deliberate dosing.

Warren waved off the warning. "It's been a while since we had a good health scare. The publicity from a fatality or two among the Brethren will keep everyone else in line. Those that don't die will be much more inclined to get with the program." Warren leaned back in his chair and settled his chin against his chest, satisfied.

"If you are sure, Sir."

Warren looked at Miles, daring him to question the Minister of Health further. "Something else you'd like to say, Miles?"

"No, Sir."

"Good. Report back when the task's complete. Where are we with the rest of the incurables?"

Miles took a moment to mentally rifle through the reports on his desk and come up with the most relevant information. "The half-dozen we arrested back in September have been moved to the Infirmary."

"Protesters?" Warren asked.

"Yes, Sir."

"Anything useful from the interrogation?" Warren leaned back in his chair, his fingers rising to a steeple in front of his mouth.

"No Sir. Nothing that we didn't already know."

"Very well. Keep me updated."

"Yes, Sir," Miles said. "Be well."

Miles nodded in the Minister's direction, the polite salutation a matter of habit, not feeling. He closed the door slowly behind him as he exited the plush office.

Warren looked up at the clock on the wall, satisfied with the day's work. The hands marched inexorably towards five o'clock, and Warren allowed himself a grimace of displeasure. Sara had made dinner plans for them. Karina was bringing her latest contract candidate.

Thankfully, this one wasn't Ministry, or at least not the Ministry of Health. Warren knew too much about his employees, a fact that didn't always serve him well. When it came to his daughter's conquests, the less he knew, the better. Finance, Sara said. Something to do with the Ministry of Enterprise. If he left now, there'd be time for a shave and a shower.

No, it wouldn't do to have the guy think he was worth that kind of forethought. Better to show up late, harried and unshaven. Warren turned his attention to straightening the papers on his desk. Twenty minutes later, he called Deirdre to have his driver pull the car around.

Sara tutted when she saw Warren walk through the front door, but didn't comment. She did, however, straighten Warren's tie and smooth her gloved thumb over his eyebrows. Her hand rested for a moment against his cheek and Warren closed his eyes. They held the posture for the length of a breath, the picture of a beleaguered bureaucrat and his long-suffering wife.

"What's this one's name?"

He sighed. Sara dropped her hand.

"Iason."

Warren looked at Sara with one eyebrow raised in comment. Sara went on, explaining, "like Jason but with an I."

"Why doesn't anyone have normal names? What's the matter with Peter. John. Charles. No one is named Charles anymore." Warren sighed in resignation. "Is there at least a drink in the house?"

Sara gave Warren a look that contained an entire diatribe. They'd been married long enough to know the argument and the rebuttal, both of which could now be expressed in the tilt of a chin or the set of the shoulders.

"You got a shipment from Texas yesterday," Sara said, resigned.

"You didn't mention it." The complaint was in his tone, but it wasn't seriously meant or seriously taken. Sara objected to Warren's indulgences, but even she was reluctant to antagonize the Minister of Health. She only took her disapproval far enough to forget to mention a shipment when it arrived, but not so far as to keep his vices from him.

Warren left Sara in the entrance and descended the stairs to the basement where his wet bar stood far from her daily notice. A bottle of whiskey was cradled in a nest of shredded cardboard like a rare bird. Warren broke the seal, uncorked it, and reveled in the sound the bottle made when it touched the glass.

He threw back one shot, then a second. Heat rose from his belly to his shoulders. With one hand on the bottle and the other on the glass, he closed his eyes and leaned against the wall. *One more for the road,* he thought. *One more to pull me through dinner. One more to see me to bed.*

Dinner was as miserable as expected; it always was with these dumb kids, half in awe of the Minister, half trying to sound more impressive than they were. Jason or Iason was no different. Thankfully, Maggie sat on his left and as soon as Iason turned his attention back to Karina, Maggie began talking Ministry business.

Her tone was bright, but her eyes were watchful. Maggie's hobby was Ministry politics; she dropped names and waited for her father's reaction. Warren leaned back in his chair and listened to the voices around him, not the words, but the tones, the rhythm and cadence of questions and answers, platitudes and evasions. Sara asked Maggie leading questions and Warren nodded where it seemed appropriate.

"You agree, don't you dad?" Maggie asked. Warren made a muffled agreement and tried to pay closer attention. It did no good. He mumbled and nodded his way through until everyone stood up from the dinner table and made their excuses. Maggie watched the absence in her father's face and decided she needed to get in to see Miles sooner rather than later.

"Do you think Maggie will sign up any time soon?" Sara asked later, as they were exchanging their daytime clothes for sleeping ones. "She spends too much time at the Ministry. Just like her father." Sara tried to smile warmly at Warren, but it came out more like a grimace. All her teeth showed, but there was more regret than affection in her eyes. "I'd like to have a grandchild or two sometime before I die," she said wistfully.

"You aren't in any danger of dying," Warren responded before he turned on the electric toothbrush and began working up a foam.

Four

Willow closed the door behind her and put her purse on the table inside the entrance to her apartment. She inhaled deeply. From the unscented SaniCheck to a small pot of lavender sitting in the window in the kitchen, the smell of her own space was almost enough to make her feel safe again. Almost.

She stood at the door, not seeing the white carpets in front of her. The dinosaur brain at the top of her spine told her to breathe, so she did. It told her she was unlikely to be attacked from behind, so her posture deteriorated back to the sullen teenage slouch she'd affected to annoy Mrs. Carlyle. Still hunched, she reached into her purse and felt around for the pill-shaped acrylic vial she'd been issued on the occasion of her first adult medical exam. She found it in a corner with a small collection of lint and carried it with her to the sofa.

From the safety of her living room and with no one to keep her public face for, Willow allowed the memories free reign. She could still taste the SaniCheck in the disinfected air of the Carlyle mansion...the little humiliations that Mrs. Carlyle inflicted... the afternoon Mrs. Warren Lake had come to tea.

"Of course, it's clean enough to take off your gloves." She'd paused long enough for Mrs. Lake to tug at the fingers of her left-hand glove. "But why bother removing them, if it isn't necessary."

Willow had watched from the door into the foyer, saw the exchange, and knew Mrs. Carlyle was putting the challenger in her place. Mrs. Lake—Sara, she'd offered up her given name to Mrs. Carlyle as peace offering—was a fan. By Sara's own admission, she owned every one of Mrs. Carlyle's books. Mrs. Carlyle didn't offer her own given name in return.

"Willow. Come, be polite," Mrs. Carlyle had admonished. And so Willow had entered the foyer, gripped Mrs. Lake's limpid hand, mumbled 'be well' in her general direction, and slouched into her spine even further.

Mrs. Carlyle let a huff of exasperation slip past her regimented lips and waved Willow back in the general direction of her room.

There was no telling what Mrs. Carlyle had hoped to get from Willow's adoption, but her poor posture most certainly was not it. It had taken the better part of 25 years, but Willow had finally done something to be disappointed about. Mrs. Carlyle would be spinning in her grave. Minister Carlyle, though...

It was thinking about Minister Carlyle that finally pushed Willow to tears. Mrs. Carlyle would have disowned her. The former Minister, however, would have been kind and that kindness, as theoretical as it was, destroyed the last of Willow's self-control. She collapsed in an inelegant heap of black and gray, a stain against the white sofa. *Mr. Carlyle wouldn't have stopped loving me.* It was a bigger recrimination than Mrs. Carlyle's imaginary reproaches.

Willow couldn't breathe; she just kept pushing the air out of her lungs. But she couldn't get rid of it. Not the clawing panic that was tearing at her esophagus, not the matter-of-fact tone of the doctor, not the silence pushing down on her, reminding her there wasn't anyone to save her and there never had been. When she could push no further, her breath rushed back in like the tide.

She reached into her pocket and pulled out the pill cocooned in its shatter-resistant casing. Quality of life, the Ministry called it. Sweet suicide, Kevorkian, get-out-of-jail. There were lots of nicknames, but everyone had one. Living was for those who wanted it, as far as the Ministry was concerned, and dying was a right. Willow didn't take the pill out of its case, but she put the case in her mouth and let the weight of the pill settle on her tongue. She sat there, saliva pooling under her tongue, until she either had to swallow or spit the thing out. She spit, wiped the case off and put the pill on the coffee table in front of her where she could see it.

It took a long time to will her muscles to move, and then she could only crawl across the floor in the direction of her bedroom, her coat dragging behind her. She gave no thought to the cleanliness of the coat. There was no dust to show up on the black cashmere. Of course not. That much of Mrs. Carlyle had stuck: Willow did not believe in dust.

On hands and knees, she crossed the threshold of her bedroom and sat back on her heels. Her knees sunk into the deep pile of the carpet. She peeled off her gloves first—they weren't any good to her now—and climbed into bed fully clothed. Eventually, she fell asleep with the blankets pulled close to her chin.

Hours later, her own protesting voice woke her out of a dream. She was back in the Doctor's office, telling him to check the lab results, that women like her didn't get social diseases. Her breath came in shallowly, skimming the surface of her lung capacity. There was no one to howl to or for. Mrs. Carlyle's voice echoed in her head, reminding her that it was too late to cry. But the real Mrs. Carlyle was dead, and Willow couldn't stop.

While Willow sobbed over the injustice and choked on her panic, the Herpes virus replicated where the last vertebra met her pelvic bone. It replicated and connected to itself, forming a chain wrapping around the nerves in her spine, its microscopic DNA dictating each cell to find like cells and link. Each additional cell drew a little more electricity from Willow's neural impulses. An electrical current twitched from cell to cell as the virus dug into her nerves. A storm of rapidly-firing impulses tore through the nerves between the outbreak and her spinal cord. It was like being hit from a taser, one that stung from the inside out.

She doubled over, absorbing the pain as best she could. It didn't help. She tried to remember if she'd taken the medicine from Dr. Webber, but the hours all blurred together. Willow leaned over the edge of the bed to search the pockets of her coat. The bottle discovered, she opened it and dropped a bright green pill into her palm. *Bottom's up*, she thought, popped it into her mouth and swallowed.

The pain intensified, worse than the tattoo. Her left leg ached to the bone. Her labia puffed up like the flesh around a sprain. Her lower back cramped in shock. She started to cry again, partly because of the pain, but mostly because she was getting the punishment she deserved. It was almost a relief.

Willow spent the first day of her unemployment staring at the wall and counting the hours until she was due to take another one of Dr. Webber's pills. Soon, the mere thought of putting one in her mouth was enough to trigger her gag reflex. It wasn't that they tasted bad, but once ingested, it was only minutes before the side effects kicked in. First her bones would start aching, then the joints, and finally her skin. The nausea came next, like she'd spent too long in the heat without proper hydration. Then came the restlessness. She couldn't sit still, even though moving her joints felt like she was rubbing sandpaper together. Finally, the blinding headache arrived. The light only made it worse. Even the sound of running water was too loud.

Just about the time the aftermath had receded, it was time to take the next vile green pill. Any sleep that came after taking one was tainted by bizarre, relentless dreams. She'd wake from long conversations with her dead mother only to realize that she had been conversing with a decomposing skull; a jaw that moved with India's voice.

In the daylight, Willow kept as still as the twitches in her legs would allow. She watched movies from the unsanitized era, before the Chaos and the Ministry. There wasn't much of her attention available for watching, but what wasn't taken up in her ongoing corporeal protest wondered at the dresses, the skin that the women exposed, and the way they'd just kiss anyone.

No one kisses in the movies anymore, she thought. It didn't matter— she knew it didn't matter—but she turned the words over and over. Even Hollywood wanted to set a good example. Too bad she herself hadn't lived like they did in the modern movies, with well-cut clothing and a laughing distance between costars. Too bad the death of the movie fairytale ending hadn't readjusted her wayward desires. Willow spent a long time wondering why, in the end, she hadn't been content living with the regulation space in between.

The 'if game' became her new sofa pastime: none of this would have happened if. The list was a long one. None of this would have happened if Nate wasn't trying to get me into his autoclaved sheets. None of this would have happened without those damn wires. None of this would have happened if Ven had been wearing gloves like a normal person. None of this would have happened if I had taken his willingness to touch the world as a warning instead of a reminder of India. None of this would have happened if India hadn't died. None of this would have happened…

Somewhere around three in the morning, Willow had finally taken that game as far as it would go. She was back to being born, blaming her mother for having unprotected sex out of contract and not knowing which of her clients was Willow's father. There was nowhere else to go. She had been born to a state whore. Her mother had touched and kissed her and let her crawl into bed with her after nightmares. Her mother had died. The Carlyles had taken her in. Mr. Carlyle had been kind and Mrs. Carlyle had been relentless. She'd gotten a degree, joined the Ministry, and done worthwhile work. She had tripped over some careless wires. Ven had touched her and the heat of his skin coming into direct contact with hers had made her knees weak.

And here she was, alone, in bed in the middle of the night sobbing inconsolably over something she had no hope of changing. She threw the covers back and left her salty pillows behind. She sat on the sofa and stared at the blank television, then went to the kitchen for a glass of water. On her way back, she passed her open purse. The CDs were still there, stamped with the recycling mark. Data erased and set for reuse.

Too bad they're clean, she thought. A good session of pointless statistical analysis would have done her a world of good. At the very least, it might have helped her sleep. She picked them up anyway, padded to her office, and set them down by the computer. *Everything in its place,* Mrs. Carlyle whispered in her ear. Willow returned to the kitchen, put her glass in the autoclave and went back to bed.

It was almost noon when Willow got out of bed again. She walked to the bathroom where she placed both hands on the counter and leaned in to look at herself in the mirror. The face looking back at her was the same as always. Maybe the circles under her eyes were a little darker, but her bones were unchanged. Willow checked one angle, then the other, looking for traces of India, but she couldn't see any.

She thought of Devan, who was always crowing to the other women about what she'd read in the latest pop-psychology self-help bullshit. A while back, she'd extolled the virtues of self-love, praising the profound experience of looking at oneself in the mirror and staring into your own eyes. Sometime after you'd connected with your aura and before you went cross-eyed, you were supposed say out loud how much you love yourself. Willow thought the theory was not appreciably different than masturbating, which had its place but was most definitely not a transformative experience.

But Devan's voice came back to her now, and Willow leaned into the mirror, her eyes shifting from one to the other, as if there were some secret to discover in the reflection. *Still bullshit,* Willow thought. *It doesn't matter if I love myself. I don't love anything.*

At least that's the direction her thoughts were taking when she became aware of a different sensation in her hands. It wasn't the tattoo. That had been blissfully silent since she'd closed the door behind her several days ago. This was in her fingertips where they pressed against the cool stone surface of her vanity. She pulled her hand back as if burned and the sensation disappeared immediately. She examined both sides of her hands, but there was nothing unusual. Willow placed her hands back on the vanity, fingertips first, then palm down. There was no mistaking it: the material under her hand was seething.

Willow reached one hand to the mirror and the other to her cheek. The mirrored cheek was as warm as the one made of flesh. She closed her eyes and felt her cheekbone under the base of her fingers, the soft curve of her cheek against her cupped palm, her jaw pushing back against the heel of her hand. The mirror felt exactly the same, except shallower, sharper. Something giving in the palm, but brittle too, like you wouldn't want to push it too far.

She snatched her hands back and returned to the bedroom. Sitting on the edge of the bed with her hands palm-down on the mattress, she half-waited for the sheets to come to life. They didn't feel the same as the granite. The granite felt deep and somehow internally wet. The sheets, however, were shallow. Little currents extended from her fingers and back, constantly at crossroads where the warp and weft met. Willow pressed down more firmly. The springs in the mattress were dull as a rusted axe. She could feel their edges where they scraped and tore at the flimsy fiberfill that ran in all directions. *Like foolish thoughts running around pillars of conviction*, she thought.

In the kitchen, she began opening drawers, taking two knives out and holding one in each hand to see if there was an appreciable difference. She closed her eyes and felt the irregular vibe of wood give way to the bright feel of the metal. She pushed it further, feeling the thin slide of the edge of the blade.

The one in her left hand needed sharpening, so she left it sitting on the countertop.

The next morning, Willow didn't look at the time when she got up. She didn't take a pill either: she had an agenda and debilitation wasn't on it. Instead, she went to the bathroom, touching as few surfaces as possible, and turned on the shower as hot as it would go. The metal protested as it rubbed against itself in the turning.

Willow tried not to notice.

When the bathroom was so steamy she couldn't see the mirror, she undressed and stepped into the stream of scalding water. Her skin reddened immediately, but she didn't turn the faucet back to cool. If she was going to go out in the world, she'd need to be as disinfected as possible. Her gloves would cover the tattoo reasonably well, but she felt dirty in a way that SaniCheck wasn't going to cure.

She dried herself, patting at her most recent lesion as if to keep the virus from soaking into her towel. Drying that part came last. When she was done she threw the towel in the general direction of the clothes destined for the washing machine.

Willow dressed carefully, but not before she swabbed SaniCheck full-strength on the breakout. The stinging pain buckled her knees and she sank to the floor of the bathroom breathing heavily. When she felt able to stand again, she followed the SaniCheck with some Vitamin E ointment and stumbled to her closet.

She dressed indifferently, paid no attention to her hair or makeup, and finished her preparation for the day with a jacket pulled tight around her. Dressed, she pulled out a new pair of gloves, picked up her purse and left her apartment. Her weight shifted impatiently as the elevator relocated to her floor. As the doors closed around her, a slender blond got up from where she'd been sitting in the doorway of one of Willow's absent neighbors. The girl opened up her cell phone, typed in a brief text message, called the elevator back to the eleventh floor and mimicked Willow's impatient swaying.

The grocery store was a riot of sensory input after long days in the silence of Willow's bedroom. There were people there. Too many people. She watched them nod at each other, maintaining a precise distance between themselves, as if everyone carried a measuring tape to ensure no one got too close to their fellow shoppers.

It wasn't enough for Willow. She flinched every time someone came near. She was sure they were all looking at her, wondering why she was in the grocery store at this time of day. She hadn't used her voice in almost a week, except when crying, and she waited for someone to speak to her with longing and dread. Normal people said small things. Willow wasn't sure she could be trusted with banal niceties: a disinterested 'how are you' could earn a full confession of the past week.

Willow pushed her left hand into her pocket and wandered the store in a state of overload. The lights overhead were viciously bright and her tattoo started buzzing every time she got near a door.

Eventually, she realized she needed a cart so she made her way back to the front of the store and pushed the button to extract a shopping cart from the disinfecting chamber. The gears whirred into motion and the chain that gripped the wheels of the cart slowly drew it towards her. The cart ejected onto the floor, still dripping with SaniCheck.

Willow grabbed it with both hands, but each reacted differently. She took a few steps forward and knew why: the right wheel was broken somehow. Even more impatient, she turned the lopsided cart back to the front of the store and shoved it back into the disinfecting chamber. She pushed the button to call out a second cart and waited for the whole process to repeat itself.

When the second cart ejected, she placed both hands on the handle and waited. Whatever it was in her hands came through evenly. She pushed the cart into the morass of edible choices and began grabbing everything that caught her attention. By the time she got around to the final aisle, frozen foods created a mound on top of everything and she was wedging her last items into the small spaces between.

At the check-out counter the cashier glared at Willow, looking at her with the disdain reserved for overly prolific mothers. Willow didn't begrudge the cashier her assumptions. She *should* be seen differently. She wasn't the overburdened professional seeing to the efficient management of the Republic; she wasn't a guardian of public welfare. She was on her way to being the kind of woman who cooked her own meals. The fall was spectacular.

It took a full ten minutes to empty all of the items. The bagger, a stooped old man with a white mustache, just kept shaking open biodegradable, antibacterial bags. The re-packed cart was just as full as its disorganized predecessor. Looking at it, it occurred to Willow that she wouldn't be able to walk back to her apartment with all the food.

She pushed the cart outside and turned in the direction of the taxi-requester on the opposite side of the grocery store doors. Her reflection wavered in the glass windows.

For the love of penicillin she thought. *How would anyone know that I'm not one of those women with not enough make up and too many children?* A taxi arrived. The driver got out and shuffled over to help Willow with her bags.

"Afternoon, Miss."

Willow looked at him again. He looked like your average aging citizen, but his voice reminded her of Mr. Carlyle. Deep and commanding and as warm as a toasted marshmallow.

"Let me help you with that," he added, reaching out for a bag. She handed it to him. Together they filled the back of the car. "Mmm. That'll do," he said as he closed the trunk. "Now, what did I do with those damned keys?" He patted his jacket pockets, and then the sides of his trousers.

Willow climbed into the back seat and the automatic disinfectant dispenser sprayed a cloud of SaniCheck sufficient to fill the car. Willow coughed a little and the driver apologized.

"It's regulation now, you know?" he said. "Personally, I'm a little nervous about the stuff. You never know what goes into these newfangled disinfecting products... but like everyone says, you wouldn't want to go back to the way things were before the Ministry. Where to, Miss?"

Willow gave her address. "Nice neighborhood," he said. "Me and the

Missus, we live further out. Not quite at the Wastes, but close enough. Been there fifty years, Gracie and me. We don't have downtown money, but we're just fine where we are. Can almost see the stars from our backyard." The cabbie fell silent. She didn't feel like talking, but she wanted to listen to him. The trick of lubricating small talk had never been easy for her. There was nothing interesting about the weather or the news. Instead, she asked the first question that came to mind.

"What was it like?"

The question confused the cabbie. "What was what like?" he returned.

"Life before the Ministry," she said cautiously. She'd broken one of the unspoken rules of etiquette: direct questions are impolite. But she didn't retract it. Instead, she waited.

"Life before the Ministry." It wasn't a question, it was a rumination. He gave his answer careful consideration. "Well, you were welcome to ruin yourself any way you saw fit. Lots of selfish people drinking and driving, smoking cigarettes, eating themselves into oblivion. We haven't cured that last one, though I hear the Ministry is going to start limiting how much the farmers can produce to keep our calories under control.

Basically, the Ministry has been a big success, what with the ban on liquor and all the tobacco companies ordered to make biofuel. A lot more people used to die, but then there were a lot more people then. The '89 pandemic really changed everything, you know? Most of the population gone. It was a tragedy, of course, but an opportunity too.

Makes me glad I'm married, though. All this disinfecting, the plastic bags bumping into each other and calling it a good time... You'll forgive my frankness, no? Well it seems unnatural. But then I'm an old geezer."

His speech brought them to the half-circle driveway in front of Willow's building. He got out slowly—the Ministry's free nutritional supplements to stave off aging didn't seem to be doing much for his joints—and opened the door for Willow like an old-fashioned gentleman. Impulsively, she pressed her cheek to his. Not quite a kiss, but close. He smiled down at her, a fellow conspirator against the Ministry in this small unhygienic gesture, and shuffled to the trunk.

Willow and the cabbie unloaded her groceries onto the pavement in front of her building.

"Would you like help in?" he asked.

"I'll manage," Willow responded, though they could both see she couldn't possibly carry everything in front of her. "The concierge will help," she added. Truthfully, the old man didn't look like he'd do her much good, and the idea of a man inside her apartment, even an elderly man, did not appeal.

"Very well," he said, and climbed back into his taxi. Willow watched him drive away. With no one there to distract her, she noticed the aching in her hand. *Damn sensors*, she thought to herself. Had she been able to set the knowledge aside for even half a second, the tattoo provided a fail-safe. There was no forgetting. It was an unintended side effect of the protocol, but Willow supposed it only made the stigma all the more effective. She turned back to her groceries.

2006/01

"Warren, I'm in trouble." It was November and cool, but Duane was sweating. Profusely. And shaking too. Warren was deliberately perfecting a reputation for never asking the obvious, so he just looked at Duane expectantly.

"I think I've got it, Warren. That thing," he said in a desperate whisper. When Warren still didn't respond, Duane went on. "Herpes, Warren. The one that's burning people alive."

"Shit," Warren finally responded. It was the obvious answer, but he said it anyway. "Shit."

"I know." The terrible thing spoken, Duane had stopped shaking as much, though a bead of sweat still quivered at the tip of his nose. "What do I do? What if Jailyn finds out?"

"Start at the beginning. Where did you get it?" Warren's voice was calm, detached again. Duane was grateful. Only one of them could be blinded by the enormity of the situation.

"A party. For that stupid paper I got published on homegrown fuel. The faculty put on a party. Jailyn was out of town. There was a woman. Short skirt, big tits." Duane looked at his feet, ashamed.

"Did you fuck her?" Warren asked.

"Blow job. It's not cheating if you don't fuck." Duane said this last sentence more for his own benefit than for Warren's. Warren had his own piece on the side. It wasn't like he had the moral high ground. "I thought I was protected. I was supposed to be protected."

"Mouth to genital transmission," Warren said to himself. "Interesting."

"It's not 'interesting,'" Duane exploded. "It's my fucking life!"

"Oh, calm down you dumb fuck. It's always the professor-types. They think they're too smart to pick the wrong one. What happened to the girl?"

"Dead." Even Duane's voice was defeated. "She was a friend of one of the History professors. Died two weeks ago."

"And this happened?"

"A month ago. It was just a blow job, Warren. No one should die over a blow job." Duane's tone pleaded for agreement. Warren didn't oblige.

"People die for less. All the time," Warren replied coldly. He let silence fill the space between them as he watched Duane tremble. Finally, he spoke.

"I've been working on something. If it works, it will mutate the virus to something harmless." Duane's head jerked upright, hopeful. "I should warn you, it hasn't been properly tested yet."

"I don't care. I'm going to die anyway. Give it to me. Now. Before this gets any worse." Desperation made Duane's voice hoarse and raw.

"You sure? You'll have to sign release papers. Regulation. You know the deal." Warren watched his friend's face with interest: it was taut with fear.

"Of course. Anything. Just give it to me."

Warren walked Duane back to the Ministry building and into his second-floor lab, closing all the doors behind him and locking the last one after pulling it shut. Duane removed his jacket before the lock clicked into place and started unbuttoning the cuffs of his shirt. Warren walked to the lab's fridge and pulled out a single vial filled with amber liquid. From a drawer, he extracted a syringe in its plastic wrapping.

Duane rolled up his shirt-sleeve and perched on a lab stool, watching as Warren injected the needle into the vial, drew out the full contents, then tapped the syringe and ejected the air trapped inside.

"Do you want to know how it works?" Warren didn't look at his friend, so it didn't register when Duane shook his head. At the silence, Warren looked up.

"Just give it to me, damn it."

Unperturbed, Warren held Duane's arm to control the shaking and punctured his skin.

"Then let the games begin." Warren said.

FIVE

Ianthe waited. She was running out of time and anonymity. Clearing the surveillance video was no issue. Clearing people's memories was much harder. The concierge had seen far too much of her in the past week and her ruse of checking up on an out-of-town friend's apartment was wearing thin.

She'd been trailing the target for weeks, all at Marshall's direction, so she had as much understanding of the woman as could be gleaned from observation. Her previous habits and dress identified her as a typical Ministry conformist. Gloves? Check. Sober outfits and demure heels? Check. Aloof air of superiority? Check. Fucking Ministry through and through.

But the sudden shift in habit the week before—first the clinic visit, then the coddled hand, and finally her rapid exit from the Ministry building—told Ianthe this wasn't surveillance as usual.

Ianthe didn't care. The mission still chafed. She wanted to be doing anything but this: hiding in a doorway, the heels of her running shoes pressed to her ass, waiting.

Maybe Marshall was losing it. He knew better than anyone that she wasn't good with people. She preferred doing. Huddling into her bike, some message or another tucked into her back pocket, weaving her way up and down the east coast. In motion.

It didn't matter that staking out a target was an upgrade in responsibility. Any other time, she would have been eager to please, but all this waiting gave her time to think, which meant thinking about Kiri. All the evidence pointed in a direction she wasn't prepared to accept. Marshall, who was known for his bullheaded tenacity, had started talking about Kiri and the other Camellias at the protest in the past tense.

When the target had closed the door to her apartment and not reappeared again for several days, Ianthe had gone back to Marshall and begged to be pulled from the mission. Staking out women was Ven's specialty, not hers. Ianthe had argued hard.

Marshall had refused. And so she'd been sitting on her ass in a dark hallway, picking at her cuticles until they bled, when the door had opened and a hunched figure stepped into Ianthe's view.

Ianthe had scrambled to catch up with the target after the elevator, finally glimpsing the back of the target's head on the street. She'd followed her to the grocery store, then returned to the building. There would be a rare opportunity to make contact when she came back, assuming she had her hands full.

Something's working in my favor, Ianthe thought when she saw Willow exit the taxi cab overburdened with grocery bags. The question was whether to wait for the target to struggle first, making the offer of help more attractive, or to step right in immediately.

Fuck it, Ianthe thought as she crossed the sidewalk to where Willow was standing.

"Can I help? I'm headed up to the third floor." Ianthe gestured at the building. Willow startled visibly.

Long before Marshall, Ianthe had learned the fine art of eliciting trust. There had been days when her ability to appear harmless, fragile even, had kept her fed. She used it now without even thinking about it. There were some advantages to being mistaken for the thirteen year old she once had been. Her face fell easily into a wide-eyed innocent expression.

"Do you mind?" Willow hesitated.

"It's no problem," Ianthe said, her tone light.

"I'm on the third floor too." Ianthe could see the woman's posture relax slightly. "I appreciate the help."

Ianthe filled her arms with grocery bags as Willow did the same, then watched Willow's face as they approached the building. The closer they got to the glass doors, the more Willow's mouth narrowed. *Goddamn Ministry,* Ianthe thought. She remembered the way her own tattoo had felt like sharp gravel under her skin every time she'd approached a sensor.

The concierge opened the door for the overburdened women, trailed them to the elevator, and pushed the button for the third floor. Exiting the elevator, they waddled to Willow's door.

Willow assessed the girl out of the corner of her eye. She looked harmless. Emboldened by the success of her last interaction with a breathing human, Willow decided to let her inside.

She pressed her eye to the biometric lock and motioned for Ianthe to precede her through the door. To her surprise, the girl walked the bags into the apartment, set them down on the floor, and made no movement to leave.

Willow considered her options, caught between two competing impulses. The first was legacy from both mothers: politeness always won. The other was fear.

But this girl had done her a favor and Willow knew she needed the practice interacting.

"Can I get you something? Tea?" Willow offered awkwardly.

"Sure," the girl said. "I'll take tea."

Ianthe shifted from one foot to the other, deeply conscious of the difference between herself and the stark white apartment around her.

"My name is Ianthe, by the way." She didn't know what to say next, so she took a step toward the living room.

The move unsettled Willow, but she forced herself silent as she busied herself with the teapot. At the very least, she could manage tea.

With the tea kettle on to boil, she followed Ianthe into the living room.

"You live here alone?"

Willow looked more closely at the blond wisp of a girl in front of her. Ianthe's shoes, taken in isolation, were white. But against Willow's carpets they were obviously dingy and worn. Even the Ministry of the Interior had better-dressed employees, and that was saying something. She shifted her weight from one foot to the other and her eyes scanned the room like she was looking for valuables. Willow murmured her confirmation but started calculating how long it would take to get back to the kitchen and some sort of usable weapon.

"Wow. Nice place." Ianthe paused. "I thought rich people would have more..." Her voice trailed off as she realized how rude she sounded. She looked around for photographs, searching for ways to identify the target's family or acquaintances, but only saw her image staring back at her from cold surfaces. "Friends," she finished. "I mean, where are the photographs. There's no color here, it's all surface." Ianthe looked around the room again. She shoved her hands into her pockets lest she leave a fingerprint behind.

A timer rang in the kitchen. Willow turned reluctantly. "Just please don't..." She didn't finish the sentence. The list of things she didn't want the girl doing was too long.

"How long have you lived here?" Ianthe called toward the kitchen.

"A few years."

"Humph," Ianthe breathed. Louder, she said "it looks like the kind of place that gets featured in Architect and Style. Except for the carpets. The carpets are very rebel of you. Don't you know how many allergens live in carpet?"

"I vacuum," Willow said, annoyance creeping into her voice.

"Oh, it's cool with me," Ianthe rushed to add. "Carpets are a little miscreant bad-ass, you know?" She looked around at the sparse furnishings. "I just thought you'd have polished concrete. You know…something that can hold up to SaniCheck once a week."

Willow glanced at the clock. She was late for Dr. Webber's medication. She poured herself a glass of water and opened the bottle she'd left on the counter. The pills rattled against each other as they cascaded into her palm. Too late Willow realized it wasn't a sound that could be mistaken for anything else, and this girl was clearly cat-curious. She shoved the bottle behind her back as Ianthe re-entered the kitchen, covering the distance between them in three steps.

"What's that?" Ianthe's face was no longer schooled in benign concern.

"Nothing." Willow's hand closed over the green pills.

Ianthe held out her hand like a mother with a misbehaved child. Willow glared at her. Ianthe glared back.

"Listen sister, I already know. I've got it too. You might as well let me see it." Willow gaped at her. "They still handing out those vile green pills?"

Willow dropped the bottle of pills into Ianthe's outstretched hand.

"Shit. You'd be more effective with raw garlic. It'll make you fart toxic waste, but this shit," she shook the pill bottle for emphasis, "this shit will really fuck you up."

Willow snatched the bottle back. "It's regulation," she said. "And who the fuck are you?"

Ianthe raised a scarred eyebrow at the curse word. The woman in front of her didn't wear the right clothes for cursing. Even for grocery shopping, she looked pressed and starched. She was a waste of Ian's time.

"You really bought the Ministry bullshit didn't you? I should have known from this," Ianthe waved her hand vaguely at Willow's apartment. "Seriously, have you ever had a non-regulation thought? You must have. You aren't taking those for fun. That shit makes everyone want to die... Ianthe paused for a minute, then smirked. "Who was he? Or she?"

Willow just glared at her, her knuckles white around the pill bottle.

"Fine. I'll go first," Ianthe continued. She leaned against the counter for a second before placing both hands on the surface and hoisting herself to sit right where Willow normally cut her carrots. Her dirty shoes banged against the cabinet doors. Willow cringed.

"I got tattooed when I was thirteen. No, I wasn't that badass. My mom just married a creep. He stopped sleeping with her. Told her he couldn't get it up. He started fucking me instead. They caught the Herp in me on my first annual testing event… Trust me, however you got it, it isn't as bad as that." Ianthe looked at Willow as if daring her to contradict.

"I don't think you can be blamed." Willow spoke carefully. Her undergrad training was the only reliable guide she had, and it urged neutrality when interviewing a subject. Unfortunately, everything else in her wanted to grab the blond by the back of her thin hair and eject her from the apartment.

"Honey, ruined pussy is ruined pussy whether you asked for it or not. The tat is the same no matter how you acquire it. Anyway, you get over it." Ianthe looked at Willow closely. "I mean, you clearly haven't, but the rest of us come to some sort of a living arrangement with our busted party parts."

"The rest of us?" Willow could see her interviewing methods teacher standing in front of the classroom, instructing them to keep the subject talking. She needed the space to think.

"Yeah, that's why I'm here. I'm going to take you to meet the Camellias. We all have the Strain."

"What do you mean, the Strain?" Willow deliberately extracted tea bags from a cardboard box as she tried to absorb it all.

Ianthe went on. "You should know at least some of this, smarty pants. I read your dossier… You went to school for this shit." Willow looked back at Ianthe blankly. "The different strains of the Herp, right? You know, the mouth one, the pussy one, and then the real strain."

"There are only two strains of Herpes. The third was so virulent, it killed everyone that contracted it." Willow stepped to the stove and pulled off the kettle. The knife she'd left out earlier sat at the far end of the counter. Too far to lunge for.

"Well, I'm pretty sure you got it, so you're gonna find out." Ianthe followed Willow's gaze and languidly stretched out her hand. The knife began to quiver. Finally, as if shaking off a pervasive lethargy, it slid across the counter and into Ianthe's waiting hand. Willow watched in silence, her eyes wide.

"Anyway, from the looks of things, you need us. If only to put some names into your address book." Ianthe didn't look at Willow for this last statement; she was too busy examining the knife.

"Hold on a second," Willow spluttered, her eyes on the knife in Ianthe's hand. "I have no idea what you're talking about, but that's no reason for violence."

"Oh, get over yourself." Ianthe twisted her mouth in derision. "I'm not going to hurt you. My orders are to bring you back to Marshall." Ianthe gestured casually with the knife.

"Look, I direct the social diseases department at the Ministry. I'd know if what you are saying was true." Willow's voice shook as she spoke; she generally abhorred people who used their titles to intimidate, but desperate times… She could feel her heart beating double-time in her ears. She placed a hand on the kettle from the stove. "Kill me if you have to," she said, bracing herself to swing. "But I'm not going with you."

Ianthe grew still; it wasn't just that her heels stopped tapping softly against the cupboard. Even her breathing froze. "You study what?" She stared at Willow as the pieces fell into place. She should have known better than to think that Marshall was using this mission to distract her from Kiri's disappearance.

Ianthe looked down at the knife in her hand and opened up her palm in a gesture of reconciliation. The knife didn't slip. She turned her palm to the floor, fingers splayed, and shook her hand. The knife didn't budge. She began to laugh convulsively, her fear of losing a suddenly priceless target compounded by the ridiculousness of her predicament. "Some help here?" she asked when she could catch her breath, her arm extended towards Willow. Willow snatched the knife from the Ianthe's hand then retreated to the far side of the kitchen, knife at the ready.

"Listen, I'm sorry," Ianthe said, her tone softened. "I didn't mean to scare you. The Camellias understand what's happening to you. We just want to help. You don't need to go through this alone."

"I don't need anyone to help me deal with … with … with this thing." Willow gestured vaguely at her pelvis.

"Oh," Ianthe said. She'd heard that tone before and her reflexive anger flared beyond her control. "What you mean is you don't want any group therapy because you aren't like us, because anyone with the Herp is automatically a whore, an idiot, or both."

"Yes. Not you, of course. But yes." Willow stumbled over the words.

Even if the protocol never used those exact words, the labels hovered under the clinical terms: sex workers, risk-takers, fringe movements.

Ianthe forced herself to breathe past the red. Marshall needed this woman. She needed her. "Yeah, the newbies do that," Ianthe shook her head. "So busy damning themselves for what they think they did wrong that they can't help but damn everyone else."

Willow interrupted. "I study these statistics for a living. Your chances of contracting the disease go up by 50 percent if you know someone who is infected."

Ianthe burst into laughter. "Of course your chances of catching it go up when you know someone with the virus. How do you think you got it, dum dum? You didn't pick it up sitting on a toilet seat somewhere." Willow glared at the vagabond girl sitting on her counter top. Ianthe went on anyway. "Not that you've sat bare-assed on a toilet seat in your life. I bet you hover with your purse dangling from your neck."

She kept talking, undisturbed by Willow's narrowed eyes. "Let me tell you how you avoid getting the Herp, or anything else for that matter: lock yourself in your sterile little apartment. Never laugh with anyone, never kiss. Never drink from a public fountain. Never put your bare feet in the grass. Never make love, never fuck just for fun. Just die in here now and wait for your heart to catch on."

Willow pointed the knife at the door. "Get out." Willow repeated herself, louder this time. "Get out of my house."

Ianthe followed her gesture with her eyes and slid off of the counter. She turned her attention back to Willow. The tip of the knife betrayed the shaking in Willow's arm. Of course she was scared. For the first time, Ianthe saw beyond her immediate needs and remembered how it had been for herself at thirteen. Her anger turned inward. *Couldn't I have just trusted Marshall?*

With nothing left to lose, she walked forward slowly. It was as much of an apology as Ianthe had in her.

Willow flinched but stood her ground. Ianthe stopped within arms' length. "If you aren't ready for a slow suicide, then you'd better get on with learning how to live," she said gently.

Willow's grip on the knife softened.

Ianthe took another half step forward and kissed Willow gently at the corner of her mouth.

"I forgot how rough the first few weeks are." She touched Willow's hand. The tattoo tingled under the surface of Willow's skin.

"I could get rid of this for you," Ianthe offered, hoping for some measure of redemption.

Willow jerked her hand back.

"Don't." Willow's voice was sharp and biting. "Don't touch me. That tattoo is for public safety. I'd report you if I had any credibility left."

Ianthe sighed deeply and backed away. "Suit yourself, but you haven't really lost your credibility, you've just gained a different kind," she paused. "You'll see." She turned slowly and walked out of the kitchen, closing the door to the apartment softly. She stood in the hall, slumped silently against the door frame, certain the door wouldn't open to her again.

Six

Ianthe slid her fingers off the key and revved the engine. The smell of the exhaust filled the air and she breathed deeply. Somehow, it was a scent that didn't get old. She'd parked far enough out that MOS thugs were unlikely to pick her up. There were no neighbors to disturb or to call the Ministry of Security and report her. She eased the clutch out and the back tire bit into the concrete.

She wasn't looking forward to her conversation with Marshall. He'd put her faith to the test, and she'd failed. She'd treated the target like a target, like an obstacle to her real purpose. She'd failed, not just Marshall but Kiri too. The back of her eyes burned with a need to cry.

She wove through the empty streets just for the hell of it. Her knees didn't have to work to grip the body of the bike through the turns. She was the bike, attracted and fixed through the forces of mutual attraction. No one rode better than Ianthe. No one dared more, or succeeded.

The big abandoned houses gave way to smaller row houses with their roofs slouching in. Deflated balls collected rain in the front yards, some in black and white, others in a grilled orange. Doors clung to their rusting hinges at broken angles. Eyes shiny as marbles looked out from some windows: feral cats more than likely. Out here, the Ministry didn't have as much control over the reproductive lives of its denizens, be they two-legged or four.

Derelict neighborhoods morphed into an industrial area bisected by train tracks. Beside the tracks, a white road gave her plenty of room to maneuver. Ianthe folded at the waist, allowing the bike to pull her closer, and opened up the throttle. The trip would take long enough at an unreasonable speed, and Ianthe wasn't known for her patience.

The Camellia's headquarters sat like an oversized brick at the end of a gravel road. Three bay doors gave off no reflection in Ianthe's headlights. The gray aluminum siding was just a shade lighter than the surrounding darkness. Only the glass in the door threw a little light back at Ianthe.

She didn't bother shutting down the engine. Marshall would know she'd arrived as soon as she opened one of the bays to put the bike away. She rode up to the side of the building, pulled her hand off the handle bar and punched in her code. The door lurched and began to draw itself upward. Ianthe bent over the gas tank and ducked in before the door had opened halfway.

Marshall was waiting in his office, pacing. When he heard her footsteps in the hall, he forced himself to sit down and assume a posture of dominance. He leaned back and let his knees fall wide.

This office was Ianthe's favorite place in the whole building. Much like him, it was imposing yet warm. Rough around the edges. But mostly, Ianthe liked it because Marshall was there.

Ianthe opened the door without knocking and sank into a worn leather chair.

"You could have told me she was critical."

Marshall took his time in replying. "I wouldn't have sent you if she wasn't."

"I lost her." Ianthe looked up at Marshall with empty eyes. "I fucking lost her. I wasn't cuddly enough. I challenged her when I should have patted her on the head."

Marshall raised a questioning eyebrow and Ianthe looked back at him. She couldn't help it; she blamed him for the fuck up too. "If you had told me who she was, I would have handled it differently."

"What would have made you handle yourself differently, Ian? Wasn't the fact that I asked you enough?"

Ianthe slouched back into her seat and covered her face with her hands. "For fuck's sake, Marshall. She could have led us to Kiri."

Marshall didn't react to her anger – he knew her well enough to know it was just a cover for her anger with herself. "Salvageable?"

He liked Ianthe. She'd never been particularly guarded, but her anguish was written all over her, from her hunched posture to the way her eyes couldn't stop looking around the room. If he believed in favorites, she would have been at the top of his list.

He waited while Ianthe thought through her exchange with Willow, but truthfully, Marshall wasn't any more patient than Ianthe.

"What is it Ian?"

"It didn't go well." Ianthe laughed bitterly. "But take the evidence. Her apartment didn't have a single photo in it. No family, no friends. She's lonely." Marshall watched as Ianthe processed. "She didn't get infected by herself. That tells us she isn't as indoctrinated as she thinks she is."

Across the desk, Marshall nodded. "And there was something. Uncertainty, I think. When she was telling me that there were only two strains of the Herp. All I can hope is that something I said will get through to her. If there's a crack in that wall, maybe doubt will seep in."

"Or she's had all the adventure she can stand," Marshall considered aloud. He closed his eyes and cracked his knuckles one by one. "She's important. I just don't know how."

"Why didn't you send Ven? Ministry freaks are Ven's specialty – not mine." Ianthe spoke of Ven with derision. She didn't have anything specific against him, he just played too close to the Ministry, and did so with a flexibility that came too easily for Ianthe's taste.

"Because Ven infected her," Marshall answered quietly. "I sent Ven to Atlanta on a reconnaissance mission."

"You let him infect someone?" Ianthe's tone was disbelieving.

Marshalls look told Ianthe that she should have known better than to ask. "Of course not. He was supposed to get information at that damn conference. No one, not even Ven, will ever get clearance to infect someone just because they feel like it."

"Sorry," Ianthe mumbled. Marshall had too much honor for that, and Ianthe knew it.

"I got a message from Kiri that she'd seen him leave the conference with that girl. You've confirmed the diagnosis. There's no other explanation. Shortly after Kiri's dispatch, I got a message from Ven saying that MOS had picked up the Camellias and he was in trouble."

Ianthe struggled to take a deep breath. She secretly thought of Marshall as the replacement for her unknown father. But even her surrogate father had other priorities: Marshall's affection for Ven was singularly palpable and unwavering, as firm as a father's love for a prodigal son. She honestly didn't know if the hollowed-out version of Marshall she'd seen since Kiri disappeared was because he'd lost six of his own or because he'd lost Ven.

Ianthe chose her words carefully. "Do you think he targeted her because she knows something?"

Marshall swiveled his chair back and forth. "She has to know something," he said. "It's just a question of what."

"The Infirmary, Marshall," Ianthe's voice caught an up-current of hope. "Maybe she knows. If she can help us we might be able to find them both." Her thoughts turned to Kiri and her hands tightened into fists. Marshall looked up at her, his face softening.

"Ian, you understand that the likelihood..." he started.

Ianthe's eyes welled up in tears. She put her hand up to stop him from speaking further. "Don't," she said. "I know I can get through to her. It know it. I'll go back. I'll find an opening. Please," she begged, "just give me another chance."

SEVEN

Willow's life settled into a new normal. Old era movies, some on repeat. She gave her mother's old VHS player a permanent home next to the TV with a hundred videotapes of television shows that were no longer available in stores. She wallowed in the old British Broadcasting Company's faithful interpretations of books that had long since gone out of fashion.

As her body reacted more and more strongly to the Malvexitran, the lights in the house got lower and lower. With the curtains closed, the ancient characters projected from her television screen and seemed to seat themselves on the edges of her furniture as they carried out their painfully polite interactions. Willow watched Anne Elliott's disappointment and redemption for reasons to hope—hope for what wasn't clear.

When one thought followed the next in a relatively sensible fashion, they inevitably returned to her conversation with Ianthe. As each pill brought on more misery, Willow considered, then dismissed, then reconsidered the girl's casual dismissal of the Ministry's medicine.

Willow had not been taunted for her ignorance often. Ianthe's teasing reminder that, for all her expertise, Willow knew nothing about what was happening to her, had struck home. Somehow, having spent the last ten years working in the field of social disease and four years before that in school on the same basic subject, hadn't educated her. She knew the names, the DNA sequences. The statistics and the history. But it was all theoretical; it assumed a world where things just are with no origin, no reason. She had never asked questions about the details, the lives.

How did each hash in the statistical tabulation actually live? It was a new thought. Thirty percent of the population was infected in one way or another, but who were they? Six percent of infected people died, a statistic that undergirded every public information campaign. *It might kill you. Stay away from the unclean. Wear your body condom, every partner, every time. Wash your hands. Wear your gloves. Don't kiss.*

The bottle was only half-empty when a new ache, this one coming with dual prongs on either side of her spine, began. She had to go back to her textbook on anatomy to check her suspicions. The positioning was right: her kidneys were objecting. The drugs were the obvious culprit, but with no slip in the bottle documenting side effects, she had no way of telling if kidney failure was normal. She picked up Dr. Webber's bottle with the evil green pills and shook it. The remaining pills clattered against each other.

She carried the bottle back to the office with a glass of water and typed the name of the drug into her search engine. MALVEXITRAN side effects. She hit the return key and the computer blinked into darkness. Willow set the bottle down, turned the machine off then back on and waited for it to reboot. When everything was back up and running, she typed the letters back into the computer and hit return again. *Ministry bastards,* she thought to herself. *Not inventive enough to lie; they just pull the plug on anything they don't want known.*

The computer crashed for a second time. Willow picked up the bottle again as she waited for the computer to reboot, and considered it. She withdrew a pill and allowed herself to really feel it in her palm. She closed her eyes and measured its weight against her skin. It felt wobbly and uncomfortable from the inside out. Ianthe's mocking words came back to her: *You'd be better off with garlic.*

Willow looked down at it and put it back into the bottle.

Over the next three days, Willow filled up a notebook with precise handwriting. History, alternate treatments, famous people who were thought to have suffered from Herpes in the old era, Willow read it all. When she was sobbing and unable to sleep, she went back to digging. The initial throbbing sore subsided, only to be followed by a subtle itching in the dermal layer of her labia. Every time she got up to pee, she'd recheck herself, probing for an ache, a thickening of the skin, anything that might possibly be evidence of an upcoming outbreak.

It didn't take too long for the thing to erupt, this time on the right side with the same pain, the same electrical current flowing through her spine. She lay down on the floor behind her desk and stared at the ceiling, willing the pain to subside. When it finally receded, she got up off the floor and walked the worn path back to the kitchen.

The raw garlic wasn't easier to swallow, but she didn't immediately feel like her body was under siege either. Just for good measure, she placed a slice of the white bulb on her skin where the blister was forming. She looked at the time. Midnight. She walked back to her bedroom and crawled into bed smelling distinctly like a spaghetti kitchen.

She dreamed of a camellia blossoming inside a kaleidoscope. It burst open and morphed, changing from white to green to yellow, then collapsed into itself and re-burst in pink with a thin texture like bubbles stretched thin and ready to erupt. It pushed itself outward and took on a blue hue as it stretched, expanded to exploding and shrank down, first to a manageable size, then further, down to a microscopic wiggle that shook and buried itself into the palm of her hand. Willow opened her eyes to absolute darkness.

She ran her hands over her body, then clasped herself close at the elbows. Willow could feel the virus glowing like a phosphorescent jellyfish in her spine, circles of bioluminescent lights chasing each other around, the tentacles drifting in the blood-tide. She followed each tentacle until she found the one thread that had attached itself to the underside of her skin. Willow closed her eyes and visualized herself examining the thread from the inside, feeling for its weak point and snapping it in two. The phosphorescent lights spun faster, but no further tentacles drifted to the underside of her skin and attached. Willow released her elbows, rolled over, and fell back asleep.

In the morning, Willow fished the slice of garlic out of her drawers and flushed it down the down the toilet. The skin underneath was smooth and she felt no pain, no kitten-claws tearing at her skin from the inside. She looked herself in the mirror, let the electrons in her hands react to the vanity surface—still reasonably solid—and came to two inevitable conclusions: first, she was clearly going crazy, and second, she needed to talk to Ianthe again.

The days blurred together. A recommendation from the internet had Willow taking enough Vitamin C to burn holes in her underwear. Even her farts were acidic. Combined with the raw garlic, she could barely stand her own stench. Even so, it was better than the sickly green pills the Doctor had given her. She could think and function, and her olfactory nerves were rapidly growing immune to the smell of her skin.

She woke up whenever her eyelids broke open. With nowhere to go, the alarm seemed pointless. She showered or she didn't, mostly depending on whether she was breaking out. The cycle of blisters and unblemished skin seemed to run by hours, not days. According to the official Herpes website, this wasn't normal, but Willow had now run out of faith in the Ministry's unfailing knowledge.

The website didn't say anything about feeling the atomic structure of the physical world either, and Willow's hands hadn't stopped transmitting information she had no logical reason to feel. She did know that what she was dealing with was different than the things shown in the literature. She compared what she saw on her own body, hunched over herself with a flashlight and a mirror, with the photographs on the Ministry sites where the victims had broad swaths of oozing blisters. She was lucky if she got a lesion the size of a pin to justify the excruciating pain.

After exhausting the sanctioned literature, she ventured out looking for the unapproved websites. The Ministry had done a remarkable job in denying access to the internet, but those who wanted to host unapproved material were ingenious too. Roving IP addresses, data buried in a flood of random information... When Willow managed to uncover one, she wrote everything down.

The Ministry didn't approve of alternative healing and their "misinformation" eradication campaign was thorough and fast. As she discovered websites, she began noticing that many shared one thing in common: a minuscule white flower embedded somewhere in the page. Willow looked up white flowers until she found a photograph similar enough to count: a Camellia in full bloom. Apparently the Camellias did more than provide physical shelter.

They weren't the only people with an alternate explanation to the Ministry's story, but they were the only ones who weren't selling anything. If you wanted to spend your money on salvation, there were plenty of people selling magic pills, potions, and creams. Willow resisted the urge to purchase.

At least once a day, Willow tried to leave the house. The grocery store was more than she could handle most of the time—all those people, the relentless cheer of the cashiers, the bright lights, row after row of colored boxes with the Ministry stamp of nutritional value. But there was a vitamin shop about a mile away, a designated open space three blocks to her east, and the odd pastime of getting to know her city.

Never had she had so much time alone, so much time to think, so much silence. Walking had the advantage of giving her something else to think about. Bricks and buildings and street names and the river. She walked to the University Hospital, took her gloves off, and touched the rough bark of the trees. The students looked at her with indifference.

In her wandering, Willow hadn't seen anyone that looked like a Camellia, though she had no idea what someone from the underground would look like. Shabby like Ianthe, she supposed, but she couldn't just approach any shabby person she saw walking down the street. Instead, she went back to the internet, following the white flower from site to site.

She joined a discussion board full of conspiracy theorists and rebels, and posted her own message: ISO Camellia Ianthe, then put her building number and street name. Willow didn't know what else to do.

Eight

Willow had been out walking again, this time towards the river because the path she took home led her past the vitamin shop. She had returned with a brown paper bag and a hundred capsules of Vitamin C, escaping the chill October weather for the shelter of her building. With her eyes on the ground in front of her as she stepped through the door, Willow's gaze caught those grungy white shoes. She looked up. "Ianthe," she called, and Ianthe turned her head.

"You rang?" Ianthe said in a hopeful tone when Willow had reached her. She sounded as young as she looked.

"Tea?" Willow offered, her voice only slightly sarcastic.

Relief flooded over Ianthe and she smiled in spite of herself. "No. You need to meet the Camellias. And Marshall wants to meet you." Ianthe gave Willow a quick half-smile in apology. "I got in trouble for fucking up our last conversation."

"Can I at least take this back to my place?" Willow raised the brown paper bag and the tablets rattled within the bag.

Ianthe nodded her assent. "More of that toxic shit?" She asked once the elevators closed around them.

"Vitamin C," Willow answered.

Ianthe smiled broadly. "So you were paying attention."

"Don't let it go to your head." Willow retorted.

"You will come with me," it was a statement, but posed with the intonation of a question. Ianthe held her breath, cursing herself for being too direct. Kidnapping had crossed her mind, but the bike wasn't likely to handle a kicking and screaming passenger.

Willow was silent, thinking through her options. If she said no, she risked losing access to an alternate source of information, one that was rapidly sounding more reliable than the Ministry. If she said yes, she knew that there'd be no going back.

Ianthe waited anxiously. A hundred beginnings hovered on her tongue, but something Marshall said to her before she left kept her quiet. "Whoever talks most, loses, Ian. Every time." So Ianthe held her tongue and let Willow squirm in the silence. Standing in her kitchen with the paper bag clutched in her hand, Willow looked around at her home. There hadn't been any photographs added to the walls since Ianthe was last her guest. No prospect for new faces either.

"What's it going to be?" Ianthe finally asked, determined to press on. "Send me to my doom all by myself or have yourself an adventure?" She stood with her palms open as if to demonstrate she had nothing to hide.

Finally, Willow sighed. "It isn't like I've got anything better to do with my afternoon." Ianthe grinned in spite of herself. Willow walked from room to room, looking for things that she should take with her, but came up empty handed. All except for her personal Kevorkian. That she tucked in the change pocket of the jeans she was wearing and was glad Ianthe wasn't there to see her. Back in the living room, she smiled at Ianthe. "Ready?"

Ianthe nodded and Willow followed her back out into the wind. She seemed to know where she was going, even though Willow was quickly lost among back alleys and crooked side streets she'd not gotten to in her daily walks. Finally, they came to a dirty little motorcycle propped up against an old-fashioned light-post.

Ianthe patted her waist. When she touched the fabric outside her jacket pockets, the fabric on her right side stuck to her hand as she pulled her hands away. She shook her hand and the fabric dropped back to her body, the keys jingling inside. She put her fingertips inside the pocket and withdrew them. The keys followed, attached to her fingers, but not because she'd grabbed them.

Willow watched everything, working hard not to stare as Ianthe pulled the keys off of her right hand with her left, then rearranged them so the correct key was pointing out. Ianthe unlocked the carrying case on the side of the bike.

With the keys just sort of hanging in her palm, she pulled out one dirty white helmet and handed it to Willow. The metal buckle on the end arched toward Ianthe's skin.

"Put it on." Ianthe handed the helmet to Willow, who heard the SaniCheck jingle dance its way through her ears. Willow was pretty sure that Ianthe had never seen the wet end of a SaniCheck stick.

Nevertheless, she did as instructed and watched for Ianthe to procure another for herself. None was forthcoming. "What about you?" Willow asked.

"Meh. I'll be fine. Lisa," she patted the bike "is almost like an appendage. I trip less on her than I do on my own two feet." She threw a leg over the seat then scootched up to give Willow room. Willow mimicked the action, but more gingerly. Where Ianthe seemed to be indifferent to the mud and oil caked onto the side of the bike, Willow was very aware of a compelling need to keep her jeans clean.

"Hang on," Ianthe said as she turned the ignition and revved the engine. Willow put her hands on Ianthe's waist lightly. Her palms were sweating inside her latex gloves. She tried not to hang on too tightly, afraid her grip might reveal her own fear. Motorcycles were deliberately rare as the Ministry did not approve. Too dangerous. Licenses were hard to come by and all the used models were modified to limit speed. Tampering with an engine to make it go faster was a crime that could earn you jail time. Nothing newly-built on two wheels went any faster than 25 miles an hour, and Ianthe was courting a huge fine if she was caught with no helmet on. Willow had never even seen a motorcycle in person, let alone ridden one. Her pulse accelerated and throbbed against her neck.

Ianthe pushed the bike off its kick-stand and took off. The jerking motion nearly threw Willow off the back of the bike. She reacted instinctively and clutched at Ianthe's middle. Ianthe snickered and opened up the accelerator.

They were on a twisty road in a nearly-abandoned neighborhood far from the city center, it wasn't quite the open road, but Willow wanted to giggle at the sensation of freedom. *I could get used to this*, she thought to herself as she leaned into Ianthe for a corner. Even with her borrowed sense of bravery, she held on tight. Underneath her and beyond Ianthe's magnetic field, the girl's cells buzzed happily against Willow's skin. Apparently, the joy of a bike and a little speed didn't lose its impact with wear.

Ianthe knew where she was going even if Willow was completely disoriented. She wove her way through neighborhoods at the fringes of the city, each more abandoned than the last, until finally they were on an empty road that ran straight into nowhere. Willow could feel the pleasure thrumming through Ianthe's body.

Willow's hands were on Ianthe's hips, and she could name the very instant that Ianthe had gone from a tense alertness to a relaxed union with the bike. It wasn't in Ianthe's posture, it was in her neurons. Willow turned to the scenery. Through the bare trees, she could see buildings that were being taken over by vegetation.

The Ministry had done some television programs on this, the benefits of allowing nature to reclaim the space around the cities to provide a true buffer between the urban areas and the vast farms in between. It had seemed romantic on the television, all that ivy breaking down the stainless steel of the capitalist era, the daisy-chain of parking lots cracking under the pressure of tree roots pushing up from below, grass breaking down the asphalt until the white lines marking parking spots gave way to the chaos of wildflowers. The Ministry didn't seem to mind the anarchy, so long as it didn't involve people.

Willow craned her head around Ianthe to look at the speedometer. It was creeping upwards, 45, then 55, then 65 miles per hour. Willow forgot about appearances and grabbed Ianthe around the waist for real. She thought about the Ministry of Security and its speed regulations, but there were no MOS troops on this forgotten road. No one to enforce the Republic's policy of prejudice against drivers.

The Ministry had long since restricted or banned anything that led to people dying in completely preventable ways cars and cigarettes topped that list. The Ministry was okay with people dying sensibly, rationally, in control of their own destinies. It was not okay with expensive, sloppy deaths. There'd been too many of those in the epidemic of '89.

They'd done a good job of convincing the population; all the old ads, the ones that had built a nation of drivers who associated freedom with a full tank of gas, had been thoroughly parodied. The Republic had drawn the direct link between emissions, global warming, and a virus-friendly environment. Indeed, of the myriad of causes for the '89 pandemic, the Ministry blamed the car as a primary factor. Now, motor vehicles were nearly extinct. If you had to go somewhere, you took a taxi or the train.

So this was Willow's first motorcycle, but it didn't take long to begin questioning the Ministry's judgment in this too. She was in love. Once the speed didn't feel quite so reckless, she took her hands from Ianthe's waist and placed them behind her, bracing herself on the seat. The machine had a whole new hum to it. Willow closed her eyes and probed it a little. Its electrons felt smooth and worn like Willow's oldest jeans. The bike knew what it was doing—it practically purred. Willow smiled a real smile, her first in forever, and put her hands back on Ianthe's waist.

Willow's face hurt from smiling. All those muscles had been woefully underutilized. Even in her week with Ven, she hadn't really smiled, not the same way, at least. *Fleming's ass,* she thought to herself, *this must be what joy feels like.* She played with the muscles in her face to relax the tension from her grin, but it didn't help. Moments later, her cheeks were back to aching.

The sun was murky behind the black trees by the time Ianthe pulled off the pitted main road and down a gravel drive. The back tire fishtailed in the loose stones, but Ianthe quickly brought the bike back under control. Willow looked over her shoulder at the speedometer. They were down to 50 mph from the 76 they had been doing as they wove through the cracks and craters in the main road. Willow's back and shoulders complained about the awkward posture, but she was too busy watching everything to care. The trees on either side of the road leaned into each other, creating a leafy arch above their heads. Darkness gathered in the leaves and intensified. Willow held on a little tighter.

Ianthe took them through several more turns, some of which seemed to double back on themselves, before they arrived at Camellia headquarters. Light from the windows on the front face of the building pushed the darkness back a little ways, enough to dispel Willow's apprehension. She could see shadows moving against the walls of the rooms within. One light blinked to life. Another disappeared. No one seemed to note their arrival even though one of the first-floor bay doors lurched against its steel tracks and retracted into the ceiling above. Ianthe drove straight into the building.

The door rolled into place behind them as Willow's eyes slowly adjusted to the indoor lighting and she looked around. There were more bikes like Ianthe's, and white buckets with dirty spare parts piled on top. In one corner, a startling variety of stained tools stood out against the white wall. Saws with rusted teeth hung from nails; hammers dangled between two pegs on a board lined with holes. Ianthe followed Willow's eyes and answered the unasked question.

"That's the workshop. We build what we need."

Willow looked back at the battered assortment of motorcycles. The floor under them was stained with black puddles. Willow remembered that she had started her adventure clean and smoothed her latex-clad hands down her thighs.

"You might as well throw those things away," Ianthe said, watching Willow's gesture. "No one here wears them." Ianthe leaned the bike to one side, bracing it with her leg while she knocked the kickstand into place and returned the bike perpendicular to the floor. "I was sure I would have to beg," Ianthe added as she pried her hands off of the handlebars. "No one is expecting me back this quickly. I think Marshall was kidding, but he did tell me not to come back without you." Ianthe didn't offer one of her lopsided grins.

"How am I going to get home?" Willow asked.

"When they're done talking to you, I'll take you home the same way we came."

"How long are they going to talk to me, and who is 'they'?" Willow's stomach clenched.

"They is Marshall and whoever else he drags in. You're kind of a big deal." Ianthe smiled at Willow, who had gone pale. "You're from the Ministry of Health. We've never had one of you before." Ianthe said it like this was a zoo and Willow was an unheard of species.

"What are they going to do to me?" Old rumors about Ministry interrogations popped up uninvited. The Ministry liked extracting information, through DNA if necessary. The Ministry always protected the comfort of their specimens, but a lot could happen while you were under anesthetic. She wondered how the Camellia's tactics differed from the Ministry's.

"Nothing bad, I promise," Ianthe answered. "Everyone likes Marshall. He'll just ask you a few questions."

Willow tried to calm her rising sense of panic. She should have pushed Ianthe on why the Camellia's wanted her so badly before she agreed to get on the bike.

"Let's go surprise someone." Ianthe climbed off the bike as if extracting herself from a glue trap and took off across the cavernous room towards a gray door in the back wall. Because there wasn't much else to do, Willow followed. She saw a trash can by the door and dropped her latex gloves in it before she passed through. In the dry air, her sweat evaporated quickly, leaving her fingers cool.

The door led into a hallway lit with struggling fluorescent lights. Willow thought back to the Ministry buildings with their regulation 60 percent natural light sources. *At least the Ministry got that much right,* Willow thought. *These buzzing lights should be outlawed.*

Here, the concrete floor was littered with tumbleweeds of dust but no oil slicks. Its drab surface was scuffed with black heel marks that stood out against the pasty gray background. The walls reflected light off painted, pocked cinder block.

"What was this place?" Willow asked quietly, keeping close to Ianthe as they moved through the echoing corridor.

"When?"

"Before you moved in." There wasn't much to see, but Willow's eyes darted from wall to wall.

"As best we can figure, it was a building supply company of some variety. The shop area was stacked to the ceiling with doors." Ianthe's voice was calm. Matter-of-fact. It didn't help.

The two women walked the length of the hallway and came to a door that opened into a stairwell. They began climbing.

Two long flights of stairs later and Willow's legs burned. She kept her weight within regulation and always passed the fitness tests at the Ministry, but they hadn't had any stairs in those. Ianthe didn't seem to have any trouble breathing, but Willow was wheezing like the kids on the asthma treatment commercials from her childhood. They burst through another door and into a room littered with worn sofas and chairs.

The space was nearly as large as the shop below but with a lower ceiling. A dying fluorescent light flickered in the center of the room. Little circles of light from a tattered collection of table lamps illuminated clusters of seating. The faces in the chairs were revealed in halves and quarters, their eyes turned toward the open door, wary.

Only a few of the Camellias—at least Willow assumed they were all Camellias—sat straight. Most lounged at odd angles, leaning into and on each other, their bodies sagged against the furniture like rag dolls discarded by some petulant child. Willow squared her shoulders and stood taller. No one said anything.

"Nice to see you too," Ianthe muttered under her breath. "Where's Marshall," she asked to no one, louder this time.

"Office," a voice called from across the room. "Is that her?"

Ianthe didn't answer. Instead, she grabbed Willow's hand and started walking. Willow followed, but she wasn't watching where they were going. She had noticed a kid half-way across the room.

He was long and lean with an awkward case of late-adolescent acne. He wore a long black jacket and the hem of his jeans didn't quite reach the top of his dingy tube socks. A yo-yo without a string dangled off his outstretched hand. It spun into a blur in the dim light, fast enough to throw sparks, as if its friction with the air were enough to catch fire. It hung there, suspended and spinning, far longer than was possible. Then the kid flicked his wrist and it whirled itself back up its nonexistent string and back into the palm of his hand.

That isn't fucking possible, she thought.

She had just about picked her jaw off of her chest when she noticed another male: this one also caught between adolescence and adulthood, old enough to grow a full beard but not solid enough to call a man. In a squared black hat, black suspenders, and narrow black trousers, he stood by the window, the arc of lightning in his hands reflecting off the pane of glass. He passed the bolt from one hand to the other, as if he was juggling a particularly bright comet.

"In the name of Fleming, what is all this?" Willow murmured, her head turned half-way around as Ianthe dragged her through another door.

"The Camellias," Ianthe replied quietly. "We all have the Strain."

"The Strain?" The door closed behind them, but Willow still whispered.

"I told you that you aren't a normal Herp. You've got the Strain, like me. I'm like a magnet. Malachi plays with lightning. You... I don't know, but I'm sure you do something." They passed through a second door then came to an abrupt stop in front of a door with frosted glass in its top half. It looked like the door you'd see in a detective's office in one of India's old movies. Ianthe knocked.

The voice that was speaking within stopped for a moment, then bellowed, "Come in."

The women walked through the door. A man Willow assumed was Marshall cradled a phone between his shoulder and his ear. He held up a blunt finger.

While his attention returned to his phone call, Willow studied him carefully. His head was nearly bald. What little hair remained was white and stood at strict attention. Bushy eyebrows framed clear brown eyes. His shoulders were broader than his chair, and he could have rested his arms on his belly had he been so inclined. He wore a zipped sweatshirt over a fraying tee shirt. They didn't match.

"I've got to go," he said into the receiver. "Call me when you have something." He didn't bother to say goodbye. Dropping the phone into its cradle, he turned to Willow and Ianthe.

"Ian," he nodded in her direction, his shiny head reflecting the sickly fluorescent light, "this had better be Willow Carlyle."

NINE

For the first time since Willow had met Ianthe, the younger woman looked intimidated. "Yes, Sir," she responded. "This is Willow."

Marshall stood and Willow got a sense of exactly what she was dealing with. He was huge. Standing, his shoulders were nearly as wide as a bull's and with the same stubborn muscularity. He extended a hand to shake. Willow reached out, taking his hand, then jerked back in surprise. She looked down at her hand, half expecting to see the skin blistering from the heat coming off of Marshall's skin.

He chuckled, but the laughter didn't reach his eyes.

"Sorry about that. The heat can be a shock if you aren't expecting it. Sit," he gestured at an empty chair. "Make yourself at home." He turned to Ianthe. "Have you asked our guest if she's hungry, Ian?" Ianthe slowly shook her head. "Well?" It wasn't so much a question as order. Ianthe ducked out of the room and disappeared.

Marshall examined Willow from under heavy eyelids, looking at her longer than was polite. Willow stared back.

"How long has it been," Marshall finally asked.

"Since what?"

From the tone in his voice, he might have been asking how long it had been since she last sacrificed innocent children.

"Since the diagnosis."

That. If membership depended on positive test results, then it made sense that eventually, someone would ask how long you'd been part of the club. Still, she didn't want to let the words cross her lips.

"Almost two weeks." Her voice wavered a little.

"Still feel like you've been skinned?" There was something like compassion in Marshall's tone, which unnerved Willow. She looked down at her hands again, suddenly afraid she might cry.

"In a way, you're as bad off as Mal." Willow looked up as if to ask what he meant, but Marshall went on without prompting. "Malachi, our poor little Mennonite. You might have noticed him on your way in. Weird beard, black pants, hat..." Willow nodded. "The poor kid doesn't know what to do with himself. It's been close to two years now and he's still breaking out all the damn time, just because he's so obsessed with the state of his dick. He hasn't even begun to wrap his head around the Strain, let alone the Herp. He comes from farm country in the Wastes south of here."

Willow started diagramming social networks in her head, conceptually trying to construct a theoretical chain of causality. Marshall kept talking.

"He started blistering up, the poor fuck, and didn't know what the hell was going on. To top it all off, he was standing in the field just before a storm and got hit by lightning three times in about three minutes. His brother was there to see it and told everyone in the colony. He had to leave before they married him off to the purist girl available. He was the residential miracle. Picked the Herp up in a whore house when he was supposed to be selling grain." Marshall paused. "Dumb kid."

He fell silent for a moment, thinking back to the terrified boy that he'd slung over the back of his bike. Better to take him in than to leave him where he was, sitting in the Wastes under a cracked blue and red sign that read Greyhound. "He did the right thing, coming with us," Marshall went on. "You just can't go around infecting a Mennonite." Willow filed the term away for looking up later. "Their immune systems aren't up to it. Could kill someone like that..." Marshall let his words trail off, then shook his head. "Right. That's not what you came for."

"Actually," Willow broke in, "I don't know what I'm here for."

Marshall leaned back in his chair, his arms across his chest. Something in his eyes cooled as he stared at her. Willow's shoulders rose towards her ears. She looked back at him, their eyes locked in an exchange Willow wasn't sure she understood but knew she couldn't afford to lose. She didn't break the stare. Finally, Marshall spoke.

"So how's the Minister?"

His voice was low and lined with contempt.

"Excuse me?" Willow responded, confused. First, it wasn't a question she'd been expecting. Secondly, if this man knew anything about the Ministry, he'd know that only the most senior of Ministry employees spent time with the Minister.

"The sonofabitch that runs the Ministry of Health. How is he?" The expletive flowed off Marshall's lips like water over stone.

"I don't know Minister Lake. At least not personally." Willow took a deep breath and forced her shoulders down again. She rearranged her body in the chair, giving her best nonverbal indicators that she had nothing to hide.

"Fine. Tell me about the Infirmary." His eyes were on her, watching every twitch, every breath.

Her face betrayed genuine surprise.

"Your testing facility. I need to know where it is."

Willow shook her head in response. "I don't know what you're talking about."

Marshall watched her closely for a tell; a touch to her face, a change in her blinking, eyes that shifted like she was looking for the truth. Nothing. He changed tactics.

"What's new at the Ministry?"

Willow thought carefully, checking her loyalties. The annual security training she'd taken every year since she'd started at the Ministry came back to her: be calm, be neutral, make a show of being open and reveal nothing. She didn't owe anything to the Ministry now, but she didn't owe anything to this Marshall and his collection of vagabonds either. She decided on appeasement and offered innocuous information in her calmest voice. "If there is something specific you want to know, just ask. But your question is too broad." Willow forced herself to react as she would have to Nate or even Nate's boss: calmly, forcing specific questions, and answering in facts, not feelings.

"I want to know everything." Marshall replied cryptically. He didn't clarify, so Willow offered up the most benign answer she could think of.

"Fine. I'll tell you about working for the Ministry. That should convince you I'm the wrong girl." Willow sighed. "The Ministry is like any other bureaucracy. One part of the organization has no idea what the other part is doing. There's always a fight for resources and research funding. Sometimes some parts of the organization have the Minister's blessing. Sometimes you get ignored completely.

The scientists there are incredibly dedicated. Those that aren't dedicated get promoted. Politics, infighting, idiots and assholes... the same as everywhere. And then you go to work one day and a project that you've been working on for years clicks into place. You've got the right funding, the right personnel and suddenly you're making a difference for the Republic and you're on top of the world."

"Which department were you in?" Marshall prodded.

"Social sciences. Predicting the erratic." Willow almost smiled at the memory. If only she'd been as effective at predicting the outcomes in her own life.

"And?" Marshall pushed.

"I went to work. My team did good work and I did my best to protect them from the bullshit that always seems to roll downhill. I avoided my boss as much as possible, I worked policy and statistics, and tried to do it all a little better every day." Willow looked up from her hands and into Marshall's eyes. "Look, I'm sorry that I don't have more for you. I was just another bureaucrat, another inch of red tape. I don't know anything of value."

"I'll be the judge of that." Marshall responded aloofly. He let his eyes drift shut as if bored with the conversation. "Where is the Minister's office?"

"Thirty-third floor, but that's not classified. You probably already knew that."

"That's not the point."

"So tell me what the point is." Willow's patience was wearing thin.

Marshall's bipolar routine had left her unsure what she was dealing with. The empathy that had marked his voice at the beginning of the conversation certainly lined up with the man Ianthe had described, but Willow had dealt with too many men in power to trust either persona.

"You're here because you caught the Herp, and you caught it from someone with the Strain, which makes the likelihood that you got the Strain shoot straight through the roof." This girl wasn't as bright as he'd expected for a Ministry chit.

"I've spent most of my adult life studying the networking of social diseases, but I've never heard of the Strain." The other word still stuck in her throat, so she didn't say it out loud.

Marshall leaned back in his chair and ran a hand across his bald head as if expecting to encounter hair. "You know the basic virology, right?"

Willow nodded, then clarified. "But it isn't my specialty."

"Strain, 101. The virus makes its home in the nerves in your spine. Something happens, your immune system is compromised, you have a stressful day, whatever, and the virus flares up, travels along the nerves and expresses itself as an outbreak. Painful," Willow nodded in agreement. "Annoying, but not the end of the world.

With the Strain, the virus changes those nerve cells. They start bunching together and acting like electrical circuits in your spine. Eventually, they reproduce enough that your entire body starts reacting to electricity differently. Mal, the poor schmuck, attracts lightning but it doesn't kill him.

Kiri," here Marshall paused, checking to be sure Willow was keeping up, "you haven't met Kiri."

Marshall's face betrayed a pain that had no visible antecedent. "Kiri's like a human battery. She sucks electricity in and stores it. You wouldn't want to let her hang on to your hand too long. Would take a good week to get squared away after that." He paused for long enough that Willow was beginning to wonder if he would start talking again.

Finally, he went on. "Ian has her own electromagnetic field. If you threw her at a fridge, she'd stick. Everyone reacts differently."

Willow leaned into the hard frame of the chair and waited for the light-headed feeling to pass. She tried to ignore the irregular cells of the wooden arms under her fingers and the certainty that the chair's maker had not used enough glue in the joints.

"In the 1980's, people started dying. Before that, there were deaths—rare instances where the virus erupted on someone's liver- but for the most part it was pretty survivable. Then people started dying in greater numbers and the government took notice. It was the first mutation of the strain. People died from overheating—their electrical system burned hotter and brighter until it burned right out. But not before they could pass it on."

Willow tried to keep up with what Marshall was telling her while testing it against what she knew from her work. "And?" she finally prompted, not really wanting to hear the answer.

"And then someone survived. We all trace our viral DNA back to the Source. He's the first one with the Strain. Before him, everyone that got the Strain died. After… well, we're not exactly normal but we're alive." Marshall didn't elaborate. Every time he explained this to a newly infected person, he got stuck here. He had no one to officially finger as the culprit, but nevertheless, he was sure that the story didn't add up. Maybe mutations did happen, but not like that. Not so quickly.

"Then what happened?" Willow watched Marshall's face in the silence, wondering what drew his eyebrows together in such unshakable concentration.

Marshall released a breath he didn't know he'd been holding. "Then the Ministry started disappearing us. It started slowly, at the beginning, one person here or there. The pace has picked up, though."

"How can they make you disappear?" Willow asked incredulously.

"If someone gets picked up by MOS, there was a system. We used to get arrested all the time when we'd protest. I could look up the location, go to the jail, and bail the kids out. Not now. My Camellia's just started vanishing. I lost another six in September. I think the Ministry's been studying the Strain in secret. Can't let the general population know that some of us are more special than others." Marshall refocused, seeing Willow again as if for the first time. "And so here we are."

"Here we are..." Willow repeated.

"At an impasse. The Ministry can't eradicate us..." Marshall leaned back in his chair, the picture of confidence.

Willow snorted, her first unguarded reaction since she'd sat down in Marshall's office.

"The Ministry can eradicate anything." She continued. "Trust me, there's a reason why you're still here and it isn't because you are beyond the Ministry's reach." Willow wasn't certain of much, but she would happily wager everything on this: the Ministry's control of the Republic was damn near complete. Even the Brethren, the biggest fringe group in the New Republic, could be wiped out should the Ministry wish.

"Spoken like someone who's been thoroughly brainwashed." Marshall shook his head. "Not everything curtsies when the Ministry enters the room, missy. The Ministry can't predict human behavior, it can't predict the path of a virus. It can't disinfect an idea away, as much as they'd like to believe otherwise."

Marshall punctuated his words with a finger. "If the Ministry's power of prediction worked so perfectly, they wouldn't have bet on you, and we wouldn't be having this conversation."

"Look," Willow interrupted. "I'm not trying to say the Ministry is perfect, but you do exist because they allow you to. I don't mean to be offensive, but it's true." Willow had gotten out of the habit of defending the Ministry and the words felt strange in her mouth now that she had no stake in the argument. But the truth was still the truth.

Marshall leaned forward, his composure fraying. "Why do you think they started the tattooing system? They are terrified of us. The tattoos give them the sense that they can see us coming. We've got Ian. Even that program backfired. How do you think I got so many Camellias? Without the tattooing, each and every one of them would have kept their dirty little secret from friends and families and lived with a buried truth. If only the Ministry knew how badly they've misjudged us..." Marshall let the sentence hang between them, derisive and certain.

Except that he was wrong. No one could have known that as well as Willow. Her stung pride loosened her tongue and injected her voice with bravado. "A decent theory, but it shows how ignorant of your so-called enemy you really are. The tattooing program didn't come into being so we could arrest your army of freaks; it started because people couldn't be trusted to disclose their status before entering contractual relationships. Your little rebellion only proves that my postulate was sound. Had you not flagrantly broken the law by removing the tattoos, I could have chosen differently for myself." Willow leaned forward, her face flushed with adrenaline.

"What do you mean 'my postulate?'" Marshall's tone was accusatory. He leaned forward too, his elbows propped on the desk in front of him.

"I wrote the policy," she admitted. It wasn't like the evening could get any worse with the truth.

Marshall narrowed his eyes, assessing her credibility, then shook his head. "Now there is the kind of irony you don't know you can pray for."

Willow didn't respond and Marshall continued. "Proud of yourself, now that you're on the receiving end? Now that you can't wash your hands in public for fear of the emergency canisters of SaniCheck being sprayed in your face? Now that you are afraid to visit your mother in case she might see what you've done?"

Marshall stood, a great hulk of a man, moving as if all his rivets were full of rust. For a fraction of a second, his face betrayed him, revealing just how much effort he expended on snapping his joints into place. He started pacing anyway, as if sitting in her presence was enough to make him sick.

"My mother is dead," Willow said coldly. "If you'd done your homework, none of this would be news."

"A true Ministry diehard," Marshall mused aloud. "I don't know if I should save you or order you drawn and quartered for betrayal of humanity."

"I didn't come to be saved," Willow said, then wondered to herself if that was entirely true.

"Does it still hurt like a son of a bitch every time you walk through a reader?" Marshall asked.

"The magnetic formula isn't quite as strong these days, but yes, it still hurts." Willow's voice was flat.

"It couldn't happen to a more deserving person." Marshall kept pacing, though his office wasn't wide enough for more than ten steps in either direction. "I suggest you not mention your genius plan for fucking us all over if you want Ian to get rid of it for you."

"I'm keeping the tattoo. I'm not afraid of paying for my consequences or doing my civic duty. Now, what else do you think I can do for you?" Willow was done with the conversation. She wanted food, a dark corner to sleep in, and a little solitude. She hadn't used her voice this much in weeks and her throat hurt from all the talking.

"One of my assets has disappeared." Marshall stated matter-of-factly.

"I thought you were losing them by the handful," Willow taunted, then immediately regretted the words. Even with her faith in the Ministry's overall benevolence, it wasn't likely to be kind to individuals that got in the way of the Republic's health and hygiene. Whatever had happened to the lost Camellias, it wasn't likely to be fun.

"This one wasn't out protesting and he's too smart to get caught." He stopped mid-pace to look Willow in the eye. She sat in the chair, her legs crossed, looking up at him from under thick brown lashes. She was sallow under his fluorescent lights and her clothing hung off of her shoulders. Marshall wondered if she realized exactly how vulnerable she looked.

"Assets?" Willow countered, unwilling to let her empathy be used against her. "Let's be honest here. You aren't running a first-class intelligence operation. You've got a bunch of kids playing with broken yo-yos."

Marshall glared at her, his sympathetic tendencies beaten back by concern for his tribe and his pride. "Don't underestimate me. I've got the best in the Republic at my disposal." He started his pacing again. Like a caged wolf, any walls would have been too close.

"So which of your 'assets' have you misplaced? Can he open his mouth and transmit radio waves, or is there something really dangerous he can do?" Willow's voice mocked him, but Marshall ignored her.

"An old friend of yours." Marshall's voice lowered. "Actually, I believe you've seen considerably more of him than I have." Marshall let the insinuation sink in. "You remember Ven, don't you?" He paused to watch her flinch.

She regrouped, calibrating her voice to match Marshall's: insouciant, defiant.

"Are you sure you know who is playing who in this game?"

"What's that supposed to mean?" Marshall shot back.

"He's a CI officer." Marshall looked at Willow blankly. "Counter Intelligence" she explained wearily. "He works for the Ministry."

Marshall didn't need Willow's definition of CI. He needed time to think. His bullshit detector was infallible. He wanted to think she was bluffing, but there was no mistaking the truth in her. A lie would have been preferable.

"Of course," Marshall said with feigned confidence. "He was infiltrating the Ministry for us."

Willow looked back, disbelieving. His face was impassive, his posture daring her to challenge him. "I need to leave now," Willow finally said, doing her best to sound bored and indifferent. Fuck the broken roads, fuck the darkness, fuck everything. She wanted her bed and a bath and solitude.

"I'm sorry, but I can't let you go."

Willow shifted her weight, her heart struggling against her ribs. Her feigned bravado abandoned her, leaving a tide of rage and panic in its wake.

"Whatever you're looking for, I'm not the one."

"I think you are," Marshall replied. All doubt her revelation had introduced was burning off, leaving a charcoaled edge to his words. Maybe the Ministry thought they had Ven, but Marshall had spent too long with him. If Ven were a Ministry spy, Marshall was certain he'd know.

"We'll find you a good place to sleep and maybe you'll feel better about your memory in the morning." He grinned at her like a man who had already won.

"No." Her tone was final. "I'm through with you stupid fucking men deciding how things are going to be for me. First Ven, then Nate, now you. Well fuck you. And fuck what you want. I'm going home."

Marshall smiled at her, crossed the room and wrapped one meaty hand around the hair at the back of her neck. His fingers sunk into its thick mass with no resistance. Long-buried hunger for a woman woke up and looked around, but quickly realized this was business and went back to sleep. He pulled slightly, the tension at her scalp tugging her into a standing position.

"You will do as I say, and if you want to keep your dignity, you'll do it quietly."

Willow kept pace as Marshall propelled her along the corridor that Ianthe had walked her through not even an hour ago. She refused Marshall the satisfaction of dragging her. They took a new turn and Marshall ushered her into a dismal room with a bed and a sofa and a minuscule bathroom.

"I'll be back for you in the morning." Marshall closed the door behind him. Willow heard the grate of the key in the lock and she watched the inside of the handle turn. She stepped to a wall, closed her eyes and let her awareness infiltrate the peeling paint to the cinder-blocks underneath. Dusty and irregular, like gravel in her teeth, but still solid. She slumped down on the bed and decided not to cry.

Kiri preferred the dark. Always had, even as a kid, but now it was a physical craving. She wasn't worried about whether or not she could see them, but whether they could see her. She'd moved her cot to the wall under the cameras, but they'd just moved it back in the fifteen minutes they allocated for showers. She had smiled a little when she came back and found the cot right back where it had been the day before, because it meant they thought she'd expressed a preference. It meant they believed they'd denied her. The more they felt like they were in control, the better for Kiri and her compatriots.

With the sheet covering her completely, Kiri pushed her hand between the mattress and the wall and walked her fingers to the socket hidden behind her bed. She inserted a paper clip that she had straightened then bent into a U: slowly, into the socket, just a little bit… She closed her eyes against the light pouring through the striped sheet over her head.

The electricity coursed through her as the lights flickered slightly. One by one, she felt her fellow prisoners plug in. She relaxed for the first time since they'd been taken. As long as they could plug in, they could survive. Kiri willed the reassurances down her arm and into her fingers, feeling through the line to check on the Camellias one by one.

2006/02

Jailyn died quietly. Warren had sent the Ministry's best expert on pain to Duane's house to provide whatever it took to keep her comfortable. Jailyn had finally slept under the specialist's ministrations, and Duane had lain next to her, afraid to touch her, but also afraid to leave her alone. She'd died while he was crouched on the other side of the bed, watching her face closely for any sign of change.

Now, splinters from the coffin bit into Duane's left shoulder, but he kept walking. Jailyn's brother had his hand clasped around that same shoulder, and Duane's hand cradled his brother-in-law's shoulder in return.

He'd considered suicide, but refusal to kill himself was both an act of penance and of cowardice. It didn't matter what the Ministries said about what followed death, Duane was pretty sure his penance wouldn't end just because he'd died.

It had been at least a week since he'd eaten, but his body refused food. His throat closed up and whatever he put in his mouth turned to ash. Instead, he had consumed great quantities of alcohol. Having a Ministry insider as a friend had its advantages. The Ministry had warehouses of the confiscated stuff, so much that a bottle here or there wouldn't be noticed.

Warren had been generous.

He was also walking behind Duane, shouldering a quarter of the burdened casket as they walked to the hearse.

With no Brethren in either family, there was no one to promise heaven as consolation at the simple graveside service. Duane didn't trust his own voice, didn't trust himself not to confess his guilt to the entire gathering. Warren spoke instead. Duane scooped the first handful of dirt and dropped it on her coffin. The other pallbearers picked up shovels and together, they covered Jailyn.

Warren offered to take Duane home to Sara, but Duane didn't think he could bear to interact with a wife, especially one that wasn't his. Instead, he drove back to the empty house and stared at the walls. When he thought he might go mad with the silence, he removed his wedding ring, set it on his dresser, and walked out the front door.

He walked into the city center, to one of the recently opened virtual sex clubs. Semi-transparent spheres hung from the ceiling by thick cables. They swung gently against each other, whether from the thump of sound waves coming from 8-foot speakers or from the gyrations of the people inside, Duane couldn't quite tell. He also couldn't hear himself think, which was a relief.

Duane found a place on the wall and leaned against it, watching the other patrons mingle and preen for each other. Eventually, a woman came and leaned next to him.

"It's all a bit strange," she said. "Our parents didn't do it like this."

"No," Duane said.

"It doesn't really work, does it? All those electrodes and adhesives. I miss skin." She shifted to look at Duane as she said it. Duane turned to return her gaze, and she smiled at him, inviting.

"My name is Morrigan."

He reached out and touched her bare shoulder. She paused, looking him up and down.

"I'm feeling old-fashioned tonight," she said. "How about you?"

TEN

"Ma, do you have to start this?" Ven looked at his mother with a mixture of annoyance and affection. She glared back at him, her chin tilted upwards to bridge the difference in their heights.

"Well, you haven't proven worthy of an inheritance. Give me a grandchild so I have someone to leave all this to." She waved her hands in a sweeping motion, indicating the room, and by extension, the house around it.

"Can I kidnap one, or do you need flesh and blood?" He was teasing her, though he knew better. At her age, she deserved a little respect, but Ven wasn't prepared to give it. Not when he'd been home for less than 24 hours and she was already on him.

"Zachey." Her voice was disappointed and whining. Perpetually disappointed.

Ven looked up at the cracked ceiling. The chandelier was attached to the rafters above by a wire joint capped by red plastic. He thought briefly about leaving his mother tied to a chair under it and then dismissed the thought. Not that he wasn't capable of it, but because he'd have to clean up the mess. A brown water stain made a Rorschach blot around the hole where the fixture used to be attached. Ven saw cigarette smoke from his childhood—blue swirls that turned into nicotine stains—but he didn't want to consider what that said about his flawed psyche.

"Sure Ma, whatever you want." It wasn't an argument either one of them could win.

She dropped her hands, the motion punctuated by a dramatic sigh. Little puffs of dust blew out of her pockets. Her blue eye shadow had settled into the wrinkles under her eyes. Dry frosted peach lipstick bled into the creases around her lips. Ven looked away.

"Why don't you bug Zelde?" Ven went on, trying for a little peace. "She's got nothing better to do. I'm not fit to be a parent." That last part he meant.

"That's because you're selfish. Too busy for your mother. Too busy to look after your childhood home, your birthright. Always running off without so much as a razor or a change of clothes. People will think you were raised by Wastelanders. Find a woman. Settle down. Give me grandchildren before I die."

His mother marked her melodramatic diatribe with equally melodramatic hand gestures. Her chipped fingernails described a dire fate for them all. Temporarily distracted by a hunger for nicotine, she fished in her pocket for a crumbling cigarette, then reached into her bra and pulled out a lighter. She fussed with lighting it but her hands shook too much to raise a flame.

"Help me, Zachey." She was vulnerable again, happily dependent on a handsome man to save her. Her lips twisted to speak while she held the cigarette in the corner of her mouth. Ven grabbed the lighter, flipped it open and produced a flame with one hand. His mother leaned in and lit the tip. She inhaled deeply.

"That's my Zachey, my good son." The argument over, she considered her only son with an appreciative eye.

Ven snapped the lighter shut with an expert flick. Given the choice between facing the Ministry and facing his mother, Ven wasn't sure he'd made the right choice. On one hand, there was the Atlantic to be had at his derelict childhood home. The Atlantic and solitude, at least while his mother was sleeping. Awake, she crossed the border between sanity and lunacy like a smuggler carrying the past. The Ministry, on the other hand, had the same advantages it had possessed years ago when he ran away from the circus to join the establishment.

Zelde wasn't due to visit until tomorrow, so Ven did the only reasonable thing: he went upstairs to make his bed, leaving his mother in a soft cloud of cigarette smoke. The laundry closet was just where he'd left it, but now the door was hanging from the hinges. It groaned when he pushed it open, protesting as only rusting metal can. On either side, shelves ran to the top of the room, each overburdened with sheets, pillows, and blankets.

Ven reached for a pillow, dragging it off the shelf. From its center, a nest of writhing mice dropped to the floor and scattered. He bit back a scream as he jumped, hitting the opposite shelf with his shoulders. Clouds of dust decorated with dead moths exploded off the shelves. He resigned himself to his fate. There was no shortcut available, so he climbed down the wide staircase and into the pantry where he rummaged for a step ladder and light bulbs, then made the long climb back up the stairs.

He was back again a few minutes later with relatively unmolested bedding to put through the antique washing machine. While he waited for the bedding to dry, he washed a glass, poured himself a generous serving of red wine, and walked out the back door and across the broad lawn to the stairs that led down to the ocean. His breath in the late October air resembled the dust that had blown off of the linen closet shelves. He stayed out as long as he could without risking frostbite, then went back inside to make his bed.

It was three in the morning when he woke up with a start. He lay in the absolute darkness, listening through the frosted night and trying to remember where he was. Then the scratches that inevitably preceded the music on the old phonograph gave in to the wail of Miles Davis.

Even lying in bed, he could see the scene: his mother in a tattered gown strewing sequins around the room while she danced with an invisible partner. He turned and clutched a pillow to his gut and hoped that there was nothing toxic in the detritus that sighed out from between the feathers, nearly choking him.

Eventually, Ven gave in and walked down the stairs in his socked feet and worn blue jeans. The light in the ballroom flickered off of his bare shoulders. "Oh my, Zachey," she said when she'd turned in her imaginary lover's arms and caught a glimpse of him. "How handsome you've become." Ven crossed the room with his gallant hand out for her. In the candlelight, she wasn't any different from the woman he had adored as a child. Always the life of the party, hosting the unofficial speakeasy for the elegant and devoutly frivolous rich displaced by the Ministry's rule.

The money was left, but few companions brave enough for decadence. Zanna, Ven's middle sister, saw to the family business from the safety of the Independent State of Texas, but it was a different world. The rich didn't drink in ball gowns; they drank in business suits. There was no glamour, no beauty to it, just a naked need for chemical relief.

Their mother was an anachronism and so was the house, a shambled mansion on Long Island just waiting for a hurricane to wash it out to sea. Ven allowed himself the vision of him and his mother continuing their waltz under water, the moonlight shimmering off of fish, the weight of the house imperceptible above them.

Together they spun and turned, the fishtail of his mother's dress making swirls and eddies in the dust on the hardwood floors. She rested her cheek on his chest and danced until the phonograph gave in to static. When she raised her head again, a line of false eyelashes dipped dangerously against her cheek when she blinked.

"Oh Zachey, I don't remember when I've had so much fun."

The sound of a key scraping in the lock woke Willow. She sat up, startled. There was no light coming in from the window and the room was black. She heard the knob turn, and then a sliver of light encroached on the linoleum floor and widened. Marshall reached in and turned on the overhead fixture, leaving Willow blinking against the sudden brightness.

He had someone in tow, a petite, stooped woman with long bony fingers and an air of peace about her that only highlighted Marshall's anger. It was the kind of peace associated with the Brethren and their faith in the irrational. The woman's eyes didn't focus on any one thing, and her lips turned up at the edges like her face had frozen while gazing at a particularly pleasant child.

"Willow, I want you to meet Kassia. Kassia, Willow." He was gruff. All business. Willow gave a brief nod in Kassia's direction and refused to acknowledge Marshall.

"Be nice, Willow. At least shake Kassia's hand. She came a long way to meet you." Marshall sounded remarkably like Mrs. Carlyle; disappointed, like his star pupil had decided to fail a pop quiz. Willow protested silently, but extended her hand to shake, a gesture she regretted immediately.

Kassia had a death-grip. Her lips stayed turned at the edges, her eyes watching everything in soft focus, but the older woman clutched Willow's hand in a vise as inescapable as the urge to breathe.

Images came to Willow and slid past too fast for her to catch more than one or two at a time. A snapshot of India on the gurney as one of the biohazard men zipped the body bag, his mask fogged from the exertion of picking it up and carrying it into the hall. The moments before Ven left the bed, the warmth of his appreciative hand on her belly and his insouciant grin as she watched his naked body move in the morning light.

Mr. Carlyle's private funeral, the one before the official Republic affair. Mrs. Carlyle hadn't cried, but the look on her face was worse than tears. A repeating dream from her early days at the Ministry, two moving walkways with bars in-between and a copy of herself on the other side looking in. Which was the prisoner? Such were her nightmares, trapped and unable to tell which side of the bars held freedom. She lost all sense of time looking at the place where her skin met Kassia's. In reality, it took no more than a few seconds until Kassia released her again and turned to Marshall.

"It's not going to work. She might have the pieces, but until she puts them together, we aren't going to be any wiser for it." Marshall swore and turned on his heel to exit the room. Kassia followed him, flipping off the light as she closed the door. She didn't look back.

Willow sank into the bed and wrapped her arms around herself. She rocked back and forth on her tailbone much as she'd done as a child waiting to know what to do about her mother's dead body. There was no anger left, no outrage. She couldn't cry or breathe. She just rocked with the primordial rhythm of an amoeba new in the discovery that it's the only one.

ELEVEN

"What brought you back this time?" Zelde asked, irritation and resentment written all over her face.

"Seemed like a good idea at the time," Ven answered, reluctant to get into it with his sister. She'd found him on the steps down to the beach, where he'd been watching the waves armed with a thermos of good, old-fashioned hot chocolate flavored with a healthy dose of schnapps. It was his favorite place on the whole estate, suspended between land and water, the possibilities of both fully available to him.

"You just make it harder, you know. For as long as you're here, she's ecstatic. She gets out of bed, eats breakfast, and parades around the house with a feather duster as if she knew which end to point at the dust or where to begin. It's great. Until you leave." Zelde had stopped looking at him and looked at the Atlantic instead.

"There's nothing for me here," he said, shrugging.

"So don't come back." Zelde's tone was bitter, her face contorted by the impossibility of harsh words directed at her younger brother. "It takes months to get her back to normal when you leave."

"Normal?" Ven turned to look at his sister, the half-a-grin that got him both into and out of trouble hanging on his mouth.

"What passes for normal with her." Zelde rolled her eyes. "Spare me the sarcasm, Ven. You don't live with it. You come and go when you please with no consideration for the consequences. You can't be half in and half out forever."

"I wouldn't be so sure about that." He took a long drink of hot chocolate. It had been years since he'd spent any time with his favorite sister. Even if she was preaching, he was glad to see her.

"One of these days you're going to have to stop blaming your life on her. Father is gone and you've long since passed the age where hating your parents was interesting." Zelde looked back at Ven, her face now softened.

"I don't hate them," he said coldly, his sister's rebuke turning him sullen. "I just don't want to be them."

Zelde snorted in unladylike fashion. "They've got the same power over you they've always had. As long as you hold onto the past, you're still living a life that's defined by them."

Ven reacted predictably. "And what are you doing here?" he snapped angrily. "You live in an abandoned town because you can't stand to live in the same house as your mother. There isn't another soul for hundreds of miles, no one for you to talk to, but you're here to make sure she doesn't starve. And you think your life isn't limited by them?"

Zelde sighed. "Here's the difference, Ven. I sleep well. I look myself in the mirror and I don't hate the person who looks back at me."

Ven turned his eyes back to the sea. Zelde studied his profile, startled at the lines that were beginning to form beside his eyes. No matter how much Ven loathed the man, the resemblance to their father was unmistakable.

She reached out and ruffled his hair, the gesture signaling the end of the argument.

He refused to look back at her.

She got up to leave. "Just let me know before you take off," she said flatly, unable to find any words of comfort to bridge the distance between them. "At least I'll be able to plan for it."

"Sure," he replied, his eyes fixed on the waves.

"Does she know?" Ianthe threw herself into the chair that Willow had occupied the night before and turned her eyes to the floor. She already knew the answer from the set of Marshall's jaw and she didn't want to see the worry on his face any more than he wanted to see the terror on hers.

"We're no further than we were," Marshall kept his voice matter-of-fact.

"Kassia couldn't get anything out of her?"

Marshall shook his head.

"Then why hold her? I'll take her home and we can start again." Ianthe sounded tired, as tired as Marshall felt.

"Because she's better than nothing."

"Keeping her doesn't bring Kiri back," Ianthe stated flatly.

"Kiri isn't the only one that's lost, Ian. There were others with her." Marshall's voice didn't invite disagreement. Ianthe didn't care.

"Marshall, we aren't any better than the Ministry if we hold her just because we can."

Marshall slammed his fist into the wood in front of him.

"Goddamn it, Ian. I've been at the head of this organization for a long fucking time. I've lost more people than I can count. Good people. People who are loved still, and missed. This woman is the closest thing I've got to a real lead. I don't know how I'm going to use her yet, but I don't answer to you or anyone else. If I see fit to lock her in a room and starve her until she talks, you will not tell me otherwise."

Ianthe's throat closed around her voice and she found it hard to swallow.

"I thought we were better than them." She choked out the words defiantly.

Marshall wouldn't meet her gaze.

She stood and left quietly, closing the door to Marshall's office just in time to hide her tears. Not even Marshall got to see her cry.

"Damn it Hadrian, I didn't bring her here for this fucking bullshit." Ianthe's muffled voice broke Willow's concentration on the wall. She sounded desperate, her voice registering a high-pitched panic. "At least let me in."

Willow heard a murmured reply but couldn't understand the response. "I don't care if God said she wasn't to have any visitors, you will let me in." Another murmur. "Because if you don't, I'll bite your dick off, you cretin piece of shit."

Willow watched the door, but the knob didn't turn. Willow heard Ianthe's screeching invectives fade down the hallway and turned back to the wall. The longer she left her eyes open, the more colors she saw in the white paint. With her concentration otherwise occupied, the rest of her attention traced a circular path.

Maybe if she could just bring the Camellias to the Ministry, then all would be forgiven. Her old life could be hers again.

But did it fit anymore? There hadn't been a Willow without regulation. Could the spilled milk be siphoned back into the carton? Latex gloves. Autoclaves. The faint scent of SaniCheck on her clothing and in her bed…

"What do you want, Willow?" Her mother's voice was seeping through the wall. Willow scrunched her eyes closed then opened them again. The bluish tint to the white paint disappeared. *I don't want anything,* she thought in reply. *I don't want the noise of my regulation heels clicking off my steps. I don't want to be watched by everyone in the office. I don't want to carry the name Carlyle with me, with all the questions and expectations. I don't want to go forward and I don't want to go back.*

Having reached an end to the thought, if not a conclusion, Willow started again. With the right prize, she could go back. Her office, her sharpened pencils, orderly numbers marching across her desk. Forgiveness. Maybe a place on the waiting list for the cure when it was found. Her heels punctuating the rhythm of the day. But for what? Had it brought her anything worth keeping? An empty bed. Blank walls. A single page in her address book sufficient to document her whole social network.

The light from a single high window had shifted from clear yellow to the smudge left after a word has been erased. The circle she'd been in turned to a spiral which wound down to a single point: if there was nothing she wanted, then the walls she was in were as good as any. She curled into a ball and went to sleep.

She awoke again to the sound of scraping in the lock. A stiletto of light invaded the room as the door opened, then retreated with the sound of the door clicking shut.

"Willow?" She recognized Ianthe's voice. "We've gotta go. Now."

"Where are we going?" Willow mumbled.

"Quiet," Ianthe hissed cracking open the door.

Most of the lights were turned off in the corridors, but Willow still blinked against the artificial light. Ianthe walked on the balls of her feet, silently pressed up against the walls. When Willow didn't move fast enough for Ianthe's liking, she reached back and grabbed her hand, dragging her like a disobedient zombie.

The halls were abandoned, the hour late enough that all but the most uneasy of the Camellias were asleep, but Ianthe proceeded cautiously and Willow imitated. They crept past Marshall's office. A single light illuminated the window in the door. Ianthe crouched and walked under the window like an overburdened babushka. A faint snore rumbled from inside. The women moved a little more quickly.

Ianthe led Willow back through the common room. From the opposite direction, Willow could see closets behind the door they'd entered through the day before. Ianthe kept to the darker shadows, so Willow followed. Willow assumed Ianthe was headed straight for the door, but she walked to the closet instead. From inside, she pulled out two heavy coats and threw one at Willow.

Willow gasped in surprise as she reached to catch it, and Ianthe shushed her as she pushed her through the door into the hall that lead to the shop. As Ianthe pulled the door closed behind them, Willow saw a light at the far end of the room flicker on. She grabbed Ianthe's hand and pulled to help Ianthe disconnect her fingers from the door knob.

Minutes later, they were moving through the mechanical room, using the feeble light of the exit signs to navigate the motorcycles and parts.

"Where are we going?" Willow whispered.

"I'm taking you home," Ianthe replied, her voice tight and muted. "And then I'm going to find Kiri."

Ianthe paused to survey the space, then crept to the outside door. Beside it, there were two bikes half-cocked on kickstands with helmets dangling, one on each pair of handlebars. Willow followed Ianthe to the bikes.

"I don't know how," Willow whispered frantically.

"It's easy. We roll them out. They make too much noise to start in here." Ianthe walked up to the familiar bike and threw her leg over the side. Willow mimicked her with the second bike. Ianthe rolled hers off the kickstand. Willow attempted the same, throwing her weight forward then rocking it back, trying to get enough momentum to get the weight of the bike onto its wheels. The third time, the bike settled onto the tires with a lurch that made Willow's stomach drop. Ianthe opened the side door and pushed her bike over the threshold.

"Keep coming," Ianthe whispered, and Willow obeyed. When they had rolled a few hundred feet from the building, Ianthe gave a Willow a quick tutorial.

"You rode a pedal bike when you were little? Ianthe asked. Willow nodded.

"Well, it is like that. Sort of."

Willow looked blankly at Ianthe.

"You'll be fine." Ianthe half-smiled at Willow and Willow was struck with the thought that the crazy bitch might actually be enjoying this.

"Ready?" Ianthe asked. Willow nodded in nervous agreement. "Okay, put the bike in neutral and start it. Follow me." Ianthe turned her engine over. Willow did the same and the bikes both roared to life. Ianthe had a relatively sedate take-off, while Willow gripped the handlebars with white knuckles. She turned the gas too far and the bike wobbled and fishtailed under her. The forward motion of the bike did not correspond with a forward motion in her shoulders. Her body jerked back and she let go of the gas. The bike sputtered to silence.

"Fuck, fuck, fuck." Willow's eyes trailed Ianthe as her tail light floated in front of her. Lights went on in the building behind them. Willow turned and looked back then twisted the key in the ignition again.

This time she closed her eyes, concentrating on the feeling of the machine underneath her. From where her thighs pressed up against the bike to the handles against her palms, the bike was a riot of information. She felt the metal's pleasure in the friction of the engine's pistons, felt its desire for the purr, the speed, the gentle touch to encourage the clutch back into place from neutral. This time, it worked. The bike eased into motion.

She looked behind her again. More lights were turning on in the compound. Willow opened up the throttle and the slender trunks of the Aspen began to blur against the darker backdrop of forest.

TWELVE

Warren James Lake kept a book in his desk in a secret compartment built for this single, specific item. The book was black and blank, but there was a photograph pressed between the thick pages. In this photograph, a beautiful woman looked back at him.

Her shoulders were bare because she was naked, but only he knew this and he only knew it because he had been the photographer over thirty years ago, back when cameras had negatives and you could send away for private development. It was the only thing he owned of her, his state-sanctioned mistress and the ghost he'd carried for decades.

They had broken rules together, the rules he was there to uphold, and she'd encouraged him. Younger enough to count, she'd laughed and danced and teased his already rigid heart into melting, cupped as it was between her hot hands. He'd laughed too. Really laughed with a deep baritone that she swore she could feel in her bones. He never laughed like that with his wife. He had never laughed that openly with anyone, not before and not since.

She'd falsified her records, giving him more than the sanctioned hour sessions. They'd played, sometimes forgoing lovemaking in order to talk. She'd protested the regulations he was creating, the shifts in curriculum, the mandates and the oversight. "This antiseptic world," she complained. "How can anything worthwhile grow from such a barren place?"

"That's the point," he reminded her. "The devastation of the old government and all its chaos and rampant capitalism. Nothing was ever solved because there was no money in solving it. They could have cured the diseases long before they decimated the population, but there just wasn't the will. Now we've got the will and we've got the control. You remember how it used to be, with the military budget taking over everything. Our priorities are where they belong now: a healthy population is a productive population."

"But at what cost," she'd muttered under her breath. Even if he did love her wildly, she knew better than to cross him or take her protests too far. He still paid her way. Warren played his part, pretended he didn't hear her, and went to work distracting her with acts he spent his days writing out of the population's sexual repertoire.

Years later, he could still hear her whispering in his ear. *What can grow in such a barren world?* What indeed. Certainly not the chaos, and that was all that mattered. Like a meditation to work over prayer beads, Warren counted the diseases eradicated or denatured: HIV, Malaria, West Nile, Influenza, Staph bacterium, and Lyme's Disease. Hell, thanks to findings borrowed from the Trust, they even had effective treatment for most forms of cancer.

There were more cures lined up in his lab, but their release was carefully timed for shifts in the leadership of the Ministries and bad news days. Still, what an accomplishment. So much suffering relieved now that the public's health was no longer entrusted to the profit boards of large pharmaceutical companies. Minister Lake fingered the worn edge of the photograph.

He only regained awareness of his surroundings when a knock sounded at his door. He closed the book carefully and set it into the fitted compartment where it belonged. He lifted a stack of files from his desk and settled it on top of the trap door, then closed the drawer softly. The knock sounded again. "Yes," he answered, barking and authoritative. "Enter." The door swung into the room, slowly inscribing an arc into the plush carpet. Miles stepped into the room already stammering.

"So sorry to disturb, Sir. You asked for an update on the Brethren when I had one."

The Minister looked at Miles blankly.

"The Brethren were refusing vaccination. We deployed H1N1..."

"Ah, yes." The Minister leaned forward eagerly. "Do go on."

"Sir, the virus has spread rapidly through the Brethren. Only those who were vaccinated were spared. Of the unvaccinated, there has been a 15 percent mortality rate." Miles voice was grave and disapproving.

"Ha!" the Minister barked. "Their immune systems weren't prepared for it. Means our microbial reduction program is working. Good news. Good news indeed."

"Among the survivors, there is a marked increase in the number who are having their children vaccinated." The Minister nodded sagely at Miles.

"I knew it," the Minister gloated. "They just needed the right incentive.

Leverage." Miles didn't comment on the irony of expecting the Brethren to trust the Ministry when the Ministry had willfully infected them. One just didn't comment when it came to Warren Lake.

"One more thing, Sir." Miles went on, bracing himself. "I just got word on an employee you asked me to keep an eye on."

Warren sat straighter in his chair and leaned forward, wrapping one hand around the other. "Go on, Miles." The jovial, self-congratulatory Minister was gone. Now, Warren Lake was deliberate. Imposing.

"Willow Jane Carlyle. She's been released."

"Released, Miles?" His tone was a warning, his voice suddenly slow and dark like molasses in January.

"Nate made the decision, Sir. Two weeks ago. He thought it was in the best interest of the Ministry." Miles shifted from foot to foot. Leading with the good news first might have been a mistake.

"Who the fuck is Nate and who empowered him to think for the Ministry, Miles? I do not recall directing anyone named Nate to think." Warren rose as he spoke, his voice becoming quieter and more deadly.

"Sir, he says she rendered herself unsuitable to protect the best interests of the Ministry and therefore the Republic." Miles clung to calm neutrality. Not that it helped.

"And how exactly would our best employee render herself unable to protect the interests of the Ministry?" The Minister asked slowly, so as not to be mistaken in the question or its implications.

"She became infected, Sir." Miles knew better than to question whether or not Willow Carlyle had been the Ministry's best employee at this juncture.

"Infected. With. What." Warren let the silence punctuate each word.

"The Herpes virus, Sir. I had her sample brought back to the lab." Miles' calmness was in no danger of cracking: the more pressure the Minister placed on it, the more resolute it became.

"And no one thought to tell me? Two fucking weeks later?" The Minister's voice rose to a point of rage that frankly, Miles found ridiculous. "Where is she? Where was she last scanned?"

"Unfortunately, Sir, she seems to have dropped off the grid." Miles knew just how impossible this was. He cringed as he said the words.

"Explain, Miles. Now. No one with a tattoo drops off the grid. We find people who are infected with syphilis by testing the water from the fucking urinals. No one 'drops off the grid.'" Miles was grateful the Minister was re-establishing a modicum of self-control. The screeching rage eroded Miles' respect for the man and set his teeth on edge.

"I'm sorry, Sir. Willow Carlyle has disappeared." Lying to the Minister wouldn't improve anything, so Miles clung to his story.

"Find her, Miles. Find her now. And bring me this Nate."

Nate was rather pleased with himself. He didn't know why he was being summoned yet, but it didn't matter. He'd made a career at the Ministry and he was getting called up to the Minister's Office. The Minister had become more reclusive in recent years, issuing directives through his Chief of Staff and entering and exiting the building through a private elevator. Nate had only met the Minister twice, both times at eradication parties nearly a decade ago. Getting invited to his office was the biggest thing that had happened to Nate. Ever.

He stepped into the elevator and found a beautiful woman already inside. She was wearing a thick cashmere coat and she looked exotic. Maybe from the Slavic Federation of States. Nate mentally unfastened the silver buttons on her coat and shrugged it off her shoulders. He imagined pushing his thigh between her legs to part them, running his hands over her perfect breasts and nuzzling her neck. The elevator doors slid open, interrupting Nate's fantasy. The woman stepped out in front of him and turned to the right. Nate readjusted his semi-erect cock in his pants and turned left.

The carpet on the 33rd floor made no noise. Nate scuffed his feet against it just to be sure. Silence. He smiled to himself and pictured himself in a position where he worked with the Minister. Maybe he was here for a promotion. A promotion would be better than anything. It would move him one step closer to being Minister himself.

Nothing could possibly top that, not even boning the woman in the elevator. Nate checked his hair in the brass around the door to the Minister's office. He teased it forward and up to just the right angle and sauntered into the room.

The Minister's secretary looked him like she'd just discovered a cockroach on the carpet—assuming that a cockroach still existed somewhere. He remembered the commercials from his childhood, before the Ministry had eradicated them. Dirty little vermin carrying who-knew-what diseases. Nate refocused.

"The Minister asked to see me?" He used his charming voice, hoping to coax a smile out of her.

She was a severe woman with a blunt haircut. Her clothing was all cut out of a sober shade of gray, except for the black accent of her shoes. When she didn't smile at him, Nate classified her in his mental 'frigid bitch' box. She nodded her gray head in the general direction of the door.

Nate walked through it, but it just led into another corridor and a second door at the end. That opened into a little room with a sofa and three doors leading off of it. The one in front of him read Warren Lake, Minister, so that is the one he approached. It opened from the inside, automatically, or at least Nate thought it was automatic until he noticed the Minister's Chief of Staff.

Nate dismissed him immediately. A rabbit in Nate's opinion. Timid and flighty with decidedly the wrong approach to dressing. Internally, Nate mocked the man's formal vest, the watch chain dangling from a button and leading to his pocket. He laughed at his balding head and decided that, were he Minister, he'd turn the Ministry's considerable resources to curing baldness.

"Wipe that asinine grin off your face," Miles whispered. Despite his disdain for the man, Nate immediately put on a grave expression and walked to the center of the room and faced the Health Minister's desk. The massive chair swung around revealing Warren Lake. He was thinner than when Nate saw him last. A sobered Nate thought briefly about the awesome responsibility and power that came with the Minister's position, but that line of thought was cut short by the Minister's harsh voice.

"Willow Carlyle."

Nate's face constricted. The Minister had no business with employees at Willow's level. Indeed, Nate was astonished that the man even knew her name. "She was released two weeks ago, Sir."

"Fifteen days, to be exact. Why was she released?" The Minister's voice sounded reasonable, his fingers made a steep tent under his nose, and he drummed them against each other as he waited for Nate's response. Nate cleared his throat.

"She came back with the tattoo, Sir. Herpes. It was a lapse in judgment that called into question her fitness to serve." Nate shifted from foot to foot, his hands wringing each other behind his back. He couldn't decide if he was going to be praised for this or fired, but his belief in the rightness of his decision remained unshaken.

"I see." The Minister's voice was as calm as the eye of a hurricane. Nate breathed a sigh of relief and began to preen under the Minister's scrutiny. The pause stretched long. "Did it occur to you that she might have been useful to the Ministry?"

Nate's face fell. "No Sir."

"I see. And did it occur to you that a dismissed employee with Herpes might be a danger to the Ministry?" The Minister's fingers stopped their motion and he leaned forward as he spoke, gripping the arms of his chair.

Nate blanched. "No Sir."

"I see."

That icy 'I see' was beginning to grate on Nate's nerves.

"And did you consider that a dismissed employee with the Herpes Simplex Virus might be vulnerable to the influence of forces of chaos and disease?"

"No Sir. Willow Carlyle is so regulation. I figured she'd go home and never be seen again."

Warren's blood pressure rose and the veins at his temples began to throb. "Excuse me?"

If the Minister had yelled, Nate might have shut up and taken the verbal abuse, but the low tones unnerved him. He knew he was on thin ice, but there was nothing to do but keep talking.

"Sir, I fully expected she'd just go home and die from shame." Behind Nate, Miles shook his head and looked down at his shoes, unwilling to watch the train wreck unfolding in front of him.

"You sent a Ministry employee to go home and make use of her voluntary death dosage?" The Minister spoke slowly so there was no mistaking his words or the threat behind them.

"She has the Herp, Sir. Her life is over."

Behind him, Miles put a hand over his own mouth, willing Nate to shut up. The arrogant prick had no idea what a shit storm he was creating for himself.

Warren turned to Miles, his voice cracking under the strain of controlling his rage. "Get him out of my sight." Nate turned to look at the rabbity Miles, now looking for support. Nate found no comfort there.

"Sir," Nate spoke again. "It was the Herp, Sir. You don't get the Herp by leaving your gloves at home. She knowingly fucked someone with a tattoo. Even my twelve-year-old nephew knows better."

The Minister's face, already red, grew purple. With all the dexterity of a much younger man, the Minister escaped the confines of his desk and crossed the room, his hands at the ready to wrap around Nate's pale throat.

"Sir..." Miles voice echoed distantly in the Minister's head. It was enough to keep him from strangling Nate. Instead, the Minister grabbed both of Nate's perfectly pressed lapels and lifted him off the floor.

"You fucking maggot. You are ruined. Do you hear me? Ruined." Nate looked into the Minister's eyes and saw something there he'd never speak of again.

"Sir?" Miles interrupted, reasonable as always. "Let me take care of this."

Warren dropped Nate like a corrected puppy. Nate looked between the two men, unsure which was his safer bet. There had been whispers in the Ministry regarding what exactly Miles would do for the Minister. Nate didn't want to find out if the rumors were true.

Miles gestured for Nate to move out of the Minister's office. Cowed, Nate watched his feet sink into the carpet as he walked out of the room.

"Don't go too far, and don't talk to anyone about this meeting," Miles said quietly to Nate, then he closed the door leaving Nate to walk the long hallway alone.

Inside the Minister's office, Warren Lake glared at Miles, having lost the true target of his anger.

"Sir?" Miles asked.

"Put a year's severance pay in her account. Find her. "Yes, Sir." Miles stopped to contemplate the wisdom of his next words, but spoke anyway. "You know, Sir, she has the Carlyle fortune. She won't starve."

Warren glared at him, his mouth narrowed into a thin line.

"One year's severance. Yes, Sir." Miles said, not turning his back as he walked backwards out of the room.

"And send Lena in." Warren barked.

Alone, the Minister leaned into his chair and sighed. He closed his eyes for a moment, then leaned forward again to extract the picture of India. A soft knock came at his private door and Warren froze. "Come," he said. The door opened as he straightened his posture. Lena extended a long, bare leg through the door first. Within three steps into the room, the silver buttons of her cashmere coat were undone, revealing the slender, pale body underneath. Dropping the coat to the floor, she walked confidently toward the desk, her heels sinking into the floor with every step.

Once at the Minster's desk, she wiggled herself between the chair and the wooden furniture. She propped herself up on the desk, bare ass cheeks warm against the cool edge of the wood, and spread her thighs. Warren Lake, Health Minister and chief enforcer of the public good, leaned forward and rested his forehead on her belly. It was a gesture of defeat, and Lena ran her long, bare fingers through his hair.

Miles Walker was a man capable of great abstraction and few scruples. He believed in the Ministry, he believed in better health through greater distance. There were few people he touched in his daily life and this suited him just fine. Indeed, he was more Ministry than the Minister himself, for while they both believed in the rightness of the system, the Minister wasn't capable of living regulation while it was all that Miles Walker wanted out of his life.

Everything in its place, a sufficient air gap between items and people, and the peace that came from a nation doing exactly as it ought. Nevertheless, the Minister was the force behind the Ministry, the glue that bound it together, and Miles was the administrator. They'd had years to settle into their roles, the vision and the inspiration the Minister's, the execution falling to Miles. Miles, who had no discernible weak points, covered for the Minister, who had many.

One of which was behind the door to the Minister's office, performing acts that kept the Minister's façade from cracking. Lena was always near, a vestige of the early days of the Ministry when they hadn't worked so hard at eradicating vice, only at standardizing and controlling it. The Minister had her on retainer. It meant she was available at short notice on days when the past threatened to seep through the tightly woven fabric of the Minister's façade. Why the Minister didn't take comfort in his wife was a bit of a mystery to Miles.

In Miles' opinion, Sara Lake was a handsome woman – handsome enough that Miles had speculated more than once on what it might be like to take the Minister's place in their home. Not only was she arresting to look at, she was committed to regulation just like Miles. In Miles' world, women's thighs were much alike. It wasn't the body one was involved with, it was the mind. And minds were not exchangeable. The only woman Miles had met that came close to Sara's commitment was her daughter, Maggie.

But while Sarah was loyal to the idea of the Ministry and her Minister husband, Maggie's loyalty was not to the appearance of things; it was to the thing itself. Miles could relate.

Privately, Miles had lost respect for the Minister. Whatever seething underbelly still existed in the New Republic of America, Miles attributed directly to the Minister's hypocrisy. That was his private opinion. However, there was nothing to be gained in airing dirty laundry, so there was no greater advocate of the Minister and the Ministry than Miles.

Miles contemplated their roles as a clinical fact, not as an emotional complaint. There was a certain pleasure in noting the moving parts and arranging them in the pattern that best served the Ministry, and Miles was good. Very good. Stripping the emotional content from the situation, identifying what was, not what he wished it would be, and acting accordingly. Indeed, if there was anything Miles took pride in, it was this—his ability to see past his own desires to reality and acting with cool logic to the mess other people's emotional and illogical reactions made.

Miles couldn't remember the last time he'd experienced a real emotion. Not hope, not despair, not desire. If satisfaction counted as a feeling, then Miles would allow himself that. The task at hand, he approached with all the distanced pleasure of one about to pop a zit. It might be messy, it might hurt, but it was going to be satisfying as well.

Finding Willow was going to be satisfying. Miles ran his tongue over his teeth. Finding Willow was going to be very satisfying indeed. She was a loose end, and Miles liked trimming loose ends. He walked across the thick carpet to his office door, conveniently situated to the right of the Minister's, and began planning his strategy.

Whatever else Willow was, she was going to be highly emotional. Emotions could be exploited. She would have no strategy and Miles could outthink anyone. At his desk, he called his counterpart at the Ministry of Security.

"Carson? Miles here. I'm going to need you to run another trace for me."

Thirteen

Ianthe put on her indicators and turned away from the wide, cracked road that they had traveled the day before. Willow followed until Ianthe finally cut her engine in the shoulder where the road intersected a two-lane highway and waited for Willow to catch up. Ianthe pulled off her helmet and shook her hair out. The gesture had more in common with a dog shaking after a nap than a seduction worthy of the television advertisements Willow had watched with her mother. Willow cut her engine and did the same.

Ianthe watched as she struggled to run her fingers through her matted curls.

"Take this road," Ianthe gestured to her right. "Follow it straight. No turns. It will take you back to Philadelphia."

Willow sat, unblinking. "I don't want to go back," she replied flatly.

"What do you mean? You have to go back." Ianthe hadn't expected this. "You can't just sit here and wait to get picked up by MOS. Where else would you go?

Willow stared blankly into the distance where the sun had just begun to slip over the horizon. "What's the worst that could happen? It's not like it matters anymore." The resignation in her voice was complete. Ianthe fingered her helmet strap, looking for something to say.

"Who's Kiri?" Willow's tone was still distant.

"What do you know about Kiri?" Ianthe's close attention to Willow sharpened..

"Nothing," Willow said, her eyes finally refocusing as she looked back to

Ianthe. "Marshall just said the name."

"Kiri is my girlfriend." Ianthe flinched at the name, even though it was her voice that had said the word. "She disappeared at the September protests right around the time Ven infected you."

"You knew Ven?" Willow's voice wasn't disembodied anymore.

Ianthe studied the woman in front of her. She was definitely not Ven's type. "Of course. He's one of the Camellias," Ianthe felt Willow's attention sharpen.

"Do you know where he is?"

"No. He's disappeared too."

Willow turned her attention down the road. Finally, she spoke. "What do you think happened to them?"

Ianthe let out a heavy sigh.

"MOS... There are rumors that there's a secret Ministry facility. The Infirmary. Sound familiar?" Ianthe struggled to keep the hope out of her voice.

Willow shook her head. "Marshall mentioned it, but I've never heard of it."

"Well, it's all we've got to go on." Ianthe paused to swallow her fear. "If I find the Infirmary, I find Kiri."

"Where do you think it is?" Willow asked.

Ianthe's shoulders slumped. "No idea." They sat in silence, each measuring out options and courses of action, their breath twisting upward like plumes of smoke in the cold air.

"What about the Source?" Willow's question cut through the silence.

Ianthe looked up at Willow as if she'd lost her mind. "Where did you hear about the Source?"

"Marshall said he was the first survivor—that everyone with the Strain traces their DNA back to him."

"Yeah, supposedly he's a crazy old man who lives in Oregon Territory. The Camellias have tried to talk to him. No one's ever been able to get an answer out of him."

Willow didn't respond, but Ianthe could see her thinking intently. Willow waited for Ianthe to say something, Finally, she gave up and made her proposal: "Help me find the Source, and I'll help you find the Infirmary."

Ianthe didn't answer.

Willow watched Ianthe, picturing her grungy sneakers, a dirty smear against her snow white carpets. "So what's is gonna be?" she said slyly, echoing Ianthe's challenge back to her. "Are you going to send me to my doom all by myself or have yourself an adventure?"

"Fuck you." Ianthe glared back at her. Her voice was rough, but there was warmth in her eyes. She studied Willow, watching the transformation from empty and hopeless to directed and proactive. Willow looked back at Ianthe expectantly.

It was a long shot. But what alternative did she have? Even doing the wrong thing was better than doing nothing. Ianthe kicked back the kickstand and revved her engine. "You'd better be ready for a long ride."

Willow smiled.

FOURTEEN

Like most of the citizens of the New Republic of America, Willow had spent very little time considering the Wasteland. It was a theoretical notion, as theoretical as the idea of seeing light in the sky from stars that had long since burnt out.

Everyone knew that there was land between the five remaining city-states, but few had a sense of what that really meant. To Willow's wide eyes, it was a ghostscape populated by haunted houses and barns built for livestock-shaped memories. At first the climb was imperceptible, then she had to hold on to the bike just a little tighter to keep her seat. The occasional sign pointed in the direction of an abandoned town, but Ianthe's helmet didn't turn like Willow's did.

As it got darker, Willow leaned closer to the bike, looking for a little extra warmth from the bike's engine. The frigid air smelled like snow, and the headlights parted the darkness just far enough for Willow and Ianthe to steer clear of the potholes and cracks in the road where grass and trees were growing through. They rode past the point where Willow's back was cramped and kept riding. Willow was beginning to think they were going to ride until the wheels fell off when Ianthe suddenly pulled off of what used to be the main highway and onto a series of two-lane roads.

Willow played with her bike as they rode, testing how different components felt from the inside as she pushed her awareness through the handlebars and into the body of the bike. The engine was older, but the pistons still slipped through their chambers smoothly and there was no rust.

They'd been climbing steadily for a while, but the incline peaked and they descended around sharp turns. Willow followed Ianthe's example and crouched closer to the bike, leaning into the curves and keeping her center of gravity low. Dawn broke through the trees as Ianthe turned off the road and up a long driveway. When the bikes were stopped in front of a dark stone mansion, Ianthe and Willow took off their helmets and ran their fingers through their sweat-soaked hair.

"Where are we?" Willow asked, painfully straightening her back into an upright position.

"Outside of Pittsburgh," Ianthe replied, as if the answer were obvious. Willow looked at her blankly. Ianthe went on. "It's a city from the era of the United States before all the flu shit went down. The Ministry closed it when they were consolidating the population."

"So why are we here?" Willow asked.

"Fuel, a place to sleep. I know the guys that live here." Ianthe smiled in spite of herself. "They're harmless—even if they don't think so."

Willow followed Ianthe as she climbed the stone stairs to the blackened door. The house was unlike anything Willow had ever seen. Beyond the size, Willow had no words for the architecture. It had gray stone walls and huge windows with glass in the shape of diamonds. The entrance door dwarfed them, but Ianthe didn't seem to notice. She picked up the circle hanging from a lion's mouth and shook it free of her hand. It fell, making a dull thump against the wooden door. The muffled sound of drums seeped from under the door.

"Who lives here?" Willow asked, suddenly apprehensive. She and Ianthe had an alliance, but it occurred to Willow that Ianthe's idea of harmless didn't match her own.

"Friends of mine." Ianthe didn't elaborate.

Willow frowned at the back of Ianthe's head. They waited, but nothing happened. Finally Ianthe placed her hand on the knob and turned it.

"Cover your ears," she said over her shoulder as she pushed on the door. Willow did as she was told just in time to keep the piercing howl of the alarm from puncturing her eardrums.

Ianthe pushed the door all the way open, revealing a great, dark entrance. To Willow, it seemed like people were coming from every direction; something about the guns they held seemed to multiply their numbers. Willow hid behind Ianthe, whose posture was erect and unafraid. Ianthe put a hand on her hip and tapped her foot impatiently. "Are y'all paranoid schizophrenics done yet?" she yelled over the din.

"Aw, fuck," another voice emerged out of the ruckus. "Turn the alarm off, it's just Ian." Moments later, a thick silence fell on the group, which consisted of one woman, three men, Willow, and Ianthe. The girl spoke first.

"Why the hell didn't you knock, bitch?" Her tone was friendly, even if the words weren't.

"Bitch," Ianthe replied. "I did. Y'all just didn't hear me. Now can we come in or what?"

"We?" the girl asked. Ianthe grabbed Willow's arm and pulled her out to face the crowd.

"We. This is Willow," Willow waved with her left hand, then realized what she'd done and covered it quickly. Not quickly enough, though.

"Cool."

The group of four pressed forward eagerly. "Will she infect us?" one of the boys asked.

"No, you fucking groupies, she's not going to fuck you." Ianthe answered, both amused and annoyed.

"Why do they want to fuck me?" Willow whispered to Ianthe, who laughed.

"Ask them," she gestured at the residents of the house. "Boys? Why do you want to get into Willow's pants?"

The tall boy spoke first. "The Strain. Duh. I'm good now, but with the Strain..." He sounded wistful.

Ianthe rolled her eyes and interrupted. "They think the Strain would make them better hackers. As hard as it is for you to believe, in certain circles, we are superheroes. With fan clubs and groupies and everything." Ianthe grinned at Willow, whose face contorted into something between amazement and horror.

Ianthe turned her attention back to the pale, wide-eyed crowd standing in front of her. "She hasn't been indoctrinated yet, so it's up to her what she wants to do with her hoo-ha. But because none of you know what to do with someone who doesn't have some kind of social interactive disorder, I wouldn't get your hopes up."

In a rush, all four began explaining why Willow should fuck them.

"I've got a 9-inch cock," the tall one said.

"They don't know their way around a pussy. I do," the young woman protested.

"I can make you cry," the second guy said. "In a good way." His skin was gray from too little sunlight and he had a bit of a paunch, but his eyes were brown like cloves.

"They are all full of shit," the third man added. "Ares is small" he pointed at the first one. "Wulf will come before you're even naked," he pointed at the one with a paunch, "and Mel is all about the dick. Mine to be exact. I'm the only one with any real experience or know-how. Those other two jerk-offs just fantasize to internet porn. And Mel will forgive me if I bone you."

"I thought that was illegal," Willow protested, clinging to the safest subject she'd heard.

Ianthe laughed. "You can still bone, I think."

Willow blushed.

"I meant internet porn." Willow practically choked on the word. Polite people just didn't.

"Hon, these are hackers. Nothing is illegal."

Willow looked to Ianthe for an explanation. "Hackers," Ianthe explained in a tone that suggested Willow wasn't much better than a six year old when it came to an understanding of the world. "They break into computers. Flynn is the big mouth," Ianthe gestured at the man who had claimed all the prowess.

"This is Melia," Ianthe pointed at the girl, who gave an exaggerated curtsy. "This is our own little god of war, Ares." Ares stepped forward to shake Willow's hand. She had to fight to get her hand back.

"And that leaves Wulf," Ianthe continued when Willow had finally extracted her hand from Ares' grip. Wulf waved and grinned, revealing very sharp teeth.

The introductions complete, the group stood in the entrance hall staring at each other awkwardly. Finally, Mel and Ianthe caught each other's eye. After a lengthy nonverbal exchange, Mel sighed. "Y'all hungry?" she asked as she turned in the direction of a narrow passageway. Willow and Ianthe followed past a room with a massive stained glass window and through a swinging door into a cavernous kitchen.

There were enough chairs around the table to accommodate everyone, even though none of the chairs matched. Willow conducted a surreptitious assessment of the chairs' cleanliness before selecting the most sterile-looking chair to settle into.

"The train just made its drop a couple of days ago," Mel said as she opened up a battered refrigerator. "We've got steak."

Willow's mouth began to water at the word. She'd not had steak since Mr. Carlyle died. Red meat was not on the Ministry's approved diet. Unless, of course, you were Minister.

"Flynn, fire up the grill," Mel ordered as she rummaged. "We're gonna eat well tonight."

Willow watched the proceedings with interest. Finally, she worked up the courage to speak. "How do you..." her words trailed off. There were too many things she wanted to know. Ianthe's upper body was sprawled across the table, her head resting on her arms. Wulf was standing over the counter, chopping something with a large knife. He stopped at her words and turned to the table, knife still in hand.

"How do we what?" Wulf asked. His knife punctured the air as he spoke.

"Everything..." Willow said. "Electricity, food, money... How did you get it out here? I didn't know anyone could survive so far from one of the Republic's city centers."

"Solar panels, train. And hacking is pretty lucrative if you do it right," Wulf said, turning back to his chopping.

"The Ministry is our usual target," Mel picked up where Wulf fell silent.

"That's you?" Willow asked, incredulous. "We hate you." Willow's words hung in the air as she considered the implications. "The Ministry hates you," she clarified, then looked down at the table.

"Of course they do," Mel said. "We find everything they want to keep secret." Melia eyed Willow suspiciously. "If you're so Ministry, what are you doing with that?" Mel waved in the direction of Willow's hand. "Or is that a fake for authenticity in your foray into the underground?"

Willow snorted, unguarded. "I wish."

Ianthe interrupted though she didn't raise her head from where it rested against her arm. "It's the real deal."

Mel and Wulf looked at Ianthe carefully. "She's with me, alright? Let it drop." Ianthe got up from the table and pushed her way forcefully through the swinging kitchen door. Ares backed away from the door's rebound, and then entered the room.

"Uh," he said uncomfortably. "Anyone want a tour?"

Both Wulf and Mel looked at him like he was a particularly annoying specimen of younger brother. Willow glanced at each of them and stood.

"Sure," she said. Willow followed Ares out of the kitchen and into the room with the stained glass window. The room was murky and gray, the sunlight obscured by clouds. "The house was built in 1884," Ares said. "Back when there were servants and stuff, this was where they hung out when they weren't cooking or polishing the silver." He gestured to the room. "Now, it's more like our break room." Willow looked to the right. The stained glass window reached as high as the ceiling. Muted purples and reds glittered like vintage jewelry. Ares pointed out curved stairs to their left. "Servant's stairs," he said. "Some of the floor boards are loose. We're waiting for the Tinkers to pass back through."

"Tinkers?" Willow asked.

"NeoRoma." Ares answered, turning to look at Willow's face. She looked back at him blankly. "God," he said, amused. "You don't know anything."

Ares sighed and started walking towards the hall where Willow and Ianthe had first entered the house.

"There are four main pockets of resistance to the Ministry. The Camellias, you've met. Now you know a few hackers. You've probably heard of the Brethren." Willow nodded her assent, even though Ares wasn't looking at her. "The NeoRoma were probably both the first and last to form. The first because there have always been drifters and nomads. The last because they're basically anarchists."

"Aren't hackers anarchists?" Willow asked as she followed Ares to the right into a room with a stone fireplace.

"Not really. Libertarian. It isn't the same thing." Ares went on before Willow could quibble. "Anyway, this is the dining room," Ares said. "Now we use it for dancing at the solstices."

"Solstices?" Willow asked.

"Twice a year, we try to get people together. An informal Hacker convention. The Camellia's hackers come and if the Neo's are around, they come too. Of course, the Brethren believe anything to do with organic belief systems is of the devil. They don't think much of us." Ares crossed a threshold into a second room, this one filled with shelving.

"Our library," he said simply as he navigated the book shelves.

Willow wanted to stop and touch and read, but there wasn't enough light and Ares wasn't slowing down. He crossed into a third room which was partially subdivided by a sliding door.

"This is where the magic happens," Ares explained. Desks lined the walls, with monitors stacked two high and three wide at each desk. Each desk was a unit. Flynn was sitting in one, which was tilted back to allow him a reclined posture while he worked.

Flynn didn't turn his head. "It's about time," he said, looking up at one of the six monitors that surrounded him.

"About time for what, asswipe," Ares responded, sounding bored.

"I'm not talking to you." Flynn said. "Willow. What's your account on the cloud?"

"Willandway" she replied.

"Service provider?" Flynn spoke in a perpetual monotone. Willow wondered if he was bored or just full of himself.

"Ministry."

"Password?" Willow looked at him suspiciously. Everyone knew that giving away your password was asking for trouble. "I can hack it, or you can save me some time." Still that same monotone.

Willow considered the likelihood that she'd be using her Ministry account again. There had never been anything personal stored on it and she hadn't cast her allegiance with anyone else; however, it clearly wasn't with the Ministry anymore. She had nothing to lose in sharing the information. "Casablanca." She said, finally. "The a's are at signs."

"Wow. Not the strongest password ever. Civilians..." Flynn said derisively and turned the whole of his attention back to the screens in front of him.

"I'll take you upstairs," Ares said as he turned to exit back into the entrance hall. "You probably want some sleep."

Willow followed Ares up the narrow stairs. The upper floor was even darker than the first had been. She watched her feet as they climbed. At the landing, Ares turned right and down a narrow passage that mimicked the one that led to the kitchen downstairs.

"This would have been the servant's wing," Ares explained. "We use it for spare bedrooms." He opened up one door and pushed a button that turned on a light bulb hanging from a string. "Bathroom," he said simply. Willow looked at the black-and-white tiled floor. A dust ball held together with shed hair bounced across the floor. Willow wrinkled her nose.

He pointed at a door across the hall. "That's above the kitchen. You'll sleep better in here." Ares opened a second door. Willow stepped inside and pushed the top button in a worn fixture. The light bulb above flickered into obedience. She turned her attention to the bed. The sheets looked like they were meant to be white, but had been neglected into a dull gray instead. She looked at the floor, which was populated by fornicating dust bunnies, and turned to Ares.

"A nap sounds lovely." As dismal as it was, the sight of the bed was enough to remind her how bone-tired she was.

"Suit yourself," Ares said, shrugging. He stepped out of the room and closed it behind him. Willow looked around again, removed her shoes, and turned the light off. She lay down gingerly, and was almost instantly asleep.

She woke in the dusty light of the winter afternoon, not because her body was recovered from the long day, but because there was a hand on her breast and an erection pressed against her ass. "Please," a familiar voice behind her whispered. "Please? Just once. I'll make it worth your time." Ares started thrusting his pelvis against her.

"Get. The. Fuck. Away. From. Me."

"Are you sure?" he asked, his palm rubbing against her breast. "I could make you see God."

"If you don't get your hands off of me I'm going to scream my head off. One... Two..." He pushed himself off of the bed. "Now," Willow said, "get out."

"If you change your mind..." he offered as he backed out of the room, "I don't just want you for your power. I think you are beautiful too."

Between the urge to vomit and a rising sense of hysteria, Willow didn't know what to do. She waited for a few minutes, then made her way to the bathroom. From there, she tested the door opposite to hers. Ianthe was sprawled across the bed, one leg kicked free from the covers, one arm dangling precariously from the edge of the bed. Willow closed the door quietly and let Ianthe sleep.

Later in the evening, when they were both awake, Willow told Ianthe the story. Willow was still outraged, but Ianthe just laughed. "These ones don't come with social skills. You're lucky he did more than grunt and point at his penis. Speaking parts aren't in high demand in this crowd."

Ianthe reached out and tousled Willow's hair.

"Have you talked to Flynn yet?" she asked.

Willow gave her a dirty look, then tried to smooth her unruly hair back into place. "Not yet," she responded.

Willow followed Ianthe through the old house, her hand reaching out of its own accord to touch peeling wallpaper, chair rail molding, and worn banisters. Under all the dust, Willow felt the weight of the house, the age of it, its unshakable foundation, the heft of the materials that went into the walls and the floors. There was a kind of love there that Willow hadn't encountered before, the wood in the banister still reveling in its straight grain, the walls still deliberate in their rigid posture.

Flynn hadn't changed positions from when Willow and Ares had encountered him earlier in the day. He grunted when Ianthe and Willow walked into the room.

"Did it work?" Willow asked.

"Define work," Flynn asked, his voice as monotone as it was the night before. "I got into your computer. You're pretty boring for a Camellia."

"I'm not a..." Willow started, but Ianthe glared at her, so she bit off the denial. "I'm not all that interesting," she amended.

"Well, you could be." He typed a command and a spreadsheet appeared spread across three screens. "What does all this mean?"

"I don't know," Willow responded, contorting her head to look more closely at the data.

Flynn turned to Willow, whose neck was twisted at a broken angle to see the numbers on the screen. "Hold on," he said as he pushed a joystick and the desk and chair unit rotated back to perpendicular with the floor. Willow stared as if mesmerized by the screen and Flynn ducked out of her way as she sunk down in his seat. She scrolled up and looked at the top row, then scrolled left to look at the first column.

"Where was this?" she asked.

"On your computer," Flynn said.

"I've never seen it before."

"I got it off of the CD drive," Flynn offered. "Anything in there?"

"Shouldn't have been, just a wiped disk..." Her words trailed off as she raised a finger to trace a line of numbers from one screen to the next.

"What is it?" Ianthe asked.

"I think these are study findings. This column looks like a case identifier. The ones that follow look like incremental results." For the first time since the horrible encounter with Nate, Willow was in her element. Dormant connections in her brain fired up, searching out patterns and meaning in the data.

"What does it mean?" Ianthe asked as she watched Willow's face. It had transformed somehow. Ianthe was getting used to thinking of Willow as a developmentally disabled older sister, older in age, but less competent in the real world. The roles were reversed, at least temporarily, as Willow studied the data in front of her. Even her shoulders seemed more confident as she leaned forward to look more closely.

"I don't know," Willow finally said, her voice all business. "You'd be tracking something here. Efficacy, change of some variety. Most of these numbers seem to slide, then level out. Some of the number series stop, but those have two different entries. Like two different events happened to end the data. They were tracking something."

She ran her finger across the first row in the spreadsheet. "It's in some kind of a code, so I'm not sure what each of these mean."

"Look at the footers." Flynn clicked on the sheet to reveal an alphanumeric code: N3899W7712. "Mean anything to you?"

Willow shook her head. "That's not any naming convention I've ever seen used at the Ministry."

"Do you think it's important?" Ianthe asked impatiently. "We don't really have time for statistics."

Willow looked back at Ianthe, a little hurt at her dismissal. She set the feeling aside. "It could be, but I'd need to break the code."

"I've got a program for that," Flynn interjected.

"How long?" Ianthe asked.

"Dunno," Flynn said, running scenarios in his head. "Maybe a week?"

"We don't have a week. We have to get going." Ianthe's tone was final. "But first we have to get rid of that tattoo." She reached out for Willow's hand.

Willow instinctively cradled her hand to her body.

"Why?"

"Because there's a bolo out for you," Flynn said. Both women turned to look at him. He'd been watching the proceedings with detached interest.

"Bolo?" Willow asked.

"Be on the lookout," Ianthe explained. "For you."

"Who wants me?"

"The Ministry, Genius. That's what Flynn just said." For being such a smart woman, Ianthe thought, Willow could be incredibly slow.

"They have a reward offered and everything. So far it isn't out officially, just for the Ministry's information. But all of your accounts are flagged," Flynn explained.

"They haven't frozen my money, have they?" Willow's stomach hit her pelvis like she'd just been dropped off a cliff. It wasn't like she used the Carlyle inheritance, but it was a safety blanket.

"No, but they'll use it to track you," Flynn explained. Willow looked from Ianthe to Flynn, the old panic settling in.

"I broke it up and moved it to a bunch of new accounts." Flynn went on. "Heavy lifting." he said, keeping his tone indifferent.

Willow looked at the floor and blushed a little.

"What aren't you telling me?" Ianthe's voice was suddenly suspicious.

"Have you ever thought about my last name?" Willow asked, cringing inwardly. She wasn't ashamed of the Carlyles, but being the adopted daughter of a former Minster didn't exactly confer credibility in the circles she was now drifting in.

Flynn cleared his throat and both Willow and Ianthe turned to look at him. "Um," he said. "I'm gonna go get something to eat, okay?"

Neither woman bothered to respond, and he left the room.

2006/03

"But you love him." It wasn't a question, but India nodded in reply.

"He's a mean son of a bitch." Duane's voice didn't register any particular resentment. It was pronouncement, not commentary.

"He's your best friend." India countered, shrugging. Duane sighed, then lay his head in India's lap.

"It's different for guys. We aren't supposed to care if you're an asshole or not, just as long as you aren't an asshole to us. You're a woman. Things like that are supposed to matter to you." Duane spoke into the room, his eyes unfocused but registering as much red as if he were looking through his eyelids at the sun. Red paintings, red cushions, a red carpet, red throws, and an extravagant burst of red roses sitting on a red tablecloth.

India shrugged again and ran her fingers through Duane's hair. "It isn't like I set out to love Warren. I'm not the one in charge here."

Duane thought about the statement and its implications. Warren commanded India's attention just as surely as he commanded a small army of researchers and bureaucrats at the Ministry. After all, the Republic's cadre of whores answered to everyone. Everyone except themselves. Monthly check-ups, quarterly cleansing, an appointment ledger subject to audit by regulators, policemen and Ministry minions, trash inspections, condom quotas... Duane was certain someone was in charge, and just as certain India wasn't the one.

"Are afraid of him? You should be."

"Of course," India replied. "But he is what he is. You can't have the good without the bad. He loves me. That has to count for something." India smiled, her straight white teeth bright against her coffee-colored skin.

"I don't know what he loves," Duane muttered.

"How is the..." India let the words die. They both knew what she was talking about, and neither had a taste for the word. The other conversation had run its course before; there was nowhere for it to go. At least this subject gave Duane an outlet.

"Warren's a wonder. No one ever thought there'd be a cure."

"No side effects?"

"Every time I cut myself shaving, I can watch the skin heal up. It happens that fast. I started cutting deeper just to see what would happen, but then I scared myself so I stopped. And I'm hot all the time. It's like my body is burning from within. At least I know how to deal with that. The memories are harder."

Instinctively, Duane drew his knees closer to his chin. India let her hands settle, one in his hair, the other on his shoulder.

"I should have made him give her the cure." Duane took a deep breath to fuel the words that came next, but India stopped him.

"It doesn't do any good, Duane. Everything happens for a reason. We all have a path and a purpose. Maybe it doesn't make sense now, but there is a reason."

Duane snorted derisively. "You better not let Warren hear you talk like that. You're as bad as the Brethren."

India smiled above Duane's head but didn't argue. The Ministry's regulations were adding up daily, but they hadn't yet found a way to stamp out philosophy—maybe from the schools, but not from between India's ears.

"Are you seeing anyone?" India asked. Duane laughed again, bitterly. "What does that mean?" India pressed.

"I don't want to see anyone. And no one wants to see me," he lied. He thought of the woman he'd been seeing since the day of Jailyn's funeral and winced. In the blindness driven by desire, everything disappeared. In the rush of hormones, the immediacy of carnal need, he could find a bit of relief. There had been quite a few someones.

"It doesn't have to be a death sentence, you know..."

The words hung in the air, palpable. India imagined stuffing them back into her mouth, pulling them from Duane's ears like yarn.

Duane sat up, then stood.

"I'm sorry, Duane." India stammered. "I didn't mean..."

Duane cut her off. "Don't worry about it. It's about time for your next appointment anyway. I should be going." He didn't look at her, didn't soften his words with a rueful half-grin, didn't turn to say goodbye, he just closed the door behind him.

India checked the time: just enough to shower and arrange the pillows before the earnest Colonel arrived. Thankfully, this one liked her hair wild. It wouldn't take long to be ready to welcome him.

India rolled her eyes even though no one was there to see the derision. Being the novelty act, the physical embodiment of the darker passions, had its advantages, all of them monetary.

"It's a job," she said out loud to no one in particular. "It's just a job."

FIFTEEN

"I inherited." Ianthe sank into the closest chair.

"No shit," Ianthe said.

"Willow nodded.

"Hot damn. I didn't know you had Carlyle money. With all of that loot, what the fuck were you doing working for the Ministry?" Ianthe's eyebrows crowded each other as she tried to sort out how this changed things.

"Being an heiress gets boring after a while," Willow said. She put on her best half-smile, a familiar habit from her days of trying to relate to college roommates and other acquaintances.

Ianthe took a deep breath and set the revelation aside. There were other currencies in the Republic, all of which got you further than money. "Whatever," Ianthe said dismissively. "Flynn moved everything and knowing him, he left a trail that will keep the Ministry chasing its own hot air for years. You can still get to your money if you need it."

Ianthe turned her attention back to the immediately important issues. "Now, we've got to ditch the tattoo. Even in the Wastelands, if we hit a sensor, we're fucked." Ianthe held out her hand to take Willow's. Instead of extending her arm, Willow cradled it protectively.

Ianthe lost patience. "What's your attachment to the ink anyway?" she asked roughly.

Willow held her silence for a moment. "It's for the protection of society," she mumbled.

Ianthe snorted. "Trust me. We won't be able to even help ourselves if we get shipped off to the Infirmary. I'm not going down like that."

Willow looked at Ianthe.

"MOS won't take us to jail, hon, and I'm not sure you could take the beating they'd give you if they did."

Willow's mouth twisted dismissively. "Listen, I know you've lost your friends, but I promise, they're a bunch of scientists, not monsters."

Ianthe snorted. "Tell yourself that. I'll even listen to the fairytale while I wipe the tat."

Willow continued to press her tattooed hand to her body. Ianthe looked at her impatiently with a hand extended, waiting for Willow's surrender.

"I wrote the protocol," Willow said finally.

Ianthe reacted like she'd been gut-punched. She snatched her outstretched hand back as the color all drained from her face. "You?" Ianthe paused, disbelieving. "You mean you're the sanctimonious bitch that decided we should all be marked like cattle? I was thirteen!"

"I didn't know you." Willow was defensive, her shoulders back up near her ears. "People weren't being up front about their status. We were looking at the statistics. The spread was out of control. The new infection rates dropped by 50 percent in the first year of the program. The tattoo works. It keeps people safe."

"At what cost?" Ianthe gripped one hand in the other, restraining her urge for destruction. Her voice was low and deadly.

"I don't know." Willow's eyes were hot and dry, like they were draining all their moisture to fill up her tear ducts. *The protocol was sound,* she thought to herself. *It made sense; it worked.*

"Yes you do. You're one of us now. What's the cost?" Ianthe stepped forward again, leaning in like an irate parent chastising a wayward child.

"Privacy. Autonomy. I guess." Willow reacted sullenly, repeating the expected answer with a voice that was anything but contrite.

"You guess?" Ianthe was suddenly shrill. "You still think it's a good idea?"

All of Willow's resentment bubbled up: the betrayal, first of her body, then of the carefully governed world she'd known. Ianthe might have been angry, but Willow was angry too. Her protocol had been designed to protect people just like herself.

"Absolutely." There was nothing conciliatory in her tone now. "I'm sorry that you got caught up in it, but people have the right to know what they are getting in to."

"Would you tattoo every liar?" Ianthe asked. "A new symbol for everyone that has ever dyed their hair? Every woman who wears a girdle? Anyone who says they're fine when they aren't?"

Ianthe's voice carried down the hall, and the residents of the house crept down the hallway to listen in. "Do you know how many people checked out with the diagnosis? I wasn't old enough for sweet suicide, but I'd have taken it."

Willow slouched back in her chair. She had no fight left for Ianthe; if nothing else, Ianthe was her only remaining link to anything. Without her, it seemed possible that Willow would just float off.

"I know," she said finally. "I almost swallowed mine too. But it's this or chaos." Willow's voice was pleading as she unfurled her left hand in evidence.

Ianthe stood up and resumed her pacing. "I hate to be the one to burst your bubble, but it's chaos anyway. All you've done is decide who an entire category of people can be. You don't let them prove themselves. You don't let them fail, so they have no chance at succeeding. You don't let them choose."

"That's no reason to give in. Anyway, the Camellias do the same thing—they won't let you infect anyone even when they ask. It's no different," Willow defended herself flatly. Her eyes followed Ianthe's dirty shoes, but never ventured further up than her ankles.

"Yes. It is." Ianthe punctuated her words with her fist striking her open palm. "I choose the Camellias and their ethics every time I get an offer. Which would you rather have? A world where people prove themselves better than you expect or one where you steal their ability to determine their own path? Do you want someone who has to be good or someone who chooses to respect you?"

"It worked."

Ianthe stopped and glared at Willow, who finally met her eyes.

"At least it would have worked if you hadn't wiped Ven."

"It debases everyone. You can't have humanity's best if you don't allow its worst." Ianthe's words came quickly. She'd been having this imaginary argument for the better part of a decade; she'd had time to figure out exactly what she wanted to say.

"It was designed to safeguard the population," Willow paused to wrestle her desperation under control. "Fleming's ass, it was designed to protect me. Maybe you've got a right to be mad, but I could be just as pissed at you."

"Bullshit," Ianthe bit out. "Why are you so mad about Ven? I gave him back his choice, and he made a bad one. That's got shit to do with me. Are you mad because he fucked you? As far as I can tell, you really needed the fucking. Or are you pissed because he decided the outcome for you before you had a chance to consider what it meant? Is it only uninfected people who should have the right to choose? Because from here, it looks to me like you did the same thing to thousands of people you'd never met. At least Ven made you feel something first. At least he knew your name."

Ianthe blinked and saw herself as she had been at thirteen, her disbelieving pediatrician with one of the early tattooing devices in his hands, his eyes tearing up. Ianthe hadn't cried, but Doctor Arthur had.

"It isn't the same. He ruined my life." Willow was crying now, the hot tears falling faster than she could collect with the back of her hand.

"What the fuck do you think you did to me, you and your little protocol?" Ianthe had the physical memory of herself stuffing pink pens into a backpack. Pink pens and snacks from her mother's kitchen, when all she could think of was her need to run away. She shook her head to clear the memory. "Ven didn't ruin your life; he took a sledgehammer to your mausoleum. You should kiss his ass in gratitude."

Ianthe paused, reloading. "What about all those wasted lives?"

"That's not my fault. We all have the right to choose our death. They could have chosen not to end it then."

"No? Was it their fault they got infected?" Ianthe's tone dared Willow to blame them.

"For the love of penicillin, this isn't something you get by sitting down in a taxi. If they slept with someone with the tattoo, then yes. Everyone has to make a choice. Everyone lives with the consequences."

She doesn't understand, Willow thought. If there wasn't a clear chain of cause and effect, then there was no control, no predicting the outcome. Even as bad as things had gotten since Ven, at least she knew that she had some control over the outcome. If the world were truly random, what did that leave her with? Consequence might be harsh, but no means of control was terrifying.

"Like living with the virus isn't consequence enough," Ianthe said, more to herself than to Willow. "What about all the people who are raped?"

"Rape doesn't happen anymore. The MOS eliminated it." Willow spoke like someone reciting a lesson in school.

Ianthe snorted. "Wouldn't that be nice." Her tone dripped with icy sarcasm. "I promise you, I never agreed to fuck the bastard my mother married." Ianthe's memory drifted to the smell of the man her mother had chosen, his acrid after-shave pushed against her nose, and refused to follow that thought any further.

"You are an exception." Willow pressed her fingers to her temples. She wanted the conversation to be over, she wanted the raw edge of Ianthe's voice gone. She wanted the bike, the bumps in the road, anything but Ianthe's relentless insistence that the world they occupied was as uncontrollable and unpredictable as a sun storm.

"You just don't get it, do you?" Ianthe stopped mid-pace and looked at Willow, forcing Willow to look up and hold her gaze.

"We are all exceptions. Your simple abstraction of hookers, whores, and idiots has a thousand faces and a thousand stories. Marshall got it decades ago from a girlfriend who had been raped. Kiri was kissed by a relative—a chaste kiss at the corner of her mouth. What about someone who just fell in love and took the risk? What about you?" Ianthe's posture changed, a sarcastic mimic of a confident woman's swagger. "You are a smart girl, a regulation girl. Even you slipped. You could have insisted on a condom."

Willow's shoulders slumped as Ianthe spoke aloud the one truth Willow couldn't get away from. Maybe, if she just shut up, Ianthe would stop her barrage.

"Give me your hand." Ianthe said, her voice deadly. Willow looked her in the eye and held onto her tattooed hand.

"I can leave you here, or you can give me your hand." Willow sat, unflinching. "Or I can take you back to the Camellias, but I am not going down with you. You have caused enough damage for one sanctimonious know-it-all."

The two women looked at each other. All the words were used up but the battle hung on. For long moments, they stared into each other's eyes.

Finally, like a three year old giving up a purloined toy, Willow thrust out her left hand. Ianthe grabbed it with an uncompromising grip. The tattoo tingled. After a couple days of no sensors and feeling nothing from it, Willow had nearly forgotten what it felt like to be read.

Ianthe began rubbing the tattoo with her thumb. It was an oddly intimate motion, given their argument, but Ianthe's anger infused it with an edge of violence. Willow watched the tip of Ianthe's tongue stick out in concentration and pictured Ven sitting in her seat, eager to get the hated tattoo removed, eager to get back to fucking unsuspecting women.

Ianthe rubbed harder than was necessary, the friction of skin against skin burning both Ianthe's thumb and Willow's palm. But Ianthe kept rubbing. Soon, Willow's whole hand felt like it was smoldering. The heat made her stomach queasy, but she didn't speak up. The blood drained from Willow's arm and her legs grew restless.

Ianthe was totally focused. Willow watched as a smudge of dark ink spread on the surface of her skin towards her wrist. When Willow's palm and wrist were covered in ink and she felt like she couldn't possibly sit still any longer, Ianthe dropped Willow's hand.

"We leave at four," Ianthe stated and walked out of the room.

Willow looked at her hand. It was sore and a thin crust of plasma and blood was drying where the tattoo had been. Otherwise, she was clean. She waited for a sense of elation, like she'd been declared clean for real, not just in appearance. It didn't come.

She waited. When it had been long enough that the chance of meeting Ianthe in the hall was slim at worst, she left the computer room and made her way back to the room she had slept in earlier. Exhausted, she closed her eyes and pretended to sleep, as if the walls were expecting a show.

Instead, she sifted through her memories to the last time she felt competent. She'd been working from the safety of her former Ministry office, with its ergonomically correct workstation and carefully ionized air. Everything had made sense. The theoretical world could be divided with little impact; people were hash marks on a research form and could be rearranged like a marble in a shell game. No names, no stories, no messy details.

In the Ministry's world, the protocol worked. It worked in the real world too, so long as you drew a thick line between people with a social disease and those without and assumed everyone on the side of the clean deserved to stay that way, and everyone on the side of the infected deserved isolation. As much as she felt like her entire worth was bound in the delta between her thighs, as far as she'd wandered outside the boundaries of regulation, she couldn't make the conviction that this was what she deserved stick.

The question was academic at best. Her unmarked hand, even more than the original tattoo, meant she could never go back to her old life. Getting infected with Herpes wasn't illegal. Removing the tattoo was. Not that her life had been on a path back to the good old days, but the illusion was nice.

Willow wrapped herself around the ache, oblivious to the grimy sheets and the dusty wall. The rationalizations didn't work; even at their best, they were irrelevant. Willow's whole body flushed hot and cold simultaneously, her adrenaline still racing with nowhere to go. She'd been robbed, though there was no dollar amount to cite or inventory of the missing items to point to.

Once again, she went through the parts of her old life that she valued and tried to ignore a small voice that reminded her how lonely she'd been. She'd written the protocol to isolate the unclean and had boxed herself into an empty room instead.

Well, the room wasn't empty anymore.

Ven walked into the lobby of the Ministry building and looked around. The soaring black marble hadn't changed since his last visit, nor had the sober guards standing with their feet planted wide and their taser guns in easy reach. Ven walked between them and over to the guard sitting at the receptionist's desk.

"I'm here to see Miles Walker," he said to the woman behind the desk. She turned a surly eye on him.

"And I'm here to see the Queen," she retorted.

"Seriously. I'm here to see Miles," Ven pressed, annoyed. It was always the bottom of the security ladder that took what sliver of power they had the most seriously.

She looked down at her calendar, checked a log that was buried under fifteen pages of notices and looked back up at Ven. "You aren't on the list. If Mr. Walker wanted to see you, you'd be on the list."

"Miles isn't expecting me, but I promise he wants to see me. Call him. Get his secretary to check. I'll wait here until you do." Ven offered his most charming smile, which was bound to be diminished by the number of days since he'd brushed his teeth. Ven hated being unkempt, but he didn't want to risk a trip back to his apartment. If he was going to see Miles, it was going to be of his own volition, not because Miles had MOS waiting to arrest him. The security guard rolled her eyes, but she picked up the phone and dialed the secretary anyway.

"Nina, this is the front desk. I've got a visitor who says Mr. Walker wants to see him." She paused for a second to listen to Nina's reply. "Name?" She looked up at Ven with thinly veiled loathing.

"Angelos," he replied.

The code name had been Miles' idea. Ven got the feeling that the little man liked playing spymaster. It was stupid, but whatever. If it made him happy.

He could hear a stream of chatter coming from the phone, but he couldn't understand the words. When the guard put the phone down, she looked at him with renewed interest.

"Savi," she yelled across the lobby without ever taking her eyes off Ven. A guard with biceps the size of cannonballs strolled across the room. "Mr. Walker wants this one. Make sure he doesn't get lost along the way." Savi nodded briefly at the desk guard, then gestured silently at Ven to precede him through the gate. Ven did as instructed.

They caught an empty elevator. Savi pressed the button with a crisp 33 emblazoned on it and the doors shut on their ascent. Ven weighed Savi from the corner of his eye, calculating. Between the third and fourth floor, Ven attacked. Savi was the stronger of the two, but Ven was meaner. By the 15th floor, Savi was unconscious on the floor and Ven was sucking the blood off of his knuckles. He walked into Miles Walker's office with his head high, unaccompanied.

Nina, the secretary, stood when the door opened, faltering slightly when there was no guard there to control Ven.

"Nina," Ven said, his voice dripping with poisoned honey. "It's been too long."

"Miles is waiting for you," she returned. "Go on back."

Ven graced her with his best feral grin, the one that showed all of his teeth, and walked through the door in front of him. Miles stood at his entrance and opened his mouth, but Ven wasn't interested in waiting for an invitation.

"What the fuck were Security Forces doing tracking me while I was on one of your assignments?"

"Oh, that," Miles started, then paused. "Have a seat. We've got a lot of talking to do." Ven eyed the smaller man warily but sat.

"New information had come to light. The mission needed to be aborted." Miles thought back to the revelation that had cut off the mission and the fight he'd had with Maggie after the fact.

"You couldn't have called?" Ven asked, unwilling to wait for Miles to finish his reverie.

"The liabilities were too great," Miles said with a sigh. "How did you disappear?"

"I have my ways." Ven smiled.

"Where did you go? I left messages at all the drop points."

"I went to the beach to get a tan."

Miles eyed Ven with a mixture of fear, envy, and distrust. Ven was as pale as the white walls.

"Hmmm," Miles responded. "Well, it turned out better than expected in some ways. When life gives you lemons, make lemonade. All that claptrap."

"What now?" Ven asked. Something in the Miles' statement had the man gazing into the corner of the room, contemplating. Miles shook off the distraction and returned his attention to Ven.

"Unfortunately, the political reality is that I'm going to have to detain you," Miles said with clinical detachment.

"Detain me?" Ven had been prepared for many outcomes, but not this.

"Oh, believe me, this isn't my preference, but it's only to preserve your cover. You'll be treated quite well. Indeed, for the lab that's going to house you, you're quite the cause for celebration. You'll see." Miles gave Ven an inscrutable look.

Ven stood and moved to the door.

"Oh yes, struggle if you don't mind. It will be all the more convincing." Ven's stomach sank. "And while you're our guest, it would be safest for us all—you in particular—if you didn't mention our arrangement. Yes?" Miles smiled brightly at Ven.

Ven opened the door to escape and six security guards rushed to enter the room, among them the recently unconscious Savi, who expressed his displeasure by kicking Ven in the kidney.

Willow gave up the bed. She didn't want to find Ianthe before she absolutely had to, so she took the servant's stairs, keeping both of her hands against the walls. Through her stocking feet, she allowed the wooden stairs to tell her where the soft spots were, bracing herself as she skipped several stairs that felt more wobbly than safe.

The narrow hall to the kitchen was silent. Willow stepped quietly anyway, emerging into a kaleidoscope of color bathing the white sofas that populated the hacker's break-room. Flynn was asleep, sprawled across one sofa. Mel was curled into a chair, reading. She looked up as Willow entered the room, but didn't immediately get up or comment. Willow crossed the room and pushed the kitchen door open only wide enough to slip through.

Moments later, Melia joined her in the kitchen.

"Hungry?" she asked as she entered the room. Willow was standing by the kitchen table trying to figure out where to begin.

"Yeah," Willow admitted. "Is there any steak left?"

Melia grinned. "Leave it to me," she said as she walked to the refrigerator. Willow watched her as she pulled containers out, mixing ingredients Willow had never seen before.

"Cheese steak." Mel answered Willow's unspoken question. "It's a classic."

More quickly than Willow had anticipated, she was seated at the battered table with a long sandwich in front of her. Cheese bubbled on a jagged landscape of steak.

"Thank you," Willow said as she picked up the bread.

"Anything else?"

Willow thought around a mouthful, then waited until she swallowed.

"Do you have scissors?" Willow asked. Melia looked at Willow carefully, then gave a little shrug and turned to the kitchen counter. She extracted a pair of rusty shears and placed them in front of Willow's plate.

"Enjoy," she said, though Willow wasn't sure if she meant the sandwich or the scissors. Then she left the room, leaving Willow an empty kitchen and no audience. Willow wolfed down the rest of the sandwich. When she was done, she carried her plate to the sink, then picked up the scissors and went back upstairs to bed.

Willow woke again well before dawn, but lay in bed, thinking.

Eventually, she made her way to the bathroom, where the mirror reflected a woman that Willow barely recognized. She was thinner, the shadow lines around her eyes were solidifying into a permanent feature, and her hair was running riot. Willow had never been particularly fond of her curls, at least not since her mother had been around to coax them into a half-hearted obedience.

Mrs. Carlyle had taken her to a salon within days of Willow's arrival. She'd left Willow sitting with a magazine full of advertisements for SaniCheck's latest hair care products, but Willow had put the magazine down. She needed a bathroom, so she'd gone looking. From around a corner, she heard Mrs. Carlyle tell the hairdresser to "iron the African" out of it.

Hours of solutions that made Willow's eyes water had produced fragile waves. Mrs. Carlyle had admired the beautician's work. Willow had wondered where her reflection had gotten lost. But you get used to all kinds of things, and those straightening potions were eventually replaced with a flat iron.

Until Ven, Mrs. Carlyle had been the last person to see Willow's curls. Now, Willow turned one way and the other, examining the frizz for the ringlets hidden within. Her ends glimmered gold against a chocolate backdrop. Her hair clung closer to her scalp curly, barely brushing her shoulders. Straightened, it draped down her back.

Willow took a deep breath and grabbed a clump of hair at the top of her head in one hand. She opened the mouth of the scissors wide and placed the apex against the column of hair. Looking into her own eyes, she squeezed the handles. Severed, the attached end of the curl dropped to her scalp in a tight ringlet.

Again and again, Willow repeated the procedure, blindly dropping the discarded hair into a wastebasket. When there was nothing left to cut, she turned on the water and waited until it ran warm, then bent at the waist to wet her head. She toweled what remained of her hair dry and left the bathroom.

Willow returned to her room, put on her shoes, and walked back to the front stairs.

Ianthe was waiting for her. "You're late," she said, holding out the thick coat she'd given Willow at the Camellia's compound. Willow took it from her wordlessly. They closed the massive door behind them.

"That couldn't wait?" Ianthe asked as they put on their helmets. She didn't wait for Willow's answer. Instead, she started her bike. Willow looked back over her shoulder at the massive stone house. A figure stood in an upstairs window. Willow raised a hand in acknowledgment, turned to her own bike, and followed Ianthe down the driveway.

What was left of Pittsburgh was deteriorating quickly. Willow kept close to Ianthe through the city's undulating streets, and Ianthe kept her concentration on the treacherous remains of the road. She made no allowance for Willow's unfamiliarity with the bike or its speed.

As the day grew lighter, Willow allowed more space between herself and Ianthe. Behind them, a red sun crawled through blackened trees. In front of them, the dark sky clouded like a cup of coffee splashed with cream. The more the day stirred, the lighter it became.

They escaped the last of the city streets and raced down the west side of the Allegheny mountains and into what used to be Ohio. Before the day was fully broken, Willow watched gray clots grow into decrepit barns and then wink into the past. The black dirt was stippled with lighter hashes of winnowed grain. *Like a spreadsheet in reverse,* Willow thought to herself, then wondered what the ground might be tabulating.

Ianthe wove around the cracks and potholes while Willow traveled a rougher route. Absorbed as she was in the landscape, she couldn't focus on the ground in front of her for long enough to avoid the bumps in the road. Road signs rusted by the side of the highway, announcing distances between towns with forgotten names. Some were festooned with kudzu; others had buckled under its weight.

Periodically, they'd blow through odd structures that spanned the length of the highway. Little booths punctuated the span of rusting metal. Willow nearly crashed as she watched a sharp black nose disappear into a door. She turned to peer into the booth and wobbled dangerously as she caught a glimpse of a fat red tail. Fox. She righted herself and pressed to catch up with Ianthe, grinning all the way.

Once or twice a day, they would pass through the remains of a city or town once kept alive by the empty factories on the outskirts. Rust ran down the sides of the buildings like mascara from crying eyes. In between the buildings with windows like missing teeth, there were great stretches of land. Willow had never felt quite so small. Before, insignificance was a terror to be fought with any weapon available. Now, the absence of anyone to judge whether she was significant or not was a joy she hadn't known existed.

She slouched a little over her hips and took a breath deep enough to expand her belly. Everywhere she looked, the Ministry was irrelevant. Nothing was trying for anything more than a meal and another day. Deer clustered in the barren fields, a paler shade of brown against the dark soil.

Some watched the two bikes speed by with placid eyes. Others kept their noses to lines of broken wheat.

By noon, the terrain had lost all but the barest imitation of variety. They passed a rusting sign with an oblong outline: Indiana. It looked no different than Ohio: the same crumbling structures, occasional fields with purposeful furrows. Bright red shards hung off of tall towers in paved pools surrounding low buildings. Ianthe pulled into one of the parking lots and cut off her engine. Willow pulled in beside her and stopped.

"Oil," Ianthe said and detached herself from her bike. Willow stood, still straddling her bike, and stretched. Ianthe reached into the saddlebags on the back of her bike and pulled out a plastic implement with a shiny metal cone at its head. Willow watched as she walked to a red-roofed hut set back from rows of pumps. She planted her feet and swung at the door. The glass shattered in a single sheet. Ianthe ducked under the bar to enter.

"Get over here," Ianthe called. Willow swung her foot wide to clear the bike. Her legs had seized up, so she waddled to the door. Ianthe began handing her containers: quarts of oil, packets with names on the face that Willow had never heard of, and dusty bottles of water. Willow stuffed Ianthe's saddle bags full while Ianthe ducked out of the hut again and set about checking the oil on both of the bikes.

While Ianthe looked after the bikes, Willow crunched through the broken glass to see for herself what was inside. Behind further glass doors, there were rows and rows of plastic bottles filled with brown liquid. In one case, red and white labels declared the bottles Coke. A second filled with blue and white labels announced the bottles as Pepsi. Willow reached into the second door and pulled out a Pepsi. She shook it to see if it would change color, then opened the bottle.

A weak fountain of foam ejected from the top, drenching her hand and sleeve in brown liquid. "Oh, for the love of penicillin," she said under her breath and looked around for something to rinse herself off with. A sign overhead said restrooms, so she walked down a dark hallway to a room with a rudimentary skirt on the door. The smell inside was nauseating, but Willow held her breath and turned on the water at the sink. It sputtered out, brown at first, but slowly the water turned clear. Willow rinsed her hands and splashed water on her face.

"What the fuck are you doing?" Ianthe's voice reached into the bathroom and Willow pushed the door open with her shoulder.

"Nothing," Willow answered as she bent over to get under the bar on the door. "Where to next?" she asked.

"Chicago. The train stops on its way to Kansas City. We can pick it up there and ride west."

There was nothing in Ianthe's tone that invited further conversation. She turned her back to Willow and started her bike. Willow started her bike too and followed Ianthe back onto the highway.

Sixteen

Warren sat down heavily and reached into his desk for the book. India's wide eyes looked back at him. "I won't lose her," he said to the photograph. India's expression was inscrutable as always. "I promise."

He snapped the book shut at the sound of a knock at his door, sliding the drawer shut as Miles stepped into the room.

"Report," Warren said, weariness creeping into his voice. Miles obliged.

"Her apartment is empty, but she didn't take anything with her. All of her clothes are still there, and her connection to the mainframe is still in place. The last read on her from the building has her exiting in the morning, three days ago. The cameras give visual confirmation. Her accounts were accessed twenty minutes later at a vitamin shop within walking distance from her residence. Cameras show her exiting the shop headed back in the direction of her house. We see her entering the plaza in front of her house at 10:31 a.m., then things get..." Miles paused, trying to think up the right word for what came next. "...strange," he finally said.

"Strange, Miles?" Warren rubbed his temples, eyes closed. Miles made a mental note to send Deirdre in with some aspirin.

"Sir, the cameras start wobbling out of focus. There is no record of her entrance, but there was an electromagnetic disturbance at 10:34 and again at 10:46. Then there is a trail of cameras experiencing malfunctions that starts in front of her building and weaves a path to the edge of the city. At that point, the trail goes cold." Miles cracked his knuckles behind his back, an unconscious tic that appeared when Miles faced a puzzle he couldn't immediately solve.

"And?" The rubbing stopped and Warren opened his eyes to look at Miles.

"And nothing until yesterday." Miles didn't change his coordinates in the room, but he rotated onto the balls of his feet. Warren knew Miles well enough to know that the little man was having fun, which annoyed him.

"What's the problem, Miles? Get on with it." The Minister hated having to drag details out of his Chief of Staff.

"Well Sir, here it really stops making sense. I moved the funds into her account as instructed, I also put a flag on the account to alert us of when and where a transaction was implemented. We got a notice at about 5:30 in the morning."

"The woman does need to eat..." There was a softness in Warren's voice that Miles hadn't heard in years. It unnerved him and he paused long moments before Warren looked back at him.

"Sir, the transaction took place at her house. We have no record or visual confirmation that she was even in the city."

"What was the transaction?"

"She moved all of her funds into an account that doesn't exist."

With that announcement, the Minister stood, banging his fist against his desk. "For fuck's sake, Miles. Find that damn account."

"What of the girl?" Miles asked tentatively.

"Monroe will get her for me. Just find the account. It will lead us to the vermin that are helping her. I'm in the mood for a good extermination."

Miles exited the room stepping backwards the whole way. He held his face in a neutral expression. The Minister was never to be trifled with, but Miles refused to turn his back on him when he was angry and, from the looks of it, exhausted. Miles was not a stupid man, but once he had crossed the threshold and was out of the Minister's view, he relaxed his control over his expression and smiled.

The aesthetically satisfying decay of eastern Indiana gave way to towns that had clearly died a meaner death. Wind-worn barns disappeared, only to be replaced by crumbling houses with shards of bright plastic toys stuck into the ground at odd angles, like broken bones protruding from the dirt. Brick factories stood like petrified sentries on either side of the road. Smashed out glass hung from the window sockets, and a few iridescent pigeons strutted along the sills, fat and sleek as politicians arrived just in time to lay the blame.

Willow wondered what kind of people had lived in a town named Gary, what it had looked like when the parking lots had been full and the houses had lights shining from their windows. Her imagination didn't stretch that far. Perhaps, then, some places were conceived as dingy as a worn dishrag. That didn't seem right either. Someone had to have been happy here, once.

For the rest of Indiana, Willow kept her eyes on the road. She couldn't explain her own sense of loss, the abstract grief for towns she never knew existed. It was better not to consider it, not to witness the corpse after an inexplicably savage murder. Anyway, her arms were tired of absorbing the shock of each gaping wound in the pavement. Watching the road wasn't such a bad way to spend her time.

The open land between the disrepair grew scarce. With no breathing room between, the dingy buildings pressed closer and closer still. By the time they passed a sign that said "Chicago City Limits," Willow felt a collar tightening around her throat. Claustrophobia, not just because of the leaning buildings, but from the press of all the bodies that weren't there.

Ianthe drove them straight into the burnt-out wasteland of Chicago's city center, and Willow's determined refusal to watch the decay vanished. While Indiana's industrial towns could be experienced on a personal scale, the enormity of the Chicago skyscrapers demanded Willow's attention. It was dusk now, and the buildings reminded Willow of the bare, backlit trees outside of Pittsburgh. They loomed above the street, dark watchmen with a single imperative: stand. And for the most part, they did. Whatever windows remained reflected the muddy sky back at itself, the absent windows absorbed what little light the moon let trail behind her.

At ground level, street signs read "Michigan Avenue," but they were rusting through and hanging sideways from the posts. Buildings threatened to lean on each other like wounded soldiers after a battle. To the right, she saw a vast, bare plot of land with a crumbing fountain and a small herd of deer grazing. To the left, nothing but shattered glass and buildings strung together with rebar.

Ianthe made a quick turn, the back wheel of her bike fishtailing a black swish on the pavement, bumping violently behind her as she disappeared down a set of stairs. Willow followed.

At the bottom of the staircase, Willow ran her tongue over her teeth to be sure that the jolting ride hadn't loosened them. Ianthe's muffler glimmered in the darkness and Willow followed that. Empty stores lined the tunnel, obvious only because of the overturned cash registers illuminated by Willow's single headlight. Scattered packaging drifted in the tunneled wind like silver leaves.

Willow chased Ianthe's glimmering muffler up a small incline and into a wider space with a fence and the skeleton of waiting room chairs. The floor under the chairs was covered in tufts of foam. For the split second that Willow's headlight illuminated the fenced waiting area, she saw the foam move and the flick of a long, naked tail. She opened up the throttle and caught up with Ianthe.

Ianthe led them into a low underground cave supported by blackened iron posts. Long slots cut in the concrete floor each had a numerical post standing watch. At the furthest end, a single train was beginning to make engine noises that reverberated through the cavernous space. Ianthe turned to look at Willow and gestured for her to stay where she was then peeled herself off the bike to check out the platform. Willow counted her own breath to mark the time. Thirty six. Ianthe walked up to Willow and shouted: "Third car from the last. Cut your lights." The engine was working itself up to a full roar, burying the sound of their motorcycles completely.

Willow swerved erratically on sleek flooring. Two green eyes reflected in the darkness and a gray shadow moved against the inky wall.

"Did you see that?" Willow yelled once she caught up with Ianthe. "It was watching us."

"Stray," Ianthe mouthed back, her voice disappearing as she drove through the open door. Willow rushed to maneuver her bike into the rail car behind her. Ianthe dismounted from her bike and used her weight to pull the door to the car closed.

Willow was slower to quit her seat. "What now?" Willow asked the shadow that moved around the inside of the car.

"Sleep," Ianthe replied. "You won't feel the hunger that way." Ianthe let her words echo through the car, hit the metal walls, and drop to the floor.

By the time the train lurched into motion, Willow had lost the count she'd been keeping of her breath. The steadily increasing rhythm of the wheels on the track soon made the exercise pointless anyway. The train's motion counted its own measure of time and space.

The moon shone through a crack in the box car, a thin blade of light cutting the space in two. There was no other light. Ianthe lay down, her back turned to Willow and the light. Willow lay down too. The boards under Willow's back were unforgiving, but it still didn't take long for her to fall asleep.

Ianthe quickly got lost in her recurring dream. Rows of toilets with no stalls to shield them, a classroom for scatological training with the "desks" set a precise distance apart. Toilet paper like arithmetic symbols stacked at the ready on a concrete floor. Behind the toilets, the same number of squared bathtubs in regimented rows. Facilities for a Victorian orphanage, where toilet training happened en masse, no privacy allowed, lest the residents take a solitary minute for pleasure.

It was not a new dreaming landscape for Ianthe: her step-father watched over the scene, dressed for the occasion in a waistcoat with a watch dangling from its pocket. She'd navigated this territory before, judging each toilet for the distance between her and that watch chain, for a measure of privacy counted in decimal places and the fast-moving hand of a watch.

Beside her, Willow was also asleep, falling into her own dream.

Willow woke with a start, her eyes wide against the darkness. She sat up and looked around. Ianthe was restless, breathing rapidly as if in pain. Willow confirmed her surroundings and lay back down, lowering herself vertebra by vertebra. She'd almost fallen back asleep when a new noise caught her attention. Like easy prey, she held herself still and tried to feel out the molecules around her for an indication of intent.

Willow had almost convinced herself that her imagination was playing tricks on her, when a circle of light opened up in the darkness, blinding her.

"Nice bikes," an unfamiliar voice said. It was decidedly male, but since it came from the other end of a flashlight, the face that made the pronouncement was unknowable. The light searched them, then landed on the bikes.

"Touch the bikes or us, and I'll cut off your balls."

Ianthe.

Willow breathed a sigh of relief. At least she wasn't alone. The man laughed.

"Try me," Ianthe warned, and a noise came from her direction very much like a knife being pulled from its sheath.

"Easy there, she-wolf. I'm just collecting tickets," he said, mocking.

"Tickets?" Ianthe's voice was less certain than it had been. She hadn't been expecting anyone to ask for tickets.

"Tickets for the Great Western Express. All can ride. Not everyone can survive. I either need your tickets or a good reason not to throw you off the train."

Willow could hear Ianthe stand up, but she could only see what fell into the beam of the flashlight. Ianthe extended her hands into the light as if in surrender. Pale, short fingers, ragged nails. Then she stepped forward, into the beam. The only concession her face made to the flashlight was in her eyes, which crinkled at the edges as she squinted. Then the beam became unstable in the hands of the intruder. As he struggled to hang on, the beam of light swung wildly, illuminating first a corner, then the floor, then the bikes, then Ianthe's determined face. His grip tightened but it didn't help.

The flashlight continued to twitch and fight his hand until it finally slid free of his grip, flew through the air, and attached itself to Ianthe's outstretched hand. Ianthe turned the light to face him and saw the glint of metal at his side. She stepped closer, one hand extended to keep the flashlight on the intruder, the other extended to relieve him of the gun he had in his pocket. It flew to her, leaving him unarmed.

"Holy shit." he sounded impressed. "You're one of them."

"I'm one of nobody," Ianthe replied, her voice as flat as the broad side of a saw. "Now, where is that ticket you promised me and my friend?"

"No harm, no foul." His bony shoulders shrugged. "Call it a litmus test. There's no point in y'all laying here in the cold and the dark. Everyone's eating down at end of the train."

"That's it?" Ianthe asked, incredulous. "You show up to play bad cop and the second you lose your little gun, now you're our best friend?"

He shrugged.

Except for the trembling, he was drifter-cute. Willow noted the dark smudges that merged with a scraggly beard, electric blue eyes, and a crooked nose.

"Fucking unbelievable," Ianthe muttered to herself. Willow heard her jacket rustle as she shook her head in disbelief.

"We'll follow you, but I'm keeping the gun." Ianthe's voice had regained its authority. "Willow. Give him his light back." Willow stood and reached for the flashlight, her skin coming into quick contact with Ianthe's hand. The connection was enough to tell Willow what her demeanor concealed: Ianthe was scared too. Willow pried the light out of Ianthe's sticky fingers and handed it back to the guy.

"Name?" It was as much an order as a question from Ianthe.

"Tane," he said. "And you?"

"Ian." Her voice hadn't softened. "She's Will. If you want to show us off, then let's get going. Otherwise, I'm going back to sleep."

Tane didn't answer, he just turned his back and his flashlight, illuminating a gap in the car almost big enough to squeeze through. On the other side, a similar gap in the next car. Under, a blur of railroad ties.

He crawled through the gap, placing a foot on the hitch that connected the two cars like it was as broad and stable as a sidewalk, and stepped into the next car. Ianthe followed as he turned the light back on the gap so she could see where she was going.

Willow went through last, her knees shaking. A voice in the back of her head noted that trying not to fall to your death on a train traveling 120 miles per hour was one way to put everything else into perspective.

And then her foot slipped. She reached forward, catching a handful of wooden railcar with her fingernails as she screamed. Her knee half way caught the joint between the two cars, and she hooked her foot around the metal tongue instinctively. She jerked her other leg away from the blurred ground between the rails, and hooked that foot too.

Ianthe turned quickly, grabbing the back of Willow's jacket. Tane crowded Ianthe to grab Willow's hand. Between the two of them, they managed to drag her in to the next car. Willow landed on her stomach, gasping for breath. She turned to her side and drew her knees up to her chest, soundless sobs shaking her body.

Behind her, Ianthe sagged against the wall of the car. Tane crouched on his heels, looking back and forth between the two women.

Ianthe spoke first. "Give us a minute," she said to Tane.

"Sure. Whatever. I'm no good at this," he said, gesturing at Willow.

"Leave the flashlight," Ianthe instructed. "We'll follow."

"Try not to kill yourself, if you don't mind," Tane said, and tossed the flashlight at Ianthe. It inscribed a wide arc against the sides of the box car before Ianthe sucked it in. Ianthe directed the beam of light at the far end of the car as Tane's feet disappeared into the night beyond. Willow was still shaking. Ianthe turned the flashlight off, leaving them to the rattled darkness.

"I can't do it," Willow sobbed when they were alone again. "I'm not like you."

"Pull yourself together." Ianthe said, her voice deceptively impervious.

"I can't," Willow whispered.

"Yes, you can." Ianthe considered the possible responses, from sympathetic to harsh, and finally settled on the truth. "I know you'd rather eat off the floor in a public restroom than own it, but you will always be at the mercy of the world around you if you don't start taking responsibility for yourself. You made the choices that got you here. The only way you get to be brave is by doing things you don't think you are capable of. The only way you get to be strong is by picking up more than you can carry. No one can save you but you. I sure as hell can't do it; I have a hard enough time saving myself."

Willow sniffled.

"Take as long as you need to pull yourself together, but this is your last shot at falling apart. You better make it good, 'cause it's going to have to last."

Ianthe lay down on her back within arm's reach of Willow. The minutes stretched long. Willow felt her sobbing grow progressively more ridiculous, so eventually she stopped. As soon as she was silent, Ianthe reached out and tousled what was left of Willow's hair.

"When I was six, I would have given my big toe for curly hair like yours." Ianthe said. Her voice was warmer than it had been since Pittsburgh.

"My mother was part African." Willow's voice was muffled by the hand that covered her mouth.

"What would she say to all of this?" Ianthe asked, surprised to find that she was genuinely interested.

Willow kept silent as the train clicked off sections of track under them. Finally, she answered. "She would have liked you." It was true: India would have appreciated Ianthe's matter-of-fact acceptance of the world around her, her gruff exterior and refusal to be intimidated.

"Does that mean you're ready to put on your big girl britches?" Ianthe asked, turning her head to look at Willow's furled back.

"I don't think I have a choice." Willow snorted ruefully. "It's cold in here."

Ianthe got up first, pushing herself up to standing then stepped over Willow's body. She extended a hand to help Willow up. "Just don't fall this time," Ianthe said. "You're sturdier than you look and I don't have the muscles to save your ass a second time."

Willow almost smiled, then followed the flashlight's beam to the opening between boxcars. She crossed first, holding her breath. She emerged into a very different boxcar than the one she'd just left. Ianthe was on her heels.

There was a fire in an iron bowl, and a string of chickens roasting on a spit. A collection of bodies lay around the box car. One of the men had a guitar and a tatterdemalion woman sat at his bare feet, a disciple to whatever song he was playing.

A big bottle of amber liquid passed from hand to hand, and when Willow stepped into the light, all eyes turned towards her.

"Dude!" one voice carried above the rest. "These the chicks you found?" The speaker had a beard but no mustache. Willow had never seen a beard on a man with a bare upper lip. It didn't suit him. Then again, Willow didn't think it would suit anybody.

"Mean chicks." Tane sounded chagrined.

"Yeah, but are they *hot* mean chicks?"

Willow turned to look. The speaker was a woman from the timbre of her voice, but looking at her, you'd never know. She was dressed in a collarless button down shirt, which was tucked into tweed pants and framed by suspenders. She wore wire-rimmed round glasses, and asked with indifference. When she turned back to look at Tane, Willow could see a long blond braid that fell to her waist.

"Depends on how you define hot." Ianthe said, all fearless swagger as she stepped into the firelight.

Miles continued to back out of the Minister's Office and into the hall. Habit kept his eyes on the door and he backed directly into Dr. Maggie Lake, daughter and heir apparent to the Minister. Her hands on his shoulder surprised him, not just because he wasn't expecting her to be there at all, but also because physical contact was a rarity in his world.

"Slow down there, Mister," she said to him, smiling. Her hands lingered. "I need to talk to you."

He cleared his voice as he tried to regain his composure. "Yes, we most certainly need to talk." His darting eyes took in her pristine suit under an unbuttoned lab coat, her blouse undone one button more than propriety dictated.

"Your office, I presume, considering you've gifted me with a specimen of dubious origins?" Her tone was light-hearted, but her demand for an explanation was clear.

"Of course, Dr. Lake. Just, if you don't mind, don't mention your guest to your father." Miles replied.

Maggie Lake looked at him, her head tipped slightly to the side as if contemplating what Miles was up to. The moment stretched. Miles gave in first.

"The Minister is in a foul mood. Proceed with care," he cautioned.

"Thank you, Miles. Perhaps I'll come back later. My issue isn't..." she paused for effect, running her tongue against her lips, "...pressing."

She looked down at her watch and back up at Miles.

"Your office then?"

Miles nodded.

"I'll see you in an hour."

Willow followed Ianthe closer to the fire, crouching to warm her hands. Slowly, whatever conversations that had been in process before their grand entrance, resumed. The guitar-wielding boy started playing again, but Willow didn't recognize the song. From the sound of it, his admirer didn't either, but if Willow listened beyond the tuneless humming of the girl, she could hear the sound his fingers made as they let go of a string to make the next chord sing, each metallic thread giving a gasp of surprise as it was abandoned in favor of another.

The bottle was passed from mouth to mouth around the inner circle. In the opposite corner, the boyish blond took a seat on a bale of hay and deftly rolled something green and dusty-looking into a piece of paper. The flourish she used striking the match was too theatrical to be necessary. But then every gesture was steeped in drama. She put the cigarette to her mouth and cupped her hand around the match. Her eyes rolled to the back of her head as she inhaled. Willow thought she might pass out, she held her breath so long. Finally, she released the smoke with a cough and passed the thing to the guy with half-a-beard. He did the same, and soon the boxcar was filled with threads of smoke that undulated and twisted together like bodies in an orgy.

On the second or third round of bottle-passing, someone offered it to Willow. Willow examined the amber liquid sloshing around in the bottom and looked at Ianthe for an explanation. Ianthe didn't give any indication either way, so Willow carefully wiped the opening and poured a careful measure of the contents into her mouth.

Whatever it was, it burned. She coughed and spluttered as some of it evaporated right off her tongue. She passed the bottle to Ianthe to keep it from spilling as she choked and gasped for air.

"What the Fleming was that?" she sputtered when she could speak again.

"Whiskey. Probably of the homemade variety." Ianthe looked nonplussed. "I'm surprised you didn't get it out of your system in high school."

"Carlyle," Willow answered, as if the name explained everything.

"Well, don't go overboard," Ianthe said in low tones meant just for Willow. "If you think Kassia was bad, it's worse. Drink enough and you'll have no secrets left."

Willow nodded solemnly in response, but drank again when the bottle was passed to her. The second mouthful went down like a forest fire and left a charcoal edge on her tongue. But it warmed her in places she hadn't noticed she was cold. The third taste was much improved. Several more rounds and it felt as if the boxcar was hurtling towards an improbable destination even as it spun on its own little axis. It was wonderful.

She curled up into herself and watched the people around her wobble in and out of focus and soon fell asleep.

Willow woke in a tangle of limbs, her head throbbing. She looked around her, located Ianthe in the pile of sleeping bodies, and tried to piece together the night before.

The wheels clattering against the track made Willow's head feel like an overripe melon. Someone had slid the railcar door half-open to let in fresh air. From Willow's vantage point, she could see fields of wheat blur as they rushed past the train. Distant houses blinked into existence and out again, leaving only the broken stalks behind. She extracted herself from her sleeping companions and approached the door, seating herself at the narrow window on to a world she'd only read about.

The old Union had a song about dawn's early light. The first American Revolution, rockets and bombs, something like that. Willow hadn't been particularly interested in history. But now, watching the wasteland go by, the forgotten song lodged itself in her head.

Whatever rise and fall had vexed the motorcycles between the ruins of Pittsburgh and the abandoned streets of Chicago had been thoroughly ironed out. The train ran perpendicular to a distant horizon and didn't deviate. There was nothing to shift direction for and the ruthless wheels drew them inexorably west. Behind them, the first rays of sunlight chased the tracks, burnishing the harvested fields in a clear shade of gold.

Willow inhaled deeply. She had no name for the scent that clung to the cool air. This was real air, no processing through SaniCheck filters.

It brought a longing Willow didn't know she had. She wanted dirt, clean laundry, sore muscles, proof that she'd touched the world around her, and the kind of complete darkness she hadn't known existed before she climbed on the bike behind Ianthe.

Who lived out there with a silence that Willow imagined must be hypnotic in its completeness? She wanted to meet them. To find out if they ordered SaniCheck from the regional distribution centers, or if they cleaned like her mother had, with diluted vinegar.

She wanted to ask if they felt. If their food tasted different. If they made love. Did they watch for military satellites falling from the sky? Shoot off fireworks on the old holidays? Believe in discounted fables like creation? Willow had never been so hungry for people.

It was like breathing for the first time. But then everything was for the first time. So what if she'd worn the same underwear for three days. The cows didn't care. The hair under her arms was longer than it had ever been in her whole life. Her nose shone, her feet stank, and none of it mattered. Her hair was truly awful, with tufts cut mid-curl, some threatening to dive across her forehead, others standing straight up. But it didn't matter. She was the observer in the landscape, not the observed. No cameras, no ID checks, no magnetic recorders.

Willow was off-script, out of control, and as relaxed as she'd been in her entire life. She didn't have to remind herself to breathe into her stomach or push her shoulders down from around her ears. She wasn't in charge. No one was looking at her. She didn't even know where she was going... It was the best feeling ever. Even better than Ven.

Ven. Aside from the taste of his sweat, Willow was coming to terms with the fact that she didn't know him at all. For that matter, he didn't know her either, so she supposed they were even. She tried to conjure something familiar from the memory, a sense of regret, a hint of anger, something. No, there was nothing. Willow wasn't sure if the vacancy where the idea of Ven had been was an improvement.

Beneath her, the train slowed. The wheels ground against the track in prolonged protestation. As the train ground to a halt, Willow stuck her head further out the door, then looked back inside the car at the other passengers. No one seemed to notice their sudden lack of forward motion. She looked back outside.

Further up the train, a rusted old pickup truck sat outside one of the train's cars. A narrow man dressed in overalls shuffled up to the back of the truck and the railcar door slid open. The man from the train crouched to shake hands with the driver of the truck, but they were too far away for Willow to hear their conversation.

A man came and sat down beside her. She stiffened.

"It's just me," he said. She recognized Tane, but she didn't relax.

"Take it easy," he said in his most soothing voice. "You aren't my type."

Willow's head whipped around to look him in the eye. He gave a wry shrug. "You looked cold."

Tane reached out and handed her a blanket as he spoke. Willow wrapped it around herself and took a deep breath.

"Used to be called the Great Plains," he said, answering Willow's question before she had a chance to verbalize it. "We're dropping off supplies for the settlers. Even before the pandemic it was pretty sparsely populated. Farmers, ranchers, a University or two."

Three more parcels came sailing from the inside of the cargo box, then the Wastelander jumped back into the bed of his truck to close the door of the boxcar. The train released a puff of steam and whistled an industrial mating call into the wheat fields. The settler stood in the bed of his truck and watched the cars as they slid past him in shorter and shorter blurs. Willow swore she saw him wink as they passed in the last boxcar on the train, but she didn't mention it. Instead, she turned back to Tane.

"Are you from the Wastes?"

"No, I was a history teacher. You pick up trivia." Tane's voice was carefully neutral.

"What happened?" Willow asked in spite of herself. Her first impulse was for solitude, but she surprised herself in genuinely wanting to know.

"To me or to the old country?" Tane sounded amused.

"Take your pick," Willow responded.

"I wanted to see the land I was teaching about." He paused, debating how much he wanted the girl beside him to know. "And I got fired for answering the kids' questions honestly."

"What kinds of questions?" Willow turned towards him.

"Questions about the freedoms that used to be the core of the old country's constitution before the Ministry came to power. The old bill of rights, before it looked like a medical checklist. 'The country has the right to be disease free, the country has the right to organic food, free of artificial hormones, the country has the right to be safely cocooned in a shroud of SaniCheck and organic cotton balls.' It didn't go over well." Willow could feel Tane force himself to take a deep breath beside her.

"How long ago was that?" Willow asked.

"I left three years ago."

"You left by choice?" Willow was incredulous, then annoyed at her knee-jerk reaction. Looking around at the motley crew of drifters that called themselves NeoRoma, she realized that they had probably all left the shelter of regulation by choice.

"Well, I knew it was coming. I decided I liked the truth better than anything my life had to offer." He looked out at the landscape sliding by. "There are times out here when the sound of the train fades away and you get silence. Real silence, not muffled jostling and multiple bodies breathing and the whining of heaters and fans and air purifiers and microwaves beeping and piped in music and all that stifled discontent. It's just me and the wind and I'm alive. Really alive. I didn't know what that felt like before."

Willow closed her eyes and listened to the clatter of the metal wheels. It didn't sound much like silence, but behind the sound of the train, there was something oddly still.

Tane went on. "You're here. I didn't see you riding in at knife-point."

"I was a social scientist. For the Ministry."

"You're a long way off the reservation." Tane looked at her with new interest.

Willow laughed bitterly. "My story doesn't have the same intellectual integrity as yours."

"I wouldn't say that. It really doesn't matter how you get where you are going, just as long as you end up where you belong."

Tane fell silent and Willow did the same. They both watched the wide expanse of blue sky, endless above the sunlit horizon.

Seventeen

As the day wore on, more and more of the riders woke up. The boyish blond engaged Tane in conversation, her body position blocking Willow out of the conversation just as effectively as the subject.

"The U.S.S.R. has managed to reinvent itself as an evolved communist state. Clearly, it works," the girl said.

"Come on, Engle. That is a total misrepresentation of Marx and you know it," Tane protested. "True communism has no government and the U.S.S.R. is nowhere near that."

"What would you propose instead? Capitalist democracy proved morally and socially bankrupt." Engle's tone was derisive.

"But it was salvageable. If there had been the political will for true reform, for a recognition that businesses are not the same as individuals and do not deserve the same representative rights as individuals."

"That is ridiculously idealistic," Engle retorted.

"No more so than the idea that the U.S.S.R. is moving towards a true implementation of communism." Tane sounded as if this were an old conversation, one that they'd been having for years.

"I just don't think that Marxism or its expression through communism takes a realistic approach to social management." Tane turned to Willow. "You are a social scientist. Do you think that social structures require codification through a government system, or can society arrange itself without any governmental oversight?"

Willow was unprepared for the question. "Uh..." she stammered. "If there were no function for government, then it wouldn't exist. Even splinter groups have some sort of hierarchy in place, at least if they seek to accomplish a common goal."

Engle rolled her eyes. "We do just fine without a hierarchy." Her tone told everyone listening exactly what she thought about Willow and her opinions.

"Yeah, but you aren't trying to accomplish anything," Willow argued. "If you were trying to accomplish a common goal, if there were more of you in the same place at the same time, you'd naturally shift into a hierarchy. Even dog packs have an alpha. Social organization is evident everywhere you look in the animal kingdom."

"What about sheep?" Engle asked, as if the question undermined Willow's whole argument.

"Maybe, but are sheep really the example you want to emulate?" Behind them, someone snickered at Engle's besting.

"That's not the point," Engle said. "The point is that not all social animals organize."

"Using cattle as an example isn't any more encouraging." Willow pressed the point.

Engle's lips thinned over her teeth in a tight line. "You clearly aren't capable of holding your own in a serious discussion." She turned to the other corner of the boxcar and set about rolling herself another cigarette.

The other traveling companions slowly turned back to what they had been doing before the skirmish between the two women caught their attention. Ianthe hid a smile with a half-hearted cough and Willow shrugged.

Silence hung between Willow and Tane as smoke gradually filled up the boxcar again. Eventually, Tane broke into Willow's study of the rushing landscape.

"What does a social scientist do at the Ministry?"

"Statistics," Willow answered. "I was a data wonk."

"What were you studying?"

"It was boring," Willow laughed uncomfortably. "No one is interested in that much data."

"Try me," Tane answered.

"I was looking at the way social diseases follow social networks."

"When you were at the Ministry, did you ever look at the survival rates by population?"

Willow turned away from the open door and looked at Tane for some explanation of the question.

"Survival of what?"

"The Avian Pandemic. Before the Chaos."

Tane was speaking more quietly now, as if he wasn't interested in his traveling companions overhearing what he was going to say next. "A precise ratio of people died. Too precise. If you look at the demographics from each of the areas where there were survivors, exactly 54 percent of the survivors were Caucasian. The remainder is pretty evenly split between native populations: blacks, Asians, Hispanics… City after city. It's just too tidy."

"Tane," Willow said gently. "I'll give you that there is a lot more crazy going around than I thought, but even the worst government isn't going to wipe out most of its population. What would be the point? That's tax revenue, the economy, basically everything that keeps a government going. What could they possibly be after?"

Tane leaned back, disappointment showing through the scruff covering the lines around his mouth.

"I guess you're right," he finally conceded, though his tone said he wasn't sure.

Ianthe watched Tane and Willow, their heads gradually bending more and more towards each other. There was a pang of something, Ianthe refused to call it jealousy. Or at least it couldn't be jealousy because Willow was talking to someone new. If it was jealousy, then she was jealous of seeing someone else on the cusp of a friendship or whatever. She and Kiri had talked like that, oblivious to everyone around them.

Willow was still at the door to the car when one of the straggly NeoRoma girls announced a game of poker. Ianthe stood and joined the game. There wasn't anything else to do with the time. The playing deck was comprised of worn cards from a dozen different decks. Sticks and stones stood in for chips, and the players each offered up the best they had to raise the stakes.

Indifference strengthened Ianthe's hand, and she won a tattered collection of semi-prized possessions, which she gradually lost or re-won in subsequent rounds. Someone traveled the length of the train and returned with a communal dinner siphoned from the settler's supplies. As the day darkened, Willow made her way around the outside of the group to an empty blanket next to Ianthe.

"How well did you know him?" Willow asked Ianthe quietly as the rest of the riders lazed about picking their teeth in the piles of straw.

"Know who?" Ianthe feigned ignorance as she grasped at the edges of her righteous anger, trying to keep it close.

"Ven." Willow stumbled on the name.

"Oh." Ianthe fell silent for a moment, caught between answering and ignoring Willow, then measuring out her words. "A little. He was gone a lot. We weren't … Close."

"What was his story? How'd he join the Camellias?" Willow asked, dreading the answer.

"It's a little late to be asking," Ianthe returned.

"Maybe." Willow conceded, then went on anyway. "Marshall doesn't seem to have really known him. I certainly didn't." She forced her voice to sound as neutral as possible. She'd not said out loud just how much of a stranger Ven had been, and didn't want to spend a lot of time talking about it now.

Ianthe closed her eyes, thinking back to when she'd first met Ven. When she opened them again, she stared at the fire, not really seeing it. "One of the Camellias introduced him. He wanted to date her, but you know Marshall's rules. If you aren't infected, you've got to be pretty damn certain before you get involved."

Willow's imagination immediately drew up a lusty redhead with unheard of beauty. "Did I meet her?" Willow asked when she felt like she could trust her voice again.

"Nah," Ianthe replied. "She took off for Texas a couple of years ago. But Ven was already one of us by then. He and Marshall are tight." Ianthe tried to sound indifferent.

"Did anyone ever hear him say that he was a double agent?" Willow asked.

"A what?" Ianthe forgot herself in her surprise and turned to look Willow full in the face. Willow met her gaze, blinking but clear.

"He was listed in the Ministry's records as a Counter Intelligence officer. Marshall tried to act like Ven had been a plant, but I don't think he knew." Willow drew her knees up to her chest, rested her arms on her knees, and laid her head on her arms. "I certainly didn't know."

"Doesn't surprise me," Ianthe offered, imitating Willow's fetal posture. She watched the flames twist around each other like different strands of the same truth. "I wonder if he knows..." Ianthe started, then fell silent.

"Knows what?"

"Knows where the Infirmary is." Ianthe let the bald words hang between them, unconvinced that Willow had divulged everything she knew. Willow didn't know how to address Ianthe's question, so she carried on with the conversation she knew. "I wish I'd known him better. Maybe I could have put the rest of this into context..."

"It's never going to make sense," Ianthe said, putting her frustration aside. "You make peace with it, you compartmentalize. You rationalize your way into thinking it's the best thing that could have happened to you. But when it comes down to it, it's just a thing. Bad shit happens all the time. But however you got here, you're here now. At least you're out of that disinfected bubble you were in."

Willow turned to look at Ianthe and smiled. "It sure is messy out here."

"Whatever." Ianthe said, but her energy for the fight was gone. "It isn't what happens to you. It's how you live with it that matters."

It wasn't quite a peace offering, Willow thought, but it was better than the uncomfortable silence that had hung between them since their fight back in Pittsburgh.

"So who's the Neanderthal?" Maggie was sitting behind her glass desk. Miles could see around the stacks of paper, through to Dr. Lake's exposed knees. Her skirt had slid up mid-thigh and a sliver of lace exposed itself at the hem.

"That Neanderthal was the means of accomplishing your request."

"Really?" Maggie responded with a feral smile. "I like him better already. So where do we stand?"

"Still dealing with the complications I warned you about when I tried to abort the mission."

Maggie's smile waned. "I'm not sure I've forgiven you for that."

Miles gave a gentle nod in Maggie's direction, acknowledging the rebuke. Startling, at times, how much like her father Maggie Lake really was.

"You got what you wanted, but as I anticipated, your father is allowing his emotions to rule. He is unconvinced of her unsuitability. In fact, he plans to ask the Minister of Security to help track her down. I don't know if he will secure the General's cooperation—their mutual antipathy is legendary—but the Minister is determined to have her rescued and returned."

"And the Neanderthal?" Maggie asked, temporarily mollified.

"Too much of a risk."

"Should I send him to the Infirmary?" Maggie's voice was almost hopeful.

"No, better to keep him here where we can control him." Miles thought back to the look on Ven's face and pushed aside a vision of the murderous expression in Ven's eyes as the security forces closed in on him. Miles wasn't sure the facilities in Bethesda would be sufficient to keep Ven.

"This can still go our way?" Maggie was watching Miles carefully. His attention had slipped away from her. Like a good fisherman, she let the line go slack, but not for long.

"All is not lost," Miles replied. "I'll just have to manage the outcomes as they present." His attention drifted again as permutations and contingencies scrambled into orderly lines in his head.

"We, Miles," Maggie corrected him, smiling. "We will have to manage the outcomes." Her voice was heavy with insinuation.

"My apologies, Dr. Lake." Miles peered at her from the top of his spectacles, testing the air between them for a sense of which way the wind was blowing.

"Maggie. Call me Maggie." She stood, pushed her chair back, and stepped closer to Miles. "If all goes as planned, this formality will be a little foolish." She stood close to him. Close enough to smell the SaniCheck still clinging to his skin. She inhaled deeply and smiled.

"Maggie." Miles said carefully, unsure whether he should lean into her or away. She solved the conundrum by reaching out and taking his hand. The latex of their gloves made a small protesting sound as it met. Under the protective layer, Maggie Lake's hand was small and warm.

Eighteen

Marshall had never met the Health Minister, but it wasn't for lack of desire. He'd wanted to meet the bastard for years. On nights when the insomnia was particularly bad, he'd imagined their meeting as a way to fall asleep. No peaceful attempts to reason. Marshall wanted a dawning realization in the Minister's eyes when he finally understood his enemy was formidable and evenly matched. He'd imagined stalking slowly across a posh office, wrapping his meaty hand around the coward's neck and squeezing. The pleas for mercy, the begging, the offer of clemency all ignored. It wasn't that Marshall Van Ness had started out thinking he was born to take down the Minister of Health, but he'd had to dedicate his life to something to survive.

Refusing to be silent had been one pillar of survival. Hating the Minister and all he stood for had been the other. In the early days he'd been beaten to the brink of dying by a MOS thug. Luckily, he had figured out that his Camellias could help each other regenerate by then. He'd spent a week in bed, his chosen family cycling through to lie next to him, to hold his hand, or to simply rest their feet next to his. The men had universally chosen the latter, but a much younger Ianthe had curled up in the shelter of his hulking arms and slept.

A dictatorship contradicted everything Marshall stood for. Even as benevolent as the Ministry claimed to be, Marshall's existence was a threat. His Camellias were a threat for as long as they remained outside the system. It was a system built on fear, but they were unafraid. Marshall had worked hard to make them so.

Out of nothing, he'd built his makeshift family. In the entire Union, his Camellias—named for the way the virus looked under a microscope—were among the few truly free citizens. There was no room for Marshall in the world the Ministry fought so hard to preserve, but here he was standing in an antechamber staring at the Minister's door.

There was only one explanation for the Minister extending a limited détente for a meeting. The girl. Marshall couldn't lie for shit, so the fact that Ianthe hadn't divulged her plans before they'd both disappeared was going to serve him well.

He practiced his answers for intonation, for just the right hint of helplessness. To whatever degree the Ministry underestimated him, it gave him an advantage he needed more than ever. *We extended our hospitality to the woman, but she repaid our generosity by stealing a motorcycle and taking off. I don't know where she's gone.*

Marshall even practiced the accompanying shrug. It was true enough to count. He compared the carpet under his feet with the concrete floor in his office and decided he'd rather have the concrete. At least he could hear when someone was coming.

The door in front of him swung open and a dapper little man stood in the gap. Marshall immediately stood taller.

"Mr. Van Ness," he said. "I'm the Minister's Chief of Staff." Miles cracked his knuckles, as if he were anticipating a sporting event. Marshall looked down at his bare hands and almost gave in to the naked feeling, like he'd forgotten to put on his pants that morning. One more reason to hate the Minister. "Please enter," Miles said, gesturing to the large office beyond the door.

Marshall felt obscenely large as he walked past the Chief of Staff. Taller than the man by a good foot and broader in every measurable way. His pleated trousers suddenly felt too tight. His plaid shirt felt scratchy and garish. No matter, or at least it was too late to matter. He smoothed his fringe of white hair and reassured himself with an internal reminder of what he'd gone through to arrive at this point. The little man in front of him was too much of a pussy to survive one day in Marshall's life.

Fortified, he held his chin up high as he passed through the door. Miles watched it all cross Marshall's face. No interpreter was needed. The intimidation, the internal monologue, the feigned calm, Miles had seen it all often enough. Anyone passing through the Minister's door went through the same predictable cycle, though not everyone got to a place where they'd hold their chin up high. Though professionally indifferent, personally he appreciated the courage.

Warren Lake sat in a large leather chair. Marshall noted that the arms were worn at the edge and liked the man occupying the chair just a little better for it. It shouldn't have been much against the burning hatred he'd felt toward the man all those years, but looking at him, Marshall couldn't lay his hands on his rage. He had imagined the Minister of Health surrounded by a beautiful wife and a bevy of happy children – everything that Marshall had been denied. There was one photograph on his desk of a family where each person each looked in a different direction.

This poor son of a bitch is lonely, Marshall thought to himself. He hesitated half way to the desk and looked to the Chief of Staff for direction. "Please sit," Miles directed, so Marshall finished the approach to the large desk and sat.

The Minister watched the proceedings with clinical interest. He'd read Marshall's dossier again before the meeting, looking with particular interest at Marshall's infection tree. From the timeline and the name, Warren supposed that Marshall was no more than three degrees of separation from Duane. Not that it made much difference to the issue at hand, but Warren liked knowing where things stood.

"What are your symptoms?" Warren asked. From his place by the door, Miles' head jerked upright. A brief look of confusion washed across his face and disappeared almost immediately. Were there less history between Miles and the Minister, Warren might have missed it. Instead, Warren silently congratulated himself on still being capable of surprising his chief of staff.

Marshall knew this trick. He'd used it on Willow. Surprise the subject, use their surprise to uncover a hidden truth. "I'm not sure that's your concern," Marshall allowed his amusement to show in his tone.

"I'm the Minister of Health, of course it is my concern," the Minister replied mildly. "Frequent outbreaks? What are the ancillary manifestations?" Warren watched Marshall's face redden. Good. He'd unsettled the man.

Except Marshall wasn't unsettled; he was angry at the Minister's attempt to play him. "I'll tell you about my symptoms if you tell me about the Infirmary."

Warren's face closed around Marshall's words. Marshall didn't know the man, but he knew the look. The Minister hadn't been expecting that. The silence thickened between the two men. Marshall's impatience got the better of him and he spoke first. "You didn't ask for this meeting to discuss my health. If you did, you are at least thirty years too late."

Warren nodded and let his fingers form a tent under his nose. He said nothing, letting Marshall squirm as he regrouped. Marshall's knee bounced, announcing his impatience to the room. Finally, the Minister spoke. "I have a cure. I'm prepared to offer it to you and yours." Warren was bluffing, of course. The cure wasn't ready for the public yet, but Marshall didn't need to know that.

Marshall had little beyond rage to go on when it came to preparing himself for this meeting. The summons had arrived the day before with a knock on the Camellia's compound door. The messenger had parked a gleaming black vehicle on the gravel driveway and walked to the door with no hesitation. It had unnerved him.

Their whereabouts, if not totally secret, were not supposed to be so stunningly obvious to the Ministry. Doubt had crept in, doubt seeded by his conversation with the girl. That the Minister had plots within plots didn't surprise Marshall. The direct approach, however, was completely unexpected.

"A cure?" he said, uncertain that he'd heard right.

"I have a cure and a vaccine. The vaccine will be distributed through our clinics. The cure will be handled with more delicacy. I offer it to your people first." Warren spoke as if explaining basic arithmetic to a particularly obtuse child.

"I don't understand."

The Minister sighed. Clearly Marshall was not going to make this easy on him. Warren cataloged his options and decided on a low dose of emotion. "I need Willow Carlyle back." Warren allowed a trace of desperation to infuse his voice. For authenticity's sake. "I'll trade you an absolute cure for Willow Carlyle."

"The woman? I don't have her. She escaped. I mean, she stole from us. She's gone," Marshall stuttered.

The Health Minister transformed in front of him. The sympathetic façade was gone. Steel and ice replaced bone and muscle as he stood over his seated guest. His voice was unmistakably menacing.

"If you have hurt her in any way..." Warren let his words trail off, implying a variety of threats.

"She was fine the last time I saw her. Better than she'd be under your tender loving care," Marshall stammered, hoping his conciliatory tone conveyed that, of the things he had to hide, this wasn't one.

"Why did you target her?" The Minister did not soften. He knew enough of the organization to know that most of their recruits came by luck. Mostly bad luck on the part of the recruit. He couldn't accept that Willow had fallen on her own accord; therefore, she must have been targeted. And if she had been deliberately targeted, then it only stood to reason that they knew something Warren was fairly certain was known only to himself.

"We... we didn't," Marshall replied, his eyebrows furrowed and his face pale. Now, the Minister was delving into subjects Marshall himself wanted answers to.

"You did, and you will tell me why." If Marshall was telling the truth, Warren would get more of it by pushing, and if he was lying, then Warren would get to the truth. Either way, Warren gave silent acknowledgment to Marshall's fortitude: the man had balls of steel to stand up to the Minister of Health.

"My man chose her," Marshall said, stretching his hands apart in the universal sign for openness. "We only sent him to the conference to find someone from the Ministry and get what information he could. Knowing him, he settled on a pretty face and went with it."

"You sent someone to deliberately infect one of my people?" Warren's outrage was genuine and it filled the room.

"Of course not." Marshall had a little outrage of his own. To suggest that he would be a party to such a thing was to suggest that he had no honor. "Deliberately infecting an unsuspecting partner is against our code of conduct. He was just supposed to listen and learn what he could."

"To what purpose?" Warren sat back down, and Marshall breathed a little easier.

"To get to you." Marshall wished he could take the words back as soon as he'd said them.

"That, at least, I'll believe," the Minister muttered under his breath. "Do you know where she went?" His body and his voice had softened back to near-reason.

"I've heard rumors that they are on a train heading west." Marshall thought back to the night they escaped. His mouth turned down at the corners. Willow escaping, he could believe. Ianthe's absence hurt.

"What's out west?" Warren watched Marshall closely for signs of deception, his stomach slowly filling with dread. There wasn't anything out there but settlers, a pocket of NeoRoma, and his old friend.

"Nothing. Unless they went on a fool's errand."

The Minister raised an eyebrow and waited for Marshall to go on. "The Source," Marshall explained.

Slowly, the color drained from the Minister's face. They sat in silence for long minutes as the Minister worked through all the ways that Willow's interview with Duane could end.

"He's turned away every person that's ever made it out that far. He's not going to welcome a couple of upstart girls." Marshall spoke to fill the space, violating his own good sense. "They'll be lucky if they don't get waylaid in the Wastes, some farmer in need of a wife..." Marshall shuddered. "I pity the fool that tries that trick on Ian," he said under his breath.

Warren watched Marshall digress and used the time to regroup. "You get me the girl and I'll get you the cure. I don't care how you get her; just bring her back alive and unharmed. If anything more has happened to her at the hands of your people, I swear on all that is good in this world, I will tear you limb from limb." The Minister's expression backed up his words.

Marshall considered that for a moment.

"I'll get her," he said and stood. "But not for the cure. You have something of mine as well."

Warren Lake stood as well, but slowly. "What could possibly be more important than a cure?"

"My Camellias." Marshall didn't even hesitate. "The MOS picked them up back in September. You've got them and I want them back." He'd take their bodies if that was all that was left, but if there was a chance they were still alive...

"Done." The Minister gestured towards his door. "Be well," he said by way of dismissal.

It had been a long time since Marshall had lived a life where the regulation protocol had any relevance. Among his Camellias, 'be well' was a joke. But Marshall couldn't help himself, caught up as he was in the ritual of it all.

"Be well," Marshall said in return.

When the door had closed behind him, the Minister sat down heavily.

"What do you think, Miles?" Warren asked.

"I think he's the wrong man for the job," Miles replied. Warren nodded silently.

Miles didn't elaborate and the Minister kept his own council.

"Try the Minister of Security again," he said finally, and Miles ducked out of the room to obey, leaving the Minister alone in his carefully constructed office.

Warren didn't mind admitting, at least to himself, that he used his surroundings to intimidate those who walked through his doors. The office was designed to make his visitors feel small, from the oversized door to the impractical carpet to the antechamber built to create suspense. But now, alone, Warren thought of the sofa fortresses he and his dead brother had made and craved the dark closeness, the kind of claustrophobic world adults find in a lover's arms.

Lena would see him. Of course she would. She'd clear a space on her schedule for him and be there with her slender, bare limbs. He allowed the fantasy for a minute. Even if the world would rearrange itself for Warren, even if the rules didn't apply to him, he knew his limits. He still couldn't afford to need Lena the way he'd needed India. He would have to see this through on his own.

Having Marshall bring Willow in was a fool's errand. Marshall would make a half-assed attempt at it, if he tried to find her at all. Warren also knew that Marshall's assessment was based on an incomplete understanding of the facts. Duane would see Willow and in her, he would see India. And Duane would let Willow through his door, and Duane would tell Willow anything she wanted to know. Nothing could possibly go right after that.

Warren was running out of options. Just about everything he'd ever wanted to accomplish fell within the auspices of the Ministry, but to get to Oregon Territory with any speed, he needed the General. He sighed and placed his forehead on the desk. The cool wood against his skin did nothing: a futile gesture with no comfort in it. He picked up his head again and reached for the phone. Maybe he'd call Lena after all, but first he'd have to call the General himself.

2006/04

"Have you seen Duane?" Warren asked. His ear was pressed against India's smooth belly, listening to her stomach gurgle.

"Yes." India considered her answer carefully. Warren tolerated her other clients because it fell within regulation: whoring was acceptable, but the Republic believed that emotional attachment between client and service provider was a dangerous thing. Therefore, if you wanted the protections afforded by the State, you followed regulation. Warren couldn't risk his career circumnavigating the rules and he knew it. Duane, on the other hand, wasn't on India's official schedule and Warren wasn't beyond jealousy.

"He was here on Thursday." She bit her lower lip. "He's not doing well. He blames himself for Jailyn."

"Well..." Warren's tone was an indictment.

"He wouldn't have hurt her. If he'd known, he wouldn't have hurt her."

"Come on. He got it from a woman he met at a party. He didn't even know her name. How was that not going to hurt his wife?"

India looked down at the back of Warren's head, glad he couldn't see her face. His spine was exposed under the edge of the sheet, each little nub testament to the fact he'd been working too much and eating too little. She thought briefly of Warren's wife and wondered which she'd prefer: a foolish indiscretion at a party or a semi-permanent fixture.

"He should be glad she died," Warren went on. "Do you think she'd have forgiven him if she'd lived? She would have divorced him."

"That's a little harsh," India interjected. Warren shifted positions, raising himself up onto his elbows so he could look India in the face.

"India, I know you're compassionate, but the man killed his wife—indirectly, but he did kill her—all for a blow job at a stupid party. He's my best friend, but he's an idiot. Now, do you really want to spend our last half an hour talking about Duane?" His voice dropped a register, and India responded according to script. She smiled at Warren from lowered lashes and offered her body up once more for the feast.

But while Warren settled himself between her thighs, and India made the sounds of someone who is drowning in desire, she thought of Warren's wife again. Sara Lake. By Warren's own telling, a chilly woman of few pleasures, but still his wife.

Warren knew well enough when India was distracted, and he knew how to command her attention as well. By the time he welded his body to hers, her focus was exactly where Warren liked to keep it: on the pleasure he was certain only he could bring. They rode their respective oblivion over the edge, and collapsed back onto the bed.

"It's too bad you only had one dose," India speculated absently.

"Mmm," Warren responded. "Too bad."

Nineteen

Ianthe returned to the poker game. Willow watched everything—the darkened landscape, the poker game, the other passengers—and leaned against Tane. Two passengers were in a corner, kissing. Willow poked Tane and gestured at the couple.

"Are they in contract?" she asked.

Tane laughed. "Funny. You really are regulation. I don't care what your haircut says about you. No one out here is in contract."

"But they are kissing..." Willow's voice betrayed her concern, and she felt awkward for it. No one else seemed to care.

"Yeah. And? Under the first constitution, people kissed all the time." Tane was still laughing at her, but quietly, behind his eyes.

"I saw it in my mom's old movies, but I didn't think that real people..." Willow let the words die out on her tongue.

"Real people kissed, and more." Tane grinned at her.

"They're ok with it?" Willow couldn't help but ask.

"It's fine," Tane said with a shrug. "In a week, they'll be kissing someone else."

"But what if they have something?" Willow asked this in a whisper, even though no one was paying attention to their conversation and the train's ambient clatter covered their words.

Tane looked at Willow, one eyebrow raised. "We all know the risks. The contact is worth it. You've noticed that no one wears gloves," he added.

"Gloves are different. Hands don't generally involve bodily fluids. They aren't mandated by regulation; they're just the common precautionary measure. Recommended, but not mandated." Willow heard her best Ministry voice. It sounded tinny and false, even to her own ears.

"You can have one or the other. You can either touch the world around you and be touched in return, or you can be risk-free and give up all contact. You can't have both." Tane smiled at her as if explaining a very basic concept to a dimwitted but likable child.

"How were social diseases handled before the Second Revolution?" Willow asked. If she was going to be ignorant, it might as well be on a subject that no one expected her to know anything about.

"It was different," Tane said, leaning back against the side of the boxcar. "They still weren't talked about, but the way they weren't talked about wasn't the same. Now, we don't talk about them because the precautions and fears associated with an infection permeate everything we do. The gloves, the SaniCheck, the body-condoms. It's all just second nature. Before, they weren't talked about because no one really wanted to admit that they existed at all. The stigma was the same, but you kept it to yourself."

Willow watched his face as he spoke. His eyes were half-shuttered, as if remembering something he'd read a long time ago.

"If you get into the archives, there were television shows where people got on stage and admitted to all kinds of weird shit. Anal sex with their cousin and more. The society had words for everything but dealing with the issue of STDs." Tane glanced at Willow, whose face was scrunched up in confusion. "STDs," he explained. "Social diseases were called 'sexually transmitted diseases.' HIV was the big one everyone was afraid of. They didn't even administer tests for Herpes because it was so prevalent in the population."

"Weird," Willow said.

"But that didn't stop the pharmaceutical companies from coming up with drugs and spending millions of dollars to advertise them." He went on. "Big pharm thrived on fear, so they spread it around as much as they could."

"Wait," Willow interrupted. "There were pharmaceutical companies? And they advertised? How does that make sense?" Willow was incredulous.

"Drugs made money," Tane answered.

"That's not right," Willow said. "Medication should be between you and your doctor. It isn't a money-maker; it's a basic human right." She spoke with the conviction of the Ministry. Willow was about to continue when she became aware of Ianthe standing behind her.

"I hate to break up the party," Ianthe said, "but we're about at our stop."

Duane Casimir opened his eyes to a flat, white ceiling. Every ceiling in the compound was the same, so it took him a minute to decide which room he was in. He lay there, feeling the walls, sensing. With the front of his brain focused on the space, his dreams bubbled to the surface. Her face burst on the edge of the first bubble and his concentration was broken. Jailyn. He'd dreamed of Jailyn, which meant it was Sunday or some approximation thereof, and he'd been sleeping in the shrine.

He got up slowly, tasting the air. Someone was coming. Duane felt it in the molecules disturbed by their passing. He sighed. It had been nearly a decade since the last pilgrims came to him, but that didn't matter. His annoyance was the same. If he had wanted to lead a movement, become a guru, he would have done it years ago.

Nevertheless, they were coming and there wasn't much he could do to stop them before the long climb up to his home. He left the shrine and slowly ascended the stairs to the old telescope. He placed his eye to the glass and turned it from the sky to the approach to his fortress. The road was empty. He returned the telescope to its sky-bound pursuits and took the stairs to the first floor to make his breakfast.

The bikes struggled against the incline. Willow's shoulders were cramping up and her lower back ached. Her thighs itched from the vibration of the dirty bike under her. It needed oil.

Around her though, the world was pristine. Tall pines reached for lazy white clouds that seemed just within reach. The air smelled good. Clean. Like it could fix everything that was wrong, if she could only sit still and breathe long enough.

A final turn and the road leveled off, revealing a domed white building on the edge of a cliff. Behind it, nestled into the trees, sat a jumbled series of old barrels with tubes hanging out of them. Glinting in the sunshine just beyond the building lay a glass structure full of greenery and a rust-covered flatbed truck. But the real curiosity lay in front of the building: a panoramic view of a blue river pocked with the occasional white lick of a wave and bordered on either side by evergreens. *No wonder he stayed,* Willow thought. Willow watched as Ianthe quit the bike like a fly trying to get out of a vat of honey. Even though it was expected by now, for as many times as she'd seen it, she still shook her head a little in wonder every time.

"Fucking hell," Ianthe said as Willow walked over to her.

"Fucking hell," Willow echoed back.

Now that they'd arrived, Willow was suddenly nervous.

He was back at his telescope, polishing the brass to a bright shine, when they arrived. Not hearing the knock on the door was not an option, but he took his time with the stairs, took his time putting away the telescope, took his time extracting a handkerchief and mopping his brow. By the time he finally opened the heavy door, both women were facing the opposite direction, looking back down the road they'd traveled. Women by the height. Women by their scent. Woman by their hair. One looked like she'd run an old lawnmower over her scalp. She was the one that turned. She was the one that took his breath away.

Willow turned at the sound of the door opening and met the eyes of the man who had appeared in the doorway. He was tall, with a monk's closely-cropped hair. Deep lines framed his eyes, and his generous mouth was outlined by a graying beard.

Something about his features didn't fit, like they were a disguise for a younger man. It was the eyes, she decided. They were too fiercely aware to belong to an old man.

The name fell out of his mouth like the protest of a rusty hinge opening for the first time in decades. "India?"

Her mother's name echoed in her ears. She didn't know which was stronger: relief that there was someone else in the world who knew her mother or kick-in-the-gut fear that the man standing before her had been a client. Quick as a burst of July lightning, her face betrayed both hope and terror.

"You knew my mother." It wasn't a question.

The Source nodded.

"Were you a ..." Willow looked for a word that didn't make her mother's line of work sound dirty. "Client?"

The Source reached out and pulled Willow's hand between them. It uncurled of its own accord and he drew a finger down the center of her palm.

Friend.

He hadn't spoken, but the word hung between them as tangible as news printed on a page. Willow stared at him, trying to imagine her mother in the company of someone else.

He stared back at her, parsing out her features as if there were something underneath he needed to know. Suddenly, he rushed her, wrapping her in a choking embrace.

The old man didn't let go, and as he held her, Willow gradually realized that every hair on her body was standing at attention. She waited for the panic associated with not being able to breathe freely. It didn't come. Instead, she felt safe. Safe for the first time she could remember.

Ianthe watched the proceedings with one eyebrow raised. As the seconds stretched into minutes, she shifted her weight uncomfortably from one foot to the other. She began to think that the old man was never going to let go of Willow and that, instead of laughing at her friend, she might need to intervene.

"Hi." Ianthe forced her voice into a brightness that she didn't feel. "I'm Ianthe."

The forced normality worked. The old man loosened his grip on Willow and turned to Ianthe. Behind him, Ianthe could see Willow's expression, with its wide-eyed *I don't know what just happened* written all over it. Ianthe shook his outstretched hand and tried not to let the surprise register on her face when his grip lacked the frailty she'd expected. The Source was supposed to be an old man, but his handshake was strong.

He stepped back and gestured at the building as if to offer it up to them, and then fled.

Ianthe looked back at Willow, who wasn't moving. "What the fuck was that all about?"

Willow blinked slowly and nodded, as if Ianthe's question could be answered with a yes or no. Ianthe sat down on the stoop and Willow sank down beside her.

"Whaddya think?" Ianthe was the first to break the silence.

"My empty stomach is the only thing I'm sure of."

"Well, he's not surviving on air and good company. There's got to be food somewhere."

Willow nodded her agreement, but didn't say anything. Ianthe stood up and pushed her way into the building. Willow followed.

The door opened into an empty room with marble floors. The walls were simple limestone to match the exterior. A curved staircase hugged the outer wall, one leading upwards, the other leading down.

Ianthe took the stairs down. They ended in a dark, circular landing lined with doors. Willow perched on the last step and waited. One by one, Ianthe opened each of the doors and listened until finally, she heard a rhythmic thumping from somewhere down the corridor. Ianthe followed the noise and Willow followed Ianthe.

The hall ended in a large kitchen. The kitchen had been impressive at some point in the past, but it wasn't now. A white porcelain sink dominated the counter. It stretched nearly the length of the wall, with two drain boards and a tall backsplash from which a silver faucet extended. The counters were pocked with burn marks and indented with the repeated impression of a knife. Aluminum marked the edges, and where the flashing met the surface of the counter, grime had gathered and stuck.

The Source was bent over a pile of vegetables, his back turned toward them. They sat down quietly in rickety chairs placed haphazardly around a worn farm table and watched as he flipped the contents of a frying pan high in the air and caught them again over a gas range.

Finally, he pushed two plates in front of them, piled high with vegetables. He touched Ianthe's shoulder.

Eat.

They didn't need a second invitation. When Ianthe had raised a spoon full of vegetables to her mouth, he gave half a bow and left the women at the table.

When his footsteps had retreated, they leaned into the food and began to scoop it into their mouths as fast as the heat would allow.

Ianthe paused first, her spoon laden with mushrooms, poised half-way to her mouth. "Do you feel funny?"

Willow's mouth was full, but she stopped chewing to take a physical inventory. She wiggled her toes, which seemed to be further away than was normal. Slower too. She finished chewing and set down her spoon. "Yes." But the word stretched out in front of her like a big rubber band.

"The room is breathing." Ianthe sounded outraged. "He fucking drugged us."

In Willow's ears, Ian's voice sounded heavy and low. Actually, everything felt heavy and low. She pushed her plate aside clumsily and set her head on her outstretched arm. Under her, the surface of the table danced like carbonated water, little particles jumping free, then falling back. "Why would he do that?" Willow felt like each of the words needed carving out of tar.

Far away, like somewhere in yesterday, Willow heard Ianthe say. "I can't die now." And then she barfed.

Duane didn't look forward to cleaning up, but there wasn't any other way. Hallucinogenic mushrooms weren't ideal, but better than being lied to. If Warren was behind this woman's appearance, Duane didn't have time to break their stories down to the truth.

The retching continued from inside the kitchen. He hoped it was the other one, the one that had called herself Ianthe, and not India's daughter.

The door swung open at his hand and revealed the girl sprawled across the table smiling serenely. The other one, Ianthe, was hunched over a pile of vegetable-confetti vomit. Duane started with India's daughter.

He spread the fingers on the hand that was already extended half-way across the table and ran his finger down the center of her palm again.

Who are you?

"Willow Jane Carlyle." She spoke the name easily. It wasn't unfamiliar or practiced.

Why did you come?

"Primary sources are superior when researching." She sounded like he had as a professor. Clinical and certain.

What are you researching?

"The Strain, of course. If I'm going to have to live with it, I should know what it is."

Duane snatched his hand back. So his sins knew no boundaries: as if Jailyn hadn't been enough, now he was responsible for ruining India's daughter.

Willow's companion had stopped vomiting. Duane crossed over to where she was sitting and felt her forehead. Of course she was reacting badly: why would anything in Duane's life go right? Avoiding the puddle of vomit, Duane scooped Ianthe up and carried her to a dark room with a pallet. When she was lying down, he dislodged her hand from under her and pressed his thumb into her palm.

Why did you come?

Her voice was rough from the misuse of her throat, but he couldn't mistake the words that emerged from her mouth.

"Find the Infirmary. Must save Kiri."

Duane crouched above her, as if there were further answers to be found written on the back of her skull. Finally, he sighed heavily and placed his hands on her back. If nothing else, he could pull the last of the effects of the mushrooms out of her. She'd sleep and be better for the rest.

There is no reason for anyone to have carpet this thick, the Minister of Security thought as his boot sank into it. The only purpose it seemed to serve was to throw any guest off balance worrying about whether they would trip or dirty the vast white expanse. "Fuck it," he said under his breath. "Fuck him." General Monroe had been out with his troops getting dirty serving the Republic.

He thought of the old military motto—doing more before 10:00 than the rest of you do all day. Lake had probably woken up late and had himself a dalliance with a secretary. General Monroe had kissed his sleepy wife and gotten out of bed in a dark house, dressed in the dark and met his troops in the dark. He'd arrived at a dark desk with the summons to this meeting practically glowing in its clean center. He was too curious to say no, so here he was with dirty boots.

He approached the door and raised a hand, but before he could knock, the door opened of its own accord. Lake's Chief of Staff ushered the General into the office then exited silently.

"Monroe," the Health Minister said. "General. Have a seat."

The General did as instructed. It was an order from a superior, not a request. He sat heavily as his hip gave out under him. Moving forward was never a problem—he never went back—but up and down didn't work like they had when he was a Major.

In front of him, Warren Lake didn't look much different than he had ten years before when he had been promoted to the head of the Ministry of Security. The Minister of Health's hair had been white for as long as the General had known him, but his face hadn't accumulated the map of lines that the General knew were gathering on his. One more reason to despise the man.

"What is this all about?" The General met Warren's cordial tone with impatience. He was no mood to dawdle with niceties.

"You don't like me," Warren said heavily. It was a true statement. Warren didn't care one way or the other, but the truth offered bluntly generally discomfited others. It gave Warren an advantage and he intended to make the most of it.

The General started to protest, but Warren Lake went on. "Don't deny it. You don't have to like me and we've never seen eye-to-eye. I just need to know if I can trust you regardless of your personal feelings. I'm in trouble, and I need your help."

The General couldn't have been more surprised if Warren Lake had told him he had Elvis in his closet. "What?" was all he said.

"You're all I've got," Warren said, inwardly believing the lie for long enough to be convincing.

"I'm listening," General Monroe said, but he was more than listening. He was hanging on every word.

"One of my employees, someone critical to our ongoing viral research, has disappeared." It was a close enough approximation. With that tattoo, she should be finding it impossible to travel without being tracked, but Warren wasn't content with the shoulds of the matter. As far as the shoulds could predict, Willow should have been ensconced in her apartment.

The General raised an eyebrow. He knew as well as the Minister of Health that the Republic didn't just lose citizens.

"She had just been matrixed into a specialized research project, a program her supervisor wasn't read into. Unfortunately, it seems that there was some professional envy and her superior let her go, citing unfounded rumors in justification. I have every reason to believe that she's carrying on her research outside the auspices of the Ministry."

"I'm not sure that's a task for the Ministry of Security," the General interrupted, his wariness of the Minister and his motives renewed. His MOS troops were used to quiet protests and enforce border security, not retrieve employees for the Ministry of Health.

On a usual day, this division of labor didn't bother him so long as the Ministries minded their mandates. Prisoners were supposed to stay in MOS custody. But the General was well aware that there was a bureaucratic battle going on several levels below him to find out what had become of the people Warren Lake had spirited from MOS facilities.

"You remember the Chaos of the 90's?" It was a rhetorical question. Warren knew anyone who had lived through it remembered it.

"I was a kid, but yes." The Chaos was to his generation like The Depression was to generations long past. It changed everything. The General stood and walked to the window. Thick blue cloth hung on either side of the glass. General Monroe pushed the fabric aside to clear his view.

"I lost a twin brother in the '89 pandemic." Warren raised his voice to compensate for the distance between them. "If nothing else, I learned how thin a line we walk between a reasonably functional society and utter mayhem. Maybe she isn't much on her own, but she could be a catalyst. A catalyst the Republic can't afford."

The lie was convincing enough. "So where is she doing this research?" the General asked, weary. He was already committed though he didn't know what he was committing to. The first lesson of the Chaos was that you didn't want to repeat it.

"Old Oregon territory," Warren said. "Near the ruins of Portland. I believe she is on her way to interview a man known as the Source. It sounds more impressive than it really is. His real name is Duane Casimir." Warren paused for a moment, the vision of his old friend rising unbidden in front of him. Warren waved the mirage off and continued. "He was a professor at the New University of the Republic."

"What's he the source of?" the General asked, wary again. Defending the

Republic was his duty, but it didn't require trusting Minister Lake.

"A lot of dangerous superstition, as far as I can tell." Warren had told himself this particular lie enough times that he didn't have to work to be convincing. Lake thought about Willow for a moment, then added, "Be careful with this one, General. She may be completely unknown to the wider world, but she is priceless as far as the Ministry is concerned." General Monroe nodded slowly.

"The Source was last rumored to be living in the Crowns Point Observatory. You'll find it on the archived maps, I believe." Warren finished, then looked expectantly at the General.

General Monroe dropped the hand that was holding the curtains away from his view and turned back to Warren Lake.

"Yes, Sir." He gave Warren a curt nod out of professional courtesy and strode to the door.

The heavy door shut behind him, the bottom edge fighting the drag of the thick carpet.

Twenty

In the days on the train, Willow had gotten used to the hum of the metal around her, had even adjusted to knowing when the train was about to stop simply from the way its molecules vibrated against her skin. She'd woken with the grain of the wood table impressed into her cheek and listened. With closed eyes and forced focus, her connection to the building spoke. Ianthe was alright – asleep, but okay. And the Source was in the observatory.

All the lights in the upper rooms were off. The stars were beginning to shimmer into existence as the last of the evening light disappeared.

She stopped at the entrance to the observatory. The Source was standing at his telescope, his patient fingers teasing the lenses into focus. Willow saw him hesitate when she stepped into the door frame, but he gave no other acknowledgement of her arrival.

"You drugged us." Willow's voice was clear and steady. "You nearly killed my friend, and you drugged us."

He turned to face her at that. Even in the murky darkness, Willow could see that his face registered no remorse.

"Funny thing about whatever it was that you gave us: while Ian was barfing her guts out, I walked away from my body. Odd sensation, that. While I was detached, I watched you. I watched you look after Ian, I watched you tend your greenhouse, and some things occurred to me."

The Source stood impassive, unmoving. Willow found that she very much wanted to shake this man out of his control over the situation.

"This is some kind of penance to you, isn't it? A twisted extension of some 'oh, woe is me, I'm the biggest fuck up in the history of fuckups' ego trip." Willow crossed the room as she spoke, until she was standing right in front of him.

"Answer me," she commanded. He didn't react or comply; he just looked into her eyes with the calm gaze of a monk.

"This pity party isn't good enough. You're a man, not a superhero. Whoever you are, you've never been so close to perfect that this forty-year commitment to wallowing is justified. It's fucking self-indulgent, if you ask me."

His lack of reaction pushed Willow further than she'd intended. "Who the fuck are you, anyway?" And as she asked, she placed her hands on his chest.

I'm sorry.

Her ears registered nothing, but her body. Her body reverberated with the words he hadn't spoken. "Who are you?" She asked louder this time. "I have a right to know." For half a second, she wondered if that was true, and then threw away the doubt.

Duane. I didn't mean to hurt your friend.

Willow's heart was racing and all the hairs on the back of her neck were standing, but she left her hands against his chest. They stood there as Willow considered questions to ask him and discarded them one by one. As her thoughts slowed down, she realized Duane was holding his breath. She stilled herself so she could hear him breathe and, as her own thinking fell away, her awareness of him grew.

He was like a scent, with the strongest note being a desperate effort in any direction that might make the past better. Under it, a lingering resentment of the penance; a hunger for forgiveness, though he clearly didn't know who was qualified to tell him enough was enough. Finally, threaded through it all, bafflement.

Her anger spent, Willow was left with a vacuum that seemed to be filling with compassion. Impulsively, she leaned up on the tips of her toes and kissed him. It was supposed to be a reassuring kiss, a dry press of the lips to the cheek like Willow imagined kissing a father might be like. The beginnings of forgiveness, if she was qualified to offer the benediction.

Duane did not react at all except to stiffen his posture. Willow pulled away and listened to the scattered pattern of his breathing. It told her nothing, so she repeated the gesture on the other side, kissing him at the corner of his mouth. The first kiss was her attempt at forgiveness. The second, a peace offering to show that the fight was over. The third, she had no explanation for. She leaned up one last time and drug her lips across his. She hovered over his mouth for long seconds before he kissed her back, tentatively at first, then demanding, then back to questioning.

She could feel the doubts rise in him as he scrambled through possibilities and implications: their obvious age difference and a question Willow didn't understand.

Is this desire or revenge?

There was already enough she didn't understand and this wasn't the time to pursue his doubts. She pushed the question aside.

He sighed heavily. *Are you sure you want this ragged old man?*

"Yes. Now shut up and kiss me."

He responded as she'd hoped, deepening the kiss, wrapping his tongue around hers and tasting her, all of her: contradictions, doubts, weaknesses and everything. She tasted the same in him, the weight of the lonely aching years, the self-loathing, the guilt and the rejection of the guilt too. With both hands at her waist, he pulled her closer, then pushed her down so she was resting on her heels. He bent to keep his mouth on hers.

He finally broke the kiss. *I'm an old man, older than I look...*

She laughed the low laugh of a woman who knows she is going to be consumed. "You don't look old," she said. "You don't feel old." She pressed her hands against his shoulders and her breasts against his chest. "No, you don't feel old at all" she said as her stomach came into contact with his erection.

He kissed her again, less doubtfully this time. "Take me to bed," she whispered. He stilled at her blatant request. But she started kissing his neck again.

Whatever his doubts, they were answered. He reached up and grabbed her hand, leading her down the spiral staircase and through the building to a dark room she hadn't seen.

Inside, there was only room for a bed and a nightstand. A window was carved out of the thick walls. The glass in the window was warped and pushed a little distorted light from the moon into the room. Just enough to see that the covering on the bed was rough.

Her hands were on the fastening of her jeans before the door had even closed. Duane batted her hands away. His touch was electric. Literally. As he unzipped her jacket, the side of his hand brushed past one nipple, and then the other. They tightened. He pushed the jacket off her shoulders and let it hit the floor in a soft slump. His hands reached for the button of her borrowed jeans next. That popped open with ease, then the teeth of the zipper parted willingly.

He put both hands to her hips and slid the denim off of her ass, then pushed her to the bed. She wasn't wearing anything under the denim. His dick hardened further, harder than he thought himself capable of. He pulled her shoes off one by one then removed the jeans from around her ankles. He ran his hands over her thighs and Willow watched his hands, watched a faint blue light between his skin and hers, and felt the heat that pulsed between their bodies.

Her eyes quickly adjusted to the shadowy light; she watched his face as he stood over her and pulled her back up to him. He began to unbutton her shirt, his knuckles coming into contact with the skin of her breasts and sparking. Her shirt joined the jeans and jacket in a soft pile on the floor, and he paused to consider her, this lovely young woman with optimistic breasts and a soft stomach. *It is a testament to my age,* he thought, *that I'd like to press my ear to her belly button and sleep there.* But while he was considering, she reached behind her and unhooked her bra. It slipped down and she shimmied just a little until the straps were by her elbows and it too was dropping to the floor.

Impatient, she did not wait for him to start his own undressing. She reached for his trousers, her arms pushing her breasts together. She unzipped him with little finesse, unbuttoned the waistband and let them fall to his ankles like an elevator in an uncontrolled fall. She didn't stop to consider his y-front white underwear, she slid her hands between his tee-shirt and his stomach and pushed them upward, dragging his shirt and tee-shirt with her.

He had no choice but to obey her insistence and take the two off together, but his feet got tangled in the trousers and shoes. He couldn't get himself out of them both and he stumbled onto her, knocking them both off balance and onto the bed. Willow laughed and used her position under him to draw a foot up the inside of his leg suggestively. Whatever irritation Duane had felt at the foolishness of tripping over his own trousers disappeared. He kicked one shoe off then the other and his pants fell on top of hers.

His feet freed, he pushed himself up and tucked his knees under, straddling her narrow hips and pinning her. She was breathing shallow, anticipatory breaths, but he just looked at her, her dusky breasts, her wood-chipper-cut hair spread against his bed, no different in color than his blankets, but distinct in the way it caught and held the little light from the window. Her arms were stretched above her head, positioning her nipples exactly center, exactly inviting. He lowered his body slowly, making her wait for the contact, then took one nipple into his mouth. It sparked against his tongue and she arched up.

Without breaking contact, he straightened her hips onto the bed with his knees so he'd have room to cover her body with his own. He did, taking his weight on his elbows and using his hands to gather her breasts together. He went from one breast to the other, sometimes so quickly the electricity followed him, joining both nipples to his mouth.

Under him, Willow writhed and gasped. She freed a leg to wrap around his waist, which only brought her body closer to his. The moisture that was gathering between her thighs seeped into the skin at his waist. Electricity travels quickly through water and it did not change properties just for them. A circuit formed between his body and hers, a riptide circling from her breasts to her pussy through his skin to his mouth and back into her. She came, fireworks exploded behind her eyelids and her entire body released a pulse of energy strong enough to unseat Duane and break the circuit.

He held her while she shook. When she stopped quivering, she kissed him again, the electrical current between them stronger this time. She pushed him towards the bed and took the dominant position, her back curved like a cat. She leaned over him and continued the kiss for long minutes, their bodies snapping with blue electricity. She began a lazy trail of kisses down his neck and across his chest, then down his mid-line past his belly button and to the worn elastic edge of his underwear. She allowed herself a brief smile, then pulled the elastic up to clear his dick as she tugged them down to his thighs. *Forty years,* she thought to herself. *It's a long time.* Then she took his cock in her mouth. She ran her tongue up and down the bottom of his shaft, feeling the spark chasing her tongue.

Above her, Duane clenched his teeth. She twirled her tongue around the head of his dick, rearranged herself so she was lying between his legs, leaned on one elbow and used the other hand to grasp the base of his shaft. She sucked and stroked, teased and tasted, a current passing between them like a tennis ball across a net. When he started thrusting, one hand in her hair, she held herself as still as she could, her grip on his dick firm, and waited. He came in her mouth, an exploding sensation like a salty version of the candy she'd had as a child—Pop Rocks or something like that.

She crawled up the length of his body, her breasts dragging against his skin, leaving a trail of twitching nerves behind, and settled herself above him, her wet pussy dampening his stomach, her breasts sitting on his chest like two expectant little queens. Willow grinned at him.

He growled as he turned her so she lay under him. He slid down her body, the scrape of his chin marking a clear path on her stomach. She was unshaven and unwaxed. He was glad of it—he'd never had much interest in the pre-pubescent look. With one hand, he parted her pussy lips, spreading the slick heat, then he bent his head and ran his tongue from the bottom of her labia up to her clit. Her thighs tightened around his ears and she reached down with one hand to touch his head.

Taking that as encouragement, he did it again, then settled into a tactile exploration of her pleasure. Her pussy released another wave of salt-glaze. He lapped it up and sucked at her clit to bring more. With the next wave, he thrust two fingers into her and felt the spongy, slippery walls of her pussy suck him in. His sated cock began to thicken again. He smiled fiercely.

He was insistent now. He drove her pleasure to the edge of the cliff and teased, then let it recede briefly before he pushed it again. Willow whimpered above him, a request for mercy he would not answer. He pressured her clit against his teeth with his tongue and she gasped. He curled his tongue around it and she bucked. His fingers set a rhythm that his tongue punctuated. She began to grind her hips, pushing upwards, her entire body begging for more. *Just a few more moments, my sweet* he thought, and he was right. He slowed his own actions to follow the sway of her hips and she spilled over the edge, just a little at first and finally in a flood.

Her whole body sparked and convulsed. Duane wasted no time. He was up on his hands and knees, then pressing his cock against the outside of her pussy while she begged incoherently. Holding himself up with one hand while the other held his shaft, he positioned himself at the soaking wet entrance of her pussy and waited. She opened her knees just a fraction of an inch further and pushed her body down on the bed. He met her with a single thrust that buried his cock to the balls. Her pussy was still convulsing and he felt the buzz of her nerves as they connected with his. She looked up at him with wide eyes, then reached up and grabbed his head, pulling his mouth down to hers.

The current that had formed between them before was a child's transformer set compared to this. Like the cartoons of his childhood, he felt his whole body illuminate, leaving his bones a dark skeleton in comparison to his bright flesh. Under him, the same sensation passed through Willow, though she'd not watched the same shows and had no idea how to describe the lights that were bursting within her.

With every thrust, the current grew stronger and as it grew, Willow began to see flickers of Duane's life. Midnight pushups by this bed, in this room. She felt the intensity of his grief walking beside his wife's casket. The desperation he felt standing next to Warren Lake, his shirt rolled up and the needle pressing into his vein. She felt the playful self-absorption that saw a blow job in the alley as a joke and his due. She felt his hunger for life, the speed that his body digested time and discarded it. She felt his need for her, his possession of her, the fierce demand of his desire, and she answered it.

For his part, he saw it all. Her eight-year-old struggle to work her mother into the bathtub; the callous paramedics; Mrs. Carlyle, who had no praise in her; her work and her coworkers; crippling loneliness and her secret scorn at the Ministry's fear coupled with her own paralyzing fear. Fear of everything.

They traded silent stories as they moved together more naked than skin. As the heat between them grew, their mouths lost any pretense of tenderness. They met again and again, pushing higher and closer to a shared orgasm. It ignited in her first and sizzled through his nerves a fraction of a second later.

Like two opposite magnets, they couldn't have pulled apart had they tried. Electrons long dormant fired to life. A storm of memories burst to life in a blinding explosion as the first wave of the orgasmic spasm hit them both. It spun through them, transferring from her pussy to his cock, running up his spine and growing as it flowed from his mouth into hers, back down her spine to her pussy. They lit from within, driving the room's shadows into hiding, breaking the spell of the dark and lighting themselves and the bed many times more brightly than the moon's light.

Any more would have been unbearable. The tide receded, a few neurons not caught in the storm fired little bursts, and he collapsed on top of her, spent.

Ianthe came to in a room that momentarily lit by pulsing lights.

Fuck.

She ran her standard physical inventory. The knife was still tucked in her boot. She flexed her pelvic muscles. Nothing hurt, which she took as a good sign. Her head felt like someone had been using it for the drum in a marching band, but everything else seemed in order. She forced a deep breath. Oxygen was good for everything, even poison.

She pushed herself upright, then stood. The room tilted wildly out of control, but Ianthe kept forcing her lungs until the walls and the floor stayed more or less in place. When moving seemed like a possibility, she crossed the dark room and opened the door, twisting the knob carefully.

The corridor was empty.

Where other people soothed themselves with exercise or meditation, Ianthe had her bike. For as long as she'd been with Marshall, everything difficult was made easier by time lost in the engines. She'd picked Lisa out of the pieced-together collection of bikes years ago. There was nothing on her, from her muffler to her odometer, which Ianthe herself hadn't adjusted. Other people had security blankets. Ianthe had Lisa, and it was Lisa she wanted.

She had to grip the railing harder than she wanted to acknowledge, but she climbed the stairs, found herself bathed in the quarter-light of the moon in the circular lobby they'd first entered that afternoon. Turning slowly, the door swam into focus and she pushed through it, now indifferent to how much noise she made. The bike was outside and with it, safety.

When Willow woke, she was alone. She patted the bed next to her to double check, then took a deep breath and listened to the house. Ianthe was gone and Duane was outside the building, but close. She drew the sheet closer to her chin and closed her eyes. Of the imagery that flooded her, one borrowed memory gradually emerged.

Warren escorted Duane down a long hallway lined with metal doors, each punctured with a barred window.

"State of the art." Warren sounded pleased with himself. His words reverberated against the freshly painted walls. "Two problems solved with one facility."

She watched as the scene played out before her, her body paralyzed.

"Are you sure this is what you want the Ministry to stand for?" The face was obscured and the voice was new. But those shoulders. She'd bitten that deltoid.

"This is the price, my friend. You like the idea of forever, no?" Apparently, Minister Lake had always sounded that smug.

"Of course."

"The research needs subjects and the Republic can't spare upstanding citizens."

Warren was interrupted by an animal groan slipping out from behind one of the doors.

"I thought you said they were treated humanely." Duane stopped and forced Warren to meet his gaze.

"Their pain medication is due…" Warren looked at his watch. "Any time now."

"I don't like it, Warren."

"Sure you do," Warren replied with a dismissive wave. "How else do you think I got your cure?"

Twenty One

Ianthe had flown down the road west. Even in the dark, the river to her left glimmered. The scent of cedar and pine conspired with the cold wind to clear the last of whatever shit the Source had fed them from her system. Miles and miles had passed before she could begin to draw a line between what she knew for sure, what she feared, and what she'd do next.

She had just begun to consider Willow and whether the Source had succeeded in poisoning her properly when she heard the sound of an engine echoing off of the water. It wasn't her bike making that roar. Then a second engine. She slid the bike to a halt. Above her, boughs of evergreen hung low. She couldn't see through them, but soon enough, it didn't matter. The tendrils of dawn reached through the ravine and illuminated two massive helicopters with black-clad soldiers hanging out of the doors.

Ianthe didn't bother to think a confrontation with MOS troops through, she kicked the bike into gear, fishtailed on the black pavement, and raced back to Willow.

Willow stood in the door to the greenhouse, a white sheet wrapped like a toga around her body, half waiting for an invitation. The lavender light of dawn made everything murky, only the light reflecting from Duane's eyes distinguished him from his surroundings. Duane watched her, pushing himself not to assume either her regret or her interest.

"Did I imagine," she paused, looking for a way to describe the night before. "Everything?"

Duane shook his head. *No.*

"I dreamed, or I saw you. Younger. With Minister Lake. You were in a research facility. I think it was the Infirmary."

Duane crossed the greenhouse as she spoke. He stopped inches from her and pressed a single finger to her lips. Willow stilled, but he didn't move his finger. She pursed her lips in a kiss, but forgot the gesture as the silence of the morning disintegrated.

Helicopters. Willow turned her head to the windows. Absurdly, Duane's finger didn't move.

Let it play out.

Willow turned back to Duane with questions in her eyes.

You can't outrun them. He allowed himself a fleeting grin. *You aren't dressed for a chase.*

They turned back to the windows just in time to see black ropes unfurling from the choppers above. As the first feet came into view, the front door to the building crashed against the inner wall.

"Willow! For fuck's sake!" Ianthe's voice was hoarse from her retching the night before and cracked on the words. Willow turned her back to Duane as Ianthe came skidding around the corner.

In a measure of time defined by fractions of seconds, Ianthe registered the fact that Willow was clad in a sheet clutched at a knot under her collarbone. Duane was standing behind her, his hand possessively on her hip.

She'd been duped. It was the only conclusion she could come to. "What fuckery is this? No, never mind. I don't want to know what Ministry game of cat and mouse I fell for. Let me die ignorant of my own stupidity."

"No," Willow protested. "It isn't like that…"

But no more explanations were possible. The greenhouse was surrounded by MOS soldiers with their guns pointed at the glass. The outer door swung open and a tall man swaggered through it.

"We came for that one," he pointed at Willow. "Am I interrupting?"

It will be okay. Duane's hand was still on Willow's hip. Willow looked at him with terror in her eyes.

Trust me. They can't afford to hurt you.

His assurances didn't help.

In front of them, the Commander pulled a syringe out of the pocket on his thigh, tapped the glass vial, and squirted an arc of clear liquid into the air as he crossed the room.

"No." Willow said. "No, no, no, no, no."

She turned back to Ianthe, who was now being held by a MOS soldier with a gun to her temple. Three more were standing, waiting for her to run.

While Willow had focused on the needle, more MOS troops had poured in behind the Commander. Their guns were now turned on Duane.

The commander circled behind her, pausing a fraction of a second to admire the curve of her ass. Duane didn't interfere as the Commander pinned her arm to her back and plunged the needle into her shoulder. He caught her by her armpits as she collapsed to the floor.

"Ms. Carlyle," he whispered into her ear. "When you are properly attired, the Minister of Health would like to congratulate you on a job well done." He gave a smirking nod to Duane and Ianthe, then drug Willow out of the greenhouse.

Ianthe stood under guard as Willow was siphoned away from them. The Source stood perfectly still, his face impassive as if none of it mattered. They watched Willow disappear into one of the helicopters, then their captors walked them out of the building. One of the guns commiserated with the Commander, then barked unintelligibly into his radio.

Moments later, their guards retreated, marching backwards away from them. The hollow barreled guns never wavered until, like a choreographed dance, the weapons pointed upwards and the soldiers seemed to levitate into the helicopter.

The blades started whirling until the chopper rose in front of them like heat off of August pavement. The Source stepped closer to Ianthe but said nothing. The oversized bird rose over their heads, hesitated, then slowly turned to face them.

"Fuck." Ianthe said it out loud. "Fuck, fuck, fuck." Nothing good could come of the helicopter turning back to face them. The MOS wasn't after a longing last glance.

Suddenly, she felt the Source grab her hand. She tried to pull away to run, but he wouldn't let go. She looked up at her captor, but his eyes were closed, scrunched up as if solving a complex calculus problem. The blank look had disappeared from his face and she felt something shift between them, like her heart had just lurched to the other side of her body. Just then, the machine guns on the nose of the helicopter began to fire, the staccato burst of bullets only slightly louder than the blades beating at the air.

Ianthe cringed instinctively as bullets struck the gravel under them, throwing up chips of rock that that stung her legs. The Source collapsed on top of her, knocking her to the ground. She gasped for air beneath his weight. The guns paused for breath then burst into their rhythmic staccato again.

Ianthe felt a warm oozing dripping down the side of her neck. The machine guns released one more volley and then went silent. The helicopter hovered for another minute like a giant dragon, turned south, and disappeared.

Twenty Two

Willow's body refused to obey her. She told her arms to flail and they flopped helplessly at her side. She told her feet to kick. Instead her heels drug against the concrete. Her head lolled to the side and she caught a fuzzy glimpse of Duane and Ianthe shuffling out of Duane's home at gunpoint. She told her mouth to say no; no noise came out. Her handlers shoved her at the chopper and pulled out zip ties to attach her to a seat. Panic set in and adrenaline loosened her limbs. She kicked out wildly, throwing her head back as hard as she could. It was the last protest she could muster. Willow felt the contact of bone on bone and heard a shriek before slowly slipping out of consciousness.

She awoke to discover that she was affixed to her chair like an insect pinned to a slab of Styrofoam. Frantically, she struggled against the plastic ties biting into her wrists and ankles. Willow craned her head around, looking for Ianthe or Duane. The only faces she found were masked.

She looked down. Her sheet had been replaced by a rough, grossly oversized black uniform. Blood pooled in her fingertips and she could feel them getting fat and sore, like a blood blister past the point of bursting. Her feet had fallen into a thorny sleep and her toes protested as she tried to concentrate on wiggling them through the pain.

It had started to rain, and the helicopter shuddered in the driving wind. With no freedom to move her arms, she couldn't stabilize herself. Like a rag doll, every lurch of the chopper sent her head careening into the window or snapping back against the headrest.

Finally, the helicopter turned sharply, circling around an empty suspension bridge, slipping between the spires before slowing and landing close to the water.

Once they landed, her soldiers cut her ties and quickly rebound her hands in front of her. She bent her arms at the elbows and held up her hands to let the blood drain. Willow tried to stand as they cut her feet loose, but her knees buckled under her.

The soldiers each took an arm and propped her up as they hauled her past the idling engines of a small jet. Someone pushed the door open from the inside and a set of curved stairs unfurled like an inviting tongue. A well-dressed man ducked through the door and descended the stairs. Willow had seen him around the Ministry, always walking with his body angled forwards like he was wading through a hurricane. Miles, the Minister's Chief of Staff.

One soldier cut the tie that held her wrists together and stepped back quickly as the other dropped her elbow. They immediately placed their hands on their weapons, ready to shoot should she make an unpredicted move.

"That won't be necessary," Miles said to the soldiers. "She works for the Ministry. She's not going to hurt anyone." Miles sketched a brief bow at Willow and gestured her up the stairs and into the airplane.

Willow gave the soldiers a defiant look and took to the stairs like she was used to private jets. It took a moment for her eyes to adjust from the white light of the helicopter's floodlights to the darkened, plush interior of the plane. With a hand on the wall, Willow passed several rows of seats that faced forward, and through a narrow door. In front of her, the Minister of Health leaned back against an overstuffed leather seat, his eyes closed. Willow had seen his photographs in the halls of the Ministry building, had even met him in passing at Ministry events, but she'd never been this close before. She lowered herself gingerly into the seat across from him, her whole body aching.

Six weeks ago, she would have been fawning with gratitude—Warren Lake was everyone's hero, at least everyone in the Ministry of Health. He'd taken the reins of power, eliminated the pockets of corruption that got in everyone's way, streamlined the bureaucracy, promoted the right people and generally made the Ministry a much better place.

Since he'd come up from within, he'd had the benefit of seeing the organization from all angles. From the early days of the Ministries after the Chaos, he'd always been involved, shaping the machine. There had been other leaders before him, Dr. Carlyle included. But not all of them had been as well-intentioned as Dr. Carlyle; many had personal agendas and egos to appease. Warren Lake stood out for his balance between pragmatism and single-minded dedication to the health of the Republic.

Further, Warren Lake's ego did not require appeasing. And so, under his guidance, the Ministry became a well-oiled machine with transparency and measures for progress and clearly articulated goals. Warren Lake's tenure as Minister was considered a success and Ministry employees tended to feel both reverential and proprietary about their leader.

As had Willow.

Towards the front of the plane, Willow heard the door shut again and the low murmur of a voice speaking to the pilot. Miles closed the door that Willow had just passed through and the engines ignited and began their dull roar. The plane coasted slowly at first, and then Willow felt herself pushed forward by the acceleration as it took off. When they were in the air again, Warren Lake opened his eyes.

He sighed as if it cost him. "We're going to cure you, Ms. Carlyle. We're going to treat you, give you an award for your work and promote you. You'll have Nate's job. Several more promotions and you'll be my deputy. My heir apparent. Just as soon as we get back to the lab, you'll have your old life back, but better."

"I don't want my old life back," she responded.

"Of course you do. There is nothing for you outside of the Ministry." He'd heard from the extraction crew; his old friend was dead. He'd also seen the report that Willow had been taken from Duane's arms. He didn't want to think about it.

"There is nothing for me inside the Ministry," she countered.

"You're just tired. You'll feel better after a shower, a good night's sleep, and the first round of treatment." His tone was dismissive. He watched her indirectly, appearing to stare out the window but watching the hard expression on her face through the reflection instead. India had never looked so brittle, not like that.

"I'm not tired."

"What is that supposed to mean?"

"You killed my mother. I don't even want to look at you." Willow eyed the Minister like a wolf eyes its prey. "Bring my mother back if you want to do something for me."

"I hadn't seen your mother for the better part of a decade when she died. I can't possibly have killed her. Hate me if you must, but surely you can see that." Warren thought back to reading her name in the annual roster of casualties from underground health practitioners. The flush of heat, the sinking desperation; both hovered at the back of his neck like the news was fresh.

"Oh, you killed her alright. She was going back to..." Willow still couldn't say the word. "Her old job. The only reason she would have needed a cell cleanse was to go back to you. You probably wouldn't have even taken her."

A knot that Warren didn't know he was carrying eased. His sense of betrayal at India's abandonment had convinced him that she'd just wanted to quit him, not the whole business. He'd inferred from the casualty report that India had found a new set of clientele. Even though she was long gone, something like hope flowered in him like a crocus in February. He hadn't allowed himself to consider that she had wanted to come back to him.

"You're wrong in that. I loved her." Warren massaged the bridge of his nose and closed his eyes. It had already been a long day.

"Love?" Willow spat the word out like it was rotten. "That's nice. Spare me the kind of love that keeps me a whore and cuts me loose with a child. Or maybe that's why you cut her loose. She had a kid and you couldn't stand the proof that she'd been with someone else? Is that it?"

"She hadn't been with anyone else when she fell pregnant." His tone was final. Willow snorted derisively.

"She was a state servant. A regulation hooker. Of course she had been with someone else."

Something in Warren snapped. Maybe it was the strain of the past few weeks, maybe it was the feeling that everything he'd worked so long to keep caged was finally breaking through the bars, maybe it was just the suggestion from this woman in front of him, this woman that looked so much like the love of his life, that he hadn't actually loved India. Loving India was the only thing that he was absolutely sure of.

"There was no one else."

Willow heard the conviction in his voice, the barely contained rage and the sorrow under it.

"That means..." she started, her voice mocking. "That means that I'm your daughter." The words hung between them. Understanding hit Willow like a wave of nausea. "You son of a bitch," she said. Warren made a gesture as if accepting an award. Stunned, Willow stayed where she was for a moment, then stood up and walked to a bank of seats at the back of the plane. Suddenly exhausted beyond her capacity to cope, she lay down and went to sleep. A few minutes later, Warren got up too, found a blanket and covered her with it. She slept under his watch the rest of the way to Philadelphia.

It was Miles who woke Willow when they landed and escorted her to the limousine. Warren was absent and Willow was grateful. There was too much to think about to also have to guard herself. She looked out of darkened windows, watching her city go by. Soon, she recognized the streets leading to the Ministry building. It had rained recently and in the puddles on the sidewalk, the building seemed to lean as far down as it stretched up to the sky. They stopped in front of it. Two new guards ushered her out of the limo.

She was almost pleased that she was threatening enough to the Ministry to require guns. But she didn't dare break and run for it. Warren Lake might be her father—her stomach bottomed out again at that thought—but he was still ruthless. He stepped out of the darkness behind her and took her elbow. His grip was warning enough. No matter, she wanted to see the areas of the building where a secret like her might be kept.

Her steps made new sounds on the marble floor. In her old life, slingback pumps had made a precise staccato of purpose wherever she walked. Now, her bare feet just made small smacks against the linoleum. Like a patient in a hospital.

They passed a mirrored window and Willow caught a glimpse of herself. Nothing about how she looked was familiar. The soldier's uniform hung off of her shoulders. In the humidity, her hair had turned into a giant ball of frizz. A month ago she would have been horrified at her own appearance. Now, who the fuck cared. Like the Minister could judge her. Like any of the complacent bastards had anything to say. Oh, Willow Jane Carlyle was important now, and dangerous.

The elevator doors closed in front of her like doors to a cell. Then they got to the 22nd floor and their little entourage marched past a real cell with a body caped in a blanket sitting within. Warren Lake ushered her into the next cell as if welcoming her to his home, then he closed the door between them.

"I loved your mother," he said defiantly. All Willow's plans of stoicism and imperviousness disappeared in a sudden flame of anger.

"What kind of person do you have to be to leave the love of your life to starve?"

"She chose that. If she had just listened to me. I was going to take care of everything. If she had just let me..." The old softness crept into his voice, like it was India he was pleading with, now decades gone.

"Let you talk her into terminating me?" Willow's voice was quiet, but no less dangerous for the lack of histrionics.

"I don't mean it like that."

"There is no other way you can mean it. If she had let you take her to one of your colleagues and gotten the problem 'taken care of,' you could have kept her as your regulation mistress for as long as it suited you. But whose fault was it anyway? Sex ed hasn't changed that much since you knocked her up."

"What we did and how we did it is none of your goddamn business." Warren's mouth was tight and his words clipped.

"You didn't watch her die, you arrogant fuck, bleeding from her eyes and trying not to make too much noise. Don't talk to me about my business. You killed her and you would have killed me long before I took my first breath, never mind showed up as the daughter who caught dirty dick disease."

Willow watched the Minister flinch with satisfaction. "Why don't you kill me now? No one is watching. You've got your clearances, your impeccable character. Chalk it up to self-defense and let's get the last of your little mess cleaned up."

"I ended the practice of cellular cleansing and put the whole underground out of business after she died, so don't talk like you know what matters to me and what I was willing to do about it. I didn't know where you were and there wasn't a damn thing I could do until her name showed up on the list of deceased, and then it was too late."

He regained a semblance of calm, his words became slightly more disciplined, a father explaining a point to his daughter for the third or fourth time. "I'm not going to kill you. I'm going to test you and treat you. As soon as the cure is ready, we are going to fix you and then life is going to go back to normal."

"A specimen. Your daughter, and I'm a specimen. How do you sleep at night?"

"I don't sleep. I dream of her." And with that, Warren James Lake, Health Minister of the New Republic of America and the most powerful man in the Union, turned and walked away from the cell. Willow looked down at his feet as he shuffled like a much older man. As the door closed behind him, she noticed her hands gripping the metal.

2006/05

India was asleep on the sofa when Warren entered his password into the keypad by her front door. Duane was asleep too, his head on India's lap. Warren walked into the living room, certain of his place, and stopped short at the sight of his mistress and his best friend in an intimate pieta.

He considered exploding in anger; Warren had already learned the benefits of applying his temper judiciously. Instead, he sat down and waited, staring at India in her sleep. Her head rested on her arm which was outstretched across the back of the sofa. She wore no makeup, her dark lashes pressed against her cheek, and her hand rested against Duane's forearm, warm brown skin contrasted against Duane's pale arm.

He had never seen her this unguarded. He watched the rise and fall of her collarbone, the quick flutter of her pulse at the base of her neck, and reminded himself to kiss her there.

He wasn't immediately jealous, he discovered to his own surprise. India knew better than to risk his ire with an unsanctioned dalliance with his best friend. He also discovered she was more beautiful than he'd remembered, even though it had only been a day since he'd seen her. He realized that he'd never considered what her days contained before. She'd always been there to meet him. He'd unwittingly thought of her like a pet that waited for him to come home and give it purpose.

But here she was, obviously engaging in a life that didn't include him. That, he found intolerable. Both that she had an independent existence and that it mattered to him.

Warren cleared his throat. India's eyelashes wavered against her cheek and she removed her hand from Duane's arm to wipe her mouth with the back of her hand. She looked up and into Warren's eyes.

"Darling," she said.

"What the hell," he countered.

Duane opened his eyes and sat up with a start.

"Warren, I can explain," Duane said.

"Please do."

"I came to see her, to talk. I fell asleep," Duane stammered.

"Yes, I can see that for myself."

"Warren," India said in her most conciliatory tone, the same voice she used when he spent his time with her ranting instead of making love. "There is nothing to be upset about."

"I'll decide what to be upset about," Warren said. He was enjoying his power, both of them simultaneously desperate to appease him.

"I'd never do that to you, Warren. You know that," Duane said.

"Do I?" Warren asked, now engaged in the argument for the sake of argument. "After all, you didn't have a problem with cheating on your wife."

Duane reacted as if he'd been given a kick to the stomach, nearly doubling over with the strength of the blow.

"Warren!" His name came out of India as a gasp. "That wasn't necessary. You know Duane would have never hurt Jailyn."

"Really?" Warren's tone suggested the answer. "In all of his crying about the loss of his wife, has he mentioned that he gave his wife Herpes and didn't have the decency to tell her why she was dying?"

"I know that," India said quietly.

"Did he mention that he begged me for a cure to cover up his five minute blow job in a back alley." Warren was caught up in the argument. He just wanted to win; it didn't matter what the argument was about.

"Warren, he's good enough at blaming himself. He doesn't require assistance."

India's defense of Duane didn't help. "Mmm. Did he mention that he never asked me for a cure for Jailyn? Didn't ask if I could rush one into production."

"You only had one," Duane protested.

"How do you know?" Warren turned to look at Duane. "You never asked, you selfish bastard. I could have cured Jailyn ten times over."

"But you didn't," India said, her voice flat.

"You didn't need me to cure her. If you'd fucked her, you could have saved her yourself."

"What do you mean?" Duane was wide-eyed and pale.

"I've checked your latest blood work. I didn't cure you. I just mutated the virus. If you'd made love to her, the mutated virus could have overrun the original. She'd be here and you'd be romancing her instead of my..." The word wife was on the tip of his tongue, but of course, India wasn't any such thing.

Warren stood, staring defiantly at both of their stunned faces.

"Enjoy the rest of your nap," he said as he slammed the door to India's apartment.

Twenty Three

Ianthe lay trapped under the weight of the Source, her body pinned to the unforgiving concrete. She waited while the sinister, sticky drip that was sliding down her neck slowed. As hard as she tried, her stuttering heart would not calm down. When she felt certain that the helicopters weren't going to return, she twisted herself under the Source trying to unpin her leg for leverage. Eventually she rocked them both back and forth until he slid off of her and landed face up next to her.

Once free, she turned her face to the sky and forced herself to breathe deeply as she ran her hands up and down her arms, over her ribs, up to her neck, and back again. She was unharmed.

The silence the helicopters had left behind was absolute. She turned her head slowly to examine the still body beside her. The Source's white tee shirt was shredded. Blood pooled in the hollow of his neck and his blank eyes turned to the white clouds that tumbled across the electric blue sky. Ianthe stood slowly.

She turned back to the Source's body. His face was peaceful, both old and young all at the same time. She hesitated, then crouched beside him to close his eyes.

Bethesda.

She jerked her hand back as the word materialized and whipped her head around, fists clinched. She was alone with the Source's body. She looked down at the bloody corpse. It continued to stare.

Slowly, Ianthe knelt again and reached out for the Source's hand. It was one of the few undamaged available parts of him. The moment her fingers came in contact with his skin, she had the same feeling, like an invasion of her thoughts by a voice that didn't belong to her.

The Infirmary. Bethesda.

She desperately wanted to look away but kept her eyes trained on the Source's face. *You'll find her in Bethesda.*

Ianthe's legs were starting to cramp. Everything in her wanted to be as far away from the body as possible. However, Willow's betrayal had done her more good than harm; she finally had what she came for—something tangible to go on in her search for Kiri. She didn't drop the Source's hand.

Morrigan knows. There's a map in the truck. Find Morrigan.

Ianthe turned to the rusting shell of a truck behind her, half-buried in the long grass beside the greenhouse. The word 'DODGE' was scratched and covered with mud but still emblazoned between the headlights. She ran to the door and threw it open.

With unsteady hands, she turned the latch of the glove compartment. It opened, revealing a rusty tin box. Inside, there was a map, its faded letters declaring the ground below 'The United States of America.'

Holding the map, she returned to the Source's body. Sitting cross-legged beside him, she held one of his hands gingerly and traced lines on the map with her other hand. Dark outlines ran through the Wastes. None of the city states were marked properly, just dots where the old cities had been.

East. All the way east.

Ianthe ran her finger along the crease that bisected the map. Just before the blue of the ocean, she stopped on a star marked Washington D.C. It was ringed by smaller dots with labels in tiny letters below them, and beneath one dot, slightly north and west above the star, she saw the name—Bethesda. Her pulse quickened.

No. Morrigan first.

Ianthe's first reaction was annoyance, then she remembered that he was dead.

The Independent State of Texas.

She turned her attention south to the irregular borders of the thorn in the Republic's side: the only hold out from the former Union that had refused the Republic's benevolent meritocracy.

Shorthand directions were scrawled across the words "New Mexico" and underneath, an address labeled Morrigan, Amarillo, Texas.

Morrigan. She'll help you find your friend.

Ven had lost count of the days he'd spent in his cell. Minister Lake's daughters had dosed him, first by pills, then by shots, until he couldn't even pass his hand through the cot he slept on. The virus was dying in him and with it, his ability to change the electromagnetic forces that determined the solidity of his body. Not to mention a loss of feeling in his right toes.

Initially, he'd teased and taunted Maggie. She didn't rise to the bait.

"I've got to tell you," he said, "I'm not sure the girl was worth the trouble you went to in order to get her out of your way." He paused, noting the sudden stillness of Maggie's back. "Too easy. Nothing like you." The admiration in his voice wasn't entirely feigned. "I could seduce you too. But it would take a lot longer. I'd want more money for it."

"Whoring isn't in my genetic heritage," Maggie replied. "And you aren't smart enough for me." Ven acknowledged the insult with a slight nod of his head.

"True, true," he said. "But every woman has a weak spot. It doesn't take genius to find it. Just time."

Maggie put her instruments down, held herself still for a breath, then turned and approached Ven's cell. Ven stood to meet her at the bars. Maggie reached through and caressed his face with her latex finger and Ven smiled at her as if he'd just scored a point in chess. With her other hand, Maggie reached through the bars to cup Ven's nuts in her hand and squeezed. Hard.

The pain cost him control over his mouth. "Sonofabitch!"

Maggie smiled sweetly and returned to her work. Ven retreated to the back corner.

Before Maggie left for the night, she walked back over to Ven's cage and peered into the darkness to meet his gaze. "She is a loose end that the Ministry can't afford. A tie back to circumstances better forgotten. You did your job well, but from here on out, I'd recommend your silence on this and any other topic." Maggie turned on her heel and exited the room, killing the lights as she went.

A few days later, Miles came to see him.

"It won't be long, now," Miles offered. "You'll be compensated for your time, of course," he went on as Ven glowered at him. "And once all is said and done, I'm sure we'll have more work for you, just as soon as we get you cleaned up."

"The shit they are giving me is killing me." Ven was still staring at Miles. Miles tugged at his collar and cleared his throat. There was no mistaking who had the upper hand between the two men. There was also no doubt that, if it weren't for the bars between them, Ven would have beaten Miles bloody.

"Unfortunate, I'm sure," Miles said. His voice didn't waver and he'd gotten his fidgeting back under control. "But we can't have you running around your cell full-strength. In any case, the Doctors Lake are extracting useful information from you. I'm sure you'll be fine when it's all over. Now, is there anything I can bring back for you? Some books, maybe?" Miles let the question hang for a minute, then answered himself. "No, I can't imagine you read much."

And so Ven paced. And thought. And paced. And reconsidered. He was sleeping more and more only to get less and less rest, so his annoyance was honestly felt when Warren Lake and Willow interrupted a catnap as the Minister propelled Willow into a cell next to his.

He was stepping forward and into the light when he saw her: thinner, dirtier, and with a hideous haircut, but somehow more arresting than he had remembered. She walked like she had a backbone. Ven shrank back into the shadows and sat on his cot, not knowing how she'd react and uninterested in finding out in front of the Minister of Health.

Willow didn't know it yet, but she was going to save him. Ven smiled.

Willow forced herself to breathe deeply and relax her fingers one by one. With a third breath and a fourth, she focused on the sensations coming through her palms. They buzzed a little, and she tested the current as it flowed back into her. Whoever designed the cells had done a good job— Willow could feel no fractures, no fissures, no breaking point. She pushed the current a little further but nothing came. She exhaled deeply and let the bars go. Escape might be the top priority, but she had to get her focus back first.

Instead, the entirety of India's death came back to her in a memory so visceral she heaved until she sat down on the cot in her cell and put her head between her knees.

It had been July. They couldn't afford the environmental tax that went along with air conditioning. India had gotten them into a basement apartment, so at least it wasn't sweltering. "Back when people used to smoke, they taxed cigarettes like this," India would say and Willow would think back to the illegal movies they watched together, movies where it was socially acceptable—desirable even—to smoke. The men with their rugged hands held up to their face to light a cigarette, the women leaning back and looking indifferent. Not many people knew those days even existed, but India knew, so Willow knew too.

"Now the government makes up for lost revenue by taxing environmental impact. But we are smarter, Will. We live down here." India made it sound like they were playing at skipping school days. But there was no "smarter" that explained going to bed hungry, or why Willow wore her mother's shoes, or why it was okay for Willow to crawl into bed with her mom after a bad dream.

"We're different, pumpkin, that's all," India would say when Willow asked why it was okay for them to touch skin to skin inside the apartment, but they always had to wear gloves when they went outside. "Just about everyone else is so afraid of dying they never get around to living. One day, you and me, we decided not to be afraid anymore. Bring on the germs. We aren't running scared."

But there is fear and then there is watching your kid lose weight because there just isn't enough of anything to go around. India left Willow alone with the black and white version of Count of Monte Cristo playing in the VCR and promised to be back in an hour. It was an hour and a half, but she did come home. She stumbled through the door like a drunk, but she hadn't been drinking. She was dying.

As an eight-year-old, Willow didn't know about social diseases and the lengths people will go to keep them out of their beds. She didn't know about state-sponsored prostitutes that made good money and went through painful cell cleansing procedures to ensure that they were clean enough for the high-powered politicians and businessmen that purchased their time. She didn't know about black markets, that the Ministry controlled the cleaners and if you weren't already in the records, you couldn't get one done. She'd never seen the machines, the needles in each arm, pumping blood out, bathing it in a series of chemical baths and light treatments before pouring it back into the body. And that was from the state-run clinics. In the illegal clinics, they used SaniCheck, diluted.

After all, SaniCheck had proven safe in clinical trials, and it was readily available. For a little extra, they'd clean you twice as fast with twice as much SaniCheck, slip you back into the records and get you ready to work again if you made your money lying down.

So it didn't make sense that India wouldn't allow Willow to call the Health Ministry's emergency line. Instead, India just coughed blood and cried blood and wiped it off of her skin when it broke through like beads of sweat. Willow held India's hand. What else can you do when you're eight? She died two days later. Willow pulled her from the bed into the bath, India's limp feet dragging along the carpet leaving a faint trail of blood behind. Willow washed her mother with warm water, then dried her face and put makeup on her. There weren't many ways India was conventional, but she never left the house without her mascara and Willow knew India wouldn't have wanted anyone to see the softness around her eyes.

The men in hazmat suits burst through the door an hour later, their disembodied breathing filling the house with the whirring and clicking of automatic air purifiers. Willow was bare-armed, bare-handed, her pale skin exposed to the world and all the hazards therein. She was sitting on the edge of the toilet, studying the tub where her mother had been, when she overheard the two goons in their white blimp suits commenting. "Not a bottle of SaniCheck in the house. Not even the generic shit. No wonder the bitch died."

Willow didn't cry. She wasn't even surprised. She knew what SaniCheck was. The teachers had it at school in dispensers at their hips. They took off their latex gloves, wiped their hands down with the stuff, then put on a new pair of gloves. They used designer gloves, with fingernails painted on them, and a slight tanned hue that almost passed for real skin.

But Willow saw the skin underneath: parched, flaking and old. Older than her teachers' perfectly painted faces. Her mother's hands were beautiful, even if Willow begged her mom to buy the latex gloves to be like other moms. India just laughed and kissed Willow on the forehead. Willow cringed. Other moms didn't do that either.

Sitting in the Ministry's jail, the memory was brand new, like it just happened yesterday, not almost twenty-five years ago. For the first time in her adult life, Willow understood what her mother had been trying to teach her about fear, about love, about accepting the good and the bad in the world and finding the beauty in both. Willow stayed bent over her knees and the motion sensors in the lab switched off the lights. The only sound left was the sound of Willow's heart beating in time with the clock on the wall.

And then Willow noticed something move to her left. The light was murky and soft at the edges. She turned and stared as the wall itself shifted and moved. A shape like a hand pushing through a cellophane barrier, then a knee and a foot, then the face leaning into the wall as if falling through a mattress. The figure emerged and shook, the color of the wall draining from his face gradually as the flesh revealed eyes Willow had been certain she'd never see again.

Twenty Four

Ven shrugged off the last of the wall and sat down heavily on Willow's cot.

Willow stood, her heart pounding. "You've got to be shitting me." The words fell out of her mouth before she had time to consider them.

"Will," he said, his voice cracking. "I can explain." Even with the crumbling feeling in his brain, he was clear enough to hope she didn't ask too many questions.

She backed away, putting as much distance between them as the cell would allow. "Start with what you're doing here."

Ven did a quick internal rundown of explanations and immediately decided that there was no good way to explain his incarceration. Instead, he short-circuited the story. "I need help." He coughed like old cement rattling around in a mixing truck.

"If you hadn't noticed, I'm in trouble too." Willow was pacing as she spoke, taking five steps in one direction, coming to the end of the cell and turning back to the other wall.

"They haven't drugged you yet. You're still," he gestured at her "you. Except for the shitty haircut. You go to the butcher to get that?"

His dig had the effect he wanted. She stopped pacing and balled up her hands into fists. It looked like she'd learned how to use them since he'd watched her packing in the hotel room.

"Funny. Anything else you want to say before I push you back through that wall?"

Even with the taste of cinder block still in his mouth, Ven smiled a little to himself. This was more like it. This he could work with. Already he liked her better.

"You don't have to forgive me. You don't even have to like me. But you do have to help me." He coughed again.

"I don't have to do shit for you." Willow's hands hadn't unclenched and she stood like a bull terrier just waiting for permission to bite.

"You do if you want answers. If you want out of here." Ven looked up and saw the resemblance to Warren Lake that had been missing. A challenge now, like she hadn't been before. There'd be no more ladylike hands stroking his back. No more whispering his name. She wouldn't ask permission a second time.

He tried a different tactic. She might have found her spine, but no one can excise all of their old character. Somewhere, she was still the same woman he'd wooed over dinner. He softened his tone. "Please?"

Willow's hands relaxed and her shoulders lowered an inch. "What?" she asked, her tone impatient.

Ven liked the way she barked the word out. It meant he was going to get what he needed. "Whatever they've drugged me with is sucking me dry. I've got to get my strength back."

"How do you propose doing that?" Willow's foot tapped the concrete floor.

"Make love to me?" Ven put on his best puppy dog face, hating the way it made him feel like he was trying to wheedle her into saving him, but also fully aware of how badly he needed the help.

"Go to hell," Willow started pacing again.

Ven dropped all the pretenses. Game or not, he was in trouble. "Just lie next to me. Let me borrow some of your energy. It won't hurt, I promise." He couldn't help himself, he looked up at her from lowered lashes and grinned. Adina said he'd learned that trick as a toddler. It had served him well.

Willow glared at him, weighing him against her memory of him. He had been charming and kind. A gentleman. The man sitting in front of her was not charming or gentle. But any idiot could see that he was sick.

She closed her eyes as she considered the options and the costs. An image of Duane crept up on her, first as a visceral memory of him driving her body to a pleasure that was nearly as terrifying as it was addictive, then of his face as she'd lost consciousness. She wondered why Ven had ever been compelling.

Still, if she said no, who knew if he'd have the ability to get back over to his cell. Then she'd be stuck with him and she'd have no place to lay down herself. If she said yes, he'd touch her again. As she played the scenario out in her head, she realized it wouldn't matter if he did. He couldn't touch anything that mattered.

"Down," she gestured at the cot. He held her gaze for a long minute, then fell to his side, his knees half drawn to his stomach. "I get answers in the morning," she said as she sat down in the cavity, then lay beside him, her body mirroring his. He put one hand at her waist, sliding his fingers between the button placket of her suit to find skin.

Her skin electrified; all the hair on her arms stood at attention. Clearly he felt it too; he nestled in closer, tucking his other arm under her head and cradling her shoulder. In a familiar sensation, every fiber in her body strained towards him much like the old tattoo had strained towards sensors.

As familiar as it was, it also wasn't the same. Duane had touched her with reverence and respect. He had held her, not his image of her. Ven didn't have a clue.

Willow stayed awake for a long time, listening to him breathe. *I should have paid this much attention the first time around,* she thought. She waited to feel like she was betraying Duane. Lying next to two men in such a short time period seemed like a whorish thing to do, but she didn't know what being a whore would feel like.

She woke to the heat of his breath on her neck. She lay there for a moment, testing out different emotions to see which one fit, and finally gave up. "Whose side are you on?" she finally asked, still facing the far wall. She didn't want to see his face.

He thought about his loyalties, fully aware that what allegiances he had were tentative at best. There was no good answer. "Same side you're on, I guess," he said as he played with the edge of her shirt, thinking his touch would serve to distract her.

"I'm not on anybody's side." Willow pushed herself up to sitting. Ven slid a hand between her shirt and her skin slowly making his way up to caress her ribs. She let him, more to confirm the conclusions of the night before than for any other reason she could name, then pushed his hand away and stood. Ven stood too.

"I'm not going to try and bullshit you," he said.

"That's what a bull-shitter says just before they feed you a line of crap," she retorted.

"Ask me anything you want to know. I'll tell you the truth," he offered.

"Why me?" She didn't even have to think about it. From the moment she'd confronted that empty hotel bathroom, she'd wanted to know why he'd picked her.

His own reasons would only lead to more questions so he decided to go with the conclusion he'd come to regarding Maggie and Miles' motivations. "Have you ever played cards without the joker?" he asked.

"What the fuck are you talking about?"

"Poker. Without a wild card, it's too easy." He ran his fingers through his hair, not because he cared what it looked like but for what the nonverbal gesture would say to her. "You're the wild card."

If he'd said that she was pretty, that he'd found her intellect irresistible, that he just couldn't help himself, she would have at least been able to respect his commitment to the lie. The truth was harder to swallow. She whirled around, put both hands on Ven's chest and shoved. Hard. He flailed backwards, surprised, met the wall and broke the surface, falling through to the other side.

When he regained his balance, he glanced at the clock. Almost time for the Lake sisters to show up. He dusted himself off and pressed his check against the wall. "In the old decks," he whispered through the concrete, "the Joker is the Fool. The guy that starts a journey just because he can. Everyone else tells him to stay home and stay safe, but he packs his shit and leaves anyway."

Willow didn't answer. Ven let his words settle to the floor like dust, then added: "Don't let them give you anything."

Moments later, the first pair of heels came clicking down the tiled hallway. Willow moved to the bars to see who was coming through the door. The lock turned and a lab coat pushed into the room. The patch on her white coat said Dr. Lake. She was small and serious, her face perpetually frozen into an expression of disdain and disgust, like she'd just stepped in shit. Willow recognized her from Ministry events: Maggie Lake, one of Warren Lake's daughters. A half-sister.

Uninterested, Willow returned to her cot and sat on it, leaning back against the cinder block wall. She heard Ven in his cell, moving slowly like a caged tiger with a broken leg. Finally, he sat too. Willow felt him and moved until her back was touching the same section of wall. Even his dubious company was a relief. She closed her eyes as the lab came to life around her.

Ven felt her seek him out through the wall and smiled. Fool indeed.

Twenty Five

Maggie ignored both Willow and Ven for most of the morning. She didn't speak at all, not to coax her work into submission, not in frustration or surprise. Her silence was starting to get annoying. Willow watched her posture. She held herself perfectly straight, as if someone had poured her shoulders from steel.

Shortly after she consumed a spare lunch of granola and yogurt, a second pair of heels came clicking down the hall. Willow shuffled her feet against the floor with impatience. The second lab coat revealed another Doctor Lake embroidered at the breast, Dr. Karina Lake. Together, their sleek gray faces and dark hair reminded Willow of the Siamese cats in an old cartoon she watched with India. *We are Siamese, if you please,* she sang to herself, and for a gleeful moment felt like a real younger sister.

They might have been good looking women, but not with that mix of entitlement and superiority smeared all over their faces. Willow remembered her mother telling her not to make faces just in case her face got stuck in some unattractive configuration. Sara Lake must not have been quite as whimsical.

"So that's her?" Karina Lake asked. Maggie gave a slight nod. "Pretty," Karina said. "For a slut-faced bitch." Maggie didn't look up. "Diseased?" Karina asked.

"Just like her mother," Maggie responded.

Ven felt Willow's attention shift and hone. He sat up straighter and began to pay attention himself.

"What are we doing to her?"

"Bloodwork," Maggie said. "We need a viral analysis, immune response titer, and DNA. Then we decide on the antiviral course and ship her off to the Infirmary."

"Has she been cleared for transport?"

"We aren't waiting for clearance on this one." Maggie's face was no grimmer than usual, but her lip uncurled into a flat line.

"Any special protocols?" Karina leaned against the lab table and crossed her arms over her chest, staring at Willow through the bars. Maggie didn't deign to look up from her work.

"She's not smart enough to know what's going on." Maggie's tone was dismissive.

"You sure?" Karina questioned her older sister.

"She's here, isn't she? She didn't get infected by being a genius."

Karina shook her head and went about gathering the syringe and vials to fill with Willow's blood. Willow watched her, carefully weighing her options. It wasn't like they could help who they were. She had been just like them, despite her mother's best efforts. She thought of the woman that had been unable to hold Warren Lake's affections and conjured up a picture of the pale-skinned, pinched woman she'd met at the Carlyle's.

Willow remained seated, all outward signs indicating she was oblivious or indifferent. Karina approached the cell with the magnetic key held up like a protective amulet. She swiped it and stepped into the cell with Willow.

"Give me your arm," she said. Willow was sitting on the cot, her knees under her chin. She unfurled an arm as directed and watched Karina's gloved hands fumble with tearing open an alcohol swab. She was not particularly gentle with the swabbing, but Willow didn't notice. She was seeing her own arm in the hands of the Doctor at the clinic, the dimpled skin just before the puncture. Neither the doctor then nor this woman in front of her now knew what they were afraid of, only that they were terrified.

Karina leaned over Willow's arm, looking closely at her vein. It had been years since she had drawn blood, but this was a special case. In a building of four thousand Ministry workers, she and her sister were among a small number of specially cleared researchers read into the Strain project. Anyway, an opportunity to cause the woman in front of her pain of any variety was simply too good to pass up. She pressed the sharp edge of the needle into Willow's skin.

Willow lunged forward with her tongue out. There was no exposed skin except for the Doctor's face, so that's where Willow aimed, licking a long swath of skin starting at Karina's chin and curving up towards her eye. It took half a second for Willow to settle back to her cot. In that fraction of an instant, the needle and vial fell to the hard floor and shattered. A bright blob of blood welled up on Willow's arm. Since both sisters were looking at her in horror, Willow went ahead and licked that too.

That made the hysterics start.

"Get me out get me out oh fuck get me out of here that crazy bitch has infected me!" Karina screamed. Maggie rushed to the cell and yanked her sister to safety.

"You rancid bitch," Maggie screeched as Karina howled and rubbed at her face.

"Be careful, you'll rub it in," was all Willow said.

Maggie guided Karina to the work desk and helped her onto a lab stool. "Just stay," she ordered as Karina hyperventilated. "Unless you have an abrasion, you'll probably be fine," she tried to reassure her sister as she rifled frantically through the cabinets. She threw a bottle of SaniCheck at her sister, which Karina opened with hands that were quivering erratically. She poured the liquid into her cupped palm until it was overflowing, then closed her eyes and proceeded to rub it into her face. Inevitably, the disinfectant got into her eyes which just added screams of pain to the horrified stream of curse words she was releasing, half-formed, into the room.

In the cell beside her, Willow heard Ven laugh.

The pair stumbled to the eye-washing station to try and get the stuff out of Karina's eyes and finally rushed from the room altogether.

When Maggie came back an hour later, she had murder in her eyes.

"Do you know what you've done?" she asked Willow with razor-sharp precision.

"Tell me. I'm dying to know," Willow gestured like a thirteen-year-old about to receive a piece of devastatingly fascinating gossip.

"You may have infected the greatest virologist this Republic has ever produced."

"Well, if she was such an amazing virologist, she'd know better than to panic. She'd know that the risk of transmission is only about one percent, and furthermore the kind of virus I've got only thrives in my pussy." Willow thought for a second. "I could have sat on her face. Then she'd have something to be mad about."

"You... you..." Maggie spluttered.

"Too bad you already wasted your best insults. Rancid bitch. Slut-faced bitch. I'm sensing a theme here. Perhaps something more creative next time?" Willow was insouciant.

"You fucking whore," Maggie roared.

"Nope. That was my mother, thanks for asking." Willow smiled a very narrow smile.

"You'll pay for this. She's my sister."

"Don't forget, I'm your sister too." Willow's voice was a sing-song of irony.

Maggie's face drained of all color and her mouth collapsed into a single line. "Fuck you," she said.

"Does daddy know you talk like this? Cause I'm gonna tell for real."

"He. Is. Not. Your. Father."

"Ah, Dr. Lake...but he is." Willow's voice had dropped the pretense of adolescent rebellion. What was left was poisonous.

Ven wisely kept his thoughts to himself and his mouth shut, even after the door slammed behind Maggie and he was alone with Willow in the dark.

Marshall paced his office with a hitched gate he only allowed himself when alone. He hated relying on his instincts, but there was no data. Nothing coming out of the Ministry. With all of his trusted team gone—first Kiri and her crew, then Ven and now Ian—Marshall was operating blind. He didn't like it. Not when so many depended on him. Scattered around the building, his kids. Not by blood, but certainly by his decision to take them in. Some could fend for themselves, others could not, but in aggregate, they were a family. His family.

And he was going to send his family away. It was too easy for the Ministry to get to him. To all of them.

Marshall had thought a lot about Warren since their meeting. The encounter had gone a long way toward amending his previous assessment. The man was no ideologue. He'd have come after the Camellias long before if he had been. No, Warren Lake was a pragmatist with an ideological agenda. The ground was shifting, and Marshall knew that he'd be the first pawn sacrificed.

He couldn't keep his Camellias safe.

He made the announcement over breakfast and by the time the sun set, everyone was gone. Everyone but him.

Willow stood at the bars for a long time before she forced herself to breathe deeply. She'd forgotten that a certain level of control over her emotions was required to keep the virus in check. There was only so much her body could take and, between the confrontation with her sisters and everything that had happened since she'd kissed Duane for the first time, she was past her limit. Already, she could feel the tightness in her labia, an ache that was beginning to spread down her thigh. It didn't matter much if she erupted in another blister, at least rationally. An outbreak would be just another annoyance, and she could logically afford to be neutral about it.

Nevertheless, she didn't have a logical relationship with her body. And with everything that was happening, and happening so quickly, she'd nearly forgotten. Not really forgotten, but it had slipped to the back of her mind like what she'd eaten for dinner the week before, or even her burning grief over Ven. She hadn't broken out since she first climbed on the motorcycle with Ianthe and, so long as she wasn't breaking out, there were too many other things to worry about. Still, the threat of a new blister was enough to send her through the whole whirlwind of emotion all over again: outrage, disgust, equivocation, resignation, and finally a grudging peace.

Willow forced a deep breath and then another after that. She closed her eyes and turned her attention inward, feeling down the length of her spine until she felt the spinning circuitry of the virus in her cells. She followed further, felt the thread of the virus and snapped it. The whirling circuits in her spine slowed. Finally, she returned her attention to the external world and to Ven.

"Why are you still here?" Her voice was weary.

"God, do you think I would miss a show like that?" Ven considered the balls it had taken to attack one of the Lake sisters with nothing but their own fear and respected her a little more for it.

Even so, he wished he could take the words back. As soon as she sensed that he held her in any real esteem, he'd lose all power over her. She had let him sleep next to her; she'd let him touch her skin. It was still his game to lose.

"Whose side are you on again?" Willow was no longer invested in his answer, but it seemed like it might be a good idea to know who was playing for what.

"I'm locked up. Do you think they'd lock me up if I were working for them?" Ven answered carefully. Lies were hard to track, but insinuations left plenty of room for deniability. Besides, he might be on her side. Eventually. Unless Miles came up with something sufficiently compelling.

"I don't know anything anymore." Willow fell silent. *I really don't*, she thought. *There are games within games, and I'm the only one telling the truth.*

"Which side are you on?" Ven asked casually, as if indifferent to the answer. He was, mostly.

"I'm on the side of leave me the hell out of it." Willow slumped back onto her cot.

After several long minutes, Ven said, "You were better than I expected." Willow winced as if slapped. "With some time, you and I could have been amazing together."

Willow thought back to that night and had trouble recalling the act itself, but she remembered the grimace on his face as he'd thrust into her with the last spasm of his orgasm. She'd told herself it was pleasurable, but he hadn't made her cum. She remembered that part too.

At the time, she'd laughed it off and told him that practice would take care of that. There was plenty she could say about it now, but she didn't respond. He wasn't worth the energy the conversation would take. She let herself fall asleep instead. There wasn't anything else to do.

Ven felt Willow drift off and pushed his way through the wall. He paced in her cell, watching her and considering the permutations and implications. There was much to think about, and it occurred to him that he should have asked Miles for more background before agreeing to totally discredit a Ministry employee. At the time, it hadn't mattered. It was money, it was a direct order, and Ven was without ideology when it came to things that interested the Ministry.

Now, of course, the game was much more complex. Now that the girl that he'd infected was the daughter of the Minister, and his orders hadn't been from Miles but from the girl's half-sister, the balance of power changed.

Ven wondered how much his story would be worth to the Minister, and how he could keep his role in the events concealed. He paced and examined the problem from one perspective and then another, gesturing as if arguing before a jury.

Hours later, the door to the lab cracked open.

When the lock sliding from its place broke Ven's concentration, he slipped into a dark shadow and back through the wall to an unlit corner in his own cell. Willow woke up slowly, looking around for a minute to sort out where she was. Warren Lake was standing outside her cell.

"Are you here to yell?" she asked.

"No. Unfortunately, I'm nearly certain she deserved it." Warren rubbed his temples. "They take after their mother."

"What is that supposed to mean?"

"No imagination and a cruel streak," Warren sighed.

"Way to choose a wife." Willow retorted and wasn't even sorry when she saw her father flinch. "What do they want?"

"They're Ministry employees; they want to defend the health of the

Republic. Think, Willow. You know the Ministry as well as anyone. We aren't the old government." Warren launched into a familiar speech which, conveniently, he happened to believe. "Our Union is based on the old principles of Marriage: the people are one half—the bride, I suppose. The government is the other. The husband. Here at the Ministry, we protect the people; we look out for their best interests. We are free to make the right choices for everyone because we aren't indebted to anyone. I'm Health Minister because I earned that right, not because I was voted prom king." Warren was wrapped up in the rhythm of his own speech, the metaphors and images that drove him. He swayed slightly on his feet.

"There is no vast conspiracy here. We do research. We don't tell our citizens everything we know because it serves no purpose. No one needs to know that your nerve cells are altered. It isn't relevant. The Strain isn't relevant. The only thing that matters is that this is a nuisance social virus. If we can keep it from spreading, that's good. If we can use it to modify people's behavior, that's better. We're perfecting the cure now, but in the meantime, fear of social diseases is solving a problem for us. Protected sex is the right thing for the population. It satisfies the carnal need and helps prevent the messy emotional attachments that happen through brain chemistry."

He thought briefly of his own adventures in unprotected congress, the heat of a woman wrapped around him, the way India had smelled after lovemaking. He paused, lost momentarily in both his own physicality and his latent wish that he could go without, then shook his head to clear the thought and continued.

"Those emotional attachments lead to poor decision making. Once people think they are in love, they get stupid. They have too many kids. They contract social diseases. They marry and divorce and marry again. It isn't love. It's simply a cocktail of naturally-occurring opiates. Love doesn't exist. Partnership exists. Shared goals. Reproducing the species at a measured rate is real. The rest of it is a chemical firebomb." He ended with a tonal flourish, as if he'd just given the speech to a crowd of the faithful, not his wayward, jailed daughter.

"The Ministries are the husband and the people get fucked. Fleming's ass, I hope that's not your best speech." Willow grinned at her own joke, to hell with her circumstances. "Anyway," she went on, "you don't believe that."

"It's self-evident," he replied simply.

"So you didn't love my mother?" Willow's tone dared him to deny it.

"I loved her."

"You touched her."

"Yes." What else could he say? He had touched her often, everywhere, and then again.

"You made poor choices because your brain was chemically altered."

"Yes."

"And she kept me because her brain was on love opiates." Willow softened as an image of her mother bubbled up from her memory. It must have taken a great deal of bravery to stand up to Warren.

"Yes."

"And in your own fucked up way, you looked out for me." Willow watched Warren's face, half expecting to see the answer before she heard it.

"I wouldn't characterize it in that way, but yes."

"So explain. Love is a chemical Molotov cocktail. You don't want it for the population, but you can't live without it yourself." Willow was genuinely interested in the answer, and surprised at herself for being invested.

"That's because I was imprinted young. Kids that grow up the right way can live quite happily in the world I've created. I didn't have that luxury. Your grandmother was a wreck of a woman. She swore the only reason why we'd survived the '89 pandemic was because she didn't believe in the autoclave." Warren's eyes closed part way, remembering his own mother.

"Except 'we' didn't survive. I did, but my twin brother didn't. 'Son' she'd say, 'all this hand wringing and hand washing is pointless. Have a few germs. Give your body the practice.' When a flu shot became mandatory, she'd keep us home from school and lie to the officials about our records. After William died, she almost forgot that there had been two of us in the first place. When the government collapsed and the social order disintegrated, we ate dandelion salad. She loved every minute of it." Warren shook his head.

"Where is she now?" Willow had never considered having grandparents. The absence of regular parental figures had been enough of a loss. Now she wondered what the woman who was her grandmother would be like.

"United Provinces of Canada. In a hippie commune, waiting for her time to be ejected from the group to go die in a cave with the bears. She thinks I'm the Antichrist."

"The Antichrist? What does that mean?" Willow felt dumb for asking, but the question had blurted itself out before she'd had a chance to rein it in.

"It's a saying from the old era. It means she thinks I'm evil." Warren's tone was patient and gentle. Willow had never heard him sound like that before.

"Okay, so how does my Grandmother explain anything?"

"She explains everything. She is representative of the old ways. Metaphorically, we live in a house with very thin walls. Before we turned all the scientific minds to solving the ongoing health crisis, they used to talk about chaos theory. Entropy."

"Never heard of it."

"Of course not. No one needs to know that the universe is constantly sliding into a state of greater chaos. It serves no purpose to alarm the population. The Ministry has everything under control. We are constantly releasing new cures for common ailments. Psoriasis is next. Scheduled for next month, actually."

"You schedule breakthroughs?" Willow asked, incredulous.

"We schedule everything," Warren answered.

Willow felt like she was talking about an alien organization, not the place where she'd worked most of her adult life. "When was the last time you discovered something new?"

"I'm an administrator now; I don't discover anything."

"The Ministry, then. When did the Ministry find something new?"

"A big breakthrough? 2033."

"Ten years ago?"

"Ten years, but we're close to the HSV cure," Warren admitted.

"But you've had a vaccine for the Herpes virus for ten years now?"

"Well, twelve for that. Give or take. We've got part of the cure in place. The Malvexitran is part of the cocktail. It inhibits the viral growth and keeps outbreaks to a minimum. Once the viral reproduction is under control, we can extract the infected cells. Theoretically."

"Theoretically? So why not just vaccinate people instead of tattooing them?"

"Ah, your protocol. I never did get to tell you what a useful stroke of genius that was. Immeasurably useful to the Ministry's cause." Warren paused. "The population's fear keeps them safe. It encourages behavior that is good for everyone. Look around. Child abuse is rare. Why? Because no one has accidental babies. Everyone wants the children they have. There is no overcrowding. We have the children we can afford. We have sufficient resources for everyone. The last government couldn't say that."

"That all sounds wonderful," Willow's tone was sarcastic, "but what's wrong with your cure?"

Warren sighed. He didn't like failure, didn't like the reports coming back from the lead scientist in Bethesda. "We're talking about isolating and treating nerve cells. It isn't easy and so far the side effects have been," he paused, looking for the right word, "unacceptable."

Willow looked at him, thinking through all the ways that a set of side effects could be unacceptable. "Is that what happens at the Infirmary?"

Warren looked at Willow, surprised. "What do you know of the Infirmary?"

"Rumor," Willow's tone was dismissive. "Rumor and conjecture."

Warren relaxed slightly. "Well, you've had your explanation and time to consider. We'll start you on the Malvexitran and circulate an explanation for your co-workers."

"No." She didn't even hesitate.

"What do you mean, 'no'? Marshall's already agreed to put your friends into the care of the Ministry to help us identify the cure. Your so-called Camellia friends are all on their way back to normal." Warren didn't notice the incredulity on Willow's face. Marshall was many things, but he wasn't stupid. There was no way he was going to put his beloved Camellias into Warren's care. But Warren kept talking. "You don't want to be the only one. I'll never release you if you are. We just can't afford the threat of chaos."

"This world of yours where nothing bad can grow, nothing good can grow either. I spent my whole life on the surface, on the shiny things, what was safe. Well, I've lived for real now and I'm not ready to die. I'm not saying I'm okay with what has happened," she added for Ven's benefit, "but the life you have planned for me won't erase everything that I know now. I know how thin the line between me and rock bottom is. It isn't like I can forget. It isn't like I can go back to the way things were."

"Think about it, Willow. You can go back to the way things were, except better. You'll have a perspective that is badly needed in the Ministry. You will be healthy again. We'll find you a worthy contract partner. You can have a family. You can have it all back. There is more to look forward to than you know." Warren's voice was pleading. "I'll give you a few more hours." There was a note of desperation in his voice. "For God's sake, Willow, you're all that's left of her. I'll see that you are taken care of."

"If I've learned one thing, it's that I can care of myself." She wasn't exactly defiant, but there wasn't any arguing with her either.

"Please, Willow. Do it for an old man." He turned the lights out. "Be well," he said over his shoulder as he closed the door.

"Be well," Willow said into the darkness.

Twenty Six

"How did you know Dad was the one?" Maggie asked her mother. She'd spent the night in her old bedroom, as if her presence could ease her mother's panic. Karina was still in the hospital, milking the sympathy angle as much as she could, but the bitch was right. Karina was unlikely to contract anything. No outbreaks, no genital contact. The odds were on Karina's side.

Maggie knew Karina was playing the drama out for all it was worth, but it didn't hurt the strategy. At least her mother's concern was real and Maggie could do something about that.

"Humh?" Sara Lake responded.

"Dad. How did you know Dad was the one?" Maggie repeated.

"Oh. That. Well, we both wanted the same thing. I knew better than to think that love would be enough—we were just kids when we met—but I did know that a shared sense of purpose would keep us working together."

Maggie thought about that for a minute. "What did happen?" she finally asked.

"What do you mean?" Sara was far too practiced at the blank-face game to give anything away in response to an open ended question. Early press inquiry into the Ministry and Warren's research there had taught her to deflect.

"Have you and dad been," Maggie paused, trying to think of the right way to frame her question. "Happy?"

Sara looked at her daughter carefully. "Your father is a good man," Sara said simply. "Greatness is always paired with great weakness. Your father is no exception. But look at the world around you." Sara gestured at the walls. "Your father built this society from the ground up. Never mind the other Ministers. Their best policy came from your father's hand and they knew it. I've stood by his side for over forty years because I believe in him and I believe in the stability he's given our ravaged Republic. I couldn't be prouder of him."

Maggie thought of the evidence of her father's long-standing adulterous habits, but didn't say anything. Sara Lake wasn't stupid: if she didn't know already it was because she'd chosen not to know. Maggie picked up her cup of tea and stood to leave for the Ministry.

"I'm glad, Mom," Maggie said. "I'll see you at the hospital later."

Sara nodded. "Have a good day, dear. Be well," she said.

"Be well," Maggie replied, and was gone.

✖

There was no telling exactly where Ianthe was. The Wastes, obviously, but beyond that, there was just the compass on the dashboard. The needle nodded this way and that, but that was only a direction, not a location.

It didn't really matter. Signs flew past her as the truck ate up mile after mile of ragged road, but the names meant nothing. As long as she was heading south or east, the rest was just details. One of the springs in the Source's dusty old truck seat dug into her side with the persistence of a toothache or the beginning of the thought she couldn't afford: *what if Kiri wasn't okay.*

From the highway, she saw a low flat roof, blue against the dry brown fields dulling in the dusklight. Provisions. She pulled off at the next gently curling exit and followed the side road. Under her, the springs in the seat creaked in protest every time she hit a sink hole. Her bones protested too.

A parking lot under a sign that said Walmart sparkled beneath her headlights. Abandoned cars littered the asphalt, their bumpers shining through the lacework rust. Faint white lines disintegrated as patches of grass pushed through the fractures in the asphalt underneath.

Ianthe didn't bother parking. She pulled up to the front of the store and stopped the truck with its nose touching the glass door. From the looks of it, she was the only living thing in at least a hundred miles in any given direction. Still, she pocketed the keys and groped under the seat for the crowbar and the flashlight.

Ianthe swung the crowbar at the glass door claw first. There was a grace in the swing, an almost pretty pleasure in the weight of the implement and the arc it cut in the evening air. The glass shattered and she scraped the jagged remnants out of the door frame with the handle. She ducked under the push-bar and into the abandoned building, directing the flashlight into one corner and then the next. It cut the darkness temporarily, but the inky interior just oozed back onto itself like pudding.

She started at the cash register, looking for bags. There was nothing good about having to stop, and if she could gather enough this time, she might not have to do it again. With her flashlight sweeping the floor, she rounded the sharp corners of the lane. Three skeletons lay toppled over each other like fallen dominoes, with only scraps of fabric draped over the bones to indicate that this was not some kind of ancient burial site. The floor under them was dark.

Ianthe shuddered and kept walking. The bags were there in easy reach, but she didn't want that black stuff that had once been human on her shoes. Blue strips of fabric crossed the skeleton crumpled behind the register. A gold cross dangled into the cavity where a heart would have been.

Superstitious twit, Ianthe thought irreverently, but her eyes were wide and her heart pounded. *The dead are dead,* she reminded herself. *Ghosts are a lie told by the superstitious. An anthropological artifact to help manage the uncertainty and fear felt in response to death. No more.*

The next two lanes were the same and Ianthe walked past trying not to look or to think. Finally, the fourth lane was free of corpses. Ianthe grabbed a handful of bags and walked into the thickening darkness in front of her. She could hear her own breathing, shallow and rapid as she walked.

Aisle after aisle, Ianthe walked and argued with herself about what was essential and what was too much to carry. A blanket, cans of tuna and bottles of water—these were for her. Every first aid kit on the shelf, the soap, blankets, some clothes—these were for Kiri. Ianthe didn't want to think about what it would mean if all of it was necessary.

Toward the back of the store, Ianthe turned her beam to the top of a shelf stacked high with tents and tarps. She had to climb to reach them, but she pulled the top one down and it landed with a smack against the linoleum floor. The noise echoed loudly through the store. She quickened her pace.

The crowbar made short work of the glass counter that held a small arsenal of rifles and bullets. Ianthe unfolded the tarp and piled the guns into its center, then drug it behind her as she stopped at the end of each aisle to pick up the bags that she'd filled on her way in.

Her flashlight swung into a spacious corner created by the shelves. Signs overhead said Maybelline, L'Oreal, and Cover Girl. Behind the shelves were pictures of heavily made up women, their lips lacquered in red and their eyes darkened like the raccoons that Marshall always swore at for getting into the compost pile. Her fingers relaxed their grip on the tarp and she walked in as if compelled. Camouflage. She immediately began grabbing at the plastic packaging, selecting the darkest shades of powder she could find and stuffing them into her pockets. Two aisles back, there were packages of hair dye to choose from as well. She retraced her steps and picked the bluest black she could find.

In the darkness, she fumbled with the tarp, securing it as tightly as she could across the bed of the truck. She pulled back the tab on a can of tuna and sniffed it. It smelled the same as any other can of tuna and she'd been careful to pick cans that didn't look bloated. So she ate it like a wild cat in three feral bites and started up the truck again. It choked back to life. On the sign by the side of the road, white letters announced "Thanks for visiting Tulare."

The rusty road signs said 395 and she followed them, not thinking, not seeing. When the signs for 40 east appeared, she turned east towards a place called Flagstaff. Her headlights peeled back the darkness only so far. Beyond them there was nothing at all.

And so, gradually, between the times her body forced her to stop to relieve or herself or the times the truck forced her to stop to transfer fuel from the plastic barrels in the bed into its gas tank, or the times she simply fell asleep at the wheel, the miles slid past her like chipped pearls from a string. Nevada, Arizona, New Mexico, the signs said. She crossed into the Independent State of Texas as the sun set behind her.

It should have felt like a triumph, but it didn't.

The telephone on Warren's desk rang, startling his eyes open. He hadn't been napping, not exactly, but he had closed his eyes and allowed the dream-like associations of an uncontrolled mind free reign. He blinked briefly as the shapes on the caller ID coagulated into a number he recognized and dreaded. He didn't bother with a greeting when he picked up; he knew the voice on the other end would be talking already.

"What the devil is going on down there?"

Warren leaned forward, one hand holding the phone, the other applying pressure to the bridge of his nose. "Sir, I have everything under control." But he could hear the weariness in his own voice and knew that the Elder would hear it too.

"Like hell you do. Where's Miles?"

Warren couldn't help but sigh. "Sir, Miles' loyalties have come under suspicion."

"Loyalties to whom, Minister Lake—to yourself or to the Trust?"

"I didn't know there was a difference, Sir." Warren's spine had straightened, and his voice had regained some of its usual authority.

"That all depends on you, Minister. It all depends on you."

"Yes, Sir." Warren had been dealing with the Trust much longer than he wanted to admit. He knew when arguing was pointless. But as much as they might believe he owed them, he owed his Republic more. There was sufficient time to deal with the Trust later. They always had time.

"Be well, Minister." It sounded like a warning.

"Be well, Sir." Warren replied and dropped the phone back into its cradle.

Willow could feel Ven as he moved about in the cell next to her, and hated her awareness of him. She wondered if he was equally as aware of her, then doubted it, then heard a chorus of insecurities whispering her down. *Just because he's a flaming asshole doesn't mean there is anything wrong with me,* she told herself. It helped, but not by much, because her very next thought was to wonder how she had felt this compelling connection between them, and yet he had been completely oblivious. Indifferent. Perhaps even laughing at her the whole time. It didn't bear contemplating.

Ven broke the silence first. "If I come through the wall, will you talk to me?" Ven offered.

"Did it mean anything to you?" She heard herself asking, then cringed at the sound of her own voice. Of course it hadn't meant anything. And it didn't matter if it did. She'd had better since: more respectful, more thoughtful, more appreciative. If she had to choose, she'd take appreciated over used.

"No," he said. Her stomach asserted its displeasure with his answer. She released a breath she hadn't known she was holding. At least it had been said.

It didn't matter, and it didn't change anything. What she'd said to the Minister held true even without the bravado; what's done was done. Instead of answering with another question or probing further, she changed the subject. "Why don't you break out? It might do both of us some good."

Ven considered it. She was right, but not for the reasons she'd suggested it. Whatever came next, he needed to make his own move. It was time to seek out the Minister.

A minute later, she heard the door to the lab open and close again. She was finally, blissfully alone. She pushed the fresh humiliation from her thoughts. The reality hadn't changed at all by hearing Ven confirm what she was most afraid of, and there were bigger issues to consider.

In the first solitude she'd had since leaving Philadelphia with Ianthe, she went over everything she'd experienced and learned: the electrical circuits in her spine, her ability to get the equivalent of an x-ray of something just by touching it. The prickly feeling in her skin when she touched anyone else with the Strain; the explosive sex with the Source; the look on Ian's face, thinking herself betrayed. She could count back to never having even met the Source in a matter of days, if not hours. From Dr. Webber's office to her cell, with a detour to Oregon and another lover. It had taken no time at all.

Willow didn't know how she was supposed to make sense of it, never mind how she was supposed to feel. Part of her was certain it had never actually happened. But then she closed her eyes and she could feel the rough skin of the Source's chin under her tongue. There was no way for Willow to think about it without ending at Duane telling her everything was going to be okay.

Instead, she thought about the flow of energy between her and Ven, the way it had felt rippling through her spine. Ven had been able to take energy from her and heal himself. No wonder Warren wanted the population terrified and the virus eradicated. If they could amplify themselves, the Ministries wouldn't be able to control the outcome.

It was a wonder the Ministry hadn't made all the security forces into spark plugs. She lay down, her head spinning.

Twenty Seven

Ven wasn't much for pomp and circumstance. He'd seen enough of men to know that they all crumpled when kicked in the nuts. A big office, a mahogany desk, these things did not signify to Ven as they might have to someone else. His father had possessed those things and more. They hadn't saved him from becoming obsolete or from deflating in front of Ven like a punctured balloon.

Still, Ven wasn't entirely unimpressed when he shook off the taste of the wood of Warren's office door and looked around. Warren's head was back and only the desk was bathed in the soft light of an incandescent bulb. The Minister looked like he was sleeping. When the Minister spoke, Ven jumped.

"Neat parlor trick. Have you considered a career in burglary?"

"I prefer mayhem." Ven could feel the adrenaline rushing through his veins and his heart beating in his throat even as he answered flippantly.

Warren raised an eyebrow and looked at Ven. Under normal circumstances, Ven believed in keeping his mouth shut and letting other people do the talking. However, the fine hairs at the back of his neck were all standing upright. His instincts weren't perfect, but he never looked back on the instances where he ignored them with any sense of pride. He started talking.

"There's more to the story, Sir." He hadn't called anyone Sir since his father, but he wasn't going to start dissecting that tell right then. Warren didn't look surprised. Ven tried again.

"Sir, I'm the one that infected Willow."

Warren leaned forward at the admission and Ven hurried to explain.

"It was on Miles' orders. I thought he wanted someone discredited. I didn't realize..." Ven thought through his next words carefully. "I didn't realize the implications."

Warren sighed. "I'd be a hypocrite if I didn't recognize the value of a certain moral flexibility. I'd prefer it not be used against me, though."

"It doesn't end there, Sir." Ven heard himself say 'Sir' for the third time and shuddered a little. He didn't like the way the word tasted in his mouth. Warren watched him expectantly.

"Maggie. She's working with Miles."

At the sound of his eldest daughter's name, Warren stood up and began pacing the room. "So she knows..."

"Why else single out Willow?" Ven commented as if he'd had nothing to do with it.

"They must be planning something more," Warren added as he stalked back past the front of his desk.

"A coup," Ven added simply, as if they were talking about arranging a brunch or a trip to the dentist. His stomach sank as the words left his mouth. It wasn't just sympathy for the Minister that had him, though there was some of that. But it was also the sudden certainty that no one was going to get out of this unscathed. Not even him.

"She's not safe." Warren stopped mid-stride as the ramifications played out in his head. "Can you get her up here?" The façade had dropped and what was left was an earnest father trying to do what he could before a storm beyond his control caught up with him. "There are things she needs to know."

"I'll try."

Ven used the doorknob when leaving the room instead of simply passing through the door a second time.

"We have to go."

It was the second time Ven had said it, but Willow's ears were full. She was in the process of trying to wash her hair in the sink in her cell. There was only SaniCheck and cold water, but there hadn't been much by way of privacy and Willow was desperate.

Ven finally crossed into Willow's cell and grabbed her hips. She screamed and showered them both in cold water from her hair. "We have to go," Ven explained for the third time. "Now. Your father wants to talk to you." Willow wiped the water out of her eyes as Ven dragged her along. Distracted by the stinging in her eyes, she hardly noticed when she passed right through her cell bars behind Ven. He opened the door to exit the lab and Willow stumbled after him.

"What the Fleming..." Willow started. "The arrogant ass. He couldn't come down himself?" Gooseflesh was rising on her arms.

"He's getting himself ready."

"For what? What is going on?" Willow tried to get her elbow back. Ven's grip slipped as she twisted away from him, but he turned on his heel and grabbed her with both hands on her arms, hard enough to bruise.

"This doesn't end well for him." Ven was struggling to control his urge to shake Willow. "He's your father. Stop thinking about yourself for half a second and do what he's asked."

Willow stared at Ven in stunned silence. It was the first time she'd seen him unmasked, no self-deprecating humor, no controlled seduction, no manipulation.

Ven was shaken too. Those words. Damn near exactly what Zelde had said to him before his own father died. Ven let go of Willow, turned on his heel and started running down the hall towards the stairwell. Willow ran after him.

Ven reached back to take Willow's hand. For once, she didn't protest. Not even when he stepped into a wall and took her hand with him. She stumbled a little and put her other hand up to catch herself, but it just passed through the wall too. Her body hit the surface like a spoon might breach the surface of a bowl of jello. She lost her sense of balance and fell through the other side of the wall and into Ven.

He, at least, was solid like she expected. When she was back on her own feet, she looked around. She'd never been to the Minister's office suite, but she recognized it anyway. Who else would the plush reception room belong to? Ven didn't give her time to look around. He put his hand on the next door, pushing it open and ushering her through it in the same motion.

Warren was at his desk, staring at the phone, but he looked up at the sound of the door opening.

"Willow," he said.

"Father."

They looked at each other, neither blinking. Ven watched them both, but knew better than to interject. Finally, Warren broke the silence with a sigh.

"I should have left you in Oregon. Maggie doesn't have the imagination to take on the Wastes. You'd have been safe there."

Ven whipped his head around to look at Willow and mouthed the question. "Oregon?" What the hell had she been doing in Oregon?

"Now, my only option is to leave you with him." Warren looked Ven over. "A mercenary with flexible morals and no allegiances."

Willow's mouth twisted in a half-smile. "I worked at the Ministry for long enough to know the type." Warren accepted the jab with a brief nod of the head.

"Things are unraveling. Maggie doesn't know about the Trust. They may not care much about me, but they care about the order of things. They aren't going to be happy."

Willow and Ven looked at each other to see if the other knew what Warren was talking about.

"The Trust?" Willow looked back at her father's ashen face. He looked back at her, almost pleading.

And then they all turned towards the entrance to the office. There were sounds coming from the hall beyond the antechamber.

"There's no time," Ven said as Warren started to speak.

"Willow, your mother was a wonderful woman. I loved her."

Ven pulled Willow to the wall, drawing her backwards into the drywall with him.

"Take care of my girl," Warren said to the wall as Ven melted into its blank white surface. The doorknob twisted and the door swung open.

Miles held the gun, but Maggie did the talking. Warren looked between the two of them, caught between pride in his eldest daughter, pleasure in knowing there were things they had not accounted for, the assurance of having the last laugh even from beyond the grave, and disappointment that it had finally come down to this: his daughter's coup.

Still the father, he started to warn Maggie. "There are things you don't..." but she raised her hand and he fell silent.

"It's too late, Dad. Now take out your capsule."

"How are you going to explain this?" Warren reached into his pocket as he spoke, feeling through the lint in the corners for the acrylic shell that protected the pill.

"Dementia. Alzheimer's. You didn't want your family to suffer through a slow death." While Miles' hand seemed unsteady on the gun, Maggie's voice didn't waver.

"Kind of you to paint me in such a noble light, but it isn't going to work." He gave his daughter a half-smile. "There are players you haven't accounted for."

Maggie held up her hand again. "We have it all under control. Now, take your medicine."

Warren cracked the housing around the pill and pulled it from its shell. He shook his head briefly as if to make sure it was all really happening. "I got the daughters I deserved," he said to the room in general, then looked to Maggie. "Be well," he said and crushed the capsule between his back teeth. "I'm sorry I wasn't more..." he said, and then slumped over in his chair.

From inside the wall, Willow found herself stuck. She tried to lean forward to stop the scene that was unfolding but Ven wouldn't let go of her hand. She couldn't go anywhere he didn't first lead. So with sight that lacked the depth she was used to, like her eye were the entire wall and unable to discern the difference between shadow and shape, she watched her father die and did nothing.

Maggie turned to Miles. "I'm going to get ready for the press conference." She glanced back at her father's body. "Take his pulse in a minute and, if there's nothing, call the Ministry medical staff. I'll meet you back in my office in fifteen minutes; we can go down together. She turned to leave the room, but Miles called her back.

"The papers, Maggie?"

She stopped mid-step and put a concerted effort into clearing her expression.

"Of course," she said brightly. "Our formal partnership begins today."

Miles had lowered the gun. It now dangled like a broken limb at his side. He dropped it into his pocket before extracting a sheaf of papers from his blazer. Maggie gestured to Warren's desk and Miles smoothed the papers flat against the wood. Wordlessly, Maggie signed the marriage contract, Warren's blank eyes silent on the subject of his blessing.

They signed the marriage contract with a flourish. Miles casually forged Warren's signature in the witness box, a trick learned over years of making Warren's life easier.

Miles picked up the contract and folded it. "I'll make sure this gets registered today," he said as he placed it in his pocket. His eyes lost focus as he stared adding up his to-do list when he felt his latex glove tugging at his hand. He looked down and saw Maggie's hand working her way between his curled fingers. Startled, he almost asked her what she was doing but remembered just in time: one didn't ask one's wife why she was attempting to hold your hand, you just let it happen.

"You are exactly what this Republic needs, Dr. Lake," Miles said, then gave himself a mental kick for the formality. "Maggie," he corrected himself. She stepped closer, maneuvering her body until she was facing him, her nose equal to the perfect Windsor in his tie. He put his free hand on her shoulder.

"There's no going back," she sighed.

"You are exactly what this Republic needs," Miles said again. "We've got a news conference to call." Maggie nodded, her hair brushing against Miles' chin, but stayed for another moment before she turned to the door in the corner. She was halfway across the room when she stopped.

"What is it?" Miles asked.

"Nothing. It's got to be the stress," she said, her eyes riveted to the drywall and her feet unmoving.

"What did you see?" The hairs on the back of Miles' neck stood at attention as if craning to see what Maggie was staring at.

"The wall moved, but then it didn't," Maggie said and shook her head as she finished crossing the room. "I'm losing it," she said, turning back to smile at Miles.

Maggie tried to focus on her new husband's face rather than her father's body behind him. Bodies were routine, but she'd never wanted to touch one before, to see if the skin was still warm, if he'd still bleed if she took a scalpel to his wrist, to knock on his forehead and hear the echo between his ears where he used to be. She did none of these things. Instead, she smiled a wan smile at Miles and closed the door behind her.

The day that had seemed so very far away just three months before had, in retrospect, come rather quickly. She was ready, yes. Ready to lead. Ready to push the Republic back onto solid footing, ready for the power and the responsibility. Ready to eliminate the vermin, the socially unclean. One final purge and then the mopping up operations, and finally a Republic as squeaky-clean as her mother's counters.

Someone would have to tell Sara, but if Sara had survived Warren's infidelity, she'd be just fine living through his death. For now, there was a news conference to get through. Thinking about announcing her father's death reminded her of something she'd been meaning to ask Miles. She turned on her heel and returned to her father's office.

"Miles?" She stuck her head around the door of the office, not really wanting to walk all the way back in. "Can we not announce our contract? At least not yet?"

"Of course. It will be business as usual," he agreed.

She smiled at him with gratitude. As a partner, he'd be deferential and efficient, walking one step behind her, as befitted a Chief of Staff with his Minister. If nothing else, she'd selected a worthy husband, someone who knew the rules nearly as well as she did and was equally committed to living by them.

"Be well," she said as the door closed behind her.

When she had closed the door for the second time, Miles rushed to the wall and ran his latexed hands over the smooth surface. "If you come out now, it will all be okay," he whispered to the wall. "I've got another job for you. Lucrative," he said as he tried to force his facial muscles into a trustworthy smile.

The wall gave no indication it was listening. Miles hesitated, grateful there was no one to see him. When nothing happened, he gave up and began to circle Warren's desk, trying to decide the best angle for checking the dead man's nonexistent pulse.

He finally picked up Warren's hand gingerly, like mortality were infectious or the chill of death were catching. He dropped the hand when the fingers fell into an uncontrolled curl. With a deep breath, he picked up the hand again and closed his eyes. The blood didn't flutter under his fingertips, so he placed the hand back on the desk and walked to the phone.

As he walked, he looked to the floor for signs of Maggie's heels. Warren stayed where he was, his corpse in a posture of defeat. Little puncture marks did mar the white carpet, but so did other footprints. Miles checked his watch. The cleaning crew would have vacuumed before Warren's usual 7:30 arrival time and he wasn't scheduled to see anyone. It was only now 8:15. Miles could only conclude that someone—make that two people, based on the number and variety in footprints—had been in to see Warren before they had entered the room.

Miles traced Maggie's path, scrubbing the dark holes in the carpet where her shoes had parted the threads until there were no more distinct heel-prints left, then quit the room.

Twenty Eight

Try as she might, Willow couldn't force Ven into moving. It was only when he felt certain that no one was going to rush into the room again that he stepped from the wall pulling Willow along behind him.

While Willow touched Warren for the first time, Ven rifled through the Minister's desk, feeling for false-bottomed drawers and pocketing anything that seemed secret. The search didn't last but a minute and Ven's hand was back wrapped around Willow's wrist, pulling her from the room and back through the cinderblock walls.

"Where are we going?" she managed to ask when they had emerged again into a dark stairwell and were moving as distinct entities, not part of the architecture.

"Basement. Transformers." He got the answer out just before he pulled her into another wall. The door above them squeaked open and Ministry security guards came stomping down the stairs only to re-enter the office spaces a floor below.

"What do you want with transformers?" Willow asked when her mouth was clear of the taste of concrete.

"Transportation."

"Through the transformers?" Willow's panic was palpable.

"The big wires are better than trying to use the building wiring. It goes faster."

"Ven. Be serious. Bodies can't fit through those wires. Even if it were possible, we'd never survive."

"You wouldn't have survived if you'd stayed behind." Ven paused. "Do you trust me?"

"Hell no." Willow didn't have to consider the answer.

"Well," he answered, "pretend. Your alternative is spending more quality time with your sisters. Bonding, if that's what you want to call it." Ven's grip on Willow's hand tightened as he raced her down the stairs.

The basement door was locked, but Willow felt Ven start to dissolve, his edges going all fuzzy where the skin of their hands met. Then she felt herself catch the blurring as they passed through the sharp metal door.

Ven moved effortlessly through the dark room. Hard corners brushed passed them like table legs against a cat's fur.

"Are you sure about this?" Willow protested as she stumbled behind him, trying desperately to pry her hand away. He only tightened his grip.

"Look. You think you're fingers and toes and everything in between. Your pretty little heart and your exasperated sighs and the pain that goes along with stubbing your toe. You aren't any of those things. You're the awareness of them."

Willow stared at him blankly.

"Fuck it. We're out of options," he said as he ground to a halt. "Hold up your hand," he commanded.

"You have it," she said dryly.

"Other hand. Hold it up."

Willow did as instructed and Ven placed his hand several inches from hers. Soon, a faint blue light glowed between them. Ven scanned the wall in the thin light. It was festooned with colored wires and empty sockets. He shuffled them to the right side where a wire too large for Willow to encircle with a finger and a thumb was plugged into the side of the panel.

"That's it," Ven muttered as he broke the connection and the light vanished. He reached for the cord. "This is gonna tingle," he warned as he grabbed the socket and pulled.

Willow had just enough time to register the alarm bells going off in the building and the emergency light flicker on by the door before she was jerked off her feet, her arm nearly pulled out of its socket. Every molecule felt bright and unsteady.

Vaguely, she was aware of what was her and what was not, but mostly it was like falling in love magnified, amplified, and expanded. She was enamored with everything, drunk on the overwhelming knowledge that she could, quite literally, do anything. It was like nothing she'd ever experienced. Her awareness remained the same, but there was no noticeable investment in the outcome. She simply was. And it was bliss.

Behind them, the main power feed into the Ministry of Health swung wildly, a blinded cobra with no sense of what to strike at, but striking nevertheless.

Standing in front of the podium, all the microphones clustered just inches from her mouth, Maggie felt nearly inadequate. Miles was already playing the role for her that he'd played for her father—when she'd reached the podium, there was a small platform in front of her to raise her up to the level of the microphones. Miles thought of everything.

The first bulb flashed in her face and startled her. She blinked heavily as the rest of the flashes went off in bursts of pure white light. When they finally slowed to the occasional burst, Maggie cleared her throat. The microphones picked up the noise and her own discomfort echoed back at her.

"Members of the Press," she started. Once again, her voice came back at her multiplied and wavering. At least they would all attribute it to grief over her father's death rather than nerves. She steadied herself and started again, this time stronger. More certain.

"Members of the Press. I stand before you with a heavy heart. I must relay the unfortunate news that my beloved Father, the Minister of Health, Dr. Warren Lake, has died. I am devastated by what this means for my family and the Ministry.

Until the normal protocol for identifying a new Minister of Health can be implemented, I will step into the seat of Minister of Health.

My father was a great man whose presence will be sorely missed both within our family and at the Ministry. His first priority was the health of the Republic. I share that commitment and am therefore following what would most certainly have been his wishes in stepping in to maintain stability and security for you, the citizens of the New Republic of America."

Maggie Lake was looking down to be certain of her step off of the pedestal when an explosion from the bowels of the Ministry sent the press diving under their chairs.

Maggie ducked under the podium and Miles threw himself over her back. Let no one think he wasn't 100 percent invested in the new Minister. A shower of powdered glass drummed against his back, shredding his suit but not quite penetrating to the skin beneath.

The silence behind the explosion was absolute. Slowly, carefully, Miles pulled himself off of Maggie and looked up at the Ministry building, expecting to see lights reflecting in the glass façade, but there was no glass to reflect anything. The windows had all blown out.

Willow and Ven materialized together, more or less intact, in a process that happened faster than Willow could comprehend. It felt exactly like falling through her dreams, assuming that the dream fall had been precipitated by being shot out of a cannon.

They were inside a dull chain link fence, a tall pole every sixty feet like a sentinel holding out a feeble light. She hit the gravel with an ungainly thud and was relieved to see Ven on his ass too.

There was a waterfall pounding in Willow's ears, a sharp contrast to the profound silence that had engulfed her not a second ago. She felt her mouth form the word "Ven," felt the word leave her chest, but couldn't hear her own voice. Ven shook his head at her. She saw his mouth form the word 'wait' but heard nothing.

Eventually, the immersed feeling in her head drained. As it did, she stood and started pacing. She hadn't had the chance to find her heavy jacket when the MOS troops swiped her from Oregon and she was cold. Ven held himself close, trying to keep as much heat as possible. He thought about offering to share his warmth and decided against it.

When Willow could hear the gravel crunching under her feet, she walked back to Ven. "Now?" she asked and was relieved to hear herself unchanged.

"You okay?"

"What do you think? I'm freezing my ass off."

"We aren't far from the Camellia compound. I've got a bike stashed close. You think you can make it over the fence?"

Willow looked at the fence more closely. It was at least nine feet tall with a halo of barbed wire.

"Anything you can do, I can do better."

Ven grinned and started climbing. Willow followed closely and grunted her thanks when he hesitated at the top, holding the sharp wires together to make it easier for her to throw her leg over and make the descent. Even so, she felt her pants catch and tear at the thigh. When Ven got to the bottom on the free side of the fence, he wiped his palm on his hip and left a smear of blood behind.

They didn't speak, but Willow followed closely through the darkness. Tucked into a copse of trees, just beyond view of the fence, was a shed. "Drink," Ven commanded as he threw her a bottle of water and rolled the bike out the door. She did as instructed. Ven climbed onto the bike and looked at her expectantly.

"Helmet?" she looked back just as expectantly.

"Get on the damn bike."

She resisted for another half a minute, just long enough to irritate him, then did as instructed.

Mercifully, the ride to the Camellia compound was short. Willow conceded to the cold and wrapped herself tightly around Ven's torso. She buried her face in the dip between his shoulder-blades and fought to keep her chattering teeth under control. Her grip tightened as he fishtailed up to the building where Willow had first encountered Marshall. Ven killed the engine.

"He knows," Willow said. Ven had saved her, she owed him a warning at least.

"Knows what?"

"That you're working for the Ministry. I saw your file before I got fired."

"That'll make this interesting."

Willow got off the bike as Ven held it steady. Ven pushed the kickstand down and stood himself. The v-shaped cut in his palm had darkened with clotted blood. He didn't seem to notice.

Marshall was standing in the empty workroom surrounded by spare parts and stains where motorcycles used to stand when Ven pushed open the door. He didn't give Ven the opportunity to get out a startled "hello." Instead, he crossed the room and punched him with a single jaw-dislocating fist.

He let his fist drop to his side, but didn't uncurl his fingers. He turned to Willow. "Who are you working for?"

"No one."

"Unlikely. I think Minister Lake sent you with your piece of shit lover." Marshall had had plenty of time to think and not much news.

"Warren Lake is dead." Willow didn't tear up at the pronouncement, which seemed like a good thing. She didn't think Marshall was likely to soften up over tears.

"Bullshit. Bullshit!" Marshall exploded. "Where's Ian?"

Ven stirred against the concrete, but thought better about getting up. Instead, he lay there trying to pop his jaw back into place. Willow was grateful for the distraction. She might be able to control her reaction to Warren's death. At the mention of Ian, she was pretty sure her face crumpled.

"I... I don't know," Willow stuttered.

Marshall's head whipped around at Willow's whispered pronouncement and crossed the distance between them. Before Willow could even react, he'd wrapped his hand around her throat and was backing her to the closest wall.

"What. Did. You. Do. To. My. Ian." Marshall enunciated every word clearly and slowly. "Lie to me and I'll crush your windpipe. Slowly. You understand?"

Willow nodded.

"Oh, for fuck's sake," Ven barked as he struggled to his feet.

Marshall pointed a beefy finger in Ven's direction as he held Willow. "Stay."

Marshall examined Willow's face closely for long seconds. Finally, he relaxed his grip finger by finger. "Where is she?"

"Oregon." Willow swallowed hard, just to see if she could.

"Whose side are you on, son?" He turned back to Ven, his hand still resting over Willow's windpipe for safekeeping.

Marshall had been prepared for his own righteous anger. Indeed he had counted on it as a weapon with which to beat the truth out of Ven, if necessary. But it had abandoned him. Instead, there was this nebulous sadness, a sense of betrayal, and a tiredness that slumped his shoulders. Marshall didn't call the man sitting in front of him 'son' lightly.

"I can explain..." Ven said, but Marshall interrupted him before he got his next words out.

"You are so far off the map. So far from the man I trusted. This woman," he shook Willow slightly, for emphasis. "You threw her in front of a freight train with no support structure. She's not a doll that only animates when you're in the room. She had the same rights that you had when you joined – the right to know. The right to choose."

Ven had been prepared for anger but not for this. "Marshall..." he started.

"Don't patronize me, Ven," Marshall said. "If you had any respect for me, we wouldn't be having this conversation."

Ven tried again. "I can't justify myself, except by the results of my actions. There's been more movement in the past week than in the past decade."

"Movement?" Marshall asked, incredulous. "What movement? Everyone's gone, disappeared or in hiding. We've lost an enemy we understand in exchange for an unknown adversary. Who's to say we'll even survive."

Marshall glared back suspiciously.

"I can explain, Marshall, but there's no time. MOS will be here any minute. You have to trust me."

"And why should I trust you?" Marshall retightened his grip around Willow's neck. She tried to swallow. It didn't work. She patted at his arm, hoping to remind him that she needed air.

"We'll survive, Marshall. I witnessed the murder of the Minister at the hand of his own daughter. We've got leverage. Real leverage. Things will change under Maggie. She's not pragmatic like Warren Lake. She doesn't know her own weaknesses. They will react now, and that means they can be manipulated."

"Damn it, Ven," Marshall broke in. "This isn't a chess game. You are talking about people. People with just as much right to survive as you've got."

"With all due respect, Marshall, that's where you're wrong. All these years, you've protected every sob story that landed on your door equally. It's made you too cautious. We could have brought the Ministry down years ago.. They are assets, Marshall. Assets. To be used."

"What gives you the right..." Marshall started.

"The right comes with the strategy. I'm not any different than anyone else, except that I am here talking to you, free of emotional ties to the players." Marshall stared back at Ven, then silently dropped his hand from Willow's neck. Willow settled back to her feet and put her own hands to her skin to check for bruises.

"We aren't playing the same game."

"You're playing to survive, aren't you?" Ven prodded. "To survive and fight another day?"

Marshall stepped forward, raising to his full height over Ven. He studied him, searching for the core of the man in front of him. "I'm playing for more than survival, son." He glanced at Willow who had retreated to the corner, trembling, and turned to the door of the workroom. "If you knew what was good for you, you would be too."

Ven refused to be seen rushing or concerned, but he stepped over to where Willow stood. "You okay?"

She nodded, but didn't trust herself to speak. Ven grabbed her hand and followed Marshall out the door.

Twenty Nine

Welcome to Amarillo.

Ianthe wondered if the Independent State of Texas had always been this dusty. Clearly, it had been more at some point. All along the road approaching the city limits, there were signs broken in half, the original announcements now turned on their head. Love's Travel Stop defeated by time. A few miles later, a line of cars with their ass end angled at the sky. So much like everything she'd read about the old era: taking the destructive power of the automobile and using it as a permanent fuck you, mooning the universe in a perpetual show of defiance. Ianthe shook her head and kept driving.

Amarillo was dusty too, filled with buildings that had long since bleached like bones under the sun. As defeated as the town looked, and quite unlike the other towns she'd driven through on her drive, there were signs of life. There were bright bicycles propped up alongside the buildings, but more importantly, white Camellias painted on signs and mailboxes.

The scrawl on the map told her to find an address on North Julian. She swore at it as she drove down street after street, trying to make out the microscopic printing of street names in the failing light. By the time she finally found the right street and the right house number, there was no daylight left, just what could be seen from square windows of the houses in the neighborhood.

She silenced the engine in front of a square, pale house that seemed to have some internal source of light. It glowed faintly against the pressing darkness. Inside the truck, Ianthe hesitated. Her back ached, she wanted nothing more than fresh water to rinse the grime from her eyes and, now that she was here, someone to talk to. But there was something else she wanted to absorb for a minute. Something that called to the memories she wished she'd had growing up. Quiet streets, neighbors connected by similar activities performed in concert up and down the block. Parents putting kids to bed, creeping out after dreams had overtaken their progeny to say hello to the friend next door, to light a cigar or share a glass of wine and a connection. The patchwork of windows, lights twitching on and off, something wild and mysterious lingering at the place where the glow of table lamps met the night.

Ianthe stayed in the truck longer than made sense. Eventually just sitting there began to feel silly, even to her. She stretched her limbs like the angle her knees bent at had frozen into place, twisted her spine for the pleasure of hearing it crackle and pop as the vertebra rubbed against the cartilage, and stepped out of the truck.

The front door of the house boasted a black iron knocker, a coyote with a heavy ring hanging from bared teeth. Ianthe tapped the ring against the base tentatively, then harder when the first knocks proved ineffective.

Eventually, she heard an uneven thump and muffled swear words. Then the door's hinges creaked in protest as it swung open to reveal a gray-haired woman leaning heavily on a cane.

"Whaddya want?" she grumbled.

"Um," Ianthe answered.

"We're fresh out," she said and moved to close the door.

Ianthe pressed her palm to the door to stop its outward swing. "The Source said you could help me." The old woman stopped at the name.

"Duane? Some nerve," she spat out, but she also stopped pushing the door closed. "Dirty fucking bastard. Been a good thirty years since I bothered to even think his name."

"We aren't friends," Ianthe protested, trying to keep on the right side of the situation. "Acquaintances, really."

"He's not the friendly type," she said and shuffled back into the house, leaving the door open. Ianthe stepped in and closed it behind her. "What's your name again?" The old woman kept moving as she called the question out over her shoulder. Ianthe followed her into the interior of the house. Even in the dim lighting, Ianthe could see that every surface was covered with stacks of paper and random artifacts.

"Ianthe," she answered. "Ian, really."

They arrived in a room with two short sofas facing each other. They were festooned with rich red pillows that matched the carpets piled on top of each other on the floor. By each sofa, a squat lamp let off a begrudging yellow light.

The old woman sat down heavily and sighed, then extracted a box from the table beside her. Methodically, she set about extracting and crumbling a small handful of buds and leaves, then rolling it into a pale white paper. She said nothing as she performed the ritual, not until she'd lit the cigarette, sucked on it, held her breath and finally exhaled a cloud of blue smoke.

"Morrigan," she finally offered in answer to the unspoken question. "How do you know Duane?"

"He saved my life."

"Paying penance, eh? He ruined mine." The old woman coughed on that last word, which started up a series of hacks that shook her body and bent her over double. Through it all, she kept her left hand extended, the cigarette safely away from the furniture and scattered papers. When she was done, she placed the cigarette back to her mouth and inhaled again. Another cloud of blue smoke, and she went on. "What do you want?"

"I'm headed to Bethesda to save my friends."

Briefly, Morrigan looked surprised, then closed her eyes and sighed. "I'm a little old for futile acts of derring-do."

"I wasn't expecting a partner," Ianthe amended.

Morrigan opened one eye and looked down her nose at Ianthe. "Thirty years ago, doll..." she let the thought trail away. "Don't worry, time will fuck you too. Just wait."

Ianthe didn't know what to say, so she didn't say anything and the old woman went back to smoking and coughing. When the cigarette was burned down to ash and her body had relaxed slightly, she started to speak again.

"Bethesda, eh. You one of us?"

Ianthe nodded.

"You prepared to die if they catch you?"

Ianthe nodded again.

"Must be real good friends." She paused, thinking. "You'll take the tunnels in. Come at them from the north. More direct that way. You wouldn't want to get lost trying to follow them in from the south. Too many ways to take a wrong turn."

"How do I find the tunnels?" Ianthe rearranged herself on the sofa, leaning forward.

"Tomorrow. I'll find you the maps tomorrow. I do my best plotting in the morning." She sighed. "You'll be wanting a place to sleep, I suppose."

"I can sleep in the truck."

"Don't be daft." Morrigan clung to her cane as she pulled herself to standing, then swayed on her feet. "What I wouldn't give for the days when I smoked that shit for fun," then she shuffled out of the room. Ianthe followed.

They walked a labyrinth through rooms landscaped in more papers and furniture than Ianthe had ever seen in one place before finally stopping at a back room. Morrigan turned on the light, revealing a room wallpapered in heavy red roses on a yellowed background. It was peeling from the ceiling.

"The bathroom's through there," Morrigan gestured at a door.

Ianthe slept hard, but not without dreams. She was back in the truck, trying to judge whether the puddle in front of her was safe to drive through. She took it slowly, but the puddles kept coming, each one larger than the last, until one surged under her. She braced herself in the truck with her hands over her head and her feet pressed against the floorboard as the truck fell and spun with her in it. She landed on a sandy shoal, stranded in the middle of a heaving ocean. The pounding of her heart woke her up, damp from sweat and breathing in quick shallow breaths. A needle of light slipped through the gap in the curtains. She'd slept much longer than she'd meant to.

The smell of frying bacon slipped up the stairs and ambushed Ianthe when she opened the door to the hallway. She picked her way back the way they'd come the night before, dodging statues, vases, books, stacked newspapers, and dunes of dust.

Morrigan was standing in the kitchen, another hand-rolled cigarette dangling from her mouth as she tended a hot frying pan.

"You can't keep going east the way you've been going. Bacon?"

"Please." Ian's mouth was watering. The last time she'd eaten bacon had been with Marshall, and that was years ago.

"You got anything in that truck of yours that the Ministries might object to?"

"Guns. Ammo." Ianthe thought around another bite of bacon. "The truck itself, probably."

"Well, they make allowances for vehicles in the Wastes. Guns, on the other hand... You'll want to cross the border carefully. Better make it at night with your lights off. Any chance you can see in the dark?"

Ianthe shook her head.

"Too bad. I've heard that some of us can. It'll be a quarter moon tonight, just enough to watch the road by, hard to be seen though. There's nothing for it once you're in the Wastes. Just keep yourself moving as fast as you can. And away from other people. We'll get you onto 83 up to old 70. That will put you right about exactly where you need to be for getting to the Infirmary." The old woman nodded to herself as she inhaled and exhaled smoke.

"What does Duane get out of this?" she asked as she lifted the last of the bacon onto her own plate and cracked a couple of eggs into the empty pan.

"Nothing," Ianthe forced a lie. "Unless you count me leaving him alone." She thought back to the body she'd left on the ground and tried to control the muscles in her face.

Puff, puff. "How's he holding up?"

Ianthe shrugged. "Looks pretty good for an old guy. Better than you at least." Ianthe hadn't exactly planned for that last bit to slip out, but Morrigan didn't seem to notice.

"Not surprising. He always was a fucking cat. Landed on his feet more times than a hooker lands on her back."

"You knew him?"

"Yeah, I knew him." Morrigan jabbed at the eggs savagely, breaking both yolks. "I knew him alright."

They spent the rest of the day looking at maps. Morrigan outlined a whole city that shouldn't have existed to the south and east of an area that she circled on the map.

"This is where the Infirmary is. It's a big complex. Getting there is the easy part. Finding them... well, let's hope you do." She was rolling again, the morning's cigarette stubbed out long ago. "The Ghost City is below the Bethesda facility, but you won't be taking that on. Not now."

"Ghost City?" Ian's voice cracked on the words. "The Sou... Duane wasn't forthcoming."

"He wouldn't be. Fucking rat bastard." Morrigan fell silent.

"You were saying?" Ianthe prompted.

"You want rumors or facts? There's more of the former."

"Rumor it is."

Morrigan sighed and rearranged herself in her chair. "Depends on who you ask, I guess. Some say that the research and development firms came up with a new step in human evolution before the Chaos and that this new species took advantage of the Chaos to create its own colony." Morrigan paused. "I don't buy it, personally. I've heard other people tell of running into an exact copy of someone they knew forty years ago. They always claim to be the son or niece, but it's unsettling, you know? Here you are in a body that is crumbling around you, and you meet your first love on the street and he looks just the same as he did when you were sixteen. Maybe better clothes, but not forty years of difference. Maybe it's just where the real power went to keep itself safe from the Chaos."

"Whoever it is, Duane knows. That's the kind of company he kept." She shook her head as if to clear it. "They're gonna be fortified and dangerous, which is why you want to avoid them. Keep to the tunnels and dark. Get your friends and get the fuck out."

Maggie and Miles climbed through the absent front door of the Ministry and looked around. The lobby was pristine even as a chill wind blew through the empty window-frames.

"There's no elevator."

"I'll go check on our guests." Miles sighed. He was in shape; that didn't mean he was looking forward to climbing all those stairs.

"I'll call the facilities engineer." Maggie's voice was subdued. If she was anything like her father in this, her tone didn't bode well. Maybe the stairs were the better option after all.

It took him twenty minutes, but soon enough Miles was standing in front of two empty cells. He didn't acknowledge the white-hot sizzle of fear that ran across the back of his neck.

When the engineers had gotten the generators up and running and the security cameras had confirmed their path down to the transformer room, Miles had to acknowledge the impossible. The pair had vanished. There was no rational way to explain the how, but the what was certain. Ven and Willow had observed the episode with Warren, and they had escaped.

Even with time to think during Maggie's performance for the press, Miles was at a complete loss. Of course there was the obvious: deadly force applied as quickly as possible. But the path from where he stood to there, starting with what to tell Maggie, was slightly less clear. It was this puzzle that engrossed him so thoroughly that he didn't hear his new wife unlock the door and enter.

"They're gone." Her statement of the obvious startled him out of his journey down one course of action after another.

"They're gone," he confirmed. He couldn't think of anything else to say.

THIRTY

"I want that bitch."

Miles and Maggie had walked in silence back to Miles' office. Maggie's mouth was hard set and Miles eyes were unfocused as he arranged outcomes and probabilities.

"I want that bitch," Maggie repeated. "I don't care what it costs."

"You're the Minister now. You have to care about the cost." Miles sounded tired.

Maggie looked up at Miles. His face was expressionless, his tone matter-of-fact. She'd had the marriage contract drawn up, there was none of the old-fashioned obedience bullshit in it. But he didn't look like he was trying to tell her what to do, merely commenting on the role of the Minister. She lowered her shoulders and took a deep breath.

"So what do we do?"

"We make it impossible for any of them to hide. She'll come to the surface eventually. And while we do that, we move forward. She's personal and the personal is irrelevant when compared to our duty to the Republic."

Maggie gritted her teeth at the implicit lecture but didn't argue. Instead, she reminded herself that her father would have done well to keep Miles' advice in mind and tried to sooth her own impatience.

She changed the subject. "What's our survival rate on the cure?"

"There have been no more deaths in the past two days. Of the last twenty-four, seventeen have survived but five of those are not looking likely to make it." Miles rattled off the numbers easily.

"We can't exactly dispatch the cure with a 50 percent mortality rate. Our PR arm can't spin those statistics."

"We can move with the vaccine," Miles said soothingly. "We can start. Meanwhile, we'll make a discrete raid on our friend Marshall and give ourselves more test subjects." He paused. "Perseverance, Minister Lake. Perseverance. Our Ms. Carlyle has nowhere to go but Marshall."

"Make it happen."

The Ministry of Security's soldiers didn't make noise as they moved through the woods like a black tide. When the Camellia's compound was surrounded, three intrepid bodies surged forward with a hunched run and a small battering ram. The door cracked with the first blow, splintered with the second, and swung off its hinges with the third. MOS troops swarmed in, their guns pointed and the laser sights dancing in the semi-darkness.

The company commander stood at the edge of the clearing, listening to the teams check with each other as each room was cleared. They had been led to believe that there would be a fight and prisoners to haul back to the Ministry. She was almost disappointed. Empty buildings were safer for her team, but not nearly as satisfying.

When everyone had checked in and confirmed that the building was empty, she ordered them to pull everything that might possibly be valuable to an investigation. Like a colony of ants, they marched out of the building one by one, each carrying a burden of computers and papers.

One of the black-clad bodies pulled a grenade from a side pocket. At the nodded go-ahead from the commander, the soldier removed the pin from the round body with her teeth with as much precision as one might pull a splinter, and tossed it into the building. The other soldiers melted back into the woods around the compound just as silently as they'd emerged. Inside the clearing, the Camellia's compound dropped into itself like a soufflé falling.

Ianthe had dreamed about these tunnels; they were familiar to her even though in her dreams, the arches overhead had been taller. There had been room to walk beside the tracks as well, in the dreaming version, instead of walking between them. The truck was miles behind her, nosed into a crevice where there had once been a concrete structure. Hidden enough from overhead surveillance.

Somewhere, lost in the miles behind her, was the white-blond that she'd been. While still at Morrigan's, she'd applied the vile, blue-black dye to her hair.

She didn't have the coloring to pull off black hair. The layers of gray eye shadow she'd rubbed on her face didn't help. The whites of her eyes were stark in comparison to the makeup and her blue irises looked more watery than icy.

Her journey had started three hours earlier, in a ghost town called Harper's Ferry. She'd driven to the outskirts of Morrigan's warnings, close enough to see the razor wire and the towers with their sweeping lights but no closer. Instead, she had found the entrance to the abandoned underground system, left the truck hidden, and left the murky evening behind. Ten, eleven miles—she'd run until her lungs burned, walked, then run some more.

The only obstacle had been an abandoned train. Ianthe ran her hands along its smooth curve and wondered. The flashlight uncovered a door in the face of the train. Ianthe scrambled to climb it and worked her way inside. There was an interior compartment that was locked, an open door in front of her, and, as she swept her flashlight from side to side, a car full of skeletons.

Ian's guts rebelled. There wasn't a smell to go along with the bodies, but she couldn't stop looking. In the seats spotlighted by Ian's flashlight, bones slumped against the plastic. Ianthe had a brief vision of what all of those people might have looked like riding on the train to get home after working all day. Now the leg bones crossed each other on the floor, shin bones next to thigh bones. Each pair to a seat might have died holding hands, like honeymooners caught by surprise.

She turned away and, instead of retching, kicked open the locked door. Another pile of bones, but also the controls. She nudged the bones aside quickly, with her foot, not wanting to prolong contact.

With the bones pushed into the main part of the car, Ianthe turned the flashlight to where the train operator used to sit. To the right, there was a lever. She squeezed the handle and pulled it to her. Nothing happened. She squeezed again and moved it back towards the floor. Behind her, the whole train sighed. Brakes.

She flipped some of the other switches and nothing happened, so she jumped out moved on down the tracks, squeezing past the train and trying not to think about all the bones that were above her.

On her way past, she pulled the pin that held the first car in the train to the next.

Every once in a while, the claustrophobia of the tunnels would give way to a cavernous space where Ianthe was certain that, if she breathed too loudly, she'd hear her breath echoing back at her. Not long after the ghost train, she'd stepped into the comparatively clear air of another station. As she had with every station before, she swung the flashlight around looking for the pillar that would tell her if she was there yet. When she found the sign, and it said Bethesda, her stomach sank. For as long as she was driving, running, searching, the hope that Kiri was unbroken and alive seemed reasonable. After all, one didn't run for a corpse, one ran for love.

But that next step—launching herself from the tracks to the platform, climbing the escalator in front of her, jumping the gates, climbing the second escalator and emerging into fresh air—there'd be no more hope, no more possibilities. Just the reality of each second dragging her closer to knowing. Suddenly, she wanted to rewind her own story, to be at some place prior. The windows down as she crossed a bridge, the Independent State of Texas behind her and nothing to think about beyond wondering whether or not the bridge she was crossing was going to hold.

Instead, she took the escalator steps two at a time and emerged into the darkness blinking and breathless.

It was almost like being back at the Camellia compound, the absolute quiet, the way the night fell against itself in inky folds. Ianthe blinked and turned slowly. If she was where she thought she was, there would be guards somewhere. There would be a compound, facilities, something. She turned again and saw, off in the distance, a light flickering off of a glass-clad building. That's the direction she walked and, when the starved moon slipped out from behind the clouds, ran.

Ianthe ran her hand along the rough brick, waiting to see the light waver again. Something that tasted like hope was bubbling up from her stomach. Lights flicker for all sorts of reasons—she thought back to Willow and her unfortunate taste in lovers—but one possible explanation was Kiri feeding off of the electrical current.

The light above her flickered and surged again. Ianthe grinned and found the closest door.

She'd been playing with magnetic locks since she'd first discovered that her condition came with some anomalies, so this lock didn't present much of a challenge. She slipped in the door and let it click shut softly behind her. Once inside, she stood still, breathing and waiting for any sound at all to indicate that there were guards. Somewhere, she was also hoping to feel the pull of Kiri on her skin.

There was no sound, no pull. *I guess we'll have to do this the old-fashioned way,* Ianthe thought, and started climbing stairs with a little gratitude that she hadn't had to do this in one of the larger buildings she'd passed in the dark. Her initial plan had involved a systematic search starting at the top, but there was a light peering through the window in stairwell door on the seventh floor. A light and a double set of locks. Ianthe gave up the climb temporarily and looked through the window.

Inside was an antechamber filled with a guard desk, a weapons locker, and two empty chairs. Beyond that, another locked door and the source of the feeble light. Ianthe picked the locks on the first and second door and found herself standing at the end of a long corridor. Closed doors flanked her on either side. The silence was complete. She almost wanted to shuffle her feet just to fill up the space.

Suddenly, there was a noise at the other end of the hall. There was nowhere for her to go, so she grabbed the handle on the first door, scrambled the magnetic lock, and slipped inside. With her back pressed to the wall, the watery light illuminated everything in front of her but left her taut body in the shadows. A huge, weary-looking dog raised its head, then dropped it against his paws. Ianthe stooped down and snapped her fingers together to catch the dog's attention. It looked at her and slowly, like everything hurt, it lurched to standing and walked over to sniff her. Crouching on her haunches, the dog was tall enough to rest its head on hers. Ianthe reached up to scratch behind its ears.

From outside, the muffled voices came closer.

"Let's go fuck," a male voice said.

"You gave me a bladder infection the last time," a female voice replied. "Besides, it creeps me out to do it with all the animals listening."

"Doctor's lounge on nine. I'll check the prisoners and meet you up there. You can freshen up."

There was a crack that sounded like an open palm hitting the flesh of an ass.

"Whatever, Bruce. But you better fucking last this time. I want mine too."

The door that she'd just come through open and closed a second time.

Ianthe stood up. The knobs of the dog's spine reached her lower ribs and she scratched its back absently as she opened up the door. When she stepped out, it followed her. She didn't have the heart to push it back into its cage.

With its spine still under her hand, she clicked open the door that the two guards had just walked through and followed silently behind. She was just in time to hear the door click above her as he crossed into the holding corridor above her. Luckily, he was unconcerned about how much noise he made as he tromped across the linoleum floor. Ianthe timed her movement to the sound of the footsteps. The dog seemed perfectly content to move in concert with her.

When the door clicked shut at the far end of the hall, Ianthe slipped into a hall exactly like the one she'd found below. She wasted no time. She hurried down one side of the hall quietly opening the locks, afraid to spare a fraction of a second to see who she was letting out in case Kiri wasn't among them.

The dog stayed right with her. When she'd made her way up one side of hall and down the other, she turned back to look. Some of the heads that were looking around the edge of the doors were familiar, others were not. Some doors stood empty.

Ianthe was beginning to feel the panic well up inside of her when Kiri stepped out of a cell. She was down to skin-clad bone, too thin and grim in the mouth like Ianthe had never seen, not even when she'd first come to the Camellias.

"Can you get us all out?" Kiri gave Ianthe a look that both eased her fears and added a few new ones. The old spark was there, but everything else was wrong.

"The guards are upstairs fucking. If we can get to the tunnels, we can get out."

"Tunnels?"

"I'll explain later. We've got to get to them first."

"If they're fucking, we've got about five minutes or so. That's assuming Bruce lasts." For a second, Ianthe wrinkled her nose. Kiri hadn't heard that from her. But then Kiri had been here for long enough to know, and Ianthe broke out in a wide grin. Leave it to Kiri to track the guards and their misbehavior.

Still, five minutes wasn't enough time. Kiri left Ianthe and started shooing the prisoners in the direction of the door. Kiri slipped through the crowded corridor like an eel, her body twisting effortlessly to avoid contact with the stretching limbs and confused faces. She looked into each cell and either stepped inside briefly or closed its door gently.

Her methodical survey of the cells was over quickly and, with the exception of the former prisoners standing on the freedom side of the cell doors, all looked just as it had when Ianthe had first stepped into the corridor. Kiri was standing next to Ianthe again, a brief touch on her elbow the only indication that she was a little more than happy to see her.

"Get us out of here." Kiri sounded as spent as a worn bar of soap. "Where did you find that mangy mutt?"

"Same place I found you." Ianthe surveyed the tattered crowd. Willow wasn't among them. If she'd been legit, the Ministry would have disposed of her with the rest of the Camellias.

"Can everyone keep up?" Ianthe did a quick count. An even dozen, not counting herself.

"They'll keep up," Kiri said grimly.

While Ianthe led the way in silence, Kiri varied her pace to herd the stragglers. Ianthe could hear her fierce whisper and harsh words. "Push," she hissed at the slowest of them. "You aren't going back and you sure as hell aren't taking anyone with you. There will be plenty of time to fall apart when we're out of here." Behind them, the alarm was gathering its breath for the outcry. Flashlights punctured the darkness like mutant fireflies. Ianthe began to run again.

They slowed down once they got everyone over the barriers, down the escalators and into the tunnel. As promised, everyone had kept up, but just barely. No one was dressed for the crisp night air and bare feet had forced them to stop to raid the locker room. They'd taken everything they could, from boots to the dark blue zip up uniforms to the black caps, but Ianthe hadn't let them put on the heavy boots until they were safe enough to sit.

No one was well, not even Kiri, who was breathing in wheezing gasps. Ianthe slowed even more. The dog was doing fine with the exercise, but it wouldn't leave Ian's side.

With the cavernous station behind them, Ianthe walked closer to Kiri. "Do you think they can walk the ten miles to the truck? I don't know how the hell we're all going to fit once we get there."

"We'll figure it out," Kiri said grimly.

An undercurrent of tenderness crept into Ian's voice. "How much energy do you have?"

"Enough."

"Enough to power a train?"

Kiri blinked in the darkness and set her jaw. "If that's what I need to do."

Ianthe reached out and grabbed Kiri's hand. It was balled into a fist, but fiber by fiber, her muscles relaxed until their fingers intertwined. Even Ian's flashlight seemed to glow a little brighter in the subterranean darkness.

Mercifully, they weren't far from the abandoned train. Even with the group's slower pace, it didn't take long for the back end of the train to bounce back a faint glimmer of light.

"You should know..." Ianthe searched for the right words. "It's bad. The train, it's full of passengers. Dead passengers."

Kiri squeezed Ian's hand. "We're not dead."

There really wasn't much more than skin and a thin veneer of muscle to distinguish Kiri's prison mates from the bony passengers already on the train. Ianthe helped each of them in with a grip around the wrist or a hand on their back. It wasn't the time for anger, but she was pretty sure she'd be furious when getting everyone to safety wasn't such a pressing concern. Even at its worst, the Ministry didn't starve its prisoners. Or at least it hadn't.

Ianthe closed the door at the front of the train as Kiri sat at the driver's seat. The others huddled in an alcove. As Kiri put her hands to the instrument panel, the lights above them flickered on. Their faces were almost as bad as the wide macabre grins of the skulls scattered on the floor. When the train lurched forward, all the skulls rolled towards the back of the car and the bones collapsed into further disarray. Ianthe couldn't watch, so she turned to Kiri.

Beads of sweat were breaking out above Kiri's eyebrows and her mouth was a grim line of resolve. Having gotten this far, Ianthe was suddenly struck with a feeling of helplessness. It had just occurred to her that she wasn't actually big enough to pull this off. She looked at Kiri again and the panicked bile that had been clawing at her throat settled down. She didn't have to be big enough.

She took the step that stood between her and Kiri and slid her body between Kiri and the back of the seat. Kiri didn't break her concentration, but she rearranged herself until she was sitting on Ian's lap. Ianthe wrapped her arms around Kiri's ribs and buried her face in the knobs of Kiri's spine. She felt awful. Small and brittle and empty. She smelled awful too. She stank of defeat. Old skin, unwashed hair, and defeat.

Ianthe didn't turn her face away, not for the entire time it took Kiri to power that rusty old train down the tracks to the end of the line where Ianthe had parked the truck that morning.

Miles handed the approved copy to the head of the Republic Newscasting Company at exactly 5:52. He turned and handed it down a line of producers until an associate producer placed it in the hands of Petra, the 6:00 news anchor. The orange light on the camera blinked rapidly, then glowed steadily. Petra pasted on her news anchor smile—solemn and welcoming—and began to speak.

"Welcome to our broadcast for this, the 21st of November. We begin with an update from the Ministry of Health." She began to read.

"It has come to the Ministry's attention that there is a new viral threat to our Republic that you, our fellow citizens, must be aware of; however, we also assure you that there is no need for panic. We must now confirm the rumor of a new mutation in the Herpes Simplex Virus. While safe sex practices are always mandatory between partners with no contract, the Ministry urges all consenting adults to maintain the utmost in vigilance.

The infected look much like upstanding citizens of the Republic; however, appearances in this case are misleading. They lack the identifying mark mandated for public safety and they are capable of acts that may seem wondrous but are, in reality, symptoms of their grave illness.

If you encounter someone behaving in ways that fall outside of regulation and common practice, please do not attempt to engage that individual. Instead, call the hotline that the Ministry has set up for this purpose. That number is 555-3269. Again, the number to call is 555-3269.

Please keep in mind that these individuals are dangerous and possess the capacity to apply lethal force to anyone in their way. In a single attack of striking brutality, one individual with the viral infection killed five fellow patients at a Ministry treatment facility. Upstanding citizens must consider these individuals a threat to their person and to their society.

In a fortuitous coincidence, the Ministry has just finished testing a vaccine that will protect its citizens from all strains of the Herpes virus. From the research that gave us the vaccine, we are also making rapid progress with the cure. If you suspect a loved one of being infected, rest assured: turning them in will only enable us to cure them and eradicate this threat to the Republic. The Ministry's wellness clinics will offer the vaccine immediately. Within the month, the Ministry intends to have safeguarded all of its law-abiding citizens.

As for the infected criminals who even now may be planning acts of war against the citizens of our Republic, they will be found wherever they may be hiding, incarcerated until cured, and brought to justice. Your Ministries will defend the Republic from all threats, be they in the form of a virulent virus or a human enemy."

The newscaster looked directly into the camera.

"Be well," she said.

ACKNOWLEDGEMENTS

With thanks to FEJ and WLV for the initial idea, MVW for helping me keep it all together, MS for putting up with me as I wrote the first draft during NaNoWriMo 2009, and SBS just because. Additional thanks due to my early readers for the encouragement, the brutally honest feedback, and the impetus to deal with all of the questions I didn't have answers to.

Finally, I couldn't have gotten here without the support of my best friend. She deserves a good 50 percent of the credit for The Camellia Resistance. She believed in this book when it was half the size and a royal mess. She gave up sleep to provide editing, plotting, and characterization support and advice. Not to mention the constant reassurance that publication was going to be worth almost five years of writing and rewriting. If The Camellia Resistance is worth the time it takes to read, the credit goes to her.

COMING SOON...

The Camellia Reckoning, the second book in The Camellias Trilogy.